In this immensely enter[...]
lished bestselling Scottish [...]
with up-and-coming new stars to raise money for
a very good cause. The result is *Scottish Girls About
Town*, a diverse and memorable collection guaranteed to divert and delight.

£1 from every copy sold will be divided between
Barnardo's, the UK's largest children's charity, and
the Scottish charity, Women Onto Work.

Barnardo's
GIVING CHILDREN
BACK THEIR FUTURE

WOMEN ONTO WORK

Scottish Girls About Town

POCKET BOOKS

LONDON · NEW YORK · SYDNEY · TOKYO · SINGAPORE · TORONTO · DUBLIN

First published in Great Britain and Ireland by
Pocket Books, 2003
An imprint of Simon & Schuster UK
A Viacom company

1 3 5 7 9 10 8 6 4 2

Simon & Schuster UK Ltd
Africa House
64–78 Kingsway
London WC2B 6AH

www.simonsays.co.uk

Simon & Schuster Australia
Sydney

A CIP catalogue record for this book is available from
the British Library

ISBN 0 7434 5036 1

Typeset by Palimpsest Book Production Limited,
Polmont, Stirlingshire
Printed and bound in Great Britain by
Bookmarque Ltd, Croydon, Surrey

Contents

Barnardo's

Barnardo's is the UK's largest children's charity, working directly on an ongoing basis with over 55,000 children, young people and their families in more than 300 projects across the UK. We also support a further 7,000 children through one-off sessions, and indirectly assist almost 35,000 others through our work with community groups.

Our work with women covers a wide range of age groups and issues, including homeless teenagers, mothers whose children have disabilities or have been excluded from school and women who are improving their surroundings through community development initiatives.

Cathy is just one of the many young women we are working with. Unable to live with her parents, aggressive and desperately unhappy, Cathy had twelve criminal charges against her and was at serious risk of receiving a custodial sentence.

Referred to a Barnardo's project in Scotland working with persistent and serious young offenders, Cathy initially rejected all approaches from social workers and Barnardo's staff. 'I was angry all the time. I didn't want to hear anything anyone wanted to say to me,' she says.

Barnardo's workers looked beyond Cathy's verbal

abuse and destructiveness, and met her at least twice every week. She stopped offending as they worked together to tackle her attitude and behaviour. Supporting Cathy through her outstanding court cases and Children's Hearings, Barnardo's staff also helped her to re-establish contact with her father.

Now seventeen, Cathy recently completed her Children's Panel Supervision and was praised for the work she had done with the help of Barnardo's. She has also found a flat of her own and a part-time job, as well as offering to act as a mentor to young people working with Barnardo's projects in her home town. 'Barnardo's has made me see what life is about,' she says. 'It's about being happy, not sad.'

In Scotland, Barnardo's works in partnership with others to provide fifty-four community-based services across the country. The charity supports around 7,000 of Scotland's most vulnerable children, young people and families, helping them transform their lives and fulfil their potential. We believe that the lives of all children and young people should be free from poverty, abuse and discrimination.

If you would like more information about our work, how to make a donation or volunteering opportunities, visit our website at www.barnardos.org.uk or call 08457 697 967 (local rate).

Barnardo's

GIVING CHILDREN
BACK THEIR FUTURE

Women Onto Work

Women Onto Work gave me back my self-belief, self-esteem and the opportunity of working, which was something I never believed I could do again – Former Trainee

Women Onto Work has been running in Edinburgh for over twelve years. We provide a variety of intensive pre-vocational training courses and guidance programmes to women who face the greatest disadvantages in terms of accessing employment, education and training.

The courses are free and childcare, including after-school pick-ups, is provided whilst the course is running. This makes an incredible difference to women with children, as one of the biggest barriers that can be faced is the cost or lack of childcare provision.

Women Onto Work gave me a chance to say, 'Where's my life going, what would I like to do?'– Former Trainee

Our level one course runs for 10–12 weeks and aims to build self-confidence, encourage thought about skills and interests, explore relevant opportunities and develop plans for the future. The course includes personal development exercises, assertiveness training, job-search skills, career counselling, CV preparation, visits to local resources and agencies, work experience, laughter, friendship and much more . . .

Courses are run in specific areas of Edinburgh where women generally face the most challenging barriers; in addition to these, city-wide courses are run for Black Minority Ethnic Women as well as for Disabled Women.

> The Women Onto Work course helped me to gain the confidence to get what I need and gave me a chance to believe in a future in employment. Women Onto Work was the stepping stone to take me forward
> – Former Trainee

There are many different ingredients that make our courses special; one of them is the twelve-day work placement that allows women an opportunity to try out their ideal job. The placements cover all kinds of work including retail, childcare, hospitality, health and beauty, community work. We've had everything from plumbing placements to poodle parlours.

A large number of the women we work with have been out of work for a long time, many busy bringing up children, so the placement gives them the perfect opportunity to step back into the throes of 'working' life. Other women have never worked and Women Onto Work gives them the chance to experience the realities of work for the first time.

Women Onto Work

The placements are a great dry run for what it may be like when they get a job, plus for many of our women the placement also provides an up-to-date reference to support their future plans.

> The main turning point for me was putting together my CV on the Women Onto Work course. It was a revelation to see that I did indeed have skills and experience applicable to working. The placement itself was the next big step and it was more than wonderful to have my confidence restored. Before Women Onto Work I truly believed I had nothing to offer and could never work again, let alone do a job that I enjoyed
> – Former Trainee

It is widely acknowledged that a large number of women are involved in their communities or in voluntary work; it is also clear that women are under-represented in leadership roles. Our active citizenship course 'Active Women' strives to change this.

This course is aimed at women who would like to take leading and influential roles in their communities and/or in a political context. It is designed to equip women with the practical skills and knowledge necessary to become a more informed, empowered citizen. One highlight from a recent course was a visit to the Scottish Parliament and an opportunity to talk with an MSP.

Scottish Girls About Town

> This is a brilliant course. It's given me the knowledge and opportunity to play a more meaningful role in my community in South Edinburgh. I also understand now what politicians are talking about. I am having a really positive experience of Active Women
> – Former Trainee

Women Onto Work travels confidently towards the future and will continue to provide an indispensable service to the most disadvantaged women in Edinburgh.

One of our favourite quotes comes from a former trainee; we use it in lots of our publicity material. When asked how she would encourage other women to undertake the course she told us she would simply tell them, 'This will change your life.'

If you would like more information about our work or to make a donation contact us on 0131 662 4514 or mail@womenontowork.org or write to us at Women Onto Work, 137 Buccleuch Street, Edinburgh, EH8 9NE.

WOMEN ONTO WORK

IN THE GARDEN OF
MRS PINK

Isla Dewar

Born in Edinburgh, **ISLA DEWAR** now lives in Fife with her husband, a cartoonist, and two sons. Her first novel, *Keeping Up with Magda*, published in 1995, has been followed by a string of bestsellers: *Giving Up on Ordinary*, *It Could Happen to You*, *Women Talking Dirty*, *Two Kinds of Wonderful*, *The Woman Who Painted Her Dreams* and, most recently, *Dancing in a Distant Place*.

If anyone had asked me, when I was ten, what heaven looked like, I'd have described the garden of Mrs Pink. I thought it gorgeous.

I grew up in Edinburgh, Crighton Street. A row of bungalows facing another row of bungalows. Neat front gardens, behind trimmed hedges or railings uniformly painted black or green. Windows shone, lawns were mown and people went about their business saying polite good mornings, and 'Lovely day'. Respectability was what they craved, part of their reward for their hard work, at their jobs, in their homes and gardens. No wonder, then, that number twenty-four, four doors down from my house, caused raised eyebrows, wagging tongues. Everything at number twenty-four was pink.

Pink railings, pink flowers in the garden – carnations, geraniums, fuchsias, pink clematis spreading up the walls – pink window frames, pink front door. Pink Mini in the drive. For years I didn't know the real name of the woman who lived there, everyone called her Mrs Pink. To this day, though I know she is Veronica Watts, she is still Mrs Pink to me.

In 1972 I was ten. I lived with my mother and

Grandpa Mac in 20 Crighton Street; my father died when I was two – cancer – and I have no memory of him. My mother spoke of him often, and never remarried. But his death left us in a state of real penury. For years, till the mortgage was paid off, my mother scrimped and saved and denied herself. We got by. I was a child, that was how I lived, I didn't think anything about it. It was just how things were.

Grandpa Mac had come to live with us when I was seven. Until he moved down to our Edinburgh suburb, he'd lived in Inverness. He was forgetful, he rambled about times gone by, he was messy. He coughed, he spat. He was old. His oldness had, at first, fascinated me. His hands, spotted brown, veined. His gnarled face, whiskers. The way he ate, moving food slowly about his mouth. His rumbling ancient voice. I blush to recall the way I must have stared at him. I don't know exactly how long it took me to love him, but love him I did. He told me stories, cooked me soft boiled eggs, showed me card tricks, taught me to play poker. We made jokes, played at who could make the loudest rude noise. Most of all, he had time for me. My mother hadn't.

Not that she didn't love me, she was just consumed with the gruelling business of coping. Getting by. I thought her distant. Her shoulders were always tense, her brow furrowed. She moved quickly about the house, picking up after Grandpa Mac and me. I realize now that, for years, she cared for us, and we gave back nothing. For years, nobody touched my mother, kissed her, told her they loved her. We took her for granted.

In the Garden of Mrs Pink

She worked in the supermarket that had opened not far from us, at first in the checkout, then as under-manageress. She was qualified for higher things, but the supermarket was close by so she didn't have to leave in the morning before I went to school, and she could be home in time to cook supper. And, she could walk. She didn't have to pay fares. She got discount shopping, and often the man on the meat counter would slip her half a pound of mince, or stew. The toll of penny-pinching, she was better off working at the supermarket than she would have been with a job as a secretary in town. Happier? That wasn't an issue. It breaks my heart to think of what my mother went through to keep the roof of 20 Crighton Street over our heads. The endless coping. Coping with bills, repairs, cooking, looking after Grandpa Mac, who wasn't in the best of health. And coping with me. I was, till Mrs Pink came into my life, a restless, unruly, rebellious child. What they called a handful.

I did not see my mother as a tired, lonely woman trapped in the endless, draining business of managing day after day to make ends meet. It didn't occur to me she was doing this for me, for the love of me. I saw her as someone who was constantly bad-tempered. She nagged, fretted. Money was so tight, she knew how many slices of bread were left in the packet, and exactly what she would do with those slices. It wore her down, this worrying. Her face was drawn with the burden of it. Nights she'd come home from work, cook for Grandpa Mac and me, then she'd clean the house, wash clothes, iron,

11

vacuum, dust, wipe. Exhaustion had taken over her life. Squeezed the joy out of her.

That summer, 1972, my best friend, Patricia Harrower, went abroad to France with her family for the whole six weeks of the break from school. I had nobody to play with. Grandpa Mac tried, he'd take the old cricket bat on to the back lawn and have me bowl to him. But, really, he wasn't up to playing games. He rarely hit the ball, he couldn't see it, till it was about six inches away. As for chasing, or hide-and-seek, well, he couldn't run, and if I hid somewhere, he'd look for me, then forget what he was looking for, and go sit in his armchair by the fire and fall asleep. I once spent an hour crouched at the back of my mother's wardrobe thinking I'd cleverly outwitted him, whilst he snored, legs splayed before him, the *Daily Mail* draped over his face. So, we played poker on the back step if it was fine, at the table in the kitchen if it rained. But every afternoon at about two o'clock the exhaustion of being eighty-five, bones aching, would sweep through Grandpa Mac and he'd sleep in his chair leaving me to my own devices.

I read *Kidnapped*, *The Railway Children*, *Treasure Island*. I wandered and played games on my own. There was a municipal golf course behind the bungalows at the other side of the road. Golfers saw fairways and greens, I saw a vast open space, a landscape that became whatever I wanted it to be in my playing imaginings. When I read *Kidnapped*, that golf course was the Highlands, the golfers were the enemy. They wore checked pants and Pringle

jumpers, but I knew they were really Redcoats, looking for Alan Breck. I would foil them. The first hole
was a long one. To the left was rough. I could sneak
through Mrs Borthwick's garden, wriggle through
the hedge at the end and onto that rough. I could
hide. Golfers whacked their balls up that first fair-
way, then started the walk towards them. This took
a few minutes. Long enough for me to run out, grab
the balls and disappear back through the hedge,
run the length of Mrs Borthwick's garden, across
the road, and home. When I amassed ten balls, I'd
take them to Jean Mackintosh's shop on the corner
and sell them for five pence each. She sold them
back to golfers for fifty pence. A fair profit.

'Damnedest thing,' they'd say to her. 'A little girl
ran out and grabbed the balls as we were walking
up to them.'

'Children these days,' she'd say.

'That isn't you?' she asked me.

'No,' I said. ''Course not, I found these balls. I go
looking for them every night after tea.'

I bought ice lollies and Mars Bars with the money.
I didn't think I was doing anything wrong. In my
mind, I was doing it for Scotland, and The Cause.
Like Alan Breck, I had cunning, and style. I wore
hand-me-down corduroy pants (elastic-waisted,
very chic) and T-shirts that Fiona Smith across the
road, four years older than me, had grown out of.
Her mother would hand things in to my mother.
'Just can't see good clothes going to waste, Mrs
Longmore,' she'd say. 'Maybe your Abby would get
the good of them.'

One day, the green keeper was waiting at the gap in the hedge at the end of Mrs Borthwick's garden. He grabbed me. Heart thumping, I wriggled, kicked and tried to bite his hand and got away. He went to Mrs Borthwick's door and accused her children of stealing golf balls. She got very angry, telling him she and Frank, her husband, had no children, and she had no idea what he was talking about. But she knew. Next day, she gave me such a glare and said, 'You behave yourself, Abigail Longmore.' She never told, though. So my mother never found out about my efforts to rid the golf course of the scourge of the Redcoats.

She did, however, find out about my plans to save the passengers of the Flying Scotsman from certain doom. The railway passed the end of Crighton Street, long trains going to and coming from London. Inspired by *The Railway Children*, I wrote a warning on a sheet of paper. Danger, it said, line ahead blocked. I stood by the line holding it up. The train whizzed past, only inches from my face. Nobody saw my warning, which was a good thing really, as the line wasn't blocked, and stopping the train would have caused no end of bother. But my neighbour saw me by the railway line, forbidden territory, told my mother, and I was spanked and sent to bed without any supper. That was the first, and only, time she ever hit me. Of course it was a reaction. Fear. I could so easily have got sucked under that speeding train. Death plagued her. It would have been another one lost, and she couldn't have withstood that pain. She hit me for the love of me.

In the Garden of Mrs Pink

Grandpa Mac was scolded for not keeping an eye on me. At ten o'clock that night, when Mum was in bed, he brought me a slice of bread and jam and a glass of milk. He wiped my tears with his big white hanky and and held me close, a snuffling, sobbing child. He told me I should try to be a good girl. My mother worried about me, and I was a handful. He kissed my cheek and said, 'Well, your old Grandpa Mac still loves you.' He was my best friend, ever. But, after that, I was forbidden to leave the back garden.

As back gardens go, ours was fairly boring. My mother couldn't afford to do anything more than grow a few flowers and shrubs, though she tended them with love. So, there was a lawn surrounded by flower beds and beyond that a vegetable patch where we grew onions, potatoes, beans, peas, cabbage, cauliflower. My mother was ahead of her time, growing what we ate organically. My taste in food, though, was still juvenile. I thought the best things to eat came out of a tin.

I played *Treasure Island* on the lawn, using an upturned kitchen chair as a boat. Grandpa Mac was Long John Silver, which he enjoyed. Or Blind Pew, which he enjoyed even more. Lumbering after me calling, 'The Black Spot, the Black Spot. You're doomed.' Me squealing. But always, always after lunch – an egg sandwich, or beans on toast – he'd shuffle off to his armchair, and sleep.

I wandered about, pulled petals off the roses, hid between the rows of peas, picked, shelled and ate some. But I was bored. I longed for the open spaces of the golf course. Eventually, I squeezed through the hedge into Mrs Edward's garden next door. It was pretty much the same as ours. Except she grew strawberries. So I ate some of those. And spied on her from behind her gooseberry bushes as she hung out her sheets. After that, I squeezed into the Hendersons' garden which was posh. It had a flowered sofa that hung on a frame, a canopy over it that matched the covering on the sofa. I sat on it, swinging, playing at being Doris Day. But Mrs Henderson saw me, banged on the window and shooed me away.

The next garden belonged to the Taylors. It was interesting because they never tended it. Weeds grew high as the sky. In amongst the nettles and thistles were bits of bicycle and rope and abandoned garden tools. Trouble was they had a big alsatian, Luther, tied to a post at the far end. He barked and strained at his rope when he saw me. I had to scarper, which I regretted because it would have been wonderful to explore. I squeezed, once more, through a hedge, and found myself in the garden of Mrs Pink.

Oh, wondrous place. It was laden with blooms. Large blowsy blooms, peony roses, dahlias, mostly pink. But yellows and reds, too. At the far end, where I entered, was a rose-covered arch, and beyond that a fountain made by a bronzed sculpture of a small cherub peeing. Crazy paving wound down the centre of the lawn to a patio where there were elaborate wrought-iron chairs and a table with an umbrella. On the lawn was a huge seat; wrought iron again, it was painted pink. The back of this seat was heart-shaped and in the middle of the heart were the entwined initials, VW and JD. I thought it beautiful. But the thing that brought joy to my young heart was the pond. Lilies grew round it, goldfish moved slowly just below the surface. And a ruddy-faced gnome wearing green trousers, red waistcoat and yellow pointy hat fished in it. I know, I know, Mrs Pink's garden was hideous. Kitsch. But I was ten; sophistication, subtlety were nothing to me, I thought it glorious.

After that, I visited the garden of Mrs Pink every day. I called the gnome Robert, after Redford who was my love and heart-throb. Grandpa Mac had once taken me to see *Butch Cassidy and the Sundance Kid*; though he'd slept through it, I had been thrilled. For weeks after that Patricia Harrower and I played Butch and Sundance on the golf course. She was Butch, I was Sundance, the golfers were the posse of men, led by the Man in the White Hat, chasing us across the Wild West. Once, when we made the Big Leap into the furious river at the bottom of the canyon, which in our case was into the steep bunker at the fourteenth hole, Patricia sprained her ankle. She told her mother it was all my fault, I had made her do it, the rat fink. And her mother complained to my mother that I was a tearaway and Patricia was forbidden to play with me. My mother told me not to go near Patricia, I seemed to be leading her astray. We didn't talk for about a fortnight. But then we patched things up and were back blowing up trains on the golf course.

I told Robert, the gnome, about all this. I told him about Mum and Grandpa Mac, and Patricia being away for the whole of the school holidays and me having nobody to play with. I told him about trying to stop the train and about stealing the golf balls. He understood. He had a cheery face, big smile. He was a very good listener.

Sometimes Mrs Pink would be in her garden, and I would spy on her. She always had a man with her, different men. In time, I saw that on certain days the same man would be there. She'd sit with them on the patio, or on the heart-shaped seat, laughing, smoking, drinking from a long glass, ice cubes clinking. I was in awe.

Once, when I thought she was away I sat on the heart-shaped seat, playing at being Mrs Pink. 'Oh, JD,' I said, taking long draws on a twig, blowing out pretend smoke, 'I love you. You are my own true love.'

And Mrs Pink laughed. She laughed and laughed and laughed. 'Oh my,' she said, wiping tears from her eyes, 'is that meant to be me?' Then, 'Who the hell are you, anyway? And why do you keep coming to my garden?'

This was a surprise to me. I'd thought I'd done a pretty good job of sneaking unseen up to Robert to chat to him. 'I'm Abby,' I told her.

'Abby Longmore,' she said. 'I've heard about you.'

I think this must have been because of the milk. The previous winter, when it was icy cold, especially in the mornings when the milk was on the doorsteps, I'd gone up every path in the street and poked off the tops of the bottles and sucked out the frozen cream from every one. All the neighbours had come to our door and complained about me. I hadn't thought it naughty. I'd just got carried away. I got grounded for two weeks and had to wash the dishes every night for that.

'You,' Mrs Pink said, 'have a reputation. You're meant to be a very naughty little girl.'

'I'm not naughty,' I said. 'I just do things. Then I find out the things I do are naughty. If I knew they were naughty before I did them, I wouldn't do them.'

'Excellent excuse,' she said. 'I might even use it some time.'

She looked at me. Her face underneath the layer of make-up was gentle. Her lips were painted red, blue shadow round her eyes, her brows plucked into a permanently surprised arch. Her hair was long, pinned at the back into a tight roll. Close up she looked older than she did from a distance. She must have been in her mid-forties. Older than my mum. In those days I thought my mum very old and sometimes wondered if she remembered covered wagons, and had worn a crinoline dress when she was little.

Mrs Pink offered me a drink. Brought me Coca-Cola in a tall glass, ice cubes clinking, a striped straw with a bendy bit at the end. I was impressed. I asked her if JD, the initials on the bench, was her husband.

'No,' she said. 'I'm Veronica Watts, that's the VW bit. I'm not married. JD is John Davis, the man I loved.'

'Is he dead?'

'No, sweetie,' she said. 'He just went back to his wife and kids. The way men do.'

'Do they?'

'Yes, sweetie,' patting my cheek. 'They do.'

Sweetie. Nobody had called me that before, I felt special. I looked at my Mickey Mouse watch (a Christmas present from Grandpa Mac): four o'clock. I had to go. Grandpa would be waking up soon. I swigged the last of my Coke, belched, because that's what gassy drinks did to me, and ran the length of the garden, through the hedges and home. When Grandpa woke, I was sitting on the back step, reading *Little Women*. That was my daytime literature. Nights, under the bedclothes, using a torch, I was working my way through *Valley of the Dolls*. I was learning a lot.

After that I had daily chats with Mrs Pink in her fabulous garden. I sipped ice-cold Coke, and never forgot to say a few words to Robert, the gnome. I'd stroke his cheery face, I thought him wonderful.

Sometimes, Mrs Pink would have one of her men friends with her, and she'd wave me away. I'd slip back through the gardens, and wait for Grandpa Mac to wake up and play poker with me.

Once she took me in her pink car to Portobello, to Demarco's ice cream parlour. She bought me a knickerbocker glory. A huge concoction in a long, long glass. I had to kneel on my seat to get a proper eating angle on it. It was the loveliest thing I'd ever eaten. Demarco's the most beautiful place I'd ever seen. Dark tiles round the walls, a sweeping staircase that led to the seating area above, and the lavatories. I had to climb it. When I came down, slowly, queening it, hand on the banister, I pretended I was Rita Hayworth. I'd seen her on movies, Sunday afternoon on the telly. Gilda.

Mrs Pink drank dark coffee from a tiny cup, smoked and smiled all the time I was eating.

And afterwards we walked along the sands.

'Where did you go for your holidays?' Miss Wilson, my teacher, asked me when I went back to school.

'Portobello,' I said.

Everyone in the class laughed. Portobello was only ten minutes away from my street. But I didn't mind. I'd had a grand time. Mrs Pink held my hand as we paddled.

On the way home, she said, 'Your mum must have a time of it. Looking after you and your grandpa. Cooking when she comes home. Bet she cleans the house after she gets back from work, too. I hope you help.'

I stared at her. It hadn't crossed my mind to help. I did my homework, I watched telly, I went to bed. Helping wasn't on my agenda. That afternoon, after my visit, I peeled the potatoes for supper. Mum couldn't believe it. 'Thank you, Abby. That was thoughtful of you.' She looked at Grandpa Mac. 'Did you tell her to peel the potatoes?'

He shrugged and shook his head.

Mrs Pink suggested I dust a little and maybe vacuum the living room before Mum got home. So I did. Then Mrs Pink thought it might be a good thing if I went to meet Mum when she was coming back from work and help her carry her groceries. Even though I was confined to the back garden. I did. She didn't mind at all. In fact, she was glad to see me.

Mum could hardly believe it. 'Keeping Abby in the back garden has brought about such a change in her,' she said. 'I should have done it years ago.'

I went to meet her every day. And on our walks back home together, we talked, teased one another, made jokes. She wasn't the worried-faced, anxious mum I'd always known. She seemed younger, funnier. We'd stop and stare into gardens, decide which was the prettiest. We talked about favourite things, food, television programmes, books. She told me about the books she'd read when she was a little girl. And games she'd played. My mum wasn't just a mum, she was a human being. Mrs Pink taught me that.

The only thing I didn't like about visiting Mrs Pink, was Kenneth. It was hate at first sight. We loathed each other. I think, now, that he resented me. When I was there, Mrs Pink spoke to me, and virtually ignored him. He was a tall man, thick dark hair. He wore his shirts open at the neck, with the collar flapped over the lapels of his jacket. A small curling of dark hair sprouted at his neck. His gold chain lay strangely on top of it.

If I was there when Kenneth arrived, he'd tell me to bugger off. I'd look at Mrs Pink, who would nod. 'Off you go, sweetie.' And I'd go to the hole in the hedge and make my way back home. Mrs Pink always did what Kenneth wanted. Well, she would. I later found out that 24 Crighton Street was his house. And the men who visited Mrs Pink, her clients, had all been sent by him.

Prostitute was a newish word to me. One of the first times I ever encountered it was when I read about Mrs Pink in the newspaper. It was three days before school went back, I was standing by her front gate when the police arrived. This was a huge thing in Crighton Street, the police. They never came here. Patricia and I were doing what we were going to be doing for the next few years of our lives, hanging about. Somehow, now that we were both approaching eleven, playing Butch Cassidy and the Sundance Kid had lost its appeal. We were more of a mind to stand swinging on the gate, drinking Coke straight from the tin, chatting and singing the latest Rod Stewart song.

So, there we were, swigging, singing, swinging when the police drew up, two black cars, outside Mrs Pink's house. They went in. And about fifteen minutes later came out with Mrs Pink, Kenneth and the small balding man that I recognized as Mrs Pink's Friday man. He looked very furtive and shocked. Mrs Pink stared straight ahead, as if she didn't care about anything. A policewoman held her arm.

It was in the papers next day. Miss Veronica Watts and Mr Kenneth Edwards were charged at Edinburgh Sheriff Court today with running a house of ill repute at 24 Crighton Street. Miss Watts was also charged with prostitution. There was more.

But, basically, I was quite glad I'd been reading *Valley of the Dolls*. Now I knew what prostitution was. The trial was set for the fourteenth of September.

In the weeks before the trial I visited often. Mrs Pink still sat with me on the heart-shaped seat, and we chatted. I told her about school, about my problems with long division, which I hated, and how, soon, next year, I'd be going up to the big school. I was looking forward to it. And I was scared of it.

'That's how it always is, sweetie,' she said. 'All your life you'll be scared of the next big thing. But if you don't do it, go forward, you'll be sorry. And that's worse. Besides, scary things are never that scary when you get to them. Go forward, boldly. That's the thing to do.'

She was going on trial for prostitution. She must have been scared stiff, but it never showed. She put on her make-up, she served me iced drinks, she let me chat to Robert, the gnome.

But on the night before the case came up, she said, 'After tomorrow you can't come here any more. I'm going away. I'm never coming back.'

I thought she meant she was going to jail, and started to cry. But she hugged me. Told me she wasn't going to jail. She was a first offender. She'd get a fine. 'A big fine,' she said. 'But Kenneth will pay. But I won't come back here. Kenneth is selling the house.'

'I won't see you again?' I said.

She shook her head. 'Best not to, love.'

'Or Robert?'

'Tell you what, you can have Robert. You take him home.'

'Oh no, she's not. She's not having the gnome.' Kenneth had been sitting at the kitchen table, playing patience, listening.

'For God's sake, Kenneth, let her have it. You don't want it. You never liked it.'

'That's not the point. It's mine, and she's not getting it.'

The air was charged. They were both nervous about the trial. And it wasn't that Kenneth didn't want me to have the gnome. He didn't want me to have anything. It was a revenge thing. He hated me.

'I'll play you for him,' I said. I looked him straight in the eye, and knew I could take him. He was the nervy kind, drummed his fingers, his eyes roamed the room. His lips twitched. Every thought he ever had moved across his face.

'Play?' he asked.

'Poker,' I said.

He laughed. 'Okay. Poker.' He thought he was dealing with a kid. But he was dealing with Abby Longmore whose Grandpa Mac had taught her well.

I fleeced him. I just sat there at Mrs Pink's kitchen table, I had a dreadful hand, and his was pretty good. I knew it just by looking at him. But I was still of face, this was serious, Robert's fate was at stake. I just kept my face impassive. Easy, I just thought about long division, and geography, capitals of the world. Things that bored me mindless.

Twenty minutes, three hands (Kenneth demanded

25

best of three when he lost the first one) later, Robert was mine. Mrs Pink helped me carry him along the road. It was the only time I ever left her house by the front door.

My mother was appalled. A garden gnome. She was hard pushed to think of anything she wanted less.

'But he's mine, Mum. I won him.'

'Won him? How?'

'Poker. Grandpa Mac taught me.'

Grandpa Mac was standing behind her, looking shifty. 'She plays a mean game.'

So far Mrs Pink had said nothing.

'Does this thing belong to you?' said Mum.

Mrs Pink nodded. 'I won't be needing him after tomorrow. I'm moving away.'

'I expect you are,' said Mum. 'So you've given us a garden gnome. A fishing garden gnome.'

I had my arms round Robert. 'Isn't he lovely?'

My mother didn't have to say that no, he wasn't. Her horror was there, on her face. She'd have been rubbish at poker. 'How do you know my daughter?' she asked Mrs Pink.

'Abby's been visiting me. Most days this summer, actually.'

My mother looked at me, looked at Mrs Pink, thought about the back garden confinement, and everything clicked. Mothers are like that. Things click quickly with them.

'We've had some lovely chats, haven't we, Abby?' said Mrs Pink.

I nodded. I was for it now. I'd been breaking out of the garden.

In the Garden of Mrs Pink

But, I'll say something for mothers, when things click into place, everything clicks into place. The change in me. The help I'd been giving her in the house, going to meet her coming home from work. The talk, the jokes. The new understanding. 'Well, thanks for caring for her when I've been at work, Mrs—'

'Pink?' said Mrs Pink. 'I know what I'm called round here. Lovely name. I love pink.'

They shook hands, my mum and Mrs Pink. Mum said, 'Thank you.' And kissed her cheek.

In front of the whole street, my mum kissed Mrs Pink, and people would have been watching from the dark of their living rooms.

Mrs Pink walked down the path, stopped at the gate and waved. That was the last time I saw her.

She was fined. It was in all the papers. House of ill-repute in sleepy Edinburgh suburb.

Mrs Pink had stood in the dock looking defiant. 'I don't think prostitution is wrong,' she said. 'If I thought it wrong, I wouldn't do it.' There was something oddly familiar about that. Number twenty-four was sold to people who painted the railings green, uprooted all the pink plants and replaced them with blues and yellows. I never found out what happened to the heart-shaped seat.

A year later, Grandpa Mac died. I went on to secondary school. Boldly forward, I thought. Six years after that to university. I became a lawyer. I married. I divorced. Last year my mother died, she ended her days at number twenty Crighton Street, the house she struggled to keep. She wouldn't have wanted to be anywhere else.

I live in Edinburgh's New Town. A garden flat. I'm considered to have taste, style. So nobody understands why I have a hideous fishing garden gnome, grinning amongst my delphiniums. When asked, I shrug, and I smile and say he's Robert, and that we go way back. To the summer of 1972, in fact, when I started to grow up, lost my innocence and learned from Mrs Pink that my mother loved me.

COUNTRY COOKING COUNTDOWN

Siân Preece

SIÂN PREECE was born in Wales and has lived in Canada, France and, since 1994, in Aberdeen. Her short story collection *From the Life* was published in 2000, and she is a regular columnist and reviewer for Scottish newspapers. She also writes for Radio 4, and has appeared as a commentator in the Scottish broadcast media. She is currently working on a novel.

'You'll not need a lot done,' said the make-up girl. I breathed a discreet sigh of relief – her lipsticks and pots were gluey and caked, with hairs sticking out of them, her brushes still coloured red and blue from their last use. She obviously didn't clean the tools of her trade between victims, or even between decades. In fact, the whole room was shoddy; it had been decorated back in the seventies, and no one had seen fit to change the orange carpet and peeling, swirly wallpaper since then. This television studio wasn't turning out as glamorous as I'd expected.

'You've got lovely skin,' said the girl. 'Fiona, come and have a look at her skin, it's lovely!'

'Lovely,' murmured Fiona, who was the Studio Manager on *Country Cooking Countdown*, and obviously too important to be looking at people's skin.

'What do you do for it?' the make-up girl persisted. 'What products do you use?'

'Soap and water.' I paused for effect. 'And dermabrasion.'

'*Dermabrasion!* What, where they scrape your skin off with that machine? Like sandpaper! Ugh, did it hurt?'

31

'Total nightmare,' I nodded. 'My head was just a big scab for weeks.'

'Worth it, though!' She stroked my face like she was petting a kitten. 'It's a baby's bottom, is your face.'

'Well, it was a *baboon's* bottom when they did it, and the *pain* . . .'

Before you start thinking that I'm some Botox-addicted lady-who-lunches, let me tell you what my skin was like before. *Acne*. Even the name is repulsive. We're talking purple porridge. We're talking pebble-dashing. We're talking a pus pizza with extra topping, and believe me, I heard them all at school. The other kids used to slip those *Caring for Adolescent Skin* leaflets into my satchel, not out of kindness but to see me blush, though I spent my school years in a state of permanent blush anyway. And besides, I'd heard all the remedies. My mother used to make me drink cabbage water, wouldn't let me touch chips, and, when that failed, she said, 'It's your personality that counts!' Nice try, Ma, but not when you're fourteen it isn't. If you're covered in acne, you may as well spend your teenage years in a T-shirt that reads 'Ignore me'. Or a balaclava. *Personality*, my bum – it doesn't matter how nice the chocolate bar is if the wrapper makes you boak.

Thank God for adulthood! Thank God for the hormones settling down (apart from the monthly grumble to remind you they're still there). And thank God for Dr McGregor, who said, 'We can do something for those acne scars, you know . . .' and made me cry right there in the surgery. I could have kissed him, but if you've grown up with acne, kissing people spontaneously is not the sort of thing you do. 'I know a good dermatologist in Edinburgh,' he said, writing the address down.

'In Edinburgh?' said the make-up girl. 'I'll get his name off you, yeah?'

A bell rang, making us jump.

'Oh, that's us! Time to go to studio. I'll just do under your eyes with a bit of this *tooshy clatt*.' She waved a tube of *Touche Eclat* at me (when you've had acne, you know all the concealers). '*Eevee St-Lorrent*,' she added, then dropped her voice confidentially. 'Now, we tell all the attractive women this ' I smiled the compliment away '– look out for Davey. He's a bit of a George Roper.'

'G. Roper,' clarified Fiona with a shudder. 'Groper.'

'I will,' I said. 'Thanks for the warning.' But I figured I could handle Davey Donald.

The studio was full of lights hanging from a black skeleton of girders on the ceiling, and microphones, and people with headphones who looked like they knew what they were doing. One man was skiting around on a big, wheeled camera like a Dalek, dodging the scurrying assistants and clipboard-wielders, but Davey looked as relaxed as if he were in his own front room. He lolled in a chair with a pen tucked into his thick dark hair, looking like a young Terry Wogan – at least, if Terry Wogan worked out – and wore leather trousers – and silk shirts.

Actually, strike that whole Terry Wogan analogy. He was engrossed in his notes, but when Fiona ushered me into the lights, he jumped up and POW! Out came his megawatt smile – the famous smile off the telly – like he'd just thrown a switch. He took my sweaty hand in his long, cool one and gave me a wet kiss on the cheek, and I thought of what the make-up girl had said.

'Hello, darlin'! You must be Heather, right? Are you nervous?'

I shook my head, didn't want to give him the satisfaction.

'Well, don't be – Davey's here! He'll look after you!' He put his arm around my shoulder, and I reminded myself that thousands of women (in the local broadcasting area, at least) would pawn their grannies to be where I was now. I focused on the glittering backdrop, the words *Country Cooking Countdown* with the three C's merging together into one big one. It looked tackier than it did on the television; you could see the nails holding it together, the spangled paper pinned onto the plywood. You never saw the huge studio on telly, the banked rows of the mainly elderly, mainly female audience, coughing away and sooking sweeties, with their handbags at their feet. You only saw the cosy kitchen set with its two wee cookers and two wee counters, the yellow and the orange – 'Bananas' and 'Nuts'. There it was, looking sort of familiar, but sort of not. I must have seen it on the screen a hundred times, but confronted with it now, expected to *step into* it and start playing houses for the cameras, I started to shake.

It was my friend Christine had got me here. She'd applied for both of us to enter the competition without telling me, but it was only me who got in, and she'd been in the huff ever since. Serves her right. 'I'll tell them to have you instead!' I wailed when I heard the news, but it was me they wanted because of my hobby – well, my small business these days. The beekeeping. The whole point of *Country Cooking Countdown* was to promote regional produce, and the honey I sold through local health food stores would allow Davey to subject me to the Donald Banter. Also, in the final interview, Christine couldn't be stopped from speaking in a fake American accent, pure mid-Atlantic, so that was her out. Daft cow.

There was a commotion at the door and Fiona bundled in with a distraught old lady, who quavered, 'Sorry I'm late! Sorry, sorry!' My rival cook, looking as bewildered as I felt. 'The place is a rabbit warren, so it is,' she added to me, taking her glasses off and dabbing the sweat from her face with a sodden tissue. I smiled sympathetically and offered her a dry one.

'Hello, darlin'!' cried Davey, but with less conviction this time, and I noticed that he only kissed her on the hand, though with the same wet slobber.

Fiona ushered us behind the set, and the serious business of making a television programme began. We listened while Davey warmed up the crowd, and you had to admit, the boy was a pro, had them in the palm of his long, cool hand. Though Fiona could hear him as well as us, she took her instructions from her Madonna-style headset, counted us in and 'Three – two – one – you're on!'

The audience had disappeared now, still there, but clapping unseen in the darkness. Every time I looked up, the lights blinded me, so I focused on Davey, his hand on my shoulder as he nicknamed me 'Heather Honey.' Mary, also chosen for her 'local produce' connection, was 'Mary from the Dairy'. We laughed obediently.

'Now, girls, I want a good clean fight, no biting, no gouging – *only joking*! You have five minutes to make a cold starter, and your time starts NOW!'

I laid out my ingredients and set to. It wasn't going to be a very cold starter under these hot lights, and the smell of my smoked haddie made me reel as I chopped it up for a fish mousse. Davey pestered me with questions, pretended to spill my ingredients and then sang, *'Only joking!'* That was his catchphrase – not much of a catchphrase, but he drew out the 'O's like he had a copyright on them. He was getting on my nerves, but the cooking, the routine of it, calmed me, and I answered his questions, even though he kept cutting me short with quips of his own.

'Do you get stung often?' he asked, and I got as far as 'No, only—' before he butted in with, 'Ever had a little prick in your hand?!', making the audience shriek. Pretty daring for afternoon telly, and us going out live too.

'Why, is that an offer?' I said, but he had pirouetted over to Mary and was inviting her to 'Pull the udder one'. You could see his heart wasn't in it, though, and soon he was back behind me, undoing my yellow apron strings and making a 'naughty schoolboy' face. I waved my knife at him, and he cowered in mock-alarm. *'Only joking!'* I mimicked, and the audience laughed. It felt good, I could see why he got off on it, and the time seemed to fly until the buzzer went for the end of the first round.

Mary was of the Old School and had wrought slices of salmon into intricate strips, dressed them with dill, quite beautiful. But when Davey cried, 'Well, audience – are you Bananas? Or are you Nuts?!' they held up their yellow cards, and I had won the first round.

'That was good,' he muttered to me while they played a clip, and the studio assistants scurried in to clean up the mess. 'That thing with the knife – they like a bit of flirting, the auld dears.' He waved a hand dismissively at the audience. 'Keep it up, Heather Honey!' He patted my bottom and danced away.

I shook my head. He'd seen my face, he'd heard my name, and he still showed no sign that he remembered me.

He was David *Mac*Donald fifteen years ago, had obviously dropped the Mac for television since then, or perhaps there was another David MacDonald in Equity. I'd had such a crush on him at school, it was practically medical – palpitations, sweating, the whole bit. He was the golden boy of the Academy: captain of football, leading light of the drama society.

In the summer he played golf at his daddy's club,
in the winter he skiied in Switzerland, instead of
scuffing around Aviemore in an anorak like the rest
of us. Daddy MacDonald had an engineering firm
and knew politicians, and was always writing opinionated letters about 'the work ethic' in the local
papers. Davey talked confidently to adults, charmed
all the teachers, and had had his hand shaken by
Prince Charles when he won a national design
competition. The design was published in the
Academy magazine (editor: D. MacDonald), and I
took it home to show my daddy, who worked for
Davey's father, though he had never so much as
seen his boss in the flesh.

'This Davey must be a clever boy . . .' he said carefully. 'You'd normally need years of practical engineering experience to produce something like this.'

'He is, Daddy, he's dead clever!'

'I bet he is,' he said, and gave me a strange look.

There was a photo of Davey beside the design,
and I cut it out secretly and kept it in my jewellery
box. I couldn't admit my crush on him – he was so
out of my league, I hardly even dared talk *about*
him – though my pal Christine knew. But I always
made sure I sat behind him in school, and my education went something like this: 'The square of the
angle is equal to . . . the back of Davey's head', '*La
plume de ma tante est sur* . . . the back of Davey's
head', 'The highest mountain in Scotland is Ben . .
Davey . . . *Davey* . . . *DAVEY*'!

'He's a handsome lad,' whispered Mary as we

waited to be counted back in, 'but he's painted up
like a hooer,' she added, deadpan. We burst out
giggling, and Fiona shushed us as Davey stepped
forward, slipping straight into 'host' mode again.

'Mmm-mm!' He rubbed his non-existent belly.
'I've been tucking into those starters in the break!'
The liar, he hadn't wanted to spoil his make-up.
'Now it's time for these two lovely ladies to dazzle
us with a couple more of their culinary creations!'
He singled out a pensioner in the front row. *'A
couple of culinary creations!* Bet you can't say that
with your teeth out, eh darlin'?'

The object of his wit rolled with laughter, nudged
her friends.

'Only joking! Right, ladies, you have fifteen
minutes to complete a main course, starting NOW!'

Most of the ingredients had been prepared for
us, but the time was still tight. I tried to concentrate as Davey bombarded me with questions.

'So, Heather Honey, you were telling me about
your bees in the first round . . .' I had been, but
he'd kept interrupting me. 'There's only one Queen
in each hive, right? In charge of all those men! Bit
like our Fiona!'

The camera flashed briefly to Fiona, standing at
the edge of the set in her headset. She waved, made
a wry face – this was part of their act.

'Well,' I said, 'most of the bees are actually
female. They're the Workers. But the Queen is the
only one who can lay eggs. And then there are a
few hundred Drones – they're the males.' I thought
of the audience demographic. 'They're like the

Queen's husbands, and their only job is to father the young bees. Drones don't have stings, and they can't even feed themselves – the Workers feed them, and clean the hive, and defend it against predators.'

I could practically hear Davey's brain ticking on this one, revelling in it.

'That's the life for me!' he crowed. 'Lying around all day, being fed by women, only a bit of nookie as my job description!'

It was so predictable – men always said that when you told them. I waited for the audience reaction to die down, then I added the punchline:

'But you know how a bee dies when it stings you? Well, that happens to the Drones after they've mated with the Queen. It rips their abdomens open,' I added with relish. 'If there are any Drones left by the winter, they're virgins. And they're not needed then – the Queen doesn't breed in winter – so the Workers starve the Drones, or drive them out of the hive to die. See, the minute the Drones become useless, they're told to buzz off!'

Davey's mouth was hanging open, and I couldn't resist popping a piece of chopped carrot into it. He couldn't spit it out, so he chewed it twice, swallowed it, and shot me a sour glance, but he soon rallied, like the pro he was.

'Mary!' he cried, schmoozing over to her, 'it's not like that at the dairy, eh? It's one bull to all those cows. . .'

The man was obsessed. At least I was left in peace now to make my honey-glazed chops while he quizzed Mary on the natural history of the cow.

Honey isn't a spectacular 'main course' ingredient. Mary had done much better with her cheese croquettes and this time, when Davey asked, 'Are you Bananas – or are you Nuts?' the audience voted, quite rightly, for her. It was one-all.

In the break, I congratulated Mary, then took the chance to dash to the loo. When I came out, Davey was waiting for me in the corridor.

'Ah, you see, Heather, you went too far there,' he murmured, getting right into my personal space. 'They don't mind a bit of banter, the auld dears, but they don't like to see a young woman getting uppity, eh? It's not ladylike.' He put an arm around my shoulder. 'Ah, but I forgive you, hen! Can't resist a pretty face!' He lowered his voice. 'Tell you what – it's the best of three. You could still win! With a little help from Davey . . . See, I have a lot of influence – bit of body language, a nod in the right place. I know how these things are done.' He put a finger to his nose, winked at me. 'Now, Heather, there's a little tradition on this show; I always take the winner out for a celebratory meal . . . and I can't see me sitting across a restaurant table from old Mary now, eh? So, you be nice to me . . . and I'll be nice to you!'

I pulled away from him. 'You'd really do that?'

'That's how things are done, Heather Honey!' he cackled. 'See you on set! We'll talk about the birds and the bees!'

The birds and the bees.

There's nothing like the atmosphere of a school

on St Valentine's Day. You can practically hear the hormones popping – all those gangly boys, all those puppy-plump girls, grappling with the concept of Romance, practising being In Love. The Biology teacher tried to knock it out of us with cross-sections of male and female rabbits, and frogs in formaldehyde, their poor little tummies splayed open like unbuttoned waistcoats, but still the air swam with excitement on the fourteenth of February.

I'd had the usual joke card from my daddy that morning, but I knew better than to expect one from any of the boys, and I certainly wasn't going to waste my money on sending any to them. It didn't bother me, not too much. I sat at my desk, waiting for the teacher to arrive for the first lesson, and vicariously sucked the excitement from the other girls.

Christine slipped into the seat beside me. 'I got a card!'

'Magic!'

'Not really,' she pulled a face. ' It's from Stephen Anderson – he's in the year below us! That doesn't count.'

Still, she seemed excited, and when Davey MacDonald came in she perked right up, and stuck out her little bosoms in their training bra.

Davey seemed to catch my eye. I blushed, looked away, but when I looked back, he was coming up the classroom – towards us. And he was carrying a stack of Valentine's cards! Maybe he was going to give one to Christine. Maybe he was going to give one to both of us! He had enough to give to every girl in the class, perhaps that was his plan – just the sort of flash thing he'd do – but it wouldn't matter. Just to know that his hand had fleetingly touched a pen to form *my name* would be dream material for months . . . I held my breath as he leaned over my desk – and slapped down all of the cards.

'Thanks, but no thanks,' he said. I stared at him, dumb. The cards, I saw now, had all been opened. Cautiously, I took one from its torn envelope. *To Davey, my darling, the love of my life, I long for the day when you make me your wife – from Heather.* And kisses. Not my writing, of course. I opened another. Different handwriting, but a similar message. *Davey, you're divine, will you be mine? In all sorts of weather – with love from Your Heather!* And so it went on, twenty-five Valentine's cards, all signed in my name. The whole class must have had the same idea, they must all have known how I felt! Some of them had decorated the fronts of the cards, spattering the faces of the loving bunnies and teddies with red-inked acne, exploding zits. I was vaguely aware of Christine's voice, distraught – 'Heather, I didn't mean – I didn't think they'd *all* do it!'

Davey raised his voice so that the whole class could hear. 'When I want a pizza, Heather, I'll order one.'

And even then, as I sat there melting with shame, I thought: he didn't mean to be cruel, he was just trying to save face. Everyone was laughing, and he wanted to make sure they were laughing only at me. That was all. How things were done.

'Sweets for the sweet!' cried Davey. 'You have five minutes to assemble a dessert, ladies!'

This I could make in my sleep. A real showcase of a pudding: honey and cream and raspberries, meringues butterflying around the edges, an edible edifice. Even without tasting it, I knew it would look great on television. I built up the layers carefully, added more cream, and, while I did, Davey worked the crowd for me. He dipped a finger into the honey, tasted it sensually.

'She's as sweet as the heather, the bloomin' purple heather!' he sang, and the elderly audience clapped along compulsively, like Pavlov's dogs.

Mary, putting together her fruit and whipped cream, could see the favouritism. Her hands shook as she arranged sponge fingers around her dish, trying to hold it together, but the studio lights made everything gooey, greasy, and she cried out as her bowl of cream skittered off the counter and smashed on the floor.

'Oh, too bad, Mary!' cried Davey exultantly. He gave me such a knowing smile that, before I knew it, I had snatched up my own bowl of cream and taken it across to Mary.

'Here, I've got plenty left!' I blurted.

'Thank you, lass!' She smiled into my face.

Davey didn't miss a beat. 'A round of applause, ladies and gentlemen! That's the spirit, eh?'

I returned to my own work of art, which was wilting a little by now.

'And, talking of spirit . . .' Davey added, 'as the last seconds count down, let's have a wee dram to toast our contestants – courtesy of the Skean Dhu distillery!' He poured out three clinking glasses. The audience were already primed with little plastic cups of the stuff, had their eyes on the studio clock, ready for the familiar ritual.

'Three!' yelled Davey.

'Two!' they joined in.

'One!' everyone cried together, and I put the last raspberry in place, a little glistening heart of the deepest red. Davey moved in behind me, plugging that body language, just as he'd promised.

'Well, then, are you Bananas – or are you Nuts?'

'I'm Bananas!' I cried, and I picked up my lovely, creamy, custardy pudding and placed it square in Davey's face. 'I'm bananas, Davey MacDonald!' The raspberries and honey slid down his face and oozed onto his silk shirt, and it was worth every second of the fifteen-year wait.

SOMETHING OLD, SOMETHING NEW

Leila Aboulela

Her country disturbed him. It reminded him of the first time he had held a human bone, the touching simplicity of it, the strength. Such was the landscape of Khartoum; bone-coloured sky, a purity in the desert air, bareness. A bit austere and therefore static. But he was driven by feelings, that was why he was here, that was why he had crossed boundaries and seas, and now walked through a blaze of hot air from the aeroplane steps to the terminal.

She was waiting for him outside the airport, wearing national dress, a pale orange tobe that made her look even more slender than she was. I mustn't kiss you. No, she laughed, you mustn't. He had forgotten how vibrant she was, how happy she made him feel. She talked, asked him questions. Did you have a good trip, are you hungry, did all your luggage arrive, were they nice to you in the customs, I missed you too. There was a catch in her voice when she said that; in spite of her confidence she was shy. Come, come and meet my brother. They began to walk across a car park that was disorganized and dusty, the sun gleaming on the cars.

Her brother was leaning against a dilapidated Toyota. He was lanky with a hard-done-by expression. He looked irritated. Perhaps by the conflicting desire to get his sister off his hands and his misgivings about her marrying a foreigner. How did he see him now, through those narrow eyes, how did he judge him? A European coming to shake his hand, murmuring *salamu alleikum*, predictably wearing jeans, a white shirt but somewhat subdued for a foreigner.

She sat in the front next to her brother. He sat in the back with the rucksack that wouldn't fit in the boot. The car seats were shabby, a thin film of dust covered everything. I will get used to the dust, he told himself, but not the heat. He could do with a breath of fresh air, that tang of rain he was accustomed to. He wanted her to be next to him. And it suddenly seemed to him, in a peevish sort of way, unfair that they should be separated like that. She turned her head back and looked at him, smiled as if she knew. He wanted to say, you have no idea how much I ache for you, you have no idea. But he could not say that, not least because the brother understood English.

It was like a ride in a funfair. The windows wide open; voices, noises, car horns, people crossing the road at random, pausing in the middle, touching the cars with their fingers as if the cars were benign cattle. Any one of these passers-by could easily punch him through the window, yank off his watch, his sunglasses, snatch his wallet from the pocket of his shirt. He tried to roll up the window but couldn't.

Something Old, Something New

She turned and said, It's broken, I'm sorry. Her calmness made him feel that he needn't be so nervous. A group of schoolboys walked on the pavement, one of them stared at him, grinned and waved. He became aware that everyone looked like her, shared her colour, the women were dressed like her and they walked with the same slowness which had seemed to him exotic when he had seen her walking in Edinburgh.

Everything is new for you; she turned and looked at him gently. The brother said something in Arabic.

The car moved away from the crowded market to a wide shady road. Look, she said, take off your sunglasses and look. There's the Nile.

And there was the Nile, a blue he had never seen before, a child's blue, a dream's blue. Do you like it? she asked. She was proud of her Nile.

Yes, it's beautiful, he replied. But as he spoke he noticed that the river's flow was forceful, not innocent, not playful. Crocodiles no doubt lurked beneath the surface, hungry and ruthless. He could picture an accident; blood, death, bones.

And here is your hotel, she said. I booked you in the Hilton. She was proud that her country had a Hilton.

The car swept up the drive. A porter in a gaudy green uniform and stiff turban opened the door for him before he could do it himself. (At any rate the car had been in an accident and the dented door could only be opened from outside.) The porter took his rucksack; there was a small fuss involving the brother in order to open the boot

51

and get the suitcase. His luggage was mostly presents for her family. She had told him on the phone what to get and how much to get. They would be offended, she had explained, if you come empty-handed, they would think you don't care for me enough.

The hotel lobby was impressive, the cool tingling blast of the air-conditioner, music playing, an expanse of marble. He felt soothed somehow, more in control after the bumpy ride. With the brother away to park the car and a queue at the reception desk, they suddenly had time to talk.

I need an exit visa, she explained, to be able to leave and go back with you. To get the exit visa, I have to give a reason for leaving the country.

Because you're my wife, he said and they smiled at the word. Will be my wife. Will be, *insha' Allah. Insha' Allah.*

That's it, she said, we won't be able to get married and just leave. We'll have to stay a few days till the papers get sorted out. And the British Embassy . . . that's another story.

I don't understand what the problem is, he said.

Oh, she sighed, people have a wedding and they go off on their honeymoon. But we won't be able to do that, we will have to hang around and run from the Ministry of Interior to the Passport office to the British Embassy.

I see, he said, I see. Do I need an exit visa?

No, you're a visitor, you can leave whenever you like. But I need a visa, I need a reason to leave.

Right.

Something Old, Something New

They looked at each other and then he said, I
don't think your brother likes me.

No, no, he doesn't mean to be unfriendly . . .
you'll see.

The first time he saw her was at the Sudanese
restaurant near the new mosque in Edinburgh. His
old Chemistry teacher had taken him there after
Friday prayers. When she brought the menu, she
said to them that the peanut soup was good, a
speciality, but his teacher wanted the hummus salad
and he ordered the lentil soup instead because it
was familiar. He was by nature cautious, wanting
new things but held back by a vague mistrust. It
was enough for the time being that he had stepped
into the Nile Café, he had no intention of experi-
menting with weird tastes.

He was conscious of her footsteps as she came
from the kitchen, up the stairs. She was wearing
trousers and a brown headscarf that was tied at the
back of her neck. She had very black eyes that
slanted. After that day he went to the Nile Café
alone and often. It was convenient, close to the
Department of Zoology where he worked as a lab
technician. He wondered if, as she leaned and put
the dish of couscous in front of him, she could smell
the chemicals on him.

They got talking because there weren't many
customers in the restaurant and she had time on
her hands. The restaurant was new and word had
not yet got round that it was good.

We've started to get a few people coming in from

the mosque, she told him. Friday especially is a good day.

Yes, it was a Friday when I first came here and met you.

She smiled in a friendly way.

He told her that at one time he had not known that the big building next to the restaurant was a mosque. There was no sign that said so. I thought it was a church, he said and she laughed and laughed. He left her an extra tip that day; it was not often that people laughed at his jokes.

Had it not been for his old Chemistry teacher he would never have gone to the mosque. At a bus stop, a face he had not seen for a number of years. A face associated with a positive feeling, a time of encouragement. Secondary school, the ease with which he had written lab reports. They recognized each other straight away. How are you? What are you doing now? You were my best student.

In primary and secondary school, he had been the brightest in his class, the most able. He sat for the three sciences in his Standard Grades and got three As. It was the same when he did his Highers. There was no reason at all, his teachers said, why he should not sail through Medical School. But he got to his third year in Medicine and failed, failed again and dropped out. He had counselling and his parents were supportive, but no one really ever understood what had gone wrong. He was as bewildered by his failure as everyone else was. His get-up-and-go had suddenly disappeared, as if amputated. What's it all for, what's the point? he asked himself. He asked himself the taboo questions. And really, that was the worst of it, these were the questions that brought all the walls down.

Snap out of it, he was told. And snap out of it he eventually did; a girlfriend helped but then she found a job in London and drifted away. He was simply not up to Medical School. It's a shame, everyone agreed. They were sympathetic but at the same time they labelled him now, they put him in a box; a student who had 'dropped out', a 'giver-upper'.

One day when she brought him his plate of aubergine and minced meat he asked her, Would you like to go up to Arthur's Seat?

She had never been there before. It was windy, a summer wind that carried away the hats of tourists and messed up people's hair. Because her hair was covered, she looked neat, slightly apart from everyone else. It made the outing not as care-free as he imagined it would be. She told him she had recently got divorced after six months of marriage. She laughed when she said six months not six years, but he could tell she was sore – it was in her eyes. You have beautiful eyes, he said.

Everyone tells me that, she replied. He flushed and looked away at the green and grey houses that made up Edinburgh. She had wanted to talk about her divorce, she had not wanted to hear compliments.

They talked a little about the castle. He told her about his girlfriend, not the nice one who had gone down south, but the previous one who had dumped him. He was able to laugh about it now.

She said her husband had married her against his will. Not against her will, she stressed, but his will. He was in love with an English girl but his family disapproved and stopped sending the money he needed to continue his studies in Edinburgh. They thought a Sudanese girl like her would make him forget the girlfriend he had been living with. They were wrong. Everything went wrong from day one. It's a stupid story, she said, her hands in her pockets.

Did you love him? He asked her. Yes, she had loved him, wanted to love him. She had not known about his English girlfriend. After the honeymoon, when he brought her to Edinburgh and started acting strange, she asked him and he told her everything.

Would you believe it, she said, his family now blame me for the divorce. They say I wasn't clever enough, I didn't try hard enough. They're going around Khartoum saying all these things about me. That's why I don't want to go back. But I'll have to eventually when my visa runs out.

I'm glad I'm not pregnant, she went on. I thank Allah every day that I didn't become pregnant.

After that they spoke about faith. He told her how he had become a Muslim. He spoke about his former Chemistry teacher – after meeting again they had fallen back into the swing of their old teacher-student relationship. She listened, fascinated. She asked him questions. What was his religion before? He had been a Catholic. Had he always believed in

Something Old, Something New

God? Yes. Why on earth did he convert?

She seemed almost surprised by his answers. She associated Islam with her dark skin, her African blood, her own weakness. She couldn't really understand why anyone like him would want to join the wretched of the world. But he spoke with warmth. It made her look at him properly as if for the first time. Your parents probably don't like it, she said, and your friends? They won't like you changing. She was candid in that way.

And she was right. He had lost one friend after a bitter, unnecessary argument, another withdrew. His parents struggled to hide their dismay. Ever since he had dropped out of Medical School, they had feared for his well-being, fretted that he would get sucked up into unemployment, drugs, depression; the underworld that throbbed and dragged itself parallel to their active middle-class life. Only last week, their neighbour's son had hanged himself (drugs, of course, and days without showering). There was a secret plague that targeted young men.

Despite their misgiving about his conversion to Islam, his parents eventually had to admit that he looked well; he put on a bit of weight, got a raise at work. If only he would not talk about religion. They did not understand that side of him that was theoretical, intangible, belonging to the spiritual world. If only he would not mention religion then it would be easier to pretend that nothing had changed. He was confident enough to humour them. Elated that the questions he had once asked

– what's it all for, what does it all mean, what's the point of going on – the questions that had tilted the walls around him and nearly smothered him, were now valid. They were questions that had answers, answers that provoked other questions, that opened new doors, that urged him to look at things in another way, like holding a cube in his hand, turning it round and round, or like moving around a tall column and looking at it from the other side, how different it was and how the same.

When he took her to meet his parents, the afternoon was a huge success. We're going to get married, he said, and there was a kind of relief in his mother's eyes. It was easier for his parents to accept that he was in love with a Muslim girl than it was to accept that he was in love with Islam.

From the balcony of his hotel room, he looked out at the Blue Nile. Sunshine so bright that he saw strands of shimmering light. Palm trees, boats, the river was so blue. Would the water be cool, he wondered, or tepid? He felt sleepy. The telephone rang and he went indoors again, sliding the tinted glass door behind him.

Her happy voice again. What were you doing, why aren't you asleep, everyone sleeps this time in the afternoon, it's siesta time, you must be exhausted. Did you remember to bring dollar bills – not sterling, not traveller's cheques? You mustn't eat at the hotel, it will be terribly expensive, you must eat only with us here at home. Yes, we'll pick you up later. You'll come for dinner, you'll meet my parents. Don't forget the gifts. Are you going to dream of me?

He dreamed that he was still on the aeroplane. He woke up an hour later thirsty, looked up and saw a small arrow painted on the ceiling of the room. What was the arrow for? Out on the balcony, the contrast startled him. Sunset had softened the sky, rimmed the west with pinks and soft orange. The Nile was benign, the sky already revealing a few stars, the air fresher. Birds swooped and zigzagged.

He heard the azan; the first time in his life to hear it outdoors. It was not as spectacular as he had thought it would be, not as sudden. It seemed to blend with the sound of the birds and the changing sky. He started to figure out the direction of Makkah using the setting sun as his guide. Straight east or even a little to the north-east it would be now, not south-east like from Scotland. He located the east and when he went back into the room, understood the purpose of the arrow that was painted on the ceiling. The arrow was to show the hotel guests which way to face Makkah. After he prayed he went downstairs and looked for the swimming pool. He swam in water that was warm and pungent with chlorine. Twilight was swift. In no time the sky turned a dark purple with sharp little stars. It was the first time for him to swim under a night sky.

Her house was larger than he had imagined, shabbier. It was full of people – she had five brothers and sisters, several nephews and nieces, an uncle who looked like an older, smaller version of Bill

Cosby and an aunt who was asleep on a string bed in the corner of the room. The television blared. Her mother smiled at him and offered him sweets. Her father talked to him in careful, broken English. Everyone stared at him, curious, pleased. Only the brother looking bored, stretched out on another string bed staring at the ceiling.

So now you've seen my family, she said, naming her sisters, her nieces and nephews. The names swam in his head. He smiled and smiled until he strained the muscles of his face.

Now you've seen where I grew up, she said, as if they had got over a hurdle. He realized, for the first time, the things she'd never had; a desk of her own, a room of her own, her own cupboard, her own dressing table, her own mug, her own packet of biscuits. She had always lived part of a group, part of her family. What was that like, he didn't know. He did not know her well enough. He had yet to see her hair, he had yet to know what she looked like when she cried and what she looked like when she woke up in the morning.

After they had dinner, she said, My uncle knows an English song. She was laughing again, sitting on the arm of the sofa. He wants to sing it for you.

Bill Cosby's lookalike sat up straight in his armchair and sang, *Cricket, lovely cricket at Lords where I saw it. Cricket, lovely cricket at Lords where I saw it.*

Everyone laughed. After singing, the uncle was out of breath.

* * *

Something Old, Something New

They went on outings which she organized. They went on a boat trip, a picnic in the forest, they visited the camel market. On each of these outings, they were accompanied by her brother, her sisters, her nephews and nieces, her girlfriends. They were never alone. He remembered Michael in *The Godfather*, climbing the hills of Italy with his fiancée and the unforgettable soundtrack, surrounded by armed guards and her numerous relatives. It was like that but without the guns. And instead of rolling hills, there was flat scrubland, the edges of a desert. He watched her, how she carried a nephew, how she smiled, how she unpeeled a grapefruit and gave him a piece to eat, how she giggled with her girlfriends. He took lots of photographs. She gave him strange fruit to eat. One was called *doum* and it was brown, large as an orange, almost hard as rock, with a woody taste and a straw-like texture. Only the thin outer layer was to be gnawed at and chewed, most of it was the stone. Another fruit was called *gongoleez*, sour, tangy, white chunks, chalky in texture, to suck on and throw the black stones away. Tamarind to drink, *kerkadeh* to drink, *turmus*, *kebkebeh*, *nabaq*. Peanut salad, stuffed aubergines, *moulah*, *kisra*, *waikah*, *mouloukhia*. Dishes he had eaten before in the Nile Café, dishes that were new. She never tired of saying to him, Here, taste this, it's nice, try this.

Can't we be alone, just for a bit?

My family are very strict, especially because I'm divorced, they're very strict, she said but her eyes were smiling.

Try and sort something out.

Next week, after the wedding, you'll see me every day and get tired of me.

You know I can't ever get tired of you.

How can I know that?

She could flirt for hours given the chance. Now there was no chance because it was not clear whether her uncle, Bill Cosby, eyes closed and head nodding forward, was dozing in his armchair or eavesdropping.

Mid-morning in Ghamhouriah Street, after they had bought ebony to take back to his parents, he felt a tug on his shoulder, turned and found his rucksack slashed open, his passport missing. His camera too. He started to shout. Calm down, she said but he could not calm down. It was not only anger – there was plenty of that – but the eruption of latent fears, the slap of a nightmare. Her brother had parked the car in a bit of shade in a side street. They reached it now, her brother tenser than ever, she downcast and he clutching his ravaged rucksack. He kicked the tyre of the car, f-this and f-that. Furious, he was and out to abuse the place, the time, the crime. The whole street stood still and watched a foreigner go berserk, as if they were watching a scene in an American movie. A car drove past and the driver craned his neck to get a better look, laughed. Please she said, stop it, you're embarrassing me. He did not hear her. Her voice could not compete with the roar of anger in his ears.

We'll have to go to the British Embassy and ge

him a new passport, she said to her brother.

No, we'll have to go to the police station and report this first. Her brother got in the car, wiped the sweat on his forehead with his sleeves.

Get in the car, she said to him. We'll have to go to the police station and report your stolen passport.

He got in the car, fuming.

The police station was surprisingly pleasant. It was shady, cool. A bungalow and several outbuildings. They were treated well, given cold water, tea. He refused to drink the tea, sat in a sulk. Do you know how much that camera cost, he hissed, and it's not insured?

She shrugged, less shocked by what had happened than he was. Soothed by the drink, she started to tease him. They'll chop off the hand of the thief who stole your camera. Really they will. Her brother laughed with her.

I really can't see what's so funny.

Can't you take a joke, she said and there was an edge to her voice. Afterwards they drove in silence to the British Embassy. There, they endured a long queue.

The Embassy staff heed and hawed. They did not like to hear of passports getting stolen. And as one question led to the other they were not overjoyed either to hear of people getting married in a few days' time. They interrogated her and her brother, broad, flat questions but still she felt sullied and small.

Coming out of the embassy, she was anything but

calm. What did they think, what were they trying
to insinuate – that I stole your passport? – as if I
am desperate to go back there . . .

What's that supposed to mean?

It's supposed to mean what it means. You think
you're doing me a big favour by marrying me?

No, I don't think that, of course not . . .

They do. They do, the way they were talking.
Sneering at me and you didn't even notice!

Okay, okay, calm down.

A small boy touched his arm, begging. Gnarled
fist, black skin turned grey from malnutrition, one
eye clogged with thick mucus. He flinched at the
unpleasant touch, felt guilty, fumbled in his pockets
and started to take out a two-hundred dinar note.

Are you off your mind, she said, giving him that
amount? He'll get mugged for it. She opened her
bag and gave the boy instead some coins and an
orange.

As she got in the car, she told her brother about
the beggar and they both laughed in a mocking way.
Laughing at him in Arabic, the height of rudeness.

Perhaps you can contribute to the petrol then,
the brother drawled, given you have so much cash
to spare. I've burned a lot of gas chauffeuring you
and your fiancée around, you know.

Right, if this is what you want. He yanked out
the notes from his wallet and slammed them down
near the handbrake.

Thanks, her brother said, but when he picked up
the wad of cash, he looked at it like it was not much,
like he had expected more.

She sighed and looked out of the window. It was as if the theft had brought out all the badness in them.

He thought of saying, drop me at the hotel. He thought of giving up and leaving for Scotland the next day. That would punish her for laughing at him, that would hurt her. But he did not ask to be dropped off. He did not give up. True, he had no passport and would not be able to travel, but something else made him stay.

They walked into disarray. Her house, almost unrecognizable for the sheer number of people who were distraught, in shock. A woman was pushing the furniture to one side, another dropped a mattress on the floor, everywhere weeping, weeping and a few hoarse voices shouting orders. Her uncle, Bill Cosby's lookalike, had died, dozing in his armchair.

For a moment, the three of them stood in the middle of the room, frozen in disbelief. The brother started to ask questions in a loud voice.

That's it, she hissed, we'll never have our wedding now, not in the middle of this mourning, never, never. And she burst into tears.

Before he could respond, her brother led him away, saying, The house will be for the women now, we have to go outside. Come on.

The garden was hell that time of day, sun scorching the grass, reflecting on the concrete slabs of the garage. How precious shade was in this part of the world, how quickly a quarrel could be pushed aside, how quickly the dead were taken to their graves.

Where was he now, the uncle who sang *Cricket, lovely cricket*? Somewhere indoors being washed with soap, perfumed and then wrapped in white; that was the end then, without preliminaries. He could faint standing in the sun like that, without a passport, without her, without the reassurance that their wedding would go ahead. It couldn't be true. But it was and minute after minute passed with him standing in the garden. Where was her brother now, who had previously watched his every move while she had circled him with attention, advice, plans? She was indoors, sucked up in rituals of grief he knew nothing about. Well, he could leave now, slip away unnoticed. He could walk to the main road and hail down a taxi – something he had not done before because she and her brother had picked him up and dropped him back at the hotel every single day. Death, the destroyer of pleasures.

The body was being taken away. There it was, shrouded in white, and the shock of seeing that Bill Cosby face again, asleep, fast asleep. The folds of nostrils and lips, the pleasing contrast of white hair against dark skin. He found himself following her brother into the car, getting into what now had become his seat at the back, two men crammed in next to him; an elderly man sitting in front. The short drive to the mosque, rows of men. He had prayed that special prayer for the dead once before in Edinburgh – for a still-born baby. It did not involve any kneeling, was brief, cool. Here it was also raw, the fans whirling down from the ceiling, the smell of sweat and haste.

Something Old, Something New

They drove out of town to the cemetery. He no longer asked himself why he was accompanying them, it seemed the right thing to do. In the car, there was a new ease between them, a kind of bonding because they had prayed together. They began to talk of the funeral announcement that went out on the radio after the news, the obituaries that would be published in the newspaper the next day. He half listened to the Arabic he could not understand, to the summary in English which one of them would suddenly give, remembering his presence.

Sandy wind blowing, a home that was flat ground, a home that had no walls, no doors. My family's cemetery, her brother said, abruptly addressing him. Once he married her and took her back with him to Edinburgh would he be expected to bring her back here if she, God forbid, died? Why think these miserable thoughts? A hole was eventually made in the ground, you would think they were enjoying the scooping out of dirt, so wholeheartedly were they digging. With the sleeve of his shirt, he wiped the sweat off his brow – he was beginning to act like them – since when did he wipe his face with his shirtsleeves in Edinburgh? He wanted a glass of cold water but they were lowering the uncle in the grave now. They put him in a niche, wedged him in so that when they filled the grave, the soil they poured in did not fall on him.

For the next three days, he sat in the tent that had been set up in the garden for the men. A kind of normality prevailed, people pouring in to pay

their condolences, the women going indoors, the
men to the tent. A flow of water glasses, coffee, tea,
the buzz of flies. Rows of metal chairs became loose
circles and knots, as old friends caught up with
each other, a laugh here and there could be heard.
What's going to happen to your wedding now? he
was asked. He shrugged, he did not want to talk
about it, was numbed by what had happened, dulled
by the separation from her that the mourning
customs seemed to impose. In the tent, the men
agreed that the deceased had had a good death, no
hospital, no pain, no Intensive Care and he was in
his eighties, for God's sake, what more do you
expect? A strange comfort in that tent. He fell into
this new routine. After breakfast in the hotel, he
would walk along the Nile, after passing the
Presidential Palace, hail down a taxi, go to her
house. He never met her and she never phoned him.
After spending the day in the tent and having a meal
with her brother and his friends, one of them would
offer him a lift back to the Hilton.

Late in the evening or the early morning, he
would go swimming. Every day he could hold his
breath underwater longer. When he went for a
walk, he saw army trucks carrying young soldiers
in green uniforms. The civil war in the south had
gone on for years and wasn't drawing to an end
– on the local TV station there were patriotic
songs, marches. He had thought, from the books
he'd read and the particular British Islam he had
been exposed to, that in a Muslim country he
would find elegance and reason. Instead he found

melancholy, a sensuous place, life stripped to the bare bones.

On the third evening after the funeral, the tent was pulled down, the official mourning period was over.

I want to talk to you, he said to her brother, perhaps we could go for a walk.

They walked in a street calmed by the impending sunset. Only a few cars passed. He said, I can't stay here for long. I have to go back to my work in Scotland.

I'm sorry, the brother said, we could not have your wedding. But you understand . . .

It's going to be difficult for me to come again. I think we should go ahead with our plans . .

We can't celebrate at a time like this.

It doesn't have to be a big celebration.

You know, she had a big wedding party last time?

No, I didn't know. She didn't tell me.

I blame myself, her brother suddenly blurted out, for that son of a dog and what he did to her. I knew, you see, I heard rumours that he was going with that girl but I didn't think much of it, I thought it was just a fling he was having and he'd put his girl-friend away once he got married.

They walked in silence after that, the sound of their footsteps on crumbling asphalt. There was movement and voices in the houses around them, the rustle and barks of stray dogs.

Finally her brother said, I suppose we could have the marriage ceremony at my flat. But just the ceremony, no party . . .

No, no, there's no need for a party . . .

I'll talk to my father and my mother, see if they approve the idea.

Yes, please, and after the ceremony . . . ?

After the ceremony you can take her back with you to your hotel . . .

Right.

Her father has to agree first.

Yes, of course.

He walked lighter now, but there was still another hitch.

You know, her brother said, we lost a lot of money marrying her off to that son of a dog. A lot of money. And now again this time . . . even just for a simple ceremony at my place, I will have to buy drinks, sweets, pay for this and that.

On a street corner, money was exchanged between them. He handed her brother one fifty-dollar bill after the other, not stopping until he sensed a saturation.

Thanks, better not tell her about this, okay? My sister's always been sensitive and she doesn't realize how much things cost.

His hand trembled a little as he put his wallet away. He had previously paid a dowry (a modest one, the amount decided by her) and he had brought the gifts in good faith. Now he felt humiliated, as if he had been hoodwinked or as if he had been so insensitive as to underestimate his share in the costs. Or as if he had paid for her.

On the night before the wedding, he slept lightly,

on and off, so the night seemed to him elongated, obtuse. At one time he dreamed of a vivid but unclear sadness and when he woke he wished that his parents were with him, wished that he was not alone, getting married all alone. Where was the stag night, the church wedding, invitation cards, a reception and speeches? His older brother had got married in church wearing the family kilt. It had been a sunny day and his mother had worn a blue hat. He remembered the unexpected sunshine, the photos. He had turned his back on these customs, returned them as if they were borrowed, not his. He had no regrets, but he had passed the stage of rejection now, burned out the zeal of the new convert, was less proud, more ready to admit to himself what he missed. No, his parents could not have accompanied him. They were not hardy enough to cope with the heat, the mosquitoes, the maimed beggars in the street, all the harshness that even a good hotel could not shield. Leave them be, thank them now humbly, in the dark, for the generous cheque they had given him.

He dreamed he was being chased by the man who had ripped his rucksack, robbed him of his passport and camera. He woke up sweaty and thirsty. It was three in the morning – not yet dawn.

He prayed, willing himself to concentrate, to focus on what he was saying, who he was saying it to. In this late hour of the night, before the stir of dawn, all was still, even his mind which usually buzzed with activity, even his feelings which tumbled young. Just a precious stillness, patience,

patience for the door to open, for the contact to be made, for the comforting closeness. He had heard a talk once at the mosque, that there are certain times of the day and the year when Allah answers prayers indiscriminately, fully, immediately – certain times – so who knows, you might one moment pray and be spot on, you might ask and straight away be given.

After dawn he slept and felt warm as if he had a fever. But he felt better when he woke late with the telephone ringing and her clear voice saying, I'm so excited I'm going to be coming to the Hilton to stay with you. I've never stayed in a Hilton before, I can't wait.

It was a matter of hours now.

Her brother's flat was in a newly built area, a little deserted, out of the way. One of her cousins had picked him up from the hotel and now they both shuffled up the stairs. The staircase was in sand, not yet laid out in tiles or concrete, there was a sharp smell of paint and bareness. The flat itself was neat and simple; a few potted plants, a large photograph of the Ka'ba. The men, her brother, father, various relations and neighbours whom he recognized from the days in the mourning tent, occupied the front room, the one near the door. The women were at the back of the flat. He couldn't see them, couldn't see her.

Shaking hands, the hum of a general conversation in another language. The Imam wore a white *jellabiya*, a brown cloak, a large turban. He led them for the maghrib prayer and after that the ceremony began. Only it was not much of a ceremony, but a signing of a contract between the groom and the bride's father.

The Imam pushed away the dish of dates that was on the coffee table and started to fill out a form. The date in the western calendar, the date in the Islamic calendar. The amount of dowry (the original figure she had named and not the additional dollars her brother had taken on the street corner). The name of the bride. The name of her father who was representing her. The name of the groom who was representing himself.

But that is not a Muslim name. The Imam put the pen down, sat back in his chair.

Show him your certificate from the mosque in Edinburgh, urged her brother, the one you showed me when you first arrived.

I can't, he said, it was stolen or it fell out when the things in my bag were stolen.

No matter, the brother sighed and turned to speak to the Imam. He's a Muslim for sure. He prayed with us. Didn't you see him praying just now behind you?

Did they tell you I have eyes at the back of my head?

Laughter . . . that didn't last long.

Come on, sheikh, one of the guests said, we're all gathered here for this marriage to take place, *insha' Allah*. We've all seen this foreigner praying, not just now but also on the days of the funeral. Let's not start to make problems.

Look, he will recite for you the Fatiha, the brother

said, won't you? He put his hand on his shoulder as a way of encouragement.

Come on, sheikh, another guest said, these people aren't even celebrating or having a party. They're in difficult circumstances, don't make things more difficult. The bride's brother said he saw an official certificate, that should be enough.

Insha' Allah there won't be any difficulties, someone ventured.

Let him recite, the Imam said, looking away.

He was sweating now. No, not everyone's eyes were on him, some were looking away, hiding their amusement or feeling embarrassed on his behalf. He sat forward, his elbows on his knees.

In the name of Allah, the Compassionate, the Merciful, her brother whispered helpfully.

In the name of Allah, the Compassionate, the Merciful, he repeated, his voice hoarse but loud enough. *All praise to Allah, Lord of the Worlds* and the rest followed, one stammered letter after the other, one hesitant word after the other.

Silence, the scratch of a pen. His hand in her father's hand. The Fatiha again, everyone saying it to themselves, mumbling it fast, raising their palms, Amen, wiping their faces.

Congratulations, we've given her to you now. She's all yours now.

When he saw her, when he walked down the corridor to where the women were gathered, when the door opened for him and he saw her, he could only say, Oh my God, I can't believe it! It was as if it was her

and not her at the same time. Her familiar voice
saying his name. Those dark slanting eyes smiling
at him. But her hair long and falling on her shoulders (she had had it chemically relaxed), make-up
that made her glow, a secret glamour. Her dress in
soft red, sleeveless, she was not thin . . .

God, I can't believe it, and the few people around
them laughed.

A haze in the room, smoke from the incense they
were burning, the perfume making him light-
headed, tilting his mind, a dreaminess in the material of her dress, how altered she was, how so
much more of her there was. He coughed.

Is the incense bothering you?

A blur as someone suggested that the two of them
sit out on the balcony. It would be cooler there, just
for a while, until they could get a lift to the hotel.
He followed her out into a sultry darkness, a privacy
granted without doors or curtains, the classical
African sky dwarfing the city below.

She did not chat like she usually did. He could
not stop looking at her and she became shy, overcome. He wanted to tell her she was beautiful, he
wanted to tell her about the ceremony, about the
last few days and how he had missed her, but the
words, any words wouldn't come. He was stilled,
choked by a kind of brightness.

At last she said, can you see the henna pattern
on my palms? It's light enough.

He could trace, in the grey light of the stars, deli-
cate leaves and swirls.

I'll wear gloves, she said, when we go back to

Scotland, I'll wear gloves, so as not to shock every-one.

No, you needn't do that, he said, it's lovely.

It was his voice that made her ask, Are you all right, you're not well? She put her hand on his cheek, on his forehead. So that was how soft she was, so that was how she smelled, that was her secret. He said without thinking, It's been rough for me – these past days – please, feel sorry for me.

I do, she whispered, I do.

FRIENDSREVISITED.COM

Carmen Reid

Born in Montrose, Scottish writer and journalist **CARMEN REID** currently lives in Glasgow with her husband and young family. Her first novel, *Three in a Bed*, published in 2002, was an instant bestseller. Her second, *Did the Earth Move?*, is due out in June, 2003.

It was the Saturday before Christmas and Emma was upstairs in the attic sorting through all the bags and boxfuls of rubbish up there. She was listening to the rain belt steadily against the skylight and feeling more than a little sorry for herself.

When had staying in on a Saturday night become so normal? She and Andrew had probably spent 90 per cent of Saturday nights over the last seventeen years at home, sometimes eating a takeaway in front of a video and occasionally having sex – but the kind that made her wonder why they'd bothered and had not just finished another bottle of wine instead.

Tonight, Andrew wasn't here, of course, and her two children, sixteen-year-old Dan and fourteen-going-on-twenty-one Lucy were out with friends as usual.

'It's *Saturday*, Mum!' Dan had moaned. 'I've got to go out. I can't stay at home *tonight*.'

Emma had watched him head out of the door, his oversized jeans trailing behind him, and she remembered way back to a time in her own life when staying in on Saturday was social suicide.

The strange thing was she still lived in Glasgow,

her university town, and the women she met up with on Tuesday nights at the gym and for coffee mornings and PTAs were the ones who had gone out with her every Saturday, when they were students, in glitter gloss lipstick, high heels and cropped skirts, to drink Hooch straight from the bottle and half pints of cider laced with whisky. They had chatted up boys and danced and danced until they puked or snogged, whichever came first, it didn't matter, both were the hallmarks of a successful night out.

God, every single one of them had settled down to an unforgivably dull normality, she couldn't help thinking now. She had married Andrew first, straight after they graduated. Then Margaret and Neil . . . and gradually everyone else, one by one or rather two by two, until they'd all mutated into married, with kids, working part-time or on a 'career break'. All staying at home on Saturday night. Well no, sometimes they went to dinner at each other's houses to compare notes on Jamie, Nigella and Delia recipes and how they'd turned out. And schools. Didn't everyone bloody talk about schools until you wanted to be sick?

If, just a few months ago, you'd stopped Emma in the street and asked her if she was happy with her life, she would have smiled nicely and said, 'Happy? Of course I am,' and walked on, thinking little more about it. Of course she was happy. She worked three days a week as a lawyer – Okay, she was in conveyancing, so she did the paperwork on house sales which wasn't the career of a criminal defence barrister she'd planned for herself – but it paid well and left her the time she'd felt she needed to look after Lucy and Dan and run the household to the sort of immaculate standards she'd developed over the years.

Andrew had been such a solid kind of husband, an orthopaedic consultant, but a man not ever prone to overt displays of romance or even affection. But then not many Scottish men were, she'd always told herself. They'd lived comfortably in a West End mews house for years now and anyway . . . it was almost Christmas. Why wasn't that cheering her up? Her presents were bought and wrapped, the fridge and freezer were stocked with goodies, the dining table was already laid with new candles, napkins, a green and gold ivy centrepiece.

But here she was in the attic, watching rain stream down the window and feeling tears to match running down her cheeks.

Maybe she should make a cup of tea. Or even open a bottle of wine? Something she would never normally do when Andrew wasn't at home.

She clicked open the trunk in front of her, knowing it was full of things she should have got rid of years ago, but instead it had accompanied her intact into her three marital homes.

She lifted the lid and all the neatly stacked files, folders, jotters, shoeboxes of photographs were still there. This was her trunk full of school. She had turned thirty-eight just a few weeks ago and realized it was now twenty years since she'd left school. *Twenty years* since she'd left Edinburgh, and moved to

Glasgow to study law, losing touch with all the over-ambitious, over-achieving girls she'd grown up with.

No one else from her year had gone to Glasgow Uni, everyone else had stayed in Edinburgh or chosen St Andrews or gone down south: Durham, Newcastle, London, Cambridge. They had all scattered.

There had been tears in that final, hysteria-laced week, which she remembered as unusually warm, with strawberries and Wimbledon and girls with pink, sunburned arms at prizegiving.

Everyone had exchanged addresses and phone numbers and promised to stay in touch and visit, but the closeness of school friendships had melted and disappeared in the heat of the first university terms which were about the adult pleasures – drinking, tentative attempts at sex and drugs – only whispered about at the cosy, sheltered, all-girls' school.

There had been a few letters, a few calls and the odd meeting in the holidays, but within a year or so, the old friendships seemed so over compared with the new.

Emma opened one of the shoeboxes and tipped out photos of teenagers she couldn't even name any more, all desperately trying to make their uniform look alluring with silly hair and sugar-pink lipstick.

She had absolutely no idea what had become of a single one of the peachy-keen eighteen-year-olds who had filed out of that imposing grey-stone building with the dizzying, glorious feeling that freedom and their whole lives were ahead of them, that anything was possible.

Ha! What a teenage dream that had been! Emma,

alone in her attic on a wet winter Saturday, couldn't help feeling she hadn't lived up to her own expectations even remotely. She'd imagined herself arguing in court in exquisite suits, saving innocent young men from accusations of murder, chairing law reform meetings, hosting elegant dinner parties with eminent lawyers. It was hard not to snort with laughter at all this now.

She was a conveyancing solicitor, all kidded-up, dressed day and night in M&S, married to a doctor. BORING! Well okay, it had been comfortable and nice and the life she'd thought she'd wanted, or, at least, the life that had worked out around her without her really trying.

It was this nagging feeling of under-achievement which put her off doing the thing she really wanted to do now, the thing she had been thinking about for weeks, months even.

She wanted to go downstairs into Andrew's little office, flick on the computer, dial up the internet and click on to that website, the one that would reveal where they were now, what they were all doing – FriendsRevisited.com.

But . . . but . . . the thought of having to sum up her own life with the lines: 'Married, two children, live in Glasgow, work as a conveyancer part-time'. . . Well, she just couldn't bear it. It sounded so crap. All it conjured up for Emma was the report card verdict: 'Not fulfilling her true potential. Could do better.' Why couldn't she at least have had more than two children? That would have been slightly less mundane.

In fact, she only really wanted to know about one girl, she didn't care about the rest, could predict what had become of them. This was just to see what had become of Sadie Summers. And Emma knew if she logged on and posted up her details and Sadie Summers wasn't there, she would be gutted and it would all have been a humiliation for nothing.

Sadie had finally allowed Emma to become her friend in the very last year of school. Before then, Emma had not been nearly interesting or cool enough and anyway, she'd been far too shy to ever approach Sadie, who was one of those impossibly self-possessed, self-confident girls. Totally comfortable with boys, Sadie could also talk back to teachers without getting into trouble, and on her even the school uniform looked sexy.

And *Sadie*? Imagine having parents so cool that they named you Sadie? Not Emma or Sarah or Jane.

Sadie had been the only girl in the year not going on to university after school. She would get the grades, but her father – a scriptwriter or sculptor or something equally fabulous, Emma couldn't quite remember – had told her it would be the most boring three years of her life, so she had planned a three-year world tour instead, with jobs already lined up in New York, California, Sydney.

And much as the other girls tutted, having had the benefits of education, degrees and a respectable profession drummed into them from the earliest possible age, Emma had been jealous and admiring, but also terrified that she was going to lose this brand-new, exotic friend so soon.

Sadie had promised to write, phone, visit when back in Scotland . . . But she had never even sent one single postcard. She'd just vanished with no hint of a forwarding address.

And every once in while, when a memory was stirred, Emma had grieved for the friend who that last summer term had finally turned her into a rebel. Okay, she had been the squarest sort of rebel imaginable; the worst thing they ever did was sneak out of the boarding school one summer evening to sit on the games pitch and drink a quarter bottle of vodka, washed down with orange juice pinched from the school kitchens, and smoke two cigarettes one straight after the other, until Emma felt so dizzy and sick she had to puke in the bushes.

But they had talked about the future, their dreams, the boys they wanted to fall in love with, the world-changing careers they wanted to have, their lefty-environmentalist beliefs. And it all seemed so naïve and childish now, but then it had been thrilling. They had been on the very edge of freedom, about to plunge into life, take it into their own hands for the first time and shape it in the direction they wanted.

Emma had of course planned to be a criminal defence lawyer and Sadie had wanted to become a journalist, a foreign correspondent, travelling from place to place, doing the kind of amazing stories that appeared with startling pics in the Sunday supplements. She was going to do a photography course in America, so she could be a photojournalist.

As Emma had watched Sadie toss her pale blonde ponytail as she talked, it had been impossible not to believe that this supremely confident girl wouldn't achieve everything she wanted to. And that had given Emma faith in herself too. She had begun to lose her fear of the impending exam results, her fear of starting somewhere entirely new on her own next term and some of the shyness which made her blush, mumble and rush to escape whenever she encountered the teenaged version of the male of the species.

She had missed Sadie for years. But she had to face the fact that Sadie had obviously not missed her, otherwise, surely, she would have written via Emma's parents or tried to get hold of her through the university? Instead, there had been nothing. She had gone, like dandelion fluff in the wind.

Three glasses of wine later, Emma decided she was at least going to look. Enough fannying around the issue. She was going to do it.

And then there she was, as easy as that, sitting at the desk, scanning through the lists of names, hardly able to believe she hadn't done this before. It was absolutely gripping, girls she hadn't thought about for years came jumping out of the text at her. They had become doctors and lawyers and accountants, they had nearly all married and reproduced. About thirty of them still lived within fifty miles of her, the rest had emigrated to London, the home counties and the occasional one was abroad – Canada, Australia, the US.

She couldn't help reading every entry thoroughly

from start to finish, even about the girls she couldn't remember, although this meant coming down the list very slowly, reining back the desire to just whizz down to 'S' and get this over with.

Sarah Saville, Manda Sawyer, and then . . . good grief! There it was! Sadie Summers. She could hardly read the words because of the choking, teary feeling welling up inside her.

Sadie Summers: Hello from sunny Bermuda. This is where I'm based for a year or so, working for the local paper, filing for Reuters and some of the American papers, blah blah. I never really did get off that world tour I started when I left school. I got my journalism qualifications, learned how to take pictures and that was me off! Haven't spent more than two years in the same place yet. And I have hardly been back to Britain at all. No husband, no kids, no serious lifetime partner to report. Doesn't seem to be my style. So, I guess I'm feeling a little nostalgic and would like to know what everyone is up to. E-mail me to say hello, and does anyone happen to know where Emma Holt is these days?

Emma Holt! She hadn't even thought about that name, her real name, her first name, for years. Well, of course Emma Holt was going to reply. At least briefly, at least to sound out the possibility of renewing their friendship. Could it be a possibility? Would Sadie be remotely interested in her? Had she really forgiven Sadie for never once trying to contact her before in all these years?

Carmen Reid

It took Emma almost two hours to compose the e-mail to her long-lost friend. She finally decided on:

Dear Sadie,

I logged on to FriendsRevisited in the hope that you would be there. I can't believe we've been out of touch for so long. Years and years have gone by and you never wrote, you never phoned! I'm so pleased you want to hear from me now. Compared with Bermuda and journalisting your way across the world, I'm probably the most boring person you've ever heard of.

I never left Glasgow. I married a doctor called Andrew, we have two children, Dan who is sixteen and Lucy who is fourteen. Dan is really tall and rangy like his dad. He plays in the school football team and I think maybe he wants to go into medicine too, we'll see. I made a vow when they were tiny that I would not become the world's pushiest mother and I'm trying to stick to it.

Lucy is . . . well, fourteen. You remember all that – listening to the same song fifty times a day, sulking about and buying totally inappropriate clothes from Miss Selfridge's. Yes, Miss Selfridge's still exists! But I think there is a nice, intelligent girl in there really.

I work as a solicitor three days a week and the rest of the time I make sure the kids aren't turning into delinquents, run our house in the West End, meet friends, do dinner parties. You know, normal life.

About a million miles away from filing news reports from an island in the middle of the Atlantic!

How are you??? How are your folks? (Mine are still

in the old place in Perth, but both retired now.) You must write back with all your news and adventures.

It is so good to hear from you. I've thought about you a lot, Sadie, and missed you too.

Lots of love,
Emma Holt

She re-read it. God, it still sounded pathetic. Was it a bit gushy? Did she bang on about her kids too much? Did she really need to add the Holt at the end of her name?

The answers were – yes, yes and probably not.

She closed her eyes, took a breath and sent it anyway. And now there was nothing ahead but the long wait for the reply. She powered down the computer and went back to the bottle of wine.

Emma!!! Fantastic. I can't believe I've finally heard from you. I know I've been the world's most crap friend about keeping in touch. But I've thought about you loads, missed you. Never occurred to me to write via your folks, thought they'd have moved years ago. Mine are currently retired in Southern California but they're restless!

So, Bermuda – I wanted somewhere quiet and peaceful and isolated for a while. I've done Beirut and Bosnia and lots of difficult, difficult places, so I guess I needed a rest. This is a beachy, ex-pat kind of para-dise, with evenings and weekends spent drinking, beaching, sailing, diving. It's beautiful – water, the clearest, lightest, bluest, most impossible turquoise, beach sand, the palest, finest pink. I love it here. But it does sometimes feel like I've ended up in the land of the lotus eaters. You know, it's so perfect, I've forgotten about everywhere, everything, everyone else that was once in my life.

I have friends here, Emma, I've always been surrounded by friends. But you have a husband and children – Two children! How amazing! – and a place where you belong and I bet the same people have been talking to you and coming round to your house and just knowing you for years and years and years. I miss all that. Not that I've ever had it. I feel rootless, shiftless, blown on the wind. On the one hand, I wonder how long this can go on for and then, on the other, I think I'll never be able to settle in one place with one person. It's just too late for that now. I'd be the most restless, wretched person in the world. But I would love to have a kid. Although I'm only too aware that thirty-nine is cutting things a bit fine.

Listen to me, rambling on.

I got the life I dreamed of, you know, that last summer term when we were sitting out on the playing fields in that weird Scottish twilight that goes on until dawn. Travel and adventure and excitement and my name at the top of news reports and all the things I really, really wanted. I can't be ungrateful for that. I got everything I wanted. Maybe I'm just getting middle-aged now and feel I want different things and that is the shock!

We're middle-aged, Emma! And I haven't seen you since you were a teenager. It seems absurd.

In fact, I'm going to e-mail a pic with this, so you can see what I'm like now. You have to return one, that's for sure.

Speak soon, great to hear from you, love to you and yours,

Sadie

The reply from Sadie had finally arrived twenty-four hours later and, sitting late at night in the office, in an empty house again, Emma sent back the e-mail which Sadie's deserved in response. The open-hearted truth. As she wrote, she felt nothing but sadness at the twenty years of missed friendship, which maybe could have taken them together through some of life's highs, some of life's lows.

Dear Sadie,

I suppose I didn't really feel I knew you well enough any more to tell you how things really are here.

Andrew has left me. Oh yes, after seventeen years of marriage, he turns to me in bed one night, six and a half weeks ago now, thirty-nine shopping days before Christmas (I'd heard it on the radio that morning) and says he's bored to tears, he needs out and he's begun 'something' with someone else.

I suppose I've been in shock ever since. I mean what gives him the right to leave? I'm bored too. Family life has a necessary element of boredom running through it, doesn't it?

We've had the same jobs for years, we've lived in

the same house for years, we've been married for years. We're living with two grumpy, resentful, lazy, ungrateful, stroppy teenagers. Why does our marriage have to be the thing to change, to bear the brunt of all this boredom? Why? It seems so unfair, like I've been given the blame for his boring life. Like I'm the boring person, I'm the one who has dragged us all down to this dull, dull existence . . . all about security and paying the mortgage and making sure the children get good grades and eat good food. And why is it my fault? I was trying to do the best for everyone.

Why is he allowed to leave us to it, to rent a little studio flat in the Merchant City and go out for dinner almost every night with Karen from work, to see if it 'develops'? While I'm still here, still doing the cooking, the washing, the housekeeping, the homework, the school run.

Two months ago, I'd have told anyone who asked that I loved my husband. But now, so quickly, I absolutely hate him. Loathe him for this. I think this is the worst thing anyone could have done to me. Left me here, marooned in this.

Why should I get all the hard work, when he can get free of it all?

And I'm so angry because I feel I made so many compromises for Andrew, for the children, especially with my career. And so many sacrifices for them. But it's all been thrown back in my face.

I have no idea why I'm telling you all this. Maybe because there's no one here I really want to talk to about it and you are conveniently far away . . . poor you!

Anyway, I don't want you thinking home and married family life is the perfect dream you've missed out on.

I mean, when I hear about your life, I'm the one who's feeling I've missed out, believe me.

Love
Emma

She pinged it off and clicked open the photo which Sadie had included with her message. Oh God, there she was, still slim, blonde and tanned, sitting on a veranda in a tiny white bikini, barefoot and laughing, shading her eyes against stark white sunshine, falling strands of hair down round her face. It could have been taken fifteen years ago, but there in the background of the snap was the turquoise Bermudan sea she'd written about.

It wasn't just that she didn't look her age, she looked so full of life, so full of fun. Not one drop of the essential Sadie appeared to have been diluted in the two decades of life she'd gone through since Emma knew her.

Emma pulled the latest family album down from the shelf and wondered what she would send in return.

There they were on their summer holiday in France. Lucy and Dan dressed in black, scowling at the camera under duress, Andrew in the background reading the two-day-old copy of *The Times* he'd found only after a forty-minute drive to the nearest town.

Endless photos of the sulky teens and the scenery and the picturesque farmhouse they'd rented, all taken by her, the cataloguer of family memories. The one who bought the camera, the films, the albums. She turned the pages and for a moment it looked as if there wasn't going to be a single picture of her on this holiday.

But there it was, finally; she was lying on the sun lounger by the pool in a black swimsuit, which hid the stretch marks that ravaged her stomach, breasts and buttocks, with a purple sarong round her plump thighs. There was just this one picture, taken from an almost spitefully unflattering angle by Lucy. Her pale Scottish skin was a little sun-reddened and freckled, her brown bob scraped off her face with an alice band.

She looked up at the photo of glowing Sadie on the screen and suddenly burst into tears. What would Sadie possibly have in common with this housebound, earthbound frump? What had happened to her over the years? She thought about the University Saturday-night Emma in micro silver dresses, discoing till dawn. Where did she go?

The little message box pinged on the screen. When she tapped in, there was a reply from Sadie already.

Oh my God! Emma, this is terrible. Are you going to be okay?

It read simply.
She tapped back a reply.

I don't know . . . are you there?

When the **YES!!** came back, it was strangely thrilling. They were really talking now. This wasn't letter-writing, this was their first chat in twenty years.

Sadie asked:

What are you going to do?

I've no idea . . . what do you think?

Several minutes went past before Sadie's answer dropped.

Emma, I wonder if maybe you need to go wild for a bit! Seriously! Why should you stay home and do all the dull stuff, while your rat of a husband gets to have his mid-life crisis. You need to have a mid-life crisis of your own – leave the dishes to rot in the sink, get really drunk a few times, dye your hair purple and flirt with younger men. That sort of thing. Spend a bit of that joint-account cash!

Do the teens have to live with you? All the time? Shouldn't they be with their Dad too?

Don't fuss over the teens too much. They'll only hate you for it. I was always so grateful to my parents for cutting me some slack.

And what I really, really want you to do – and give this some consideration, Emma, don't just dismiss it out of hand – is come over here in the New Year for a holiday. Just you. Leave them behind. It's a five-hour flight from London. You can stay with me, rest up and think about all this and what to do next.

I want to see you again, get to know you again. We've missed so much. Don't answer tonight, Emma. Get to sleep, it's late in Britain, isn't it? And write to me in the morning when you've thought about it.

But don't go down, come up fighting!

Love
Sadie

It was after midnight when Emma finally switched off the computer. Dan was back and she could hear music coming from his room. As she crossed the hallway to knock on his door and tell him to go to sleep now, the chorus of the song drifted over to her.

She wasn't such an uncool mum as to not know it was Dido singing in her perfect, crystal voice about seeing the world alone again, taking a chance on life again.

It sounded like a blessing. She was only thirty-eight for God's sake, still six months younger than Sadie . . . always six months younger than Sadie.

She woke up at 6.45 the next morning, grateful that it was Monday, so she could start putting some of her plans into action.

'Come on, guys,' she shooed the teens out of bed. 'Get up, sort yourselves out. I'm too busy to get breakfast for you today.'

They finally left the house at twenty to nine, probably full of pop tarts and coffee, but for once she wasn't going to care. She was busy in the bedroom, hauling her and Andrew's belongings out of the cupboards, the floor-to-ceiling cupboards right along one wall of the bedroom. How much fucking stuff did they fucking have? And when had she started thinking in swear words like this?

Ever the cataloguer, she colour-coded the bin bags with stickers, yellow for Andrew's things, red for the good stuff she was going to sell, blue for the charity shop, and on the small remaining pile were the things she would keep — a couple of work suits, her smart black winter coat, the expensive shoes.

It took the whole morning, but it felt fantastic. She started giving things away slowly, carefully, but two hours into the job, dull cashmere jumpers, sensible Jaeger suits and even all her jewellery from Andrew were divided up between Oxfam or the dress agency. Armfuls of saggy knickers, worn-out bras, greying T-shirts, frayed pyjamas and tan tights were hitting the bin pile.

Finally, the job was done. Andrew's cupboards and drawers were empty. There were eleven sack-fuls of stuff to be dumped at his bijou little place, including his fifteen pairs of – as far as she could see – identical black brogues.

On her side hung just the barest of working essentials. And she wasn't going to rush out and load herself up with more clutter. No.

Just a traveller's essentials. Traveller? For God's sake, listen to me. Where am I going to travel to?

I'm not really going to disappear off to Bermuda leaving poor old Dan and Lucy and their stupid fucking dad to muddle along? Am I?

She spent the afternoon ferrying her bin bags out to the relevant shops, then tackled other parts of the house. The attic was cleared out already, with Andrew's things bagged and boxed, so she went through the kitchen cupboards, the linen closet, the trunkfuls of stuff in the spare room. Old children's clothes . . . summer dresses . . . Jesus! Why had they hung on to all this stuff? Or rather, why had *she*? She was the keeper, the custodian of family life and family treasures. Well, it was all going now.

The house was obviously going to have to be sold after Christmas, so she might as well get on with it.

The teens drifted in at teatime, ate toast and cornflakes morosely in the kitchen and went out to friends' houses again. If they'd noticed the boxes and bags of stuff she was piling into hallways, doorways and stairwells, they didn't ask her about them.

She'd left a message on Andrew's mobile for him to call her and arrange to collect some of his things, and for once it didn't bother her one bit that he didn't call back that night. She had not cried over their split for two nights in a row now. This was progress.

The next evening, she read newly-bought magazines in the sitting room and drank hot chocolate laced with Baileys. When Dan came in at 10 p.m. and Lucy topped him by appearing an hour later, saying she'd been doing her homework at Louette's house, Emma didn't grill either of them, just said, 'Oh well, night, night then,' and let them escape to their rooms without the expected interrogation.

She didn't want to care so much any more and, rather amazingly, she found she didn't. It was that easy to let go and let your children grow up a little without hovering over their every move.

Almost an hour later, when she was sure they wouldn't come downstairs again, she went to Lucy's leather jacket in the hall and rummaged through the inside pockets.

There was the anticipated packet of ten Silk Cut.

Emma took them into the sitting room and after staring at the box for a long time she shook one cigarette out, smelled it deeply, right under her nostrils, then, without another moment's hesitation, lit it with a match from the box kept beside the scented candles on the mantelpiece. What an obsessionally perfect housewife she'd turned herself into: scented candles on the mantelpiece with a box of matches tucked in behind them.

She had given up smoking the moment she and Andrew, then a health-obsessed medical student, had become a serious item. Of all the things she had done for him, packing in the cigarettes had been the hardest. And she was bloody well throwing it back in his face now.

She took a long drag of smoke and was surprised at how easily she inhaled it down her throat and blew it out. Oh, smoking! It was still so easy and so nice!

'I'm only thirty-eight,' she said out loud to herself.

'Not fifty-eight!' What had she mapped out for the next twenty years? Hardly anything at all: staying at work until she retired, staying in the house until the children were settled in homes of their own, staying married – she hadn't doubted that for a moment – and becoming an involved grandmother.

She realised now there was nothing new ahead planned just for her . . . no move to a different country or even town, hell, even street . . . no new career plan. She had just assumed everything would 'tick along' in this vaguely unsatisfactory groove for the next *twenty years or so*.

No wonder when Andrew had told her he was getting out, she'd been furious with him for daring to change it all when she couldn't. But now, at last, she was beginning to understand it didn't have to be like that. She could change things too.

She didn't have to keep the house, keep the children, keep her job, keep her boring old routine, clothes, friends . . . bloody hairstyle. Maybe it was the hit of nicotine, but she was beginning to feel dizzy with the possibilities.

School broke up very late that year for Lucy and Dan, on 23 December. Unusually, they met up at the bus stop and travelled home together, chatting about friends, class, music and only finally exchanging a few words about what they thought Christmas was going to be like.

'Mum will want it to be just as usual – huge lunch, Nan and Gramps, Auntie Rosie and the kids. Only Dad will be missing,' Dan said.

'Oh God,' Lucy sighed, 'I don't think I can stand it. Suze has invited me round to her place in the evening. Mum better let me.'

'Well, who knows? Maybe it will be better without Mum and Dad narking on at each other all day long. I mean they were so awful together.'

'But did he have to get a girlfriend?' Lucy moaned. 'It's so embarrassing. And, you know, she just *had* to be blonde and in her *twenties*. I mean, gross.'

'Look on the bright side,' Dan said. 'Christmas presents from them both. That'll be a first.'

'S'pose.' But Lucy couldn't really work up much enthusiasm for the tasteful, expensive item of clothing she would invariably get and hate from her mother, and God only knew what her dad would come up with, since he'd never had to buy them a present before.

As they trudged up the street in the dark towards their home, they both looked at each other in wordless astonishment to see the big For Sale sign outside. The garage door was open and their mother was unloading bags from the boot of a tiny, shiny, black Ka thing which she then plipped shut with an electronic key.

'Mum?' Dan asked with more than a hint of uncertainty because this woman had spiky blonde-and-red-tinged hair and was wearing a knee-length wine-coloured leather coat and high-heeled ankle boots.

'Oh hello, guys!' she said. 'D'you like it?'

It was hard to know what she meant.

'The car?' Dan asked.

'Your hair?' Lucy said at the same time.

'It's all change,' she smiled at them.

It certainly bloody was, Dan thought. How the hell were they all going to fit into it? Mind you, that had hardly been his first thought when his dad had showed them his new BMW Z3.

'Have you sold the Scenic?' Dan asked.

'Yup.'

'Don't you think Dad will mind?'

'I don't give a fuck,' she answered, unlocking the front door, while her two stunned children did nothing to help her with her armfuls of bags.

When they were all inside, she insisted they come into the kitchen for a cup of tea and something to eat because she wanted to talk to them.

And sitting there at the kitchen table, it was impossible not to notice how different she looked. It wasn't just the hair, which was short and funky and knocked an undeniable five years off her, but she also had red lipstick on and clothes which looked sleek, expensive and groovy.

Lucy had seen the names on the bags and been impressed, convinced that her mum had finally been to the kind of shops where she would find her something decent for Christmas.

'So. I've got some news for you both,' she smiled at them. 'Christmas at this house is cancelled. Well, I just mean I'm not doing Christmas dinner here. I've taken all the stuff back and Nan and Gramps are going to go to Auntie Rosie's for a change. You guys are going to Dad's new flat and, for once, I'm going to have a bit of peace and not be stuffing turkeys and flaming puddings and all that guff.'

Sharp intakes of breath.

'I don't mean I've cancelled the Christmas spirit.' She reached over to the counter top beside her and pulled out two white envelopes, which she handed to them.

'I took your presents back. You never like the things I get you anyway, so I've decided on cheques instead.'

'Thanks,' they managed in mumbles.

'Now, there's some other stuff you need to know about. The house is going to be sold and I'm going to get a little flat. So we'll either have to squeeze in together for a while or maybe your dad will get a bigger place and you might want to stay there , we'll see.

'And the other thing is that I'm going to take a bit of a break in the New Year. An old school friend of mine lives in Bermuda now and I'm going to go and visit her . . . for a couple of months.'

As she'd anticipated, her two teenagers looked bewildered. They were obviously wondering how the hell they were going to survive eight weeks without their cook, caretaker, cleaner, driver, personal organizer. Well . . . Time they found out.

'Obviously, your dad will move back in to take care of you. And probably take care of the house sale too.'

However surprised the children looked, they weren't nearly as gobsmacked at these plans as their father had been.

She had just come back from his smug little

stainless steel, track-lit, power-showered singleton apartment. She'd turned up unannounced and of course Karen had been there and Andrew had hovered at the door, reluctant to invite her in, until she'd told him: 'For God's sake be a grown-up, I know what's going on here.'

She had enjoyed the less-than-enthusiastic look on Karen's face when she'd informed them that Lucy and Dan were coming to his for Christmas dinner and, by the way, she was leaving the country for January and February and oh . . . she thought she'd get the ball rolling and put the house on the market.

Andrew had followed her out into the wood-panelled, beige-carpeted stairwell and asked what had got into her, how could she possibly be so irresponsible?

She'd laughed in his face: 'Responsible? Is that what you thought you were being when you walked out on us and moved in here instead?'

'Fuck you, Andrew,' she'd told him, causing him to just about faint. 'You thought I would stay home and pick up all the pieces. Well, fuck you.'

'And I hate your hair,' he'd shouted venomously down the staircase after her.

'GOOD!' she'd shouted back. 'At least I *have* hair!'

How she'd giggled at the childishness of that all the way back to her tiny new car.

And as she had listened to the dreamy lyrics soaring from the radio about freedom and life and new love, she felt vindicated, which was just as well because she had been starting to wonder, what with the credit card bleeding from the day's purchases, hair treatments and final £600 whack spent at the travel agents.

But then she'd consoled herself with thoughts of the whopping house valuation. There would be plenty of money in the bank. Things were going to be different. She wanted Sadie to be proud of her.

'And one last thing,' she casually shook out a cigarette and lit up in front of her utterly silenced children, 'you'll have to sort yourselves out for supper. Because I'm going out tonight . . . with the girls.'

CROSSROADS

Manda Scott

Born and brought up in Scotland, **MANDA SCOTT** studied to be a veterinary surgeon in Glasgow. She now lives in Suffolk and writes full-time. Her first novel, *Hen's Teeth*, short-listed for the Orange Prize in 1997, was followed by three further highly acclaimed thrillers, *Night Mares*, *Stronger Than Death*, *No Good Deed*, and the forthcoming *Absolution*. Manda Scott is currently writing a fictional trilogy on the life of Boudica, war-leader of the Eceni, who led the revolt against Rome in AD61. The first volume, *Dreaming the Eagle*, was published in February, 2003.

It begins like any other day. Frances Buchanan wakes with the dawn. The sun rises over the crook of the Campsies and shines in through her bedroom window. The curtains are not drawn to shield her. There are, in fact, no curtains to draw. One of her first acts of independence on the day she moved into the spare room with its single bed and east-facing windows was to stand on a chair and take down the curtains, fold them neatly and drop them in the bottom of her wardrobe. That was two years ago. She intended, at the time, to re-hang them for the winter but the double glazing was new and effi-cient and by the end of summer she had grown used to the broad reach of the sky. So she has left the curtains gathering dust and now, on a bright morn-ing in May, the first rays of the sun ease over the edge of the hills and fall across the hollows of her eyes and tease her awake.

She lies still for a while, letting go of the noise of her dreams, and listens instead to the familiar quiet of the world at sleep. A grandfather clock ticks heavily downstairs in the lounge; a wedding pres-ent from her in-laws, that she might never forget their existence. On the other side of the wall, their son, who is still her husband, wakes with a grunt and rolls over to check his alarm clock before turning once again to sleep. Up in the loft, one of the cats drops heavily in through the open skylight. A scurry of smaller feet suggests the gift it carries may not yet be ready to meet its maker. Frances opens her eyes and watches the patterns of light shift and change on the ceiling. In time, she hears the sounds of her son's awakening; a cautious, whispered conversation with the cats, a token splash of water that passes for a wash and then the scuff of bare feet on the uncovered wood of the loft, down the ladder and across the hallway to pause outside her bedroom door.

'Finn? Come in. I'm awake.'

A dark, tousled head appears round the edge of her door. It was clear a long time ago that Findley Buchanan was going to have his mother's hair. By the end of his time at infant school, his mother had realized that what had always felt like a curse to the growing girl and the woman was going to be a gift for the boy and the man. It has taken her thirty years of trial and error to find that the only way to look halfway sensible is to ask her hairdresser to cut her hair shorter than either of them likes. Her son never bothers about looking halfway sensible. He lets it grow wild, like a thorn bush, and, on him, it is captivating. Give him ten years and they'll fall at his feet for his hair alone, whoever they may be.

The boy sidles sideways into the room clutching the larger of the two cats in the crook of his arm.

He glances at her, appraising. His eyes are brown and they melt her soul. 'Weasel wants to say hello,' he says.

'Does he? Bring him in then.' Weasel is lithe and black with green eyes and muscles of spun steel and an extraordinary capacity for killing rabbits. Frances is constantly surprised at the patience with which he tolerates an eight-year-old's haphazard affections.

'He brought me a mouse,' says Finn and he shows Frances the fresh bloodstain on his pyjama trousers as proof.

'Did he? That's nice. Was it dead?'

'The first one was.'

'Oh. Good.'

The cat reaches its threshold of tolerance and slides free of the grip on its neck. It flows out of her window like so much dark water and returns to the killing fields outside. The boy watches it go, then turns and bounces onto the edge of Frances' bed. He grabs her arm and looks at her watch. The time is five o'clock or thereabouts. He shoves her hand back where it came from. 'It's too early,' he says, 'you should still be asleep.' He is grinning and it is difficult to know if he is giving her orders or simply reading her thoughts. Either way, she is too mellow to argue.

'Is it?' She curls into an arc and lifts the corner of the duvet. 'So then, do you want to come and sleep with me until breakfast?' This is a special ritual, saved for those rare mornings when mother and son are awake and alone. The boy slides in beside her and curls in a foetal position, nesting in the curve of her abdomen. He lays his head on her shoulder and drapes his forearm across hers. The pale boy-skin lies white against the relative dark of her tan.

'Why am I whiter than you?'

'Because I work outside all day and you have to sit in a classroom away from the sun.'

'Will I be able to work outside when I'm big?'

'If you want to.'

He thinks about that. 'What happens in the winter?'

'I get cold. And very wet.' Actually, this is not true. In winter, they set up the breeding tanks under cover of the barn and do their best to keep the fluctuations in ambient temperature to a minimum. She considers explaining and decides it is too complicated for the time of day.

Finn, too, has been thinking. 'Then I'll work inside,' he says, decisively. 'But only in the winter. In the summer, I'll come and work with you outside.' He rolls over to look up at her. 'Would you like that?' His eyes are widely innocent and there are small crusts of sleep at the inner corners.

'I'd love it,' she says and this is true, if unlikely ever to be tested. She licks her thumb and wipes his eyes. He screws them up, frowning, and then relaxes when it is clear she is not going to insist on cleaning him all. 'I want to go for a walk on the hill before school,' he says.

'Maybe. If there's time. But you have to sleep some more first.'

'I want a story.'

'I know. I'm going to give you a story.'

He turns his back to her and she runs her hand through the wild hedge of his hair, dragging her fingertips lightly across the skin of his scalp and then settles to telling him stories of magic cats and even more magic mice who fall to the cat at night and are reborn at dawn the next day to relive their short lives under the sun. He sleeps before the end, his head growing heavier on her shoulder, his mouth slack. For nearly an hour beyond that, she lies awake and watches the sun move round and the clock hands with it and feels the small pool of her son's saliva collecting in the hollow beneath her clavicle. Her thoughts wander to the day ahead; to the work and the meetings and the timing of the complex jigsaw that is her life. 'I'll be late at work,' she says, dreamily, to the sleeping head on her shoulder. 'Jill will pick you up from school and you can play with Daniel. She has a friend coming for dinner so you can't stay late. I've promised I'll pick you up by six.'

The woman coming to collect the child is late, but this is not a surprise. When the six o'clock news comes and goes and she has not appeared, Jill Winter wrinkles her nose and says, 'Frances is never on time. We'll be lucky to see her before nine.'

Her guest is lying on the floor with her head cushioned on her arm and her legs crossed at the ankle. She has been lying like this for an hour and is remarkably comfortable. The night is warm and the company reminds her of her student youth, which is not so far away as to be nostalgic but just far enough that she can remember the good parts better than the bad. She remembers particularly Jill Winter when she was Jill Forsyth and unmarried. She is not so different now. Jill Forsyth played hockey for Scotland's under twenty-ones but only because women's rugby wasn't considered suitable by a father who spent a great deal of his time intimidating everyone. She studied law, because her father had studied law, then married to escape it because that was the only acceptable route to freedom and then waited until the day after Forsyth senior died before she filed for divorce. In his absence, she has mellowed. It doesn't always show.

Now, for instance, she is caught with a bottle of white Burgundy in one hand and a glass in the other and she is glaring at the clock as if it alone is responsible for the fact that her son still has his friend to play with.

Her guest pushes herself to sitting and says, 'I'll go then. The flat's a mess. I could do with an early night and then I can tidy up in the morning.'

Jill is not impressed. 'Really? I thought your body clock was set on California time, eight hours behind Glasgow, and you weren't going to get any sleep till the morning?'

'I can always try.'

'Give me a break. You're not fit to walk, never mind drive. Sit where you are and I'll make us a meal. Unless you object to sharing a dinner table with the boys?'

114

Crossroads

Jill Winter wouldn't ask a question like that if she believed there was more than one possible answer. Dinner comes and goes and the children with it; the big beefy red-head who inherited his mother's hair and his father's bulk and a double dose of bullish obduracy and is already shaping up to be a handful, and the small, wiry, dark-haired one with the quiet, knowing smile and the disconcertingly watchful eyes. There is a battle underway and a meal with a stranger doesn't count as a suitable reason to call off hostilities and so the large red-haired Viking continues to wage war on the small, dark-headed Celt with every sign that rape and pillage are on the agenda for the final onslaught. The meal is messy on the grounds that everyone knows Viking warriors only eat with their knives, which is an interesting achievement with spaghetti bolognaise. Fortunately the Celts have better table manners and are, as a result, spared washing-up duties. On reflection, the Viking's duties are deferred to a later date with a view to protecting the crockery from the inevitable fallout of war.

The children retire to plan the new campaign. The adults wash and dry and catch up on the details of the ex-husband on the one hand and the ex-lover on the other; the small minutiae of relationship-endings that never made it into the letters and the phone calls, and then they sit at the table in the kitchen – which has been declared a neutral zone on pain of an early night – and drink wine on the one hand and water on the other and wait for the mother of the small, dark-haired Celt to come and rescue her son from certain death.

The doorbell rings shortly after the start of the nine o'clock news.

'And what kind of time do you call this?'

If you didn't know Jill well, you would run from that voice. The incomer does not run and so must know Jill almost as well as her dinner guest does. She says, 'I'm sorry, Jill. You could just file for adoption papers now, it would be so much easier in the long run.' Her voice, heard from the kitchen, is dry and husked, as if she has spoken for too long without water; a west coast accent with a roughening overlay of Glasgow, the modulation of someone used to speaking and being heard, but it is the humour, the raw intelligence of it, that catches the ear.

Jill is on a roll and will not stop for someone else's humour. 'You think I want two of the little bastards? Permanently? Do I look completely insane?'

There is only one possible answer to that and it comes, dryly. 'You've been completely insane for the whole of your life, Jill Winter. It's genetic. There's no escaping it. You've only got to look at your son.'

That takes the wind from the matriarch's sails, which is all that the incomer needs. She slips up the steps into the light of the hall and it can be seen that she is slim and slight like her son and with the same dark hair but that the eyes, on an adult, have learned a guardedness that is lacking in the child. She steps forward, one hand outstretched, the other pushing the hank of hair from her eyes.

'Hello, I'm Frances Buchanan, Finn's mother. You must be—'

'Meet Grace,' Jill is never subtle with her introductions, 'Grace McLeod. Grace, this is Frances, who used to be a friend in the days before she forgot how to read the time. Her son is the body on the patio with the stake through its heart awaiting a Viking's funeral.'

Jill is grinning and Frances, who must be used to this, does not run to the rescue of her child. Instead she stands very still, as if the world has become suddenly fragile. Jill Winter's grin fades and is replaced by something quite different. She says, 'I'll go and referee the funeral pyre. You two sit here and finish the wine, or drink the taps dry of water – whichever you prefer. Let me finish the introductions first: Grace, this is Frances, she's technical director of a firm making genetically modified fish. Frankie, this is Grace, she's the international legal adviser for Greenpeace. The combination of which should prove fairly incendiary should you choose to explore it. And, yes, I have slept with you both. But not in the last ten years. Have fun.'

The door closes softly behind her.

There is a certain quality of quiet in the kitchen that comes when a crossroads has been reached and not yet passed. Two women sit opposite each other and neither knows what to say. Beyond the door, a pair of child-warriors harangue an adult who takes pleasure in altering the lives of her friends, not always to their detriment. Presently, Grace says, 'Jill can always be relied on to cut through the small talk. We could have spent the next several hours working our way round to that last fact.'

'And still never got there.' Frances is living in a dream. The ordered boundaries of her reality have folded and imploded and the world of fiction and fable is threatening to overwhelm her. She has found a chair by feel and her hand, with a will of its own, has poured her a glass of wine. 'Except that I think I've seen you once before. In Peppermints, on Great Western Road. I was a fourth-year medical student, hiding in the shadows with the others of the infant underclass and you were with Sarah Crawford and we were all wildly jealous.'

'Ah.' There is a moment's thought and old memories rekindle. Grace moves to the floor. The tiles are handmade Mexican terracotta and there is a solidity and coolness to them that is stabilizing. She is not sure, yet, if the instability is jet lag or something greater. It can't be alcohol, because she has had none, although she may need to change that shortly. 'Why were you jealous?' she asks.

Frances says, 'Everyone was jealous of Sarah She was every woman's dream; beauty and intelligence combined. And she'd just started as SHO a the Western. As I remember, we were all incredi bly impressed that anyone could come through thei houseman's year intact and have a life at the enc of it.'

Crossroads

Frances is taking refuge in the past. The blurred
patina of memory is safer than the rawness of the
present. She watches Grace, who has pulled one
knee to her chest and rested her chin on the looped
hammock of her fingers and is blowing a sudden
sigh through ballooned cheeks, saying, 'I'm not sure
you could ever say Sarah Crawford was intact. Just
that the scars were well hidden.'

In the reflected light from the floor tiles, her eyes
are oddly amber. Earlier, and in Frances' memory,
they were grey, flecked with brown. Grace is tall
and would be angular but for the unconscious grace
with which she holds herself. Her hair has grey
streaks in a sandy blonde but is otherwise the same
as it was fifteen years before. Were she an animal,
Grace McLeod would be a lioness. They had played
that game once in Peppermints and Frances, who
had been named variously as otter, seal and stoat,
had not had the courage to say what she thought.
She was much younger then. Now, she can ask the
question that has been growing inside her from the
moment she entered the kitchen. 'Are you and Sarah
still together?'

'No.' The pain of that may be old, but Grace feels
it and Frances sees it. Grace says, 'She left two
years ago. She's a consultant paediatrician somewhere south of the border. We don't keep in touch.'
And in that is a lifetime's hurt. Grace rises from
the floor and pours herself a glass of wine. She sits
on a chair, tipping it back against the wall. The
silence has fallen again and must be broken. 'You're
married?' she asks.

Grace knows this is the case because Jill has told her. Only now is it apparent why. Frances places the flat of her hand on the table, her fingers either side of the wine glass stem, and swirls Jill Winter's best Burgundy dangerously close to the rim. 'After a fashion,' she says at length. 'Neil is a friend if nothing else. We share a home. We share the occasional dinner party. We share our work.'

'And a son.'

'And Finn. He is the reason we still share as much as we do.'

'All this after evenings spent in Peppermints.' That could have been said to hurt but is not. Grace can soften her lawyer's voice when she chooses. She leans her elbows on the table and draws looped infinities in a patch of dribbled wine. 'What happened?' she asks.

'I fell in love. And then fell out of it. Finn had happened in between. I couldn't undo the past without undoing him and I wouldn't do that.' In that, too, is a lifetime's hurt and the weight of isolation without the promise of respite.

They are hovering on the cusp of the crossroads. They could say everything, or nothing. There is no half-measure in between and either way, life will be different afterwards. With a courage she was not aware she possessed, Frances says, 'In Peppermints, everyone else was jealous of you because they wanted to be with Sarah. I was different; I wanted to be her, to be with you – except you were a year past your Finals and so you had passed into the world of the adult and were beyond reach of the pond life.' She lifts her eyes from the table and makes herself look into the waiting grey gaze opposite. 'I was very young. Three years seemed like an impossible gap.'

'And does it still?'

'No.'

Their hands are flat on the table, fingertips a hair's breadth apart. It takes the smallest of movements for Grace to bridge the gap, for skin to meet skin and a thousand nerve endings to touch and connect, for hand to slide over hand and grip and change the way of the world for ever.

And then the door opens and Jill Winter enters, flanked on either side by a Viking and a Celt, and the world crashes back into place and all that has happened is a handshake. Frances withdraws her hand first. 'Jill, I'm sorry. You've had the maniacs all evening. Let me take Finn home.'

'Oh, Mummy, *no* . . .'

'Frances, you can't. Mummy, tell her she can't . . .'

'You can't, Frances. At least, not without an exceptionally good reason. I promised they could turn Daniel's bed into a long-boat and sleep at the oars.'

It is late and Frances is tired and her mind is too slow. 'What?'

Grace is smiling her long, slow lion's smile. She says, 'Finn has asked to stay the night and Jill has said yes. Am I right?'

'You are. Good woman, I'm glad one of you is still awake. Finn will stay here and I'll take him to school in the morning. Unless Frances has any serious objections, which would be bloody silly, if you ask me.' Jill is smiling as only those closest to her have seen her smile. Both Grace and Frances have been that close, if only briefly. Their eyes meet across the table and the crossroads has been passed, effortlessly and there are only the minor practicalities to sort out.

Grace says, 'The flat's a mess, I haven't been home for four weeks and I left in a hurry and there's washing-up in the sink and I have two suitcases full of clothes you really don't want to see. But it has no husband sleeping in the next room, which may give it the edge. Will it do?'

Frances smiles as she has not smiled in fifteen years. Finn is at her shoulder, not understanding, but happy that she is happy. She kisses the top of his head and runs her fingers through the wild mess of his hair. 'I think it'll do fine,' she says.

A TRUE ROMANCE

Shari Low

SHARI LOW writes regularly for the *Daily Record* and is the author of two hilarious romantic comedies, *What If?* and *Why Not?* She lives in Glasgow with her husband, John, and ever-increasing brood.

Friday morning. The *Kilcaidie Advertiser* Daily Horoscope. Sagittarius: Despite a bumpy start to the day, positive aspects will forge a new beginning mid-afternoon. Don't turn away from new ideas or challenges as your future happiness might just depend on them.

Deo placed her cup of tea and bacon sandwich down on her desk and switched on her PC. There was no putting it off any further. In the last hour she'd considered and dismissed every conceivable excuse to avoid sitting down and doing some work today. Excuse number one: raging hangover. Dismissed on the grounds that it was self-inflicted so therefore not a credible reason to avoid doing paid labour. Number two: a mountain of ironing so high that a Sherpa would get vertigo just looking at it. However, ten minutes searching for the iron had proved fruitless. It was probably underneath the pile. Desperation started to creep in. Number three: it *was* nearly a fortnight since she'd visited her mother. She could nip over for a couple of hours. After all, she was already feeling atrocious, how much worse could it be? She sighed in resignation, then gritted her teeth. Sod it. It would be less painful to sit down and put in a few hours' work. Her mother's dulcet tones on top of the hangover from hell would have her speed-dialling the Samaritans.

She blinked hard, trying to clear the fog. Which of her literary hats would perch most comfortably on her pounding head today? Did she feel like being Desdemona White, the True Romance Book Club's novelist of the month, esteemed author of such romantic classics as *He Came, He Conquered* and *His Throbbing Heart*? Not for the first time, she gave an involuntary shudder. How *had* she managed to assume the identity of someone whom her mostly aged, single readers imagined lounging on a chaise-longue, wearing an apricot kaftan and patting a shitzu while she wrote her love classics on parchment with an antique fountain pen? If they could only see her now . . . She'd be evicted from the House Of True Romance quicker than a bigamist with body odour.

A flashback seared through her trance-like state. It had all been Trudy's fault. But then, everything always was. It had been Trude's idea to write romantic slush to supplement their meagre grants at uni. It had been Trude's theory that creating personas in keeping with the True Romance Book Club's average reader would give their manuscripts a better chance of being accepted. Thus Dee became Desdemona White, a fifty-year-old spinster who passed her days in a picturesque cottage in a blustery Scottish village, tending to her four cats and her petunias as she awaited the arrival of her God of Love, who would one day, she was sure, come and conquer.

It was also Trude's fault that even now, ten years after leaving university at the age of twenty-two, Dee was still penning her fluffy pink prose for a paltry income, instead of being the hard-hitting investigative journalist that she had always aspired to be. Well, okay, so that wasn't Trude's fault at all, but in her present tender state it made her feel better to pretend it was. In more lucid moments she would admit that the truth of the matter was that she just hadn't wanted it enough. No matter how many times she'd planned the move to London or composed applications to the more respectable tabloids and the lofty broadsheets, she never quite made it to the train or put her CV in the post. Finally, in a moment of clarity on her twenty-fifth birthday, she'd grudgingly acknowledged what everyone around her had always known: she was staying in Kilcaidie. And what's more, she was happy about it.

Three train stops and thirty minutes on a good day from the centre of Glasgow, Kilcaidie was notable only for the fact that, defying a long Celtic association with the merits of alcohol, it was the only dry village left in the West of Scotland. Not a pub for fifteen miles. It was therefore completely understandable that Dee was in this fragmented condition today, she reasoned. After all, you had to make the most of a trip to Glasgow and that's

exactly what she and Trude had done on yester-
day's shopping-cum-eating-cum-drinking-cum-
rousing-three-other-passengers-and-a-dog-into-a-
sing-song-on-the-last-train-home excursion. At her
age she really should have known better. But then
that was the story of her life, she mused. Common
sense had never been her strongest personality
trait. If it were, then she wouldn't have a career
pretending to be a post-menopausal spinster on
heat, earning a salary that was barely above the
poverty line (not including, of course, a heady £100
bonus for being voted Author of the Month in
September 1998), which she had to supplement by
being Auntie Diana, author of the *Kilcaidie
Advertiser's* agony column, and the in-house
astrologer, Madame Donatella, predictor of the
population's daily fortunes. Multiple personality
disorder was more a career choice than a mental
condition.

Indecision furrowed her brow. Auntie Diana it
was. It was a warming thought that reading about
other people's trials and tribulations would
undoubtedly make her feel better about her present sorry condition.

Bacon sandwich in one hand, she manoeuvred
the mouse to the Outlook Express icon and clicked.
It pinged as it opened the program. Ouch! Good
God, when did that ping get so loud? It was vibrating round her head so violently that her eyelashes
started to tremble.

She quickly slid the mouse to the volume control
and reduced it to mute, before switching to the

A True Romance

'Advertiser – Auntie Diana' profile and clicking send/receive. The screen flashed up its progress. Dialling. Verifying password. Checking mailbox. You have twelve new messages. Dee groaned. Kilcaidie was a troubled place this week. Normally there weren't more than three or four letters in a week and they generally consisted of a lonely heart, a couple of neighbourly disputes and a complaint from George the hypochondriac about skateboarders on the high street inducing his panic attacks.

She automatically clicked on the most recent arrival.

Dear Auntie Diana,

I'm very concerned about my best friend. I think she has a serious drinking problem – every time she indulges in alcohol she has an irresistible urge to sing Beach Boys songs really loudly on public transport. Is there a support group for this condition? Please advise as to the best course of action.

Yours in deep concern,
Trudy

An amused snort escaped as Dee started typing.

Dear Trudy,

Pretend she's a horse with a broken limb and put her out of her misery – with the severity of her current

headache she'll thank you for it. And thank you for
your concern.

Auntie Di

Two minutes later the phone rang. Ouch. Dee
snatched it from the table. The caller spoke before
she did.

'Sorry, mate, I haven't got a gun. How's your
head?'

'Don't ask. And stop bloody sending e-mails to
Auntie Di – she's overworked as it is. How are you
feeling this morning?'

'Like I've spent two weeks marinating my head
in gin.' Pause. 'But enough fantasizing. I've got a
proposition for you.'

Dee groaned out loud. 'Whatever it is, you can
forget it. I'm not going to start yoga classes at the
community centre, donate my eggs or do a spon-
sored slim in aid of Save the Whale. No matter how
ironic that is.'

'Nope, it's none of those. Although, and I'm telling
you this strictly in the spirit of a best friend who
only wants what's best for you – your thighs could
definitely benefit from a session or six of Ashtanga.
Anyway, the proposition. How would you like to join
Dave and me tomorrow night for a veritable feast
of dishes from around the world as featured in the
new Jamie Oliver bible of home cooking?'

'What's the catch?'

'Why does there have to be a catch? Can't I just
invite my best friend for dinner without there being

some dark, ulterior motive? I'm *so* offended.'

'It's a proposition, Trudy, therefore there's a catch. Who is he this time?'

'Okay.' Trudy sighed in a tone pitched somewhere between resignation and defeat. 'It's Dave's new boss. He's just moved up here from London, so we thought we'd do the hospitality bit and invite him over. Can't beat a bit of grovelling to authority in the name of career advancement.'

Dee put her head in her hands. Or at least she tried to, but her aim was off and she succeeded only in imprinting her keyboard on her forehead. This was the last thing she felt like doing this weekend. Dave, Trudy's fiancé of four years (he didn't like to rush things), worked in some obscure department of Glasgow City Council. He had told her about his job a couple of times but Dee's tendency to zone out after the first two minutes meant that she was none the wiser. Another internal groan. Dinner with the remnants of a hangover (this was definitely a three-day headache) and two civil servants, one of them trying to impress the other – was this some cosmic punishment for overindulgence last night?

Trude sensed her hesitation and resorted to blatant pleading. 'Come on, Dee, if you do this, I'll never mention your cellulite again. Please.'

'Okay, okay. But I'm warning you, this had better not be a set-up. The first whiff of a blind date and I'm out of there, Trude.'

'It's not a set-up, I promise. It's just a fine example of good old Scottish hospitality.'

Somehow, Dee doubted that.

Saturday morning. The *Kilcaidie Advertiser* Daily Horoscope. Sagittarius: Today is a day for rest and recuperation and taking quiet time to recharge your batteries. For those Sagittarians who do have to venture out, avoid new social interactions arranged by friends – despite their well-meant intentions, they don't always know what is best for you.

Dear Auntie Di,

I'm very worried about my best friend. She is in her thirties now and is still single despite numerous attempts by me to introduce her to suitable men. In fact, she was downright rude when I last sprung a blind date on her (I mean, what's so bad about a nervous twitch, a train-spotting hobby and mild halitosis – nobody is perfect) and threatened to amputate my limbs if I repeated the exercise. What can I do about her anti-social tendencies and her threatening behaviour?

Yours in mortal fear,
Trudy

Dear Trudy,

Maybe your friend is perfectly happy with her single status and as her friend you should support her in this lifestyle choice. Perhaps there is something sadly lacking in your life that prompts you to take such an avid interest in other people's relationships. I suggest you look into taking up a hobby, such as basket-weaving or origami.

Yours sympathetically,
Auntie Diana

PS: Trude, you promised that tonight isn't another set up. If it is, I'll have to kill you.

Dee stared at her reflection in the full-length mirror. She should have asked Trude what to wear tonight but she hadn't wanted to appear adolescent or apprehensive. She was a cosmopolitan woman of the world. One with no dress sense, she reflected. It was so difficult trying to dress for occasions like this. If she were too casual, Dave's boss might take offence, especially if he was one of those late-fifties, dress-for-dinner, formal types. On the other hand, Trudy and Dave's kitchen dining table, which doubled as a table tennis table and, in times of decoration, the wallpaper pasting area, didn't exactly lend itself to cocktail dress and diamonds.

In the end she settled for the middle road. Dark blue hipster jeans (size 12 – who needed yoga?) with a black, low-cut T-shirt, supported by breast-enhancing bra. She clipped diamond studs into her ears and twisted up her long auburn hair, leaving some tendrils loose to frame her face. She couldn't decide if it looked Julia Roberts classy or been doing housework all day messy. Anyway, why was she caring? She was just there to make up the numbers and to reinforce the theory that Dave was a decent, normal guy who was a credit to any workplace. After all, it wasn't as if this was a date or anything . . .

The very thought sent her eyeballs rolling and a shiver down her spine. She *so* wished that Trudy would just let her get on with living her life the way she wanted to. Why must everyone on the planet be shackled up to a member of the opposite sex to ensure everlasting happiness? Why was a man (or another woman for that matter) crucial to self-esteem, image and sense of worth? Dee shrugged her shoulders. She just didn't get it. She'd tried to analyse her feeling many times over the years (especially after a few libations and in between the Beach Boys' greatest hits) but the truth was she didn't care enough to delve too deeply. Maybe it was the fact that she'd been an only child and was therefore used to enjoying her own company. Perhaps it was because the things she enjoyed doing most – reading, lying in the bath pondering life, and running in the mornings with her walkman on full blast – were predominately solitary pursuits.

She had never had her heart broken and had never crushed anyone else. And no, it wasn't down to deep-rooted self-loathing, a pathological aversion to commitment or some deep psychological scar tissue on her soul. It was simply a fact of life. Dee Statton was happy being the word that was greeted with fear, horror and loathing amongst other women of her generation: *single*. She didn't want children, she didn't want to be married and she enjoyed only emotionless flings with members of the opposite sex. As soon as they demanded any form of commitment deeper than occasionally borrowing her toothbrush after they'd spent the night, Dee would trot out the 'going too fast, maybe we should have a break' speech.

Meaningless sex and someone to be her partner at weddings, funerals and the odd trip to the cinema – that was all she wanted in a man. Was that too much to ask? And anyway (she was perched on her metaphorical soapbox now), why was it that a single, attractive thirty-something male with a job, financial security and the freedom to change partners at a whim was revered and envied by his peers, yet a female in the same circumstances was almost unanimously pitied by hers? It was one of life's little idiosyncrasies, she decided. Like why men automatically scratch their nether regions in times of deep concentration, bravado or when they think no one's watching them. God was definitely having a laugh when he created human beings . . .

Trudy opened the door and physically dragged Dee inside. 'He's here and he's *gorgeous*,' she stage-whispered through the hand that was trying to cover the grin stretching from one gold hoop to another. 'I promise, Dee, this wasn't a set-up. But he's thirty-five, was married for three years to a female who sounds like a major bunny boiler. Anyway, she ran off with the plumber who was installing their en-suite. Marble. Cream. He's been divorced for six years. No children. Earns over fifty grand a year.

Likes football, rugby and tennis, but isn't obsessed. Hates cricket. Listens to soul, Motown and also likes rock. Favourite group Oasis. No obvious halitosis or strange hobbies. Likes to travel, go to the flicks and Italian food is his favourite.' She paused for breath. 'Sorry, that's all I could find out. He's only been here five minutes.'

Dee laughed, despite an overwhelming premonition of doom. 'You forgot his inside leg measurement.'

'Thirty-four and a half inches, give or take a fraction. And you know I'm never wrong about these things.'

That summer job in the gent's tailors had left its mark.

Dee followed Trudy into the kitchen, mentally noting that she seemed to have got her outfit just right. Trudy too was wearing jeans with a black top, her blonde hair pulled up into a high ponytail. That was no surprise. Ever since their virtually inseparable childhood, they would arrange to meet and then invariably both turn up in almost identical clothes. They liked the same music, the same movies, excelled at the same sports . . . Sometimes it was almost as if they had one brain, just with extra arms and legs.

Thankfully, though, there was one area in which they differed, Dee thought, as she entered the kitchen and Dave stood up to kiss her. Men. To Dee, Dave had all the appeal of a big teddy that looked good in the corner of a room and might occasionally warrant a cuddle in times of severe stress or depression. He was sweet, cuddly and cute, but didn't set the bells ringing in her brain, or any other part of her anatomy for that matter. Still, he loved Trudy and she adored him and that was all that mattered. And one day they'd give her gorgeous adopted nieces and nephews to play with. Ones that she could hand right back at the end of the day.

'Hey, Dee, you look gorgeous,' Dave smiled as he kissed her cheek. None of this air-kissing nonsense. North of the Watford Gap, you got the full saliva-leaving, make-up-smearing, deadly suction smacker. It's been known to result in bruising.

She returned Dave's kiss, then turned to face the newcomer. He put out his hand and shook hers. 'Hi, I'm Greg, pleased to meet you.'

'Dee,' she replied superfluously.

'I know. Thirty-two, natural hair colour, journal-ist and author, single, never been married, likes *ER*, re-runs of the *Sweeney* and had a childhood crush on Tony Hadley. Hates seafood, likes Japanese, Chinese and Indian food and going to the cinema.'

Dee closed her eyes in embarrassment.

'Oh, and inside leg thirty-one and a half inches,' he concluded.

She opened one eye and contorted her face into what she hoped was an apologetic expression. Trude should carry an early warning alarm.

She half expected him to make a run on his thirty-four and a half inch legs, but no, he was still standing there with a lopsided grin. Trudy hadn't mentioned that he had a killer smile.

There was a pause, then the ludicrousness of the situation seemed to descend on all four of them at the same time and they creased into laughter.

Can't beat a bit of ritual humiliation to break the ice, Dee thought, as she offered her hand to his. 'Erm, pleased to meet you,' she laughed. And she was.

Dinner passed in a comfortable, lots-of-laughs and four-bottles-of-red-wine kind of haze. Dee made a mental note to apologize to her liver – no alcohol for a month then two blow-outs in the one week. She was going to feel like road-kill in the morning.

They ran the usual gauntlet of discussion topics. Dee was pleasantly surprised to find that other than the information Trudy had forcibly extracted from the defenceless Greg, they actually had loads more in common too. Maybe there was a bit of potential there after all. There was, if she was reading the signals correctly, definitely the hint of a mutual attraction going on. It was the little things: he listened with a smile when she spoke, was interested in everything about her and didn't cringe when a spoonful of chow-mein missed her mouth and landed in the cleavage created by her push-up bra. By midnight she'd decided that the wine was fantastic and dinner parties were great! And so was Trudy, for obviously fixing her up with this lovely man. She must remember to thank her in the morning. Good old Trude, what a star!

At one o'clock, Greg called a taxi just as she announced that she was heading for home.

'Let me drop you off,' Greg offered.

'No, there's really no need. But thanks.'

'Look, I insist.'

'Thanks, but honestly, I'm happy to walk. It's really not far,' Dee persisted.

Greg refused to listen, so eventually Dee shrugged her shoulders and succumbed. Five minutes, lots of kisses and so much winking from Trudy that she now had repetitive strain injury in her right eye, they were ensconced in the back of a Mondeo.

'Thirteen Thistle Drive,' Dee said with only a slight slur.

The driver looked at her quizzically. 'But—' he started to say.

Dee put up her hand. 'I know, but humour me. Thirteen Thistle Drive, please.'

The driver shrugged his shoulders and released the handbrake, shaking his head.

Greg looked momentarily confused by the exchange, but obviously put it down to too much wine or a taxi driver with attitude. As the car pulled away, he turned to Dee.

'I wanted to take you home because I thought we could talk on the way there without the relationship sheriff monitoring our every move,' he confessed with a smile.

Dee said nothing.

'You see, the thing is—' He was caught in mid-sentence as the driver slammed on the brakes. What was wrong with this guy?

'Thirteen Thistle Drive,' Schumacher announced.

Greg looked confused and Dee couldn't suppress a giggle.

'I told you there was no need. I live only three doors down from Dave and Trude.'

She almost felt sorry for causing his flabbergasted expression.

'But—' he stuttered. Dee cut him off by leaning over and kissing his cheek.

'Call me,' she said with a wink, as she alighted from the Mondeo and started up her path. 'Trudy will give you my number,' she continued without turning round.

As she closed the door behind her, she heard the taxi take off down the road.

Maybe there was something to this blind date thing after all . . .

Thursday morning. The *Kilcaidie Advertiser* Daily Horoscope. Sagittarius: Planetary aspects are conspiring to bring a racy time to you lucky Sagittarians. Whether single or not, emotions and passions will be running high. Brace yourselves!

Dear Auntie Di,

My best friend is going out on a date tonight for the first time in ages. It might even be decades. Anyway, since it's been so long, could you please advise her as to what is currently acceptable in the – well, *physical* sense for a first date in the year 2002, as she's obviously a bit out of touch.

Yours in helpfulness,
Trudy

A True Romance

Dear Trudy,

This is such a difficult subject to advise on as it is highly subjective and depends on the individuals concerned and the amount of alcohol consumed. I would say that most intimate activities are perfectly acceptable these days. However, games involving Batman costumes, swinging from chandeliers or using objects made from leather or chain should perhaps be saved until much further into the relationship, that is the second date.

Yours,
Auntie Di

PS. It bloody well has not been decades.

Dee poured a glass of wine as she waited for Greg to collect her. She didn't know if the feeling in her stomach was hunger or apprehension. It wasn't that dates made her nervous. If anything, the opposite was true – the prospect of great food, interesting conversation and the potential of a frolic was something to be looked forward to. No, it was more that she was beginning to doubt whether she and Greg had the same approach to relationships.

Her misgivings had started to sprout on the morning after Trude's dinner party when, despite the fact that it was a Sunday, he had managed to talk, bribe or coerce some poor unsuspecting florist into delivering twenty-four red roses to her door. She accepted them with some reticence. There was nothing she disliked more than cut flowers. It was a shocking waste! As far as she was concerned, flowers belonged in a garden with trees and bushes, not on top of her Ikea dining table amongst used coffee cups, two weeks of filing and yesterday's half eaten tuna salad. It was criminal. Florists should be outlawed.

Fortunately, she had managed not to share this train of thought when Greg called later that day to ask her out for dinner. He might think she was one of those demented tree-huggers or a closet eco-warrior.

After summoning up as much graciousness as she could muster and thanking him for the flowers, she checked her diary. Monday night: deadline for the following week's horoscopes and problem pages, so she'd be glued to her laptop. Tuesday night: Scotland was playing football against some tiny, obscure nation that she couldn't have found with the aid of a satellite navigation system. They'd almost certainly get beaten by an embarrassingly high margin (when will we accept that *curling* is our forte – half sport, half housework), but she had to be on the sofa in her tartan beret nonetheless. Wednesday: *ER* and *Friends* on telly. Nothing but death, fire or a plague of locusts would get her out of the house that night. So Thursday it was.

Greg somewhat weakly hid the disappointment in his voice. He had hoped he wouldn't have to wait quite that long to see her again. Perhaps he'd misread what he thought was a spark of mutual attraction.

He was still analysing this as he knocked on Dee's

door and manoeuvred a box of chocolates the size
of a coffee table into her hands when she answered.
Dee's smile was more of a grimace as she feigned
gratitude, the noise of another nail going into the
coffin of her healthy eating plan banging in her
head. Okay, so she was prone to the odd lapse, but
chocolates! Didn't he know that it would take three
weeks on the Stairmaster to work those off?

She grabbed her coat and followed him to the
car where they made comfortable, light-hearted
small talk all the way into Glasgow. They continued chatting as they weaved around the city's one-
way system, finally coming to a halt in St Vincent
Street. Dee almost groaned out loud. They had
stopped outside L'Amour, the restaurant with the
reputation of being the most intimate and romantic in the city. It was the type of place where men
who were floundering for inspiration or a slither of
originality took their girlfriends to propose. It came
complete with pink-silk table covers, a violin quartet that serenaded you until you were squirming in
your seat with embarrassment, and menus for the
ladies with no prices down the sides. Dee hated
those. If she was going to be charged an exorbitant
amount of money for a steak that she could get for
a tenner in Garfunkels, then she wanted to know
about it. Oh, groan.

She frantically scanned the street, hoping that
there was a Pizza Hut or TGI Friday's nearby and
she'd misunderstood where they were headed. But
no. Fate wasn't that kind. An elderly doorman in a
top hat, morning coat and with a slightly inebriated

smile held the door open for them (while simultaneously attempting to hold a lit cigarette behind his
back – the rising smoke gave his top hat the appearance of a chimney) and ushered them in. The atmosphere inside was enough to throw anyone with an
aversion to Mills & Boon into a catatonic depression.

Dee had been there once before with her mate
Charlie, who was the food critic for the *Daily
Record*. Anything for a free meal. Anyway, when
Charlie's subsequent review described the heart-
shaped pink canapés with the cherry on top as the
naffest things he'd ever seen and an insult to
puddings (and that was coming from a gay guy with
a predilection to anything remotely twee), he'd
received a curt letter from L'Amour saying he
wouldn't be welcomed back. Dee hoped they didn't
recognize her now.

She lowered her head as an immaculate *maitre
d'* with a patronizing expression, a gel overdose on
his hair and shoes with inch-thick rubber soles
showed them to their table. Right in the centre of
the room. Oh, groan, groan. Where were secluded
alcoves when you needed them? Was this the kind
of place that Greg liked, she thought in horror. And
how much would it be for a taxi back to Kilcaidie?

'I hope you like it here,' Greg said haltingly as
they took their seats. 'The guys in the office recom-
mended it.' Of course! Dee suddenly realized that
this wasn't intentional. Greg had just moved up
from London, so how would he know that this
restaurant ranked right up there with getting your
partner's name tattooed on your bottom? It was

probably some sad case in his office, the kind who spent all day sending replies to personal ads, who had suggested it. She decided to cut him some slack and visibly relaxed. She was going to enjoy herself tonight. She was determined.

A couple of hours later, she realized that she was starting to do just that. The conversation had flowed easily, although they'd avoided the hotspots of religion, politics, past relationships and worst sexual experience. There were a couple of sticky moments when Greg tried to hold her hand across the table, but she managed to avoid contact every time by reaching for the breadbasket. Her loathing of public displays of affection had now resulted in a carbohydrate overload. Nonetheless, she was just slipping into that kind of comfortable, flirty haze of sexual attraction when Greg blew it. Big time.

'So what star sign are you?' he asked with a provocative smile.

'Sagittarius.'

'I'm fascinated by star signs,' he continued. 'So tell me, what are the main characteristics of a Sagittarian?' He made a move for her hand again, so Dee jerked towards the breadbasket. Empty. She plunged her hand into the finger bowl instead, fully aware that she now looked like the lady in the Fairy Liquid advert.

It was time to be honest. The night was suddenly sinking quicker than a U-boat. And to make matters worse, the violin quartet were approaching.

'We're short-tempered, impatient, hard to please and terrible company. And we like an early night.

It's a beauty sleep thing. I think we'd better be going, if that's okay.'

Harsh, she knew, but there was no point in leading the poor guy on. They were obviously on different planets when it came to relationships.

An expression of disconcertion crossed Greg's face. He took a deep breath.

'Look, Dee, is there a problem?' he asked with just a hint of hostility in his voice. 'All night you've seemed really uncomfortable. You sounded like I'd given you a contagious disease when you thanked me for the flowers I sent, you obviously hated the chocolates I brought you when I picked you up, and now you're giving me the impression that you'd rather be anywhere else but here.'

Greg's voice was getting louder and louder. Other diners were starting to stare and the violin quartet did such a sudden about turn that they left skid marks on the floor.

Dee paused for a while. Honesty. She had to go for the direct approach. She just wished she didn't have a room full of eyes burning into her with undisguised aggression for impinging on their oh-so-romantic culinary experience.

'Greg, I'm so sorry. The truth is that I just really hate all this love and hearts stuff. I'm more of a football and Budweiser kind of girl.' May as well get hung for a sheep as a heart-shaped canapé, she decided. Plough on. 'I don't like getting flowers, I don't eat chocolates, romance makes me break out into a cold sweat and I don't believe in all that star sign nonsense.' Dee exhaled forcefully, then added,

A True Romance

'I'm sorry, Greg, but it's better that you know now. I guess I'm just not your kind of date.'

There was a long pause. Then, just as the violin quartet decided it was safe to make a covert approach, Greg leaned towards her, the look on his face inscrutable.

'Let me get this straight. You write romantic novels for a living, but you have an aversion to romance?'

Dee nodded. 'I hate it,' she agreed weakly.

'You write a daily horoscope column, but you don't believe in astrology.'

'Nope, I make them all up. I just write the first thing that comes into my head.'

She almost had the decency to look ashamed.

'And you don't want me to be openly affectionate, touchy feely, or whisper sweet nothings when we're out together?'

'The very thought makes me want to heave,' she replied. So that was it. The end of another almost started, almost beautiful relationship.

Greg took a few moments to think this new information through.

His brow furrowed. 'You know, Dee, I really made an effort tonight. I brought you to a nice restaurant and tried to make conversation about things I thought you'd be interested in. I'm a bloke, for God's sake – star signs are in the same department as knitting, netball and remembering birthdays. But at least I tried.'

She hung her head in mortification. She was an ungrateful cow and should be burned at a stake. The guilt trip was starting at her toes and working its way up. The violin quartet had disappeared, obviously on a break. How she wished that she were sitting in a dingy staff room with them, a bottle of beer and a packet of Marlboro. Instead, she was sitting with a lovely guy, gouging holes in his heart. She was relationship Satan.

'And what you're saying, after all this effort I've gone to, is that you'd rather stay in with a takeaway and watch footie, then go down the pub. You don't want me to be at your beck and call and you just want to have a bit of a good time as opposed to a commitment to one day stroll up the aisle. You don't want me to shower you with affection, except at appropriate times when physical contact is imminent. And I don't have to call you every two minutes or see you every night?'

Dee nodded. 'Sorry. I guess you want more. But that's all I do, I'm afraid. We should go now.' She suddenly wanted to be at home, away from his disparagement.

Then a slow hesitant smile started to cross his lips. 'I think I should be straight with you too. You see, the truth is, my wife said that the reason she left was because I didn't appreciate her enough, didn't treat her like she was special. But even though I tried, it just seemed that it was *never* enough. I guess I'm just a beer and footie, no hassle, no commitment kind of guy.'

Her eyes rose from the floor. He was grinning now.

'I think, Miss Statton,' he continued with a chuckle, 'that we might just make a go of this after all.'

A True Romance

She met his eyes. They really were gorgeous, she decided. Yes, there could possibly be potential here. Maybe. Definitely. The guilt trip was swept away by a tidal wave of relief.

'Glad we sorted that out,' she laughed. 'Now can we get out of here? We might just make last orders at the pub.'

Greg quickly paid the bill, not taking his eyes from hers and grinning maniacally. She was just too perfect. He couldn't believe his luck. They dashed to the door, the sounds of Vivaldi's *Four Seasons*, just a little off tune, ringing in their ears, with the same thought running through their heads: hope the pub jukebox has Oasis.

Thursday morning. The *Kilcaidie Advertiser* Daily Horoscope. Sagittarius: Jupiter and Uranus are aligning to create a period of contentment in relationships with loved ones. Relish this time and don't think it's too good to be true . . . it isn't!

Dear Auntie Di,

Once again, I write to you in concern for my friend, Miss X. She has been seeing her boyfriend for almost six months now and hasn't so much as sneaked a peek at a jeweller's window, a bridal magazine or tuned into the GMTV Plan the Ultimate Wedding Day series. Surely that's not natural? Do you think she could be missing a hormone or two? And can that be treated on the NHS?

Yours anxiously,
Trudy

Dear Trudy,

It is obvious to me that your friend is of that almost extinct, highly prized and much studied sector of the female species – Latin name: Contentimus aloneous. This rare breed finds happiness in solo habitation and does not rely on others for any kind of physical or mental support. Take comfort in the fact that you are very lucky to have this extraordinary, treasured example of womanhood as your friend.

Yours in reassurance,
Auntie Di

PS: There is no need for NHS treatment, but if you want to pop round with some Lucozade and grapes that would be fab.

Dee took a break from writing Desdemona White's latest love fest, *The Girder of My Loins,* and sat back in her chair, sipping a mug of hot chocolate. She pondered Trudy's latest e-mail. Was that really what she should be doing? Should she be starting to entertain thoughts of a more permanent arrangement with Greg? She shuddered involuntarily, mental pictures flying to the forefront of her brain: someone else's toiletries in the bathroom cupboard, toilet seats left up, having to make up *both* sides of the duvet instead of just one, double the amount of washing and don't even contemplate the ironing . . . she'd never get to the bottom of the pile.

But then . . . their relationship *was* giving her a feeling of contentment that she'd never experienced before. She loved the fact that she now had two indentations on her sofa seat after watching a football game, someone's shoulder to lean on when she was pretending not to cry at the sad bits in a movie, and an interested ear when she was throwing around ideas for the latest Desdemona plot. She smiled to herself, deep in thought. If she were honest, it wasn't just those reasons that were giving her a glow unaided by St Tropez tan in a bottle. It was also, well, just *Greg*. He was gorgeous, he was funny, he made her laugh and he wasn't all caught up in his image and the whole designer label thing like so many self-obsessed guys these days. She was actually starting to miss him when he wasn't around. That was a first! And he was so secure in himself that he didn't cling to her, demand anything of her, get upset when she cancelled dates or couldn't see him for a week. He was a totally self-sufficient, independent and together guy. Oh, and he was great in bed. What more could a girl want? Maybe, just maybe, taking this relationship to the next level (overnight stays twice a week – she didn't want to get over her head just yet) wouldn't be such a bad thing after all.

The telephone rang and she snatched it from the cradle. 'What happened to my grapes?' she asked with a smile.

'You put them around your erogenous zones and

paid someone to bite them off. The grapes that is, not the erogenous zones,' chuckled a male voice.

Dee was confused. Who the hell was this? She hoped it wasn't her doctor with the results of her latest smear test – he was being just a bit too familiar. She couldn't bring herself to speak, so there was an interminable silence.

'Dee? Dee, it's Charlie, your beloved fellow journalist and food critic extraordinaire.'

Dee burst out laughing. 'Sorry, Charlie, I was expecting Trudy to call and you threw me – I didn't recognize your voice. How the devil are you? And what do you know about erogenous zones? Your last boyfriend chucked you because your idea of passion was spending a whole day in the soft furnishings department of Habitat.'

Charlie was still laughing. 'That's right, go for the kill. Just when I was calling to invite my favourite lady to the VIP opening of Glasgow's newest, so in that it's almost out, star-studded spectacle of an eatery this Friday. All expenses paid, of course. Say yes and I'll love you for ever.'

'Flattery, flattery. What you really mean is that you can't find anyone else to take, you've been rejected by everyone including the work experience guy who does the photocopying and now you're calling me as a last resort because you don't want to sit there all night like Charlie-no-mates.'

'Erm, well, yes. That's about the size of it.'

'Charlie, you're a lucky man. The fact that I'll go anywhere for a free meal and an ogle at celebs compels me to say yes. Pick me up at eight and you can grovel in thanks all night for me agreeing to this.'

Charlie agreed instantly. 'Grovelling is my specialist subject – consider it done.'

It was only when she hung up that Dee remembered she had arranged to go to the flicks with Greg on Friday night. She rang his office and explained the situation.

'Dee, this is the third time you've cancelled in two weeks,' he replied. Did she detect a note of impatience in his voice or was it just a bad line? Must be a bad line. He did work in a council building after all – the recent cutbacks must have affected the telecoms system.

'Erm, do you mind?' she stuttered. Surely not. Total freedom was part of their arrangement. Even if she was beginning to consider the possibilities of changing the parameters.

'No, not at all,' he replied. There was a definite change in his tone now – it was decisive, positive. This was more like it. The phone system must have sorted itself out and she could hear him clearly again. 'I'll give you a call next week,' he added.

As she replaced the handset, she returned to her earlier train of thought. Yes, Greg was definitely one in a million. One who was worth hanging on to.

She dressed with care on Friday night, trying to tread the thin line between being trendy but not veering into fashion victim territory. Finally, she settled on a tan suede skirt with an obscenely tight black T-shirt. After a quick nipple check – yes, both pointing in the same direction – she ran down the path to a waiting Charlie.

They gabbed incessantly all the way to the city, swapping titbits of gossip about the others who had been at college with them. Charlie might have struggled with his journalism degree but he had attained a distinction in bitchiness. Even so, it seemed to Dee that all their classmates had done fantastically well for themselves: national magazines, broadsheets, internet publishing. The *Kilcaidie Advertiser* fell somewhat short in the glamour stakes. Still, she had a lovely, uncomplicated life with minimal stress, she could work in her dressing-gown all day and she made enough money to give her everything she wanted. Life was pretty good, she reasoned. Oh, and she had Greg too.

Bliss.

Charlie pulled to a halt in the middle of the Merchant City, the über-cool centre of Glasgow's nightlife, where fashionista police scoured the streets in search of illegal outerwear. White stilettos were a towing offence.

'I thought the restaurant was in Ingram Street?' Dee asked, realizing that they'd stopped two streets away and that Charlie would never walk more than ten yards in the open air for fear of a sudden gust of wind messing his hair.

'Yes, but the invitation says eight o'clock and it's only half past now. I can't possibly arrive this early. It would be just *too* gauche. Don't you know how important I am?' he preened in his campest voice.

A True Romance

They made their way into the Mortuary, the only bar in Glasgow with its own resident paparazzi. Charlie nearly tripped over his feet trying to ensure they got his best side.

Two vodka tonics later, they were ensconced at a suitably prominent table in the shape of a mortuary slab, Charlie trying to look as chic, cosmopolitan and interesting as possible. Unfortunately nobody noticed, as they were all too busy unobtrusively checking their own reflections in the stainless steel of the fake body lockers that lined the walls. Whoever dreamed up the concept of this place needed therapy, Dee decided.

'So, tell me all about this new man then,' Charlie probed. 'All the details, intimate and otherwise, just make it bloody fast because I'm freezing my body parts off in here.' It was true. In keeping with the theme, the bar was so cold it would be a natural habitat for penguins.

'Weeeelll,' Dee grinned coyly, 'he's tall, he's dark, he's handsome . . .'

'Oh, stop, you're making me giddy,' Charlie feigned a blood rush.

'He's funny, he's smart and he's—' Dee broke off, her attention caught by something in her peripheral vision. 'And he's sitting over there with some blonde piranha sucking on his earlobe.' Dee's heart sank to the bottom of her knee-high boots.

Charlie tried to express shock and sympathy but that was difficult to do with the smile he had fixed on his face just in case the paparazzi were lurking nearby.

What to do? Dee was steeped in horror, disbelief and trepidation. They'd agreed on total freedom, she mentally raged, but monogamy was also part of the deal. Or so she'd thought. Should she make like Dodge City and march over there, demanding an explanation? Or surreptitiously sneak out and pretend she hadn't seen him?

She was about to grab Charlie's hand and do a commando crawl to the door when the decision was taken out of her hands. Greg's eyes met hers and he jumped to his feet, leaving the piranha sucking on fresh air. He walked hastily towards them and, courtesy of her weekly copy of *Hello!*, Dee could tell that he was dressed top to toe in Armani. Greg in Armani? What was going on? She thought he shopped only in Gap.

Charlie realized what was happening and dashed to the gents, reasoning that this was no place for a pacifist.

'Dee, I'm sorry,' Greg began.

'Sorry that I saw you here or sorry that you had a blonde attempting to pierce your ear with her veneers?' Dee spat.

They stared at each other for a few moments.

Greg spoke first. 'I guess our relationship just wasn't working for me, Dee. I feel terrible about it, but I realized a couple of weeks ago that we'd run our course.'

Dee was dumbfounded. 'But I thought you said that I was your perfect woman – no hassle, no commitments, no demands. What's changed?'

'Sorry, Dee,' he repeated. 'I think, to be honest,

I know now that I need more than that. You're always so independent, so sure of yourself. You act like you need no one.'

'I *don't* need anyone,' Dee agreed with venom.

'Well, there's the difference. Maybe I do. Maybe I need some commitment. Now and again, I'd like some demands made on me – it would make me feel like I was needed. You just make me feel, well, unfulfilled.'

Dee almost groaned out loud at that one. Unfulfilled? Had he been watching too much daytime telly? To her, unfulfilled meant that she hadn't had pudding yet. To think that she had even considered stepping this relationship up a level!

A gag couldn't have halted Greg's emotional outpouring now. 'You're just too uncomplicated for me, Dee. I thought you were every guy's fantasy emotionally, the kind of woman I'd always wanted, but I know now that I'm looking for more than you want to give.'

Good Lord, would he never stop?! Dee's brain was screaming for mercy. This was exactly the kind of situation that she'd spent her whole life avoiding and now here she was, trapped by an emotionally lacking guy in front of all of Glasgow's beautiful people. This was hell. And he *still* wasn't done.

'You see, Dee, I'm at the age where I'm starting to yearn to settle down, starting to think about children, and there's no point being stuck in a relationship that isn't going anywhere . . .'

Dee closed her eyes. Greg wasn't a guy – he was a woman with an out-of-control body clock.

'So I think that we should call it a day: say goodbye while we can still be friends.'

Silence. Dee opened one eye just to check that his mouth wasn't still moving and the trauma of all this emotion wasn't simply causing her to block out his voice. No, mouth was shut. Coast clear. And further more, Charlie was making a cautious approach.

Dee leaned over and kissed Greg on the cheek, a wave of relief washing over her. Thank goodness she'd found out now what he was really like. A close escape if there ever was one.

'Good luck, Greg. I hope you find what you're looking for,' she smiled. 'And talking of demands, I think you'd better get back to your friend over there, she's starting to look demonic.' It was true. The female's expression was so murderous due to this total neglect from her date that her pout was threatening to suck up the cocktail umbrellas.

Dee grabbed Charlie's hand as they strolled out of the door – slowly, to give the photographers plenty of time to snap.

Her shoulders started to shake. For a moment Charlie thought she was crying, until he realized that it was huge chortles causing the spasms.

'You know what, Charlie? I think from now on I'll stick to gay guys and girls for company. They're much less complicated!' And with that, they strutted off into the night.

The *Kilcaidie Advertiser* Daily Horoscope. Sagittarius: The solar system has now realigned, bringing you Sagittarians who have

lost your way of late back onto your destined path. But have no regrets – recent experiences have taught you a valuable lesson. Heed it well.

Dear Trudy,

It has been very commendable to see how you have attempted to comfort your friend after the recent and very public break-up of her relationship. I do feel, however, that it is time for you to move on as it has been over a month now. I must point out that your friend had indeed recovered from the break up before she returned home on the night in question. In short, it is time for you to enrol in those basket-weaving sessions now.

Yours with love,
Auntie Di

PS: Fancy a night out – you, me and the Beach Boys?

A MIXED BLESSING

Aline Templeton

ALINE TEMPLETON has worked in education and broadcasting. She grew up in Scotland, read English at Girton College, Cambridge, and now lives in Perthshire and Edinburgh.

Aline is the author of five critically acclaimed novels of psychological suspense, *Shades of Death*, *Night and Silence*, *The Trumpet Shall Sound*, *Past Praying For* and *Last Act of All*.

'It's a mixed blessing,' my dad always used to say when he was talking about the three weeks in late summer when we would leave dirty, smoky Glasgow and go back so he could help with the harvest on the West Coast where he grew up and where his father still, at the age of seventy-five, ran his own small farm single-handed.

It confused me. The only mixed things I could think of were Mixed Boilings in the sweetshop on the corner, which were violently coloured sweeties of different flavours, and Mixed Fruit which Mum bought to make the Black Bun at New Year, and Mixed Infants, which was where my wee brother Stewart and I went to school.

I had a rough idea what blessings were, so perhaps he was just meaning all the mixture of delights the farm offered: the hay loft, where you could lie eating the penny sherbet from the local shop with a damp finger, which like your tongue then became a pleasingly lurid shade of purple or orange; the warm, rich smell of the calves as they licked your hands with their rasping tongues; the thin, half-wild kittens in the stack yard, drifting about like leaves blown by the force of their sudden fancies.

It was only later that I began to wonder if perhaps Dad didn't see it in quite the same light. I was reaching the awkward stage – not quite child, certainly not yet an adult – when I found myself becoming a sharp-eyed, unremarked spy on grown-up behaviour, noticing things I'd never been aware of before. It was strangely like my earliest memory ever of gazing over the side of my pram as it was wheeled across what looked like a sheet of red stuff, then, as it stopped, realizing that this was made up of lots and lots and lots of small pieces – gravel. Similarly, the summer I was eleven, adults – that undifferentiated mass – suddenly turned into separate and distinct individuals.

How long ago it all seems now – how long ago it was, indeed! But I've never forgotten the annual excitement of preparation, the anxious studying of weather portents for weeks in advance, the gathering of treasures which Stewart and I started a full fortnight before the date of our departure – and the difficult choices about what to leave behind when Mum pointed out it was all to be packed into one small bag that we had to carry ourselves.

Then, the night before, we were too excited to sleep properly, waking groggily to an early morning start. We had to be at the station in plenty of time for good seats on the magnificent steam train which groaned as it pulled us out of the city station in clouds of smoke and smuts, then picked up speed, roaring and clattering as if it, too, couldn't wait to leave Glasgow behind.

A Mixed Blessing

Was it always a sunny day when we made that journey? Surely not; yet when I think of it now, of the glorious scenery on the West Coast line going up to Mallaig, I can never remember looking out to the blue, distant isles of the Inner Hebrides when they weren't gilded with sunshine and lapped by sparkling seas.

Mr MacGregor's battered taxi was commissioned to meet us at the station – an annual treat, this, for a welder's wages left nothing to spare for luxuries – and before long we'd be on the single-track road leading to Auchingair, with my brother and me competing to see who could spot the first sign of grass growing down the centre which proved that we were really, truly on holiday. Whenever we saw it, we cheered, but my father always groaned and said, 'Here we go again!' That final summer holiday, I puzzled for the first time about what he meant.

Mr MacGregor, as always, dropped us on the road that ran along the sea-loch, at the bottom of the short, steep farm track which was more like a river bed than a road with its stones and potholes and cart ruts. My brother and I, eagerness lightening our load, hurried on ahead while Dad, burdened with the heaviest cases, brought up the rear.

Granny was waiting for us on the soapstoned doorstep, a spare, erect figure, grey hair ruthlessly scraped back into a wispy bun, with a flowered, sleeveless wrap tied over her dress, her arms stretched out to welcome us children as we dropped our cases and ran the last few yards.

That year, it seemed that I looked at her properly

for the first time, with a sense of shock. I had grown, of course – I was proud of that, and expecting admiring comment – but surely she was smaller? I could look straight into her face now, and what I saw there made me uneasy, as if a threatening east wind had suddenly sprung up on a warm day. Her eyes were hooded, her skin heavily wrinkled and marked with age, and there were deep-cut lines there which told a different story from her smiling mouth.

My brother let himself be hugged, then hurtled past to bag the coveted bed beside the window in our usual bedroom. I followed more slowly, heard my mother say gently, 'How have you been?' and my father, fiercely, 'More to the point, how has *he* been?'

Knowing this was not intended for my ears, I went round the turn of the stairs before I stopped to listen, knowing I shouldn't. Granny's voice, which always sounded more Highland when you first arrived, said, 'Och, fine, Davy. I manage. But it's just rare to see you all. He's doing too much, you know, with his heart, but he won't be told. It makes him – well, more irritable, but now you're here, he'll maybe be better.'

'That would be a first!' Was that my bluff, easygoing dad speaking? It sounded like a stranger's voice, bitter, harsh. 'And he still won't let me come back to work the farm?'

My heart skipped a beat. Come here, to what seemed to me paradise, instead of the crowded, noisy, smelly city?

A Mixed Blessing

Granny's long sigh finished the dream before I'd had time to shape it properly. 'Only on the same terms he's offered before.'

'I won't be an unpaid labourer, Mother, working for nothing more than our bed and board and my expectations. I'll not subject my wife and family to that.'

'Right enough, Davy, right enough. And you're a good lad to come for the harvest. Most of it would rot in the fields without you, and then where would we be next year? He won't hear of hiring help, and there's not a neighbour would do a single thing for him nowadays.'

'Small wonder,' my father snorted. 'Make no mistake, Mother, this is for you, not him.'

I heard Granny's voice falter. 'I hate to be beholden, but—'

My mother cut her short. 'Dear Gran, it's a holiday for our poor wee peely-wally townies that we could never afford otherwise. And the hams and preserves we go back with – there's been many a Thursday night before Davy gets his wages when we'd have had a poor supper if it wasn't for the Auchingair ham—'

'I've got the best bed!' My brother's sing-song chant taunted me from the top of the stairs and the conversation below broke off. Hastily I got myself to the top of the stairs, hoping no one had heard my footsteps.

'So?' I said loudly. 'When the Kelpie comes up out of the burn there in the middle of the night, he'll get to you first.'

He was old enough not *quite* to believe me, but I took an elder sister's pleasure in watching uncertainty replace smugness as I took possession of the other bed with exaggerated satisfaction.

Grandfather expected his high tea on the table at five o'clock sharp. We were all in place, hands washed, waiting around the dining-room table which was spread with a snowy cloth and covered with dishes holding Granny's lighter-than-air scones, oatmeal bannocks, gingerbread and shortbread and – a special first-night treat, this – pink meringues filled with the thick yellow cream from their own milking cows. In the kitchen, Granny stood by with a pile of breadcrumbed fish, fresh from the boats today, ready to put into the pan when she saw him coming across the stack yard.

Until now, Grandfather had featured little in our lives at Auchingair. He breakfasted before us, had his midday dinner with Dad while we were still out about our childish ploys, and it was only at high tea, when he was an awesome figure at the head of the table, that we crossed his path. We knew enough to bow our heads meekly as he said grace then to eat the delicious food in silence while he ignored our presence and, when we had finished catch Granny's eye for the nod which would release us from the torment of sitting still.

It seemed strange to me now, as this burly, elderly man took his seat, barely glancing at us all and grunting by way of greeting, that this had never seemed odd to me before. In previous years, it had just been, well, Grandfather; now I was looking at him with fresh eyes.

He had a farmer's weather-beaten complexion and cracked, horny hands. He still had a thick thatch of white hair, and his voice when he called to Granny who hadn't emerged immediately from the kitchen, 'Woman! Where's my meat?' was strong as ever.

Granny appeared, her face flushed possibly with embarrassment as much as with heat from the range, but she spoke calmly. 'Your meat's fish tonight, Murdo. You'd not be wanting it if it wasn't freshly fried.'

He grunted again and she slipped neatly into her own seat while he said the grace, then whisked back into the kitchen again. My mother rose to help her.

I had been studying him, perhaps too intently, noticing the broken veins and purplish colour in his cheeks and the signs of ill-temper about his mouth and eyes. Suddenly, terrifyingly, those faded eyes with their yellowing, bloodshot whites were focused on me.

'Well, miss? What are you staring at?'

'N-nothing,' I stammered.

'Then keep your eyes to yourself.'

My cheeks flaring, blinking back tears, I lowered my eyes to my plate.

As if he was speaking through clenched teeth, Dad said, 'She didn't mean to upset you, Father.'

'Upset me? Her?' He laughed shortly. 'That would be a fine thing! She can just learn right and proper respect for her elders, that's all, and if you haven't taught her, I will.'

I saw Dad open his mouth, but Mum had come in from the kitchen with an ashet piled with fried fish; as she passed Dad on her way to set it down in front of Grandfather, I saw her grip his shoulder, hard, and he shut it again.

Grandfather noticed too. He laughed. 'She's wiser than you, Davy lad. Knows which side her bread's buttered on.'

Mum smiled, but it was a smile that just went straight across without turning up at the corners.

My brother and I kept our heads down for the rest of the meal, but I listened hard. It was funny how much you could pick up from the tone of people's voices when you weren't looking at them. Grandfather blustered and bullied everyone. Mum's remarks were a little too bright, as if she was trying too hard. Dad sounded as if he would like to lose his temper and shout but didn't dare.

Granny was the most interesting. Anything she said was softly spoken and suitably meek, but somehow I felt that, inside, she was the only one of all of us who wasn't afraid of him.

Absorbed in this fascinating pastime, I didn't notice Stewart fidgeting and Granny nodding permission to go until Dad nudged me. I got up reluctantly for once.

As we left the table, Granny said, 'I'll just be getting your medicine, Murdo,' and came through to the kitchen with us. There were some left-over meringues on a tray in the kitchen; she took a bag and popped two of them in, winking at us. 'They'll maybe taste better in the hay loft,' she whispered, and with grown-up problems forgotten I scampered off to see if there were any new kittens this year.

It was a few days later. In the excitement of re-discovering our old haunts and pastimes, I had almost forgotten my new preoccupation, but today it was windy and wet. Stewart and I had put on our raincoats and walked the mile into the village to the 'Johnny-a'-things' where you could buy every-thing from a packet of pins to an anchor, as the saying went. I'd been saving up my meagre pocket money for weeks, and now had the pleasant prob-lem of choosing between the more expensive *Girl* or the cheaper *School Friend* plus a Highland Toffee chew. Stewart, who'd spent his long since, lost inter-est when I refused to consider the *Beano* and went off to play with one of his friends.

When I got back to the farmhouse, Mum and Granny were in the kitchen making raspberry jam from the berries we'd picked in the garden yester-day. The kitchen door was open and the sticky-sweet fragrance of the boiling fruit wafted through the house as I drifted past to luxuriate with my comic on the plush sofa in the front parlour.

I could hear their companionable voices, but lost in *Belle of the Ballet* I paid little attention until I heard my mother's voice, raised in protest.

'But you shouldn't put up with it, Gran! He's a bully, that's all, and he's getting nastier.'

Then Granny. 'Maggie, my dear, we've been married for more than forty years. I know what he's like, and I've learned to live with it.'

Belle's adventures lost their interest. I sat up, edged silently along the sofa until I was right behind the door.

'That makes it worse, not better.' Mum sounded fierce. 'Why didn't you leave him – walk out years ago?'

'Where would I have gone? How could I have supported myself and your father – for I'd never have left him here—'

My mother sighed. 'I know, I know. But you've no one to consider now but yourself, and he's getting more and more unreasonable – Davy's very worried. What if he turns violent, when you've no one here to protect you?'

'I'll be all right, don't you worry.'

'But we do, Gran! Look, we've talked it over. Come to Glasgow with us – it's cramped, right enough, not what you're used to here, but we could squeeze your bed in the bairns' room, and if you were there for them coming home from school, I could get myself a job cleaning, maybe, that would bring in a bit more—'

There was a brief silence, and squinting through the crack in the door I could just see Granny going to hug my mum. Her voice was quavery when she said, 'I used to wish I'd a daughter, but I could never have had one better than you've been to me. But no, my lass, I'll not do that.'

'But Gran—'

'Listen to me.' Granny moved back to the range where I couldn't see her, but her voice was steady, almost hard. 'If I walked out that door, you know

172

the first thing he'd do? He'd be away down to see yon lawyer in Oban, changing his will. He'd leave every penny he could to the heathens in Africa, or the cat and dog home – it wouldn't matter so long as Davy got no more than the bairn's part of the estate that's his by law. And that would mean you'd never have the farm, and we both know it's been Davy's dream all his life.'

'Mine too,' my mother said softly. 'And the wee ones would think they'd died and gone to heaven.'

'As long as I'm here, I can see nothing stands in your way. Oh, mercy! Look at this in the saucer – the jam's wrinkling already! With all this talking, I'll ruin it if we're not careful. Bring me over the jampots from the warming shelf.'

I heard the clinking of the jampots and the bustle of the two women as they discussed the filling of them. I lost interest and was just inching cautiously back along the sofa again when Granny said suddenly, 'He's not a well man, you know, Maggie, and he's worried. The doctor's told him – if he doesn't take his medicine and ease off the work, he could go at any time.'

'Then why, *why* will he not let Davy come, as an equal partner, even, if he doesn't want to retire? Davy says the farm could do a lot better, more than enough for us all, if he'd the running of it.'

'Can you see Murdo agree to that? He's thrawn enough to kill himself rather than change his mind. Now, if you pass me the wee wax circles, I'll put them in the pots and we'll get them in the larder to cool.'

I listened a bit longer, then went back to *Belle of*

the Ballet, but somehow her adventures palled beside what I had been given to think about.

That year, the harvest went well. The sun mostly shone, with a good drying wind some days, and by the beginning of our last week the dusty, peppery smell of the dried hay was everywhere and the spaces in the hay loft where we had made our cosy dens had disappeared.

With a sick feeling inside at how quickly the holiday was passing, we made the best of the fine weather, which as the week went on grew hotter and more oppressive. Even Mum and Granny joined us now for afternoons on the little sandy beach below the farm, where the water was shallow and warm for bathing, but there was always the sea breath for coolness even on the hottest day.

It was the middle of the week, three days before we had to return to Glasgow, that the storm broke. Over the tea-table first.

Grandfather seemed in high good humour that evening. Dad, his skin tanned as a gypsy, looked tired after a long day of hot, heavy labouring, but not bone-weary the way he did when he came home in Glasgow, filthy and red-eyed, from the shipyard.

'Well, you've not forgotten the way you were taught to work, Davy lad, I'll give you that,' Grandfather said as we all sat down to salad with the lettuce and cucumber picked an hour earlier from Granny's vegetable garden, home-cured Auchingair ham and hard-boiled eggs, laid that morning in one of the nests it was my job to seek out each day. With the sultry heat, though, I didn't have much appetite.

My father, who had grown more and more silent at teatime as the days went by, said stiffly, 'I'm glad we got the harvest in early this year. It's let me get to some of the other things that were badly needing done. You'll have to hire another pair of hands round the farm, Father, if it's not to go to ruin.'

'Aye.'

I risked a quick glance at him; the old man was chewing his lip, where beads of perspiration stood out. There was a long pause, then he said, 'You've turned me down before, Davy, and I swore I'd never make the offer again. But come back and we'll say no more about it.'

I heard my mother's sharp intake of breath, saw that she was trying to catch Dad's eye across the table. But he was staring directly at Grandfather.

'You'd need to make a better offer than that,' he said tersely.

'A better offer! You and your wife and two children living free, at my expense, and when they carry me out this will all be yours! That's the best offer you'll get from me!'

'Then the answer's no.'

We had all stopped eating. Even I, who had barely looked towards my grandfather since that first afternoon, openly stared from one man to the other.

Grandfather's face took on a deeper purple tinge. 'No?' he bellowed. *'No?'*

Granny murmured, 'Your heart, Murdo.' He cast her a furious look, but, still breathing heavily, said nothing for a minute or two. The silence in the room was electric.

He shovelled a forkful of food into his mouth, and nervously we began to eat again. When he next spoke, it was in a different tone.

'I've never asked any favours from you, Davy. But I'm an old man, a sick man, and you said it yourself – the farm's going downhill. The strain of it's killing me, and it's now I need my son. I raised you, fed you, clothed you, until you turned your back on the farm and me and went your own way. Even so, I've made you and your hungry mouths welcome at my table. I wouldn't have to ask if you knew your duty to your father, but I'll shame myself to beg. Help me, Davy. Come back.'

Though his voice was pleading, I could see that his eyes were narrowed and calculating. I heard Granny make a little sharp, 'Tsk!' with her tongue, as if she had seen too and it angered her, but I doubt if either of the men even heard.

Dad stared at him, his face sweaty and rigid, a muscle twitching at the corner of his mouth. The air was thick with heat and tension, and Stewart, bewildered and frightened, started to cry. Mum, who had been sitting as if turned to stone, leaped to her feet.

'Gran, perhaps the children could leave the table?' Without waiting for Granny's nod, she said to me, 'Take Stewart out and see he's all right,' then sat down again at the table.

I left with a bad grace. What was happening was frightening, but it was interesting too. Fortunately,

A Mixed Blessing

Stewart's tears dried quickly once we were safely out of the room, and he started complaining about not having finished his tea. Frantic with impatience, I grabbed some biscuits from a tin in the larder and shoved him out of the back door.

'Go and play with the kittens,' I said.

He hesitated. 'Aren't you coming?'

'In a minute.'

I shut the door and hurried back to listening at the foot of the stairs, just outside the dining-room door.

Dad was speaking. '. . . own ideas. If I can't make the changes that it needs, the farm won't thrive, and if I'm just your labourer, I'd still have to be doing it your way. I've earned my living for years now, and I'll not be the one who has to come with my hand out asking for money every time my wife needs a dress or the bairns new shoes. I'd have to be able to run the farm, Father, with a proper agreement, before I'd come back.'

Even there, outside, I held my breath. It was like the flash of lightning, which would inevitably be followed by the thunder.

It came. Grandfather's voice yelled, 'So that's it, is it? You'd rather kill your own father than lift a finger to help, except by stealing from me what's mine by right. Well, I have your measure now. You can be out of here tomorrow, the lot of you, and I'll be down to Oban to see the lawyer, and he'll see to it you never set foot in this place again. Be damned to you all—'

The voice faltered suddenly, then Granny, very

quiet and calm in the stillness, said, 'Murdo, the doctor warned you your temper would be the death of you. You'd better go and lie down. I'll bring you your medicine.'

Grandfather's voice again, but now sounding thick, almost slurred. 'Yes. Lie down.'

'Let me help you.' I heard the sound of Dad's chair being pushed back.

'Let me be! You'll – you'll not change my mind.'

The dining-room door opened. My heart pounding, I scurried upstairs to our bedroom, just across the small square landing from the front room where Granny and Grandfather slept. Shamelessly, I set my eye to the crack in the door.

Grandfather was mounting the stairs slowly, pulling himself up on the banister rail. His face was a dark, unhealthy red, and flecks of spittle had gathered at the corners of his mouth. He went into the bedroom and, without closing the door, collapsed heavily on to the brass bed, on top of the patchwork quilt.

He seemed to fall asleep. A minute later, I heard Granny's footsteps on the stairs. I thought she would be carrying the glass with his medicine in it, but she was empty-handed.

'Murdo?' I heard her saying as she went into the room, and I heard him mutter something in reply.

I have wondered all my life what really happened next. I saw her lift a pillow, but perhaps it was just to put it under his head and make him more comfortable. I couldn't see. She was between the bed and the open door, and as she came out some minutes later, she closed it. Was her face a little flushed, or is that an artistic touch I have added to my recollections?

I heard her go into the dining room and say to my parents, 'He's resting. Best thing for him.'

I heard my father say, 'Oh God, was that my fault?' and Granny's voice saying firmly, 'No, Davy. If he's made himself ill with rage, if it was anyone's fault, it was mine. It just always seemed easier at the time, to let him have his own way. I should have stood up to him years ago, when you were a wee boy, and maybe he'd have learned.'

'He didn't look at all well.' My mother's gentle voice was anxious.

'I'll go up in ten minutes and if he's not better we'll get the doctor,' Granny said.

It was a long ten minutes. I sat without moving, not knowing what to think, what to feel, until at last I heard Granny coming up the stairs. She looked composed as she went into the bedroom, but when she came out again, closing the door quietly behind her, she was crying silently, the tears coursing down her cheeks. She paused for a moment; I saw her take out a handkerchief and wipe her face fiercely before she started downstairs.

'Davy!' she called as she went. 'Davy! You'll need to go for the doctor, but I fear it's too late.'

Minutes later, with a flash and a devastating peal of thunder, the storm broke outside too.

Our lives changed completely after that. Stewart and I grew up as healthy, rosy-cheeked country children instead of pale-faced townies; I married a trawler skipper and Stewart married a local girl and went into partnership with Dad. They did well, with a salmon farm too, and so did Mum's little business of making and selling preserves made to Granny's recipes, though she and Dad have been retired for a good while now.

Granny lived to be ninety, a benevolent presence in all our lives. When I told my husband once what I had seen through the crack in the door, he was inclined to be dismissive.

'You always had a rare talent for fiction, my lass,' he said, and I suppose I have to agree with him there. But then again, you do need to start accurately observing people from a very early age if you're going to be a successful crime writer.

THE FRINGES

Jenny Colgan

Born in Ayrshire in 1972, **JENNY COLGAN** worked in the health service for six years after graduating from Edinburgh University, moonlighting as a cartoonist and stand-up comic.

Her first novel, *Amanda's Wedding*, published in 1999, was an instant bestseller, and has been followed by three further bestselling romantic comedies, *Talking to Addison*, *Looking for Andrew McCarthy* and *Working Wonders*.

Jenny Colgan lives in London.

'Well, just be careful,' Marisa was saying. 'It's the biggest festival in the world. It makes Glastonbury look like an event for dribbling two-year-olds.'

'That's exactly what Glastonbury is. Edinburgh is different.'

'But it rains all the time there too. And they have jugglers. And mimes. I saw it on BBC2. You'll hate it.'

I was going anyway. I'd never been to the festival, but I had jealous memories of our terrible student drama club at Birmingham coming back tired, skint, overweight and with glandular fever. I wanted a bit of that. So now I'd split up with boring, boring bloody Warren, that fat boring twat who put on what felt like half a stone a week throughout our nine-month relationship and still had the bloody cheek to dump *me*.

'Yes, Nat,' he had proclaimed, his chubby hand clutching a fistful of Twiglets. 'Maybe if you'd read a bit more George Orwell and watched a bit less *Big Brother*.'

He snorted as if this was the funniest thing anyone had ever said.

'What?' I said. 'But *Big Brother's* on *all the time*. There's no time for reading.'

Warren sighed, noisily. I remember seeing a picture of him at his parents' house, aged about four. He was wearing podgy shorts and a bow tie. All the other children were running around in the background and he was staring fixedly at a slice of cake. He hadn't changed very much. However, he'd added a veneer of sophistication to cover up his greedy habits, and now guzzled opera, the theatre, trendy films and the latest bars with the same open-mouthed expression he had on in that photograph. At first I'd thought he was funny, opinionated and impressive. Now I wanted to take all of those Twiglets and shove them up his nose and into his brain, thus ending his life. Funny what getting to know someone can do to you.

'I'd hoped we could grow together,' Warren had said. 'But really, I feel like I'm leaving you behind.'

'What's the fatal dosage for Twiglets?' I'd asked. But his corpulent, cord-encased posterior was already heading towards the door.

'I need to get cultured,' I'd explained to Marisa, my artiest friend. She liked hippy clothes and raffia, so I reckoned she'd know what to do. And it turned out an acquaintance of ours was taking a show up there and might let me crash on her floor for a couple of days, and I was owed holidays anyway as fat Warren had mentioned fresco-hunting in Tuscany in earlier days and I was kind of hanging on in there just in case, so I had some time off and I was raring to go. I could be cultured! And I didn't need a fat-arsed sad sack around me anyway. No! I'd met Saskia (couldn't possibly be her real name: nobody arty and hippie is actually called Saskia, surely) a couple of times before and, okay, had thought she was a bit of a mare, but hey! It was the festival!

'I'm not sure you're going to need so many party dresses,' said Marisa, looking dubiously into my suitcase. Marisa, it should be noted at this point, was wearing two skirts, one long, one short, some cowboy fringing, a lace vest and a pair of denim embroidered doc Martens.

'It's a party town,' I said stubbornly.

'On the same latitude as Moscow. Do you want to borrow a jumper?'

All Marisa's jumpers look like they've been knitted out of cereal.

'I'm sure it will be fine,' I said.

'Anyway, why do you need party dresses if you're just going for the culture? You'll be sitting in a pitch-dark audience for nine hours a day.'

I didn't say anything to that. I mean, technically I was interested in the culture, but a little bit of me saw me gracing some lovely parties in those gorgeous big terraces they have up there, and Alan (Cumming) and Ewan (McGregor) both fighting to refill my glass and take part in my witty, terribly cultured conversation. I reckoned I was going to like Edinburgh.

The skies came down to reach the sea as we creaked our way up the East Coast mainline. It was – well, it rains a lot in London, but this was wet even for me, and I wasn't exactly sure my Zara peasant look was going to make it, particularly when I looked around the rest of the carriage, where every person was wearing a pair of jeans and (if a boy) a trendy T-shirt and (if a girl) a trendy little top. Everyone had very sensible trainers on and shot funny looks at my lovely kitten heels as they walked past me to buy large gin and tonics from the buffet car at ten o'clock in the morning. People were showing off (I thought, buried in *Conde Nast Traveller* – I had bought *Atonement*, but you need a little light reading for travelling, don't you? Probably even Martin Amis reads *Viz* on planes), shouting down their mobiles about 'tech rehearsals' and 'preview tickets' and 'make sure you get the Scots man', whoever he was. I hadn't made any cultured friends *exactly* yet, but what could you expect on GNER? I'd be much better once I got to – I consulted my address book again – Pilton.

Yup. I'd be fitting in. Very soon.

I stared at the taxi driver.

'Last year,' I said, 'our mayor in London, to get cabbies out on the street after eight o'clock, he made them the richest cabbies on earth. But you have just shown them up as a bunch of rank amateurs.'

He smiled at me and looked ruefully at the meter.

'Sorry, lass,' he said. 'You're a bit further out than most of ma passengers, yeah?'

'Hang on,' I said to him. 'I have to check my friends are in.'

The Fringes

I looked around. At first, I'd been overjoyed as we'd made our way through the city. A castle on one side, and a Harvey Nichols on the other – I thought I might just have arrived in heaven. And so many people! People on stilts, people in Victorian clothing; everywhere, there was a huge human morass pushing one way or the other. And I was here! I was going to be part of it! And even if I didn't get to go to any balls, I could probably still wear my balldress in the morning!

Then we'd driven through elegant, laid out streets of tall grey houses, and I'd fantasized that each street would be mine.

Then we'd gone through slightly tattier streets.

Then we'd gone through a massive, massive council estate.

We were still there.

Everything was grey, the damp-stained walls of the low-rise alleyways, the dead grass covered in old dog shit and ash; the burned-out car at the end of the road.

'Miss, I'm not sure you should be gettin' out the car right now, aye?' said the cabbie, looking anxiously around.

I had opened the door, and was now getting soaked through, half in and half out of the cab.

'I don't want to stay here in the cab, right?'

I shoved myself out of the door. 'Just a *minute*,' I said. My heels clattered on the pavement, horribly loudly. I went up to the first set of houses. There were no numbers on them. Head down against the black wind, I ran to the next building, and the next.

"West Pilton Gardens" the street sign said, but there was nothing like a garden here now. I stumbled across the road, standing in a puddle up to my knees. My chiffon top was soaked through and I was cursing the stupid idea that had ever made me want to possibly come up here.

Finally I saw on a wall 'Numbers 138–164', and ran towards it gratefully. Saskia's friends, Herbal and Valvula, had a flat at number 150.

Number 150 was on one of those housing corridors where policemen on *The Bill* are always kicking the doors in.

I rang the bell. Nothing from inside the house although, around me, a loud chorus of what sounded like extremely large dogs started up.

I rang again. I could feel a chill running through me that wasn't everything to do with the fact that I was soaking wet. No lights could be seen through the smoked glass in the door, even though Marisa had assured me that they knew I was coming and someone would be in. I checked under the doormat just in case. Nothing. I poked open the letter box. The smell from inside the flat was of neglect, of a place nobody had been in a long time. It smelled of old carpets and mildew.

I tried not to panic. They must have left a key with a neighbour. But nobody was answering on the right-hand side, and from the left somebody shouted, 'Gan away wi yiz, ye fuckin' gadges. He's no fuckin' here ken.'

Well, that sounded nothing like, 'Come right in, have a cup of tea and here're the house keys.'

The Fringes

In desperation, I decided to get back to the cab, get him to take me to a café, and phone these people to come and get me. I turned around.

The cab was surrounded by about nine feral-looking youngsters wearing burgundy tracksuits and anoraks. They were shouting wildly at it, and the cabbie was gesticulating back. As I watched, the smallest of the children picked up a discarded Coke can and threw it so it bounced off the back window. They cheered. The cabbie was looking around in desperation – for me, I realized, in a panic. I had to get downstairs. I pounded down the narrow, dangerous staircase, skidding horribly in my heels, but as I emerged onto the street again, I heard the sickening sound of breaking glass. Closely followed by the even more sickening sound of a taxi motor starting up, and hurtling away down the street.

Fuck. Oh no. Adrenalin shot through my system. How DARE he? How could he possibly go and leave me alone out here? I was in the middle of nowhere, it was pouring with rain and – crap crap CRAP – my bag was in the car! I'd left it there to show him I wasn't going to do a runner. I didn't think *he'd* do a bloody runner. With my bag!

One of the feral creatures suddenly pointed his face to the sky, sniffing like a meerkat. I realized with horror that they were short of a prey – and in this grey landscape, under an ever-lowering sky, it was me.

I cowered behind the entrance to the flats, a distinct smell of old garbage and pee launching itself directly at me. The group were shouting at each other now; nothing specific I could make out, just the distinct, overloud, expletive-filled vernacular of under-confident pubescence everywhere. I did *not* want them to find me. Every horror story I had ever heard of today's de-sensitized, over-sexualized, dribbling-junk-food and computer-game-addict children started to run through my head. I could feel my pulse jumping through my skin. And I was starting to shiver.

'Okay, Natalie.' I told myself. 'Don't panic. I'm sure you'll be laughing about this later, when you're reunited with your baggage and sipping cocktails in one of those posh-looking hotels you passed on the way here . . . a long, long time ago.' Would they even tell Warren when they found my body? I hoped Marisa wouldn't think it was all her fault.

'WRAOUFFFFFGGGGGH!!!!!!!!!'

The noise was so startling I think I actually leaped in the air. I hadn't known anyone did that. I certainly shrieked, because the meerkats immediately pointed their tracksuits in my direction.

'WRAOUFFFFFGGGGGGH!!!!!!'

'Oh for FUCK'S sake!!' I yelled and turned round. A huge dog – more horse than dog, I'd have said – was heaving itself against the back gate, which obviously led out to some scrub at the back of the building. He was launching his enormous body with all his might, obviously desperate to get to someone wearing Zara and take a big chunk out of them. The owner must be there, right? The lovely kind owner would pop up any moment to call off the dog and save me and . . .

The rusted metal of the bars – was it moving? It definitely looked like it was moving under the onslaught of the dog's massive head.

'WRAOUFFFFGGGHHHHH!!!!!'

'What's Aul Bastard shoutin' at?' screeched one of the kids.

Oh God. No.

They started to walk towards me, carefully.

'Have you found something there, Aul Bastard?'

Was that his name? My hopes for a friendly neighbour were diminishing.

'Maybe it's a dead body, like the one doon the canal,' hollered one acned scrawn-bucket, hopefully.

'WRAUFFFGGGHHHH!!!'

The gate was definitely feeling it now. It screeched, and the bars were gently starting to give. The animal stared straight at me, hackles raised. The boys were about ten feet away on the other side of the brick arch. It was now or never.

'Who the fuck?' One of the boys turned round as I flashed past, a streak (I hoped) of wet-patterned gypsy cotton.

'GET HER!' shouted another boy, and my heart was in my throat as I pounded along the pavement, shoes in hand, praying I would miss any broken glass.

The teenagers threw themselves at me, just as I heard Aul Bastard, with a final shove, burst through the gate at last. Then there came a scream, and I looked behind me, to see the tallest boy thrown to the floor by nine stone of rottweiler. The teenagers stopped and regarded the two shows: chasing the English tart or watching their friend get his throat ripped out. No contest. They edged back towards the main show. I backed away faster and faster. One of them saw it.

'We're still going to get you, you filthy hoo-err!' he shouted.

Frustrated beyond belief, I flipped him the middle finger. Oh God, I am such an idiot. Suddenly he was racing towards me. And I made my second mistake. I threw my shoe at him.

The heel caught him right above the eye, and he staggered back in disbelief. I wasn't waiting for any more; I was running, running away, never having dreamed that those hours in the gym would ever have helped me like they were helping now. I ran and ran, past a gasworks, past a park, until – until I couldn't run any more and came to an abrupt halt, looking out at the docks.

Great. So I was soaked through – in a thin cotton dress, in what felt like the middle of winter, wearing one shoe.

A large lorry slowed down, sprayed me in water from the road and passed on its way. My eyes filled with tears. I didn't know where I was – I didn't even know Edinburgh was *on* the sea, for God's sake – I had no money, no phone, and only one shoe.

A Mondeo slowed down.

'Wanting a bit o' business, darlin?'

It was a horrible little fat man in a grey suit. I stifled a sob and turned away.

'For fuck's sake,' he grumbled. 'Shouldnae be out here then. Go back to yer mammy where you belong.' And he drove off, splashing me again.

So now I couldn't even cut it as a tart.

A burgundy van slowed down.

'Are you working?' said a soft voice.

'NO!' I screamed. 'I am NOT working, okay? And you, by the way, are DISGUSTING.'

The man didn't respond, only smiled in a slightly pitying way, I thought.

'I'm sorry,' he said. 'Bad day?'

'Oh no, perfectly normal in Wet Whore World.'

'Can we help?'

It was then I noticed what was written on the van. It said 'Community Outreach Project'. And the man certainly didn't look like a hooker-beating-up murderer. Mind you, that was always what their mothers said.

'You're not seriously suggesting I get in your van?'

'You're no from round here, are you?'

He had a nice, soft accent. He got out, with his hands raised, keeping a good distance from me, and went and opened up the back of the van.

'No!' I broke down in huge ragged sobs.

'You're shivering.'

Quietly, he handed me a big tartan rug. It smelled clean. I wrapped it around me as I coughed out the rest of my sorry tale.

When I'd finished, he held out a Tupperware box, taken from a large pile in the back.

'Hungry?'

'No.'

I was starving, but I was not – quite – at the point of taking food out of the mouths of the homeless.

'I'm Graeme.'

'Natalie,' I said petulantly.

'Where were you headed, Natalie?'

'I told you, I came up for the festival . . .'

'Ah, the festival.'

He nodded. He had brown curly hair, and bright blue eyes, which were currently crinkled with amusement.

'What's wrong with that?'

'Nothing . . . nothing . . . just takes up quite a lot of our time when we have some *real* waifs and strays to look after . . .'

'Well, I'm sorry to take up your precious day with my hypothermia.'

'Don't be like that. Where are your friends performing?'

I looked at the paper. The ink had run in the rain.

'Somewhere . . . I don't know. It just says somewhere pleasant.'

He smiled.

'The Pleasance. No problem. I'll run you there.'

'*Really?*'

'Well, have you got the bus fare?'

'No.'

He told me a little about himself as he drove me up into the city, windscreen wipers blazing. He had a job with Barnardo's, but also spent a couple of evenings a week volunteering.

'There's an Edinburgh a lot of people don't see,'

he said intensely, as we crossed what I now knew was called the New Town, although it looked old enough to me; lots of rich people's houses.

'That's great,' I said. 'Ooh, isn't that Jonny Vegas?'

I scrambled round for a closer look.

'*Especially* people like you,' he said. 'Cultural cherry picker.'

'That's not true,' I said indignantly. 'I've got the *Trainspotting* soundtrack.'

He looked at me. 'Well, we're nearly there,' he said, drawing up in front of a large sandstone courtyard hung with yellow banners and streaming with people. Everything was bathed now in an odd, watery sunlight which had finally managed to push itself through the furious clouds, which meant that, wringing wet, I looked worse than ever.

'Are you sure you're going to be okay?' he said.

'I can look after myself.'

He narrowed his eyes at me.

'Today was an exception.'

'What are you going to do about your shoe?'

I looked out of the window. A man painted silver was lurching past on enormous stilts. Across the road a bevy of transvestites and Victorian wenches were mingling, waiting to cross. A large red-haired man in a space suit zoomed by, riding a hoover.

'I think I'll probably blend in okay,' I said.

Graeme shrugged.

'Well, okay then . . .'

I turned to him.

'Thank you,' I said, and meant it, as I went to

open the door. 'I . . . you really helped me back there.'

A slow smile spread across his face.

'That's okay,' he said. 'In fact, if you ever—'

'Nata-LEEEEEEE!!!!!!!!!!' A screech echoed across the road.

'Nata-LEEEEEEE!!!!!!!!!'

That couldn't be me, could it? But before I'd had the chance to think about it, Saskia flung herself on me, all patchouli oil, leather bracelets, shawls, and ribbon-plaited hair dangling in my face.

'Babe, where *have* you been!?'

'Waiting for you!' I said, disentangling myself.

'What? Really? Where?'

I stared at her.

'What? I went down to the place you said!'

'Oh, darling,' she laughed, as if I'd done something unbelievably embarrassing by actually following her instructions. 'Don't be *ridiculous*. It's the festival! We ran into a group of Australian improvisers earlier who are letting us kip in their gorgeous pad in New Town.'

'Oh. Nice of you to let me—'

Her pretty face frowned suddenly.

'Not sure there'll be room for you, though . . .'

'Natalie,' came the quiet Scots burr from behind me. 'I really have to get on.'

'Oh yes.' I turned round.

He really was rather attractive in a puppyish way.

'This is Graeme.' I introduced him to Saskia. 'He helped me when I was lost, looking for you.'

'Oh,' she said. 'Are you in a show?'

196

'No,' said Graeme politely. 'I work with the home-less.'

Saskia looked at him blankly as if he'd just said 'I work bleurgh bleurgh blah blah.'

'That's nice,' she said. 'I saw a show about that.'

'Look after yourself,' he said to me.

'Okay,' I replied, nodding. He grinned, I stepped out of the car and he was gone.

'Now!' said Saskia. 'Have you got any money? Only I'm terribly skint.'

It turned out, in fact, that Saskia's play wasn't doing quite as well as everyone had hoped, hence the sleeping on someone else's floor and the hair plaiting. Saskia had practised on herself and was now pouncing on unsuspecting children, in between painting tigers on their faces. The idea was to get as much done as possible before the parents noticed and got pissed off at having to cough up money. There were a lot of half-ribboned children running around the town, and very few packet soups left in the local shops.

I gathered this, despite Saskia wittering on about 'possible Fringe Firsts' and 'we've had the Scots Man in' – I still didn't know who this guy was, but he was obviously pretty important – and 'building slowly'.

'It doesn't help that we're on at the same time as Ross Noble. Bloody Ross Noble. Right.' She sighed heavily. 'I suppose we'll have to comp you in then.'

'What does that mean?'

'Get you in for free.'

'Ooh, thanks,' I said, although I'd kind of hoped to see Ross Noble. But still. I was here. I'd made it. My cotton was drying out and Saskia had made a massive point of not asking what had happened to my other shoe, so finally FINALLY I was at the festival and I was going to have a great time. Okay, I was hungry, but I could visit the bank tomorrow. Now was a time to look round and . . .

'You know your dress is see-through?' said Saskia.

God. I looked down.

'Great!' she said. She pointed me towards an open-air bar/hot-dog stand that had been set up in the middle of the courtyard.

'Walk over there. Slowly. And I'll have a pint of lager.'

'What?'

But she had shoved me across the cobbles. I started to walk, very self-consciously.

Immediately, I was set upon by four odd-looking men. Two gave me flyers, flashed me wide smiles and said, 'It's great!' The other two looked me up and down with odd mocking looks. They were both slightly ugly white men in their late twenties, dressed entirely in black. I wondered if this was some kind of a trick.

'Hi,' said one. 'I'm a comedian. Here. At the festival. I have a show. I'm a comedian.'

'Me too,' said the other one. 'And I've had Channel Four in.'

'We've had Channel Four in too,' said the other, immediately. 'And the Perrier panel. Maybe.'

I stared at them.

'Would you like a drink?' said the first one. 'I

could tell you all about my show. And about me, a comedian. I'd be doing better, only Ross Noble has my time slot.'

'Well, okay,' I said. 'Can my friend have one too?'

Saskia pouted and waved.

The comedians were *very* keen to tell us everything about how brilliant their acts were. They seemed, however, to be the only good comedians in the festival. Everyone else was terrible, drunk and had stolen their material from everyone else. In a further stroke of amazing coincidence, they had both split up from their girlfriends just before they'd arrived. They also concentrated on getting an endless supply of drinks down our necks. I was all right with that, although I hadn't eaten all day, and realized I was becoming louder and distinctly happier than I'd been since I got here.

'That's a really nice bra,' said the lankier and less acned of the two.

'Thank you!' I said, slapping his arm. 'Make a joke about that then!'

He smiled half-heartedly, but stayed staring fixedly at my breast.

'Can I touch it? I need to, for research.'

'Come on!' shouted Saskia suddenly. 'We need to get there for the warm-up!'

'What?' spluttered the comics.

'My show!' said Saskia. 'It's on now. Want to come?'

'What's it about?' said the lanky one.

'One woman's journey into the path of herself,' said Saskia. 'It's called *Sisterical*.'

'Has it got periods in it?' said the spotty one.

'No thanks,' said the lanky one.

'But we just bought them all those drinks,' whined the first one.

'Maybe see you later, eh?'

'What was that all about?' I asked Saskia as we made off out of the courtyard.

'Comics,' said Saskia, 'they're like puppies, desperately trying to hump your leg all the time. Looking for innocent Oxford graduates.'

'That is *so* not us,' I said.

'Works for the free drinks though.'

I followed her, limping along cobbled pathways and round the back of abandoned buildings by the train line. This wasn't looking terribly promising. I'd rather liked the look of that nice cheery court-yard. But this was no man's land. I hadn't seen another person for ten minutes.

'It's a very good venue. Number 415. Intimate, yet a good space,' Saskia was wittering, as we pulled up in front of something which, I had to say, looked rather a lot like a row of lock-up garages under-neath a primary school.

A sullen-faced sixteen-year-old sat at the door.

'How many are in tonight, Clover?' Saskia looked excited.

Clover barely looked up from her big difficult-looking hardback book.

'Four.'

Saskia gulped. 'Well, four, four is definitely better than . . . I must do more flyering. Natalie, maybe you could flyer instead of paying for the show.'

The Fringes

I nodded, having no idea what this might mean, but, feeling drunk already, I was looking longingly at a makeshift bar in the corner. A few lost looking people were already hanging about, self-consciously, reading the newspaper and sipping gin and tonics.

'And can we just have a little advance on petty cash . . .' said Saskia, slightly desperately. Sighing heavily, Clover doled out a couple of ten-pound notes, ostentatiously making a note for the box and getting Saskia to sign it. She wasn't what you'd call an attractive girl, Clover.

Saskia sighed, quickly bought us two large gin and tonics, necked one, then disappeared.

'See you in showbiz land!' she said.

The 'stage' wasn't exactly a stage. More of a dark clearing in the middle of somebody's sitting room. Likewise, the seats weren't exactly seats. More like packing cases covered in black cloth. Even though there were only five of us in there, it still felt pretty cramped. There was a lot of traffic noise coming from outside too. Still, I had had lots of gin and tonics and was feeling pretty cheerful on the whole. Suddenly there was some horrible grinding music coming out of a pair of speakers. The sound quality was about on a par with old ice dance competitions. From behind a big pile of cardboard boxes painted black, Saskia did a forward somersault and landed (rather awkwardly) in the middle of the stage.

She was wearing black, some sort of bin liner fairy bag conceptual thing, which made a noise like a fart whenever she moved.

'I am woman,' she hissed, pushing her hands in front of her face like Hot Gossip dancers from the old Kenny Everett shows. 'I come, from the primeval swamp; warm, wet, and open.'

There was an audible groan from the audience. It was hard to tell whether this was sexual excitement, or a reviewer in despair.

'I am nurture. I am womb,' said Saskia. 'Listen. HEAR MY STORY!' Then she did another forward somersault.

'I am Eve. Look, as I begin . . .' She took out a small rubber snake and started caressing herself with it.

I wish she hadn't mentioned wombs. I don't know why, but it really made me want to go to the toilet.

By the time Saskia had given birth live on stage with lots of panting and shrieking and 'Watch as this man is torn from my womb and goes on to tear the world apart with his war!', I absolutely couldn't hold on to it any longer. But because this wasn't a proper theatre, there wasn't an aisle I could creep down and sneak out undetected. The only exit was across the stage. But Saskia had barely reached the middle ages and we had a long long way to go. It was either this or wet the seat. Nothing else.

As unostentatiously as possible, I got up. All five pairs of eyes immediately fixed themselves to me. I gave my most apologetic look, one that tried to convey 'I am so sorry, but I have been drinking far too much and must empty my bladder and it's hardly my fault that we're not in an actual theatre for people with actual bladders', but Saskia decided to make an example of me. She drew herself up from her latest woman/creature crouch and fixed me with a pointed finger.

'Whither go you, wooo man?' she said to me in a spooky voice. Oh crap, she was going to shout at me in character.

'Do you betray your sisterhood so?'

'Um, I need a pee.'

'Sit!' she said, still in the scary Egyptian Goddess voice, and started bearing down on me, finger still outstretched. 'You will hear the ways of our people!'

'I will pee myself.' I said. 'Look, Saskia, I absolutely have to . . .'

I think the rest of the audience thought it was part of the show.

'There is no Saskia here.'

Oh for fuck's sake. I inched sideways to the door, determined now.

'I'm really, really sorry.'

'You betray us! You betray us all!'

Nearly there.

'You will be cursed! You are no woman!'

Got it.

'CUURRSSSEEEDDDDDDD!' was the last word I heard before I thankfully tumbled out into the foyer. Fuck, this wasn't the foyer.

Lights shone brightly in my eyes and I stumbled forward, before realizing that I was in a room that was also a theatre – with distinctly more people in it than there had been next door. And – oh CHRIST – I was standing in the middle of a stage.

There were about nine people round me, and, blinded by the light, at first I thought they were looking at me really strangely. Then, as I blinked, I realized they were done up as clowns.

'Xlkjodijflds!' shouted one of them, and the rest joined in. The audience clapped enthusiastically. It appeared these were not only clowns, they were non-English-speaking clowns. I raised my hands.

'So sorry,' I said again, breathless now, and desperate.

'No worry!' shouted one of the clowns with a heavy Russian accent, and they all surrounded me. I could hear the audience bristle with excitement. I also saw a bright orange Way Out sign, and headed directly for it.

But whichever way I moved, the clowns would block my progress.

'Ha ha,' I said. 'Excuse me.'

Wherever I turned, though, there'd be another, horribly identical clown stepping in my way. The audience were still laughing. This was turning into a nightmare.

'Let me out!!' I yelped. The lead clown raised his arms and bowed, and as I ran towards him, the sky suddenly exploded and became full of speeding balls and batons. The clowns were juggling over my head, with what seemed like hundreds of pieces of heavy equipment. It looked like enormous, hefty hail. Reflexively I covered my head with my hands, shaking. The audience laughed on.

'Hai!' shouted one of the clowns. I absolutely could not move.

'Stop it! Stop it!' I yelled, as the cups and batons flew faster and faster. Suddenly one caught my eye as it whirled above me – oh God. It was on fire. I screamed, dropped to my knees and started crawling out between them. I could see a man just by the door and I aimed for him. The clowns were laughing maniacally but didn't – maybe couldn't – stop. I was bawling by now as I got to the door.

'There, there,' It was the man I'd been aiming for as I finally made it between one white-suited Pierrot's legs. 'Let's get you outside for a breath of air.'

I had to find a bathroom first. And splash some water on my hands and face. When I came out, my saviour was sitting on a wall outside.

'I'm sorry about that,' I said. 'It took me by surprise.'

'Not to worry, lass.'

He was an older man, very genial looking, wearing a smart uniform and peaked hat. He was sitting opposite the most enormous car I had ever seen, apart from those stupid stretch limos: a huge burgundy Bentley, which gleamed under the last rays of the sun.

'You looked a little upset, that's all.'

'Umm, yes . . . I don't like clowns.'

He nodded sagely.

'Are you sure that was the right show for you to

be seeing, then? The *Universal Clown Spectacular*?'

'No, I . . .'

I didn't quite feel up to explaining, so I told him he had a nice car.

'Ah, that's not my car. I'm just driving it for someone a wee bit special.'

'Oh! Who? Who!?'

'I couldnae tell you that, I'm sorry.'

'Oh please. I've had a terrible day.'

He smiled, then said, 'Well, you're no to tell anyone.'

'Cross my heart,' I said. 'I only know one person here anyway, and she wants to witchify me to death.'

So he leaned over and told me, and my mouth dropped open.

'You're joking.'

He shrugged, 'Well, I take them all. Doesnae mean much to me. My daughter likes to hear about it, that's all.'

Suffice to say, it was a big movie star. A really big one. I promised Gareth (the chauffeur) that I wouldn't tell anyone, so I'll just say it was someone very very like, but NOT, John Cusack. Someone I liked a lot – almost exactly as much, by an incredible coincidence, as I like John Cusack. But not him. And not only that, he was marching down the road! Towards us! Right now!

Okay, so he was surrounded by blondes, all chirruping away, and all, I noticed, wearing two shoes. But still! A real movie star! Right here! I LOVED the Edinburgh Festival.

'Hey, Gareth, how you doing?' he said, smiling

as he mooched up. The girls laughed as if he'd said
something extremely amusing.

'Very well, sir. Where to?'

'Christ, I can't remember. That place they're
having that film festival party.'

'Right away, sir. And this is my friend.'

I couldn't believe it. My knees turned to water.
The movie star turned to glance at me. The girls
turned to shoot me dirty looks, but as soon as they
saw me they clearly realized I was not entirely a
threat, so looked pityingly at me instead.

'Hey there,' said the movie star, carelessly. 'Is she
coming to the party?'

Gareth looked at me, eyes twinkling.

'I think she is, sir.'

And the blondes crossly squeezed up their skinny
behinds for me in the enormous car.

Although almost bouncing up and down with excitement, I tried to keep my head down and stare quietly
out of the window as the movie star tried to elicit
conversation from the blondes that didn't entirely
consist of giggling, without success. All I was
concentrating on was not getting thrown out of the
car, but it was only a two-minute journey until we
came out at the big beautiful square building, the
one that I'd seen when I'd first arrived – obviously
a luxury hotel, with a huge clock tower at the top.
As we were whisked through reception in the wake
of an over-excited *maitre d'*, I kicked off my other
shoe and revelled in my good fortune (I'd already
given Gareth a huge kiss). Okay, the other girls

hadn't exactly said hello or in fact done anything except giggle, but I was with a big movie star and, here we were. I looked out of the huge window, above the crowd of people there for the party, and gasped. The sun was setting over the castle, lighting up orange and yellow down through the gardens, and reflecting off the massed grey stone above them. It was the most beautiful view I'd ever seen. I lifted a glass of champagne off the waiter's tray and looked around, shiningly happy.

Sipping the champagne seemed to make my head light immediately. Everywhere very beautifully dressed people were air-kissing each other. I saw lots of people I recognized, and, in this exalted company, in this beautiful room, filled with beautiful people screaming at the top of their voices, minor TV personalities looked as nervous and gauche as I did. I smiled politely as people walked past me, or waved to each other over the top of my head. Even the waiters were about ninety times more attractive than me.

'Nice party!' I said encouragingly to a tall dark man standing next to me.

'Oof, so boring,' he said. 'Excuse me.'

'Do you know a lot of people here?' I asked a girl wearing very red lipstick, in what I hoped was a bonding moment.

'Yes, thank you,' she said. 'Excuse me.'

Also unanswered: 'Isn't this a lovely hotel?'; 'Do you work in the film industry?' ('Yes – do you?') and, 'Do you know Mindy?' (I was getting desperate). But the conclusion was inevitable. Here I was at my first sparkling event ever, looking like a hedge-drag specialist (although I knew that even scrubbed up, I couldn't outdo these women, who clearly spent their waking hours doing nothing but polishing themselves), and nobody would talk to me. Sighing slightly, I went and stood next to the big picture window and looked out. At least the view was still beautiful. The last of the golden light made the whole sight almost unearthly; it was like some Siberian midnight, the ancient windows of the houses white-blank with reflection, mount each other like a rock fall.

'It's amazing, isn't it?' said a quiet American voice beside me. I half glanced over. It was. It was the non-John Cusack. The movie star. Fuck!

I blushed. I coughed. I tried to take a sip of my drink, but buggered it up and it went up my nose and I spluttered, going increasingly red as I did so. I tried to regain my composure, looked everywhere but in his face, then finally, chokingly, said this:

'Ha ha ha aha!'

The movie star looked at me for a second.

'Yes,' he said, quietly. 'What I just said was very funny. Excuse me.'

And he drifted back into the fray, pursued by the hysterically giggling blonde harpies.

Anything. I could have said anything. I could have said, 'This is the most disgusting view I've seen since the Taj Mahal. Why would anyone like it?'

I could have said 'Are you looking at the sky or looking at me?' Crude, but potentially effective.

I could just have said, 'Yes', and we could have enjoyed looking at it for a while.

I necked another glass of champagne, wearily, and turned around. Making a beeline was one of the lanky comics I'd been talking to earlier.

'Got you now, you minx! It's payback time! Did you see my show? No? Oh, I stormed it.'

'I'm very tired,' I said. 'I think I'm going to go.'

Though I didn't know where.

'You can't go! It's the festival!! Everyone stays up really late and gets really ratted!!'

'Well, it may not be late' – it was nearly eleven actually, I'd forgotten how late it stayed light here, though it was totally dark now – 'but I think I've pretty much covered "ratted".'

'Aw, come on. Stay a bit and have some fun.'

'I've had enough fun, thanks.'

He tried to grab my arm.

'Get off, please.'

'Geez, another fucking gaghag who pretends to be above it.'

'A *what*?'

'A gaghag. You're all the same. Hang around the performers and see what you can get. That's okay darling – have a go!'

I was very tired. Bad things had happened. I'd had too much to drink. He was a dick. Four good reasons which counted for nothing with the security guards who threw me out when I threw a glass of champagne in his face.

* * *

The Fringes

I landed on my arse. I bumped down the front steps, expostulating wildly, into a sea of revellers passing by on Princes Street, to be instantly submerged into the throng, trying to avoid being trodden on, or hit on the head with somebody's backpack. Now I really didn't know where I was going, or what I was doing.

The crowd spat me out into a kind of rhombus shaped clearing above a jagged mall, with a large pointy obelisk in the middle, which seemed as good a place as any to sit while I tried to work something out. I had never felt so alone in my entire life. So, this was what happened when I tried to show Warren – who wouldn't care anyway, and I didn't really care about him – how I could get on culturally without him. I was freezing now. Starving, drunk, homeless. God, I didn't even like thinking about what I was going to do later. Could it get any worse? I sucked at this. I sucked at festivals. I sucked at life. I couldn't do . . .

A piercing scream rent the air.

Everyone passing immediately froze, desperately searching around. That hadn't been a child's yell, or a student's prank. It was a bloodthirsty and horrible sound. It came again.

Suddenly, from the flash of people passing on the pavement, a figure in a white and red top burst through into the courtyard area where I was sitting.

As my eyes focused, I realized that her top wasn't white and red – it was white, with a ghastly streak of blood running across the top. Her mouth was open in a wild banshee cry.

Without thinking, I jumped up. Almost in slow motion I moved towards her, the heads of the crowd turning to follow our progress. I could see them raise their hands to their open mouths as I collided with the girl, balletically, in the middle of the open space.

'Here, here,' I said, breathlessly, feeling her heart flutter underneath her blouse in the cold air as I put my arm around her. 'Come here.'

She felt as light as a feather and I led her over to the bench, gently sitting her down.

'Let me see you,' I said, as softly as I could. 'It's all right. It's all right. It's going to be okay.'

She was shaking and wouldn't let me see her wound.

'Don't worry now, don't worry.'

Out of the crowd rushed a young man. He belted up to us. 'I've got medical training,' he gasped. 'I can probably help . . .'

It took me a moment to focus on him properly.

'It's you!' I said. It was Graeme.

'Bloody hell!' he said. 'What's happened here?'

And we bent over the girl. There were more people now, coming out of the crowd around us.

'We'll have to get this top off and maybe make a tourniquet,' said Graeme, quickly, but calmly. 'Is she breathing?'

Jesus. I felt for a pulse in her neck, as Graeme carefully tried to examine her chest.

Suddenly, in one terrifying motion, the girl sat herself upright. I couldn't have been more scared if she'd been a zombie.

'Argh!' I shouted, moving back.

'Venue 74!' shouted the girl. 'Burke and Hare!'

At first I couldn't work out what she was shouting: was it her last death rattle? Then I heard Graeme say 'Shit!' in a disgusted tone of voice, and stand up, as a photographer started flashing photographs.

The crowd still looked on like loons, as the girl danced up and started handing out leaflets to what I belatedly realized was a festival show.

'What!' I said, my heart still pulsing with adrenalin. 'She nearly scared me half to death.'

'STUPID bloody students,' said Graeme, furiously. 'Bloody publicity stunts.'

'I thought . . . I thought . . .' I crumpled back onto the bench, as I realized how scared I'd been.

'I know,' said Graeme. He sat down beside me. Then he looked at me, and my utterly bedraggled appearance, and started to laugh.

'You're not having the best festival, are you?'

'Yes I am! No.'

At that I felt the tears prickle my eyes and my throat get all big and sore.

'I didn't think . . .'

Graeme patted me gently on the arm, as I let it all go.

'There, there. You've had a shock.'

'This whole bloody place is a shock,' I sobbed.

He laughed and put his arm around me. It felt nice. I leaned my face into his shoulder.

'Why did you come?'

'I don't know! I wanted to show my pesky

ex-boyfriend and get lots of culture and go to the right parties and have fabulous fun and . . .'

'All noble aims,' he said, nodding his head gravely.

'Just because it's stupid doesn't mean it's not true,' I sniffed, mournfully.

Graeme looked into the distance for a little bit.

'Well,' he said. 'You nearly saved someone's life.'

'There was nothing wrong with her,' I said crossly.

'Well, if there had been, you'd have helped her.'

I sniffed.

'Which I think is better, frankly.'

'I suppose.'

'It was.'

I half smiled.

'Well, there is that.'

'Absolutely. You were very brave.'

'You think?'

'If she'd really been bleeding to death, you would have got freedom of the city!'

'Yeah!' I said. We smiled at each other.

'But now I want to go home,' I said.

'Okay,' shrugged Graeme. 'We're near the rail way station.'

'Yeah,' I said. 'I'll get someone to meet me in London with the ticket money. God, probably bloody Warren. He's the only person I know with any money. Yeekh.'

'Or – ' said Graeme.

I raised my eyebrows.

'– Ross Noble's got an extra show at midnigh . . . and we might just make it . . .'

'You seriously want me to start enjoying the festival?' I asked.

He shrugged. 'Life has a funny way of being unpredictable.'

'You think?' I said.

He grinned, then he offered me his arm. And I took it.

From: *The Scotsman*, 24 August 2003

Page: 3 ***** Saskia Veldt's amazingly passionate *Sisterical*, set to be pick of the fringe.
Page 7: All-female Perrier shortlist announced.
Page 8: 'I love British Girls; they're so much fun,' says star of new movie.
Page 11: (photograph) Anastasia Hartley of, *Burke and Hare*, shown here being 'saved' during publicity stunt by kind-hearted couple.

ANGELS WI' DIRTY FACES

Miller Lau

Of Scottish descent, **MILLER LAU** now lives in Dunbar, East Lothian. She is the author of the highly acclaimed novels in *The Last Clansman* series, *Talisker* and *Dark Thane*. The forthcoming *Yiska* is the third in the series.

They're laughing again, killin' their sel's.

'Right . . . right . . . whits this?'

The wee'st one, Morna Balfour, flings back her red hair in a kinna distractit fashion. An' then – jings but ah've been hanging aboot this place too long! – ah could've swore she grinned at me! Aye! Right over tae where I'm sitting on top o' *Majoliner II*.

'What goes zub zub zub, ouch!?' She giggles nervously, an' the other two – Senga and Margaret – do the usual rolling of the eyes. Senga just smirks and waits for Margaret to do the biz.

'I dunno,' she says in that kinna sing-song voice folk use for jokes, 'whit does go zub zub zub, ouch?'

'A bee flying backwards!' Morna laughs triumphantly. 'Get it?'

'Away y'go . . . you made that up!' Margaret says. She's killin' hersel' laughin' but Senga frowns like as though she's been asked some stoater o' a scientific question.

'Naw,' she says, 'I dinnae get it. Why does it go 'ouch'?'

'Aw fer chrissake, Senga, cos its stinger goes up its ar— Morning, Mr Murray!'

Margaret and Senga stiffen and shuffle their papers trying tae look efficient. Senga's got a right beamer. 'Made you look!' Morna crowed.

'Ye wee scunner!'

Then they're all laughing again. Ah'm laughin' too which doesn'ae happen very often – 'zub zub zub, ouch!' – I like it! That wee Morna, she reminds me o' my Helen – all sassy and a bit raj. I like to see her smiling, there's somethin' real aboot it. No like that hard-faced Senga – or should I say Agnes. Silly cow.

The Allied & Northern Bank, Sauchiehall Street. No much changes aroond here 'cept this wasn'ae always the computer room. Nearly thirty years ago it wis the vault – 's funny, here's me, stuck here for ever for all I ken – chained almost tae these machines, big metal boxes wi' daft macho names – *Hermes*, *Odin*, *Zeus* – and ma 'bed', *Majoliner II* – and I dinnae have a clue whit they actually dae. Mainframes, that's what thon wee plooky guy cried them, the engineer who installed them that is. He named them an' all – told Morna that *Majoliner* was the hammer of the Viking god Thor. She blushed and giggled. Later she said to Margaret, 'I bet hes got a wee one,' and held up her pinky . . . don't think she likes men ower much. I wouldn'ae either if I was her – she come in wi a right keiker a couple o' weeks back. Said she walked inte a door, but that's whit my Helen used to say, God forgive me. Aye, I was a right bastard. Married twenty year, never once told her I loved her . . . just hope she knew. Hard man y'see; I'da walked ower hot coals rather than telt her. Daft bugger . . . That's how I ended up here – it's that Jimmy Cagney's fault . . .

Mind o' that film? The one where he gets the electric chair at the end? Aye, well – ah thought he wis dead noble when that priest came and telt him no tae be a hard man aboot walkin' tae the chair. See it wis his reputation, his credibility. Ma pals a' said you couldn'ae have got a Glaswegian tae dae a' that screamin' and they wis probably right. Me, I lived fir the movies – thought Jimmy wis the greatest. Aye, you could say he definitely coloured my thinking.

When the bank job started to go wrong, we aw panicked – I bet in the pub afterwards they wis a' saying they wis dead cool. But ah ken. When the alarm startit they ran like rabbits. It wis McEndrick that knocked the wedge oot the vault door an' by the time I breenged through it wis nearly shut. Shut oan ma leg didn't it? Ya bugger it wis sair! A' that reinforced thick steel – two tons – ye can imagine ma leg was just pulp. So here's me lyin' there and the lads were a' cursin and sweatin', running around like headless chickens. There wis blood everywhere cos my arteries were still pumpin' awa. It wis pretty sickenin'. In fact Wee Malky threw up . . .

Then came the Jimmy Cagney bit.

''S all right, lads. You go on. I'll no shop ye's, I promise . . .' I rasped. (Little did I ken I wouldn'ae hea much option!) They wasn'ae that noble onyway. They legged it. 'Cept McEndrick; he dithered for a wee few seconds, then he lit a fag and stuck it in ma mooth. I wis nearly unconscious by then but I sucked on it hard – reckon Cagney would've approved.

'Ye wee beauty, Smitty,' McEndrick muttered. Then he left.

Well, I thought the polis would be on the way didn't ah? I bled tae death. They found me in the morning in a pool o' blood and puke – a Benson an' Hedges kinna stuck to ma lip. The haul wis ower a million and I became a hero tae a' the wee low-lifers in Glasgow. The bastards never even saw Helen right . . .

It's quiet round here when the lassies go fer lunch. It's never really silent though, these mainframe things make a low pitched humming sound aw day and aw night – fer the silence o' the grave, it's no quite whit I expected. Today there's a wee snuffling noise from the corner where the lassies do what-ever it is they do at their VDU things. (Aye, that's whit they cry them – I thought it wis some kinda contraceptive device!) Think I'll jist float on over there and investigate . . .

Jings. It's Morna Balfour. Her pale face is aw red and blotchy and she's greetin' fit tae bust. I jist hate it when women greet. I gie her a wee pat on the back but she doesn'ae seem tae feel it.

I ken. I'll hie a fiddle wi the keyboard. I've often fancied a shot.

Hiya.
What goes black/white, black/white, black/white?

She jumps as she sees the letters appear on the screen and peers at them in disbelief. It's really

222

good, the key things dinnae move when I touch them but the letters appear onyways. Morna gives a wee laugh and doesn'ae seem as suprised as I thought she wid.

'That's ancient.' She types.

A pengin in an avalanche.

Ye beauty! Why did I no think of this before? I can make contact. Mebbes I can get a message to Helen. Maybe no. It might not be for the best. Morna is keying something else in.

What goes zub zub zub, ouch?

This throws me. She doesn'ae realize who I am – I suppose that's reasonable. How come she doesn'ae think her computer is hauntit? Weird. Mind you, I can talk eh? I think I'll tell her.

My name is Smitty Sawyer. I'm a ghost. Honest, doll.

'Smitty Sawyer?' she says aloud. 'The Smitty Sawyer? The bank robber?' She types again.

Sure.

I must admit, I'm fair chuffed she's heard of me. She's typing something else now.

I have to report hackers to the management.

223

What's a hacker?

You know. Go away before you get me in trouble.

Why were you crying?

This seems tae gie her a fright fer some reason. She pushes away from the screen and peers around aw furtive. By chance she ends up looking straight at me.

'Are you here now?' she whispers.

I look right into her face. She's got big green eyes an' I wish I could kiss her. She's looking at the screen again, waiting for my answer; she bites her lip – my Helen used to dae that.

What's tae say? What's that saying? Life is for the living . . .

Still, I might have anither shot o' the computer when they've all gone hame tae their men and their bairns. Hame. S'truth, I feel sick. I head back towards *Majoliner II* and lie doon. Cagney wid o' said something tae her – Bogie or Brando mebbe . . . they always got the girl, made them smile . . . Not Smitty Sawyer . . .

A one way-ticket to Palookaville for Smitty Sawyer . . .

She stares at the screen fer ages.

Payday. It's always the same – I dunno why but they reach fever pitch. Get a' excited talking aboot what they're goin' tae buy. Chattin' away aboot red blouses an' winter coats – right enough, ye need a good winter coat in Glasgow. It's like a ritual. Just when they reach the heights o' excitement, in walks Murray wi' the wage lines. I eyways think he hands them oot like he was doin' them a personal favour – a' snotty and full o' hisel'. Then there's the curious delving in the handbags. I used tae wonder why they did that, but now I ken. See, they dinnae know whit one another makes – they're no allowed tae discuss it e'n. So they kinna dip the pay line intae their handbags and tear them open in there – aw cosy like.

I ken whit they earn, least I do now. Senga, she makes the most, mainly on account o' she's been here the longest. Dunno why though, cos she's a bloody skivver. Ah think she suspects she gets the most, leastways she always looks smug.

Wee Morna, she earns the least, she's no been here very long and I seen her skelp Murray's face when he stuck his hand up her skirt , so she's only had the cost o' living rise fer the past year.

No today, though. She delves into her bag (I'm trying to hover nonchalantly nearby, by the way – aye, I ken she cannae see me but old habits die hard) and I hear a sharp intake of breath. Her wee hands are fair shakin' as she takes the pay line oot intae the light tae examine it better.

'Mr . . .' she begins.

Her voice trails off as she looks at the message.

Trust me. (Yeah, I know!) They won't miss it. Do me a favour. Keep smilin'. Get out there and live! Here's looking at you kid!

Yeah, well . . . I couldnae resist it. Mebbe old hard men dinnae die – they just go soft roon the edges. Mebbe I wanted that smile for me . . . for Helen. Mebbe Smitty Sawyer wasn'ae too late to be just a touch Jimmy Cagney.

Whea kens . . .

Mebbe I could rest now.

HAPPY HOUR

Lennox Morrison

A former translator, TV presenter and staff writer for the *Daily Mail* and *Scotland on Sunday*, **LENNOX MORRISON** now writes full-time. She is the author of a highly successful debut novel, *Re-inventing Tara,* and her second novel, *Second Chance Tuesday*, will be published in early 2004.

Born in Elgin, Lennox grew up in Galloway and Aberdeen, and now lives in Glasgow.

For the fourth time in as many minutes, Gillian Shand looked at her watch and picked at the fraying leather strap. Despite the soft upholstery and ambient music in the dimly lit basement bar, she was sitting more and more uncomfortably.

Force of habit had impelled her to arrive ten minutes early. This meant – Gillian checked her watch again – she'd had twenty-five minutes to register that the Episode shift dress and jacket in which she'd felt so chic at the Lord Provost's drinks reception in Aberdeen branded her as too dowdy for Saint Jude's, one of the hippest rendezvous in Glasgow city centre.

Thanks to a logistical operation involving her husband Brian, her nanny, her taking conveyancing work home from the solicitors' practice, staying up till 2 a.m. cooking meals for the freezer, and allowing an extra hour for late-running trains, she'd negotiated the 150 miles from Aberdeen to arrive punctually at six o'clock for cocktails with Jilly, whose elegant West End flat was at most a ten-minute drive away.

Gillian settled into her seat and let her thoughts

drift back to the first day of primary school. Jilly had been the last to arrive, smiling confidently and sliding into the little chair next to hers. 'Perfect!' Miss Yuill had said. 'The two Gillians side by side.'

Suddenly school had seemed less frightening. She wasn't just Gillian Shand, alone in a bewildering new world where other children had things like middle names, 'lunch' instead of 'dinner', and 'supper' instead of 'tea', but she was Gillian Shand, best friends with Gillian MacFarlane, the funniest, bravest girl in the class, who at breaktime drew a huddle of instant friends shocked by stories of stealing milk bottles from door steps and seeing grown-ups' bare bottoms.

Gillian Shand had taken her new friend by the hand and led her where even *she* wouldn't have dared venture, into the clanging, shiny engine room of simmering cauldrons and slapping mops where Mummies with sweaty faces and party hats scented the air with disinfectant and cabbage.

'Fit's wrang?' Mrs Shand had asked. Then her voice had become angry: 'I tellt you nae to come in here for nae reason.' She'd reached into a pocket of her blue nylon overall: 'Here.' Her voice still sounded like a telling-off but she was handing her daughter a shiny coin: 'I'll see ye at three o'clock. Off ye go and get yerselves some sweeties.'

The following week, Mrs MacFarlane, who smelled like flowers and who never raised her voice, not even when the two Gillians had raided the materials for her art students to make handbags for their dollies, asked the girls to set the table for supper. Attentive as a sorcerer's apprentice, Gillian Shand had watched her new friend perform the ritual of laying out rolled-up napkins in rings for family, and white napkins folded into rectangles for guests, on a dining table in its own room. There had been a strange but delicious dish called lasagne, and lettuce, just on its own, in a bowl.

Now, on the table in front of her, Gillian spotted a circular ashtray. She pulled it towards her.

'The two Gillians' had lasted until they were eight. At which point Gillian MacFarlane had revealed that Mummy and Daddy called her Jilly and so should everyone else. 'You can be Jilly too,' she'd suggested. They'd both known she hadn't meant it. But they'd remained inseparable.

Rolling the ashtray between her palms, Gillian considered all their shared adventures. For a few moments, a smile as bright as happy memories flashed across her thirty-nine-year-old face, bestowing a teenage glow to the unremarkable features.

She thought of the first pocket money they'd earned, as eleven-year-olds, picking potatoes. And of their first kisses – with Alan and Stuart – on the same night, shivering in the sleet, behind the youth club.

On the school trip to Paris – Gillian's first time abroad – Jilly, who'd already been to France, and Switzerland, and Italy, had insisted they skip dinner with the others and sit in a little café, smoking Consulates and sipping cognac. A man with dark eyes and a little leather handbag had asked if they were models. 'You are so beautiful you English girls,' he'd said. 'We're Scottish,' they'd chorused. 'English? Scottish?' he'd shrugged. 'You're beautiful.'

Hugging her memories like a talisman, Gillian surveyed the scene developing around her. Glances were skimming cleavages and ring fingers, smiles were lighting up to anecdotes and compliments. Silk Cuts were lit too, with hands which brushed each other, and eyes met over the rims of cocktail glasses.

Gillian fought the craving for a cigarette. Replacing the ashtray to its original spot, she used her neatly-filed but unpainted nails to remove a few more flecks of colour from the leather of the watch strap. Then, abruptly, she got up to go to the bar.

'Hi there.'

The barman's smile was engaging, but Gillian was focusing on the cigarette machine behind him.

'D'you have a drinks list?'

He handed her the cocktail menu.

'The champagne's cheaper by the way. It's happy hour.'

He offered Gillian his smile for a second time but she was busy stifling thoughts of the Private School Fund she and Brian had just set up. They'd taken on a vast mortgage to live in the catchment area of one of the best state schools in the country, but who knew what standards would be like by the time three-year-old Cameron and one-year-old Lauren were old enough for secondary?

'A bottle of house champagne,' she decided. 'With two glasses. And some olives.'

'Anything else?'

Gillian eyed the cigarette machine.

'That's it.'

Before she could change her mind, she pulled out her credit card and thrust it at him.

'I'll bring everything over,' said the barman.

His tone was polite but he'd tucked away his smile.

Gillian looked at the door, frowned at her watch, then sat down again.

The couple at the next table were smoking. She struggled with the temptation to inhale deeply.

'Shall I open it now?'

The barman had festooned her table with ice bucket, glasses and a saucer of olives and caper berries.

'No, no. I'll wait for my friend.'

Emboldened by her own extravagance, Gillian amplified: 'She's my best friend. I haven't seen her for ages.'

Saying this, Gillian was reminded of how much she'd been looking forward, after so many months of snatched telephone conversations, to seeing Jilly properly. She smiled. But the barman had already gone.

Leaning back against the grey tweed banquette, Gillian allowed herself to breathe in so deeply she sensed her lungs opening like a pair of bellows. She looked at the champagne, savouring the anticipation.

'Gillian! Hello! So sorry I'm late.'

Lips sticky with gloss brushed Gillian's cheeks.

The cloud of Silk Cut was chased away by Eau Dynamisante.

'Champagne! What a fantastic welcome! That's *so* kind of you. You *should* have.'

Gillian flushed with pleasure.

Jilly sat down. In a quieter voice she said, 'It's great to see you.'

'Would you open it? I always make a mess of it.'

'Sure.'

But before Jilly had even lifted the dripping bottle from the ice bucket, the barman rematerialized.

As he busied himself with napkin and bottle, Gillian noted Jilly's dishevelled locks, vest top, jeans and flip-flops and wondered why she hadn't made more of an effort. Jilly wondered when her friend had taken to dressing like the mother-of-the-bride.

'Thank you so much,' said Jilly, rewarding the barman with the smile which had taken her into the post-gig party at the Status Quo concert, into the coolest clique at the student union, then, later, onto the decks of yachts at Troon and the passenger seats of Porsches heading to Gleneagles, and to all sorts of places Gillian had only heard about afterwards. The one trip she'd made, twice, which Jilly had never done, had been down the aisle.

As Gillian raised her glass to meet Jilly's, a solid sparkle caught the light.

'It's beautiful,' declared Jilly.

'Brian gave me it on my last birthday.'

'What is it?'

'Diamonds and garnets. They're my birthstone.'

'Yes, but what—'

Gillian regarded the trio of bands on her ring finger with satisfaction: 'It's an eternity ring.'

'Gorgeous.'

As Jilly held her friend's hand up to the light, Gillian, who among the mothers at the nursery gate prided herself on her trim figure, realized – as she noted the Madonna-like definition of Jilly's triceps – that staying the same dress size wasn't enough. She regretted removing her jacket and, looking round, she realized that Jilly's outfit, far from making her look underdressed, was completely in tune with the effortlessly cool sound of the Buddha Bar CD flowing from the speakers.

Gillian looked down at her Kurt Geiger courts, the result of a precisely timed assault on Esslemont & Macintosh's spring sale three years ago. Normally, like her up-to-date insurance policies and pristine laundry room, the classic shoes were a source of self-congratulation. But now, next to Jilly's bejewelled flip flops, Gillian felt wrong-footed.

Worse though was the rising queasiness which had nothing to do with the creamy bubbles hitting her empty stomach. It was a feeling which, like the pain of childbirth, was soon forgotten but swiftly remembered.

Over the years it was Gillian who'd completed university, Jilly who'd dropped out, Gillian who'd become a property owner first, Jilly who'd rented far too long, Gillian who'd become a mother, Jilly who hadn't even married. And yet despite that, every time Gillian felt she'd finally caught up with the friend she'd idolized at school, it was only to find – not that Jilly had moved the goalposts – but that she'd left the pitch and was engaged in a whole new ball game.

'Did you say maternity or eternity?' asked Jilly.

'Eternity. That's what they're called.'

'Right. I just wondered if it was something new?'

'No. Just an old-fashioned eternity ring.'

'Well, it's gorgeous. Absolutely gorgeous.'

'Thanks,' said Gillian.

Looking down at her rings, she remembered how touched she'd been when Jilly had turned up at her first wedding only five minutes late, having hitched from Paris to Aberdeen.

Then she thought of her second wedding. Jilly had arrived in a low-cut white dress and had vanished before the speeches, taking the best man with her.

Gillian returned her left hand to her lap, then, with her right hand, resumed her attack on the watch strap. As she looked up again, she saw Jilly watching her.

'It's falling apart,' she explained.

Jilly said nothing.

'I know,' said Gillian, 'I should leave it alone. I'm only making it worse.'

Picking up her champagne glass, she took a sip, then turned energetically to her friend: 'So, are you seeing anyone just now?'

'You mean: 'Is there a man in my life?'' responded Jilly – deepening her voice seductively and putting one hand on her hip, like a modern-day Mae West.

'Well, *is* there?'

'Yes, there is someone.'

Gillian waited to hear more.

Jilly took a further mouthful of champagne.

'His name's Boris . . .'

Gillian made a face.

'I know. But he's tall, fair and handsome, half-Polish, brilliant cheekbones – but not tortured – very funny, very intelligent.'

'What does he do?'

'He's a theatre director.'

'Is he working just now?'

'At the Almeida. In London.'

Gillian speared an olive. 'D'you see him much?'

'He's rehearsing just now so he's been up for a few weekends. And I've been down there. When the play opens, it'll be different but . . .'

'Anyone famous in it?'

'Well, Clive Owen's the leading man and—'

'Clive Owen? Will you be meeting *him*?'

'Well, we've had dinner with him and Kelly.'

'Kelly?'

'Macdonald. She got her break in *Trainspotting* and then she was with Clive in *Gosford Park* so Boris thought—'

'I know who Kelly Macdonald is. Are they an item?'

'Not at all. They're just in this play together. It's a twenty-first-century take on the kitchen sink drama. Dishwasher drama, Boris calls it.'

'What's the title?'

'*Destination Chiswick*.'

'Hmmm.'

Jilly topped up their glasses.

'There's quite a buzz about it. Clive and Kelly were so keen on it they're doing it for Equity minimum.'

'Good for them.'

Gillian unpursed her lips to take another sip of champagne, then returned to her previous line of questioning: 'But what about you and Boris?'

Jilly smiled and shrugged her perfectly toned deltoids.

'Is it serious?' persisted Gillian.

'It's a lot of fun,' responded Jilly, in a tone to preclude any more interrogation.

'You can't have known him long?'

'Four months. Or five. You know I'm no good on numbers.'

'It's the first time you've mentioned him.'

'Is it?'

'Oh well, I'm sure you'll tell me when I need to buy a hat.'

They busied themselves with the champagne and olives. In the course of the phone calls it had taken to arrange meeting up before a legal seminar Gillian was attending the next day, they'd enquired minutely after family and run through the time-honoured litany of their mutual acquaintance.

Now, like little girls who'd spent their Sunday School collection at the sweetie shop on the way to church, they'd scant gifts with which to celebrate the rites of friendship.

'You look so fabulous and I look so mumsy,' offered Gillian.

'Don't be daft.'

Gillian, who'd been expecting a stronger denial, upped the ante:

'I feel like the mother-of-the-bride in this dress.'

'You look gorgeous.'

'*You* look gorgeous. I look about fifty.'

Jilly narrowed her eyes as she scrutinized her friend's two-small-children-and-too-big-a-mortgage face: 'You look thirty, okay thirty-two, at the most.'

Gillian's brow unfurrowed. 'Thanks.' She smiled. 'I must admit, though, there are plenty of days when I *feel* like fifty.'

'Have you got any new photos of the children?'

Gillian opened her wallet.

'Oh, they're beautiful. So sunny and glowy and rainbowy. So full of life,' said Jilly – with a smile as dazzling as the children's.

Gillian nodded.

In her mind's eye she saw Cameron and Lauren in the paddling pool in the kitchen – because the floor was tiled and why should rain stop their play – giggling and tumbling and clenching her heart with the warmest, purest ache of happiness she'd ever felt.

'They're certainly full of life. I can hardly keep up with them,' she said dryly.

Then her tone softened: 'I've got some more snaps here if you'd like to see them.'

She produced a mini photo album from her bag.

Jilly smiled and began looking through it.

In the lonely months after Jilly had dropped out of university, Gillian had persistently sent letters which were rarely answered. But when Jilly's affair with Yves came to an end, Gillian had taken the night coach to Paris and tramped three *arrondissements* in tar-melting August heat, helping her friend to flat hunt.

In the years Jilly had remained in France, detained by a series of jobs and romances, they'd always met up when she came home for Christmas. And when Gillian had been in the process of divorcing Mark, Jilly had whisked her off to Cyprus on holiday.

That week together had felt like a fortnight – to both – but despite that, in continuing phone calls, they never failed to repeat how great it would be if they could see each other more often.

Now, studying a photo of Gillian lying back on a sofa, beaming, as she let her little daughter tickle her, Jilly regarded her friend thoughtfully: 'You're happy, aren't you? I've never seen you so happy.'

'Yes,' admitted Gillian. She looked at Jilly warily: 'D'you ever wish you'd become a mum?'

'Who says I won't?'

'Oh well, I mean . . .'

'There's a lot of last-minute motherhood around. One of my clients has just had twins at forty-two and she's blissfully happy. So who knows? I've plenty of time yet.'

'Right.'

Gillian had never been sure when Jilly was being serious and when she was being flippant. Either way, the thought of life without Cameron and Lauren was so unbearable that kindness prevented her enquiring further.

Happy Hour

It also stopped her from sharing the observation Brian had made about how all her female friends were either working mothers sleepwalking through their days or childless singletons lying awake worrying about the meaning of life. 'Not Jilly, though. She'll never settle down,' Brian had noted – with a flicker of something Gillian hadn't liked but had chosen not to analyse. 'With Jilly, you can never tell,' was all she'd said, trying to forget the expression on her husband's face at that Hogmanay party when he, like every other man in the room, had been watching Jilly dance.

Men had been doing that since 1980, when she and Jilly had gone to Glasgow University to study law. Gillian had settled in easily, hoarding her energy for her studies and relying on Jilly to deliver a ready-made social life direct to the door of her room in the halls of residence.

But then, halfway through second year, Jilly had swanned off to Paris with Yves, the French film director she'd met on the underground between Hillhead and Cowcaddens. Yves turned out to be an electrician who'd once worked on a Gerard Depardieu movie. His only other connection with the cinematic world was his mission to bed more women than a posse of James Bonds.

Meanwhile Gillian was forced, after too many evenings sprawled on her single bed with her law books, to confront her shyness and make friends on her own. One evening, at the Queen Margaret Union, a podgy, but handsome and, it emerged, sharp-witted, Englishman had asked her for a light.

Mark Knowles was thirty-two, a mature student and, excitingly, already divorced, with a young daughter who was living with her mother in Weston-super-Mare.

Eighteen months later, when the rose-tinted haze induced by attracting a suitor all by herself had lifted, Gillian awoke in his dusty bachelor flat to realize the interesting older man she'd just married had a chip the size of a bollard on each shoulder – about his family, his first wife, his ex-parents-in-law and a growing succession of bosses. Worse still, he had no interest in assuming responsibility for a second family.

Too honest to trick him into being a father again, Gillian kept taking the Marvelon and was eventually rewarded with the discovery of his infidelity.

It was a one-off moment of madness, he'd protested. And he still loved her. She'd known both statements to be true. But it was the get-out clause she'd been looking for and a colleague in her first solicitors' practice had arranged the divorce with a smoothness those outside the legal profession can only dream of.

'How's business?' Gillian asked.

'Brilliant,' said Jilly who, after Gillian had spent years mired in the minutiae of conveyancing, had swept back to Glasgow, taken one look at the divorce rate and set up Happy Endings, a company offering to make divorce 'as painless as possible' for those who could afford it. With the slogan, 'When one becomes two, you need as much help as you can get', Jilly would match

242

client to lawyer, new home, counsellor, botox
doctor – whatever they needed to make it through
the split.

'I saw an article about you the other day in the
Scotsman's business section. Jilly MacFastlane, they
called you.'

'I know. Daft, isn't it?'

'It said you were thinking of expanding.'

Gillian waited to hear more. Once upon a time
they'd shared every plan, right down to the fish and
chips and ice cream they both wanted at their
wedding receptions. In the first months at university they'd agreed they'd both be advocates, and
would live in the West End of Glasgow or, possibly,
the New Town in Edinburgh.

Now, Jilly just nodded and took another mouthful of champagne.

'So what's it to be?' persisted Gillian. 'Two for
one? You'll look after both parties?'

'Well no, I don't think that would be quite ethical.'

Gillian nodded in agreement.

Jilly leaned in towards her friend. 'Keep it quiet
just now but I'm launching a new business in a
couple of weeks: Happy Beginnings.'

'Sounds like some sort of introduction agency.'
Gillian's tone was disapproving.

'Exactly,' smiled Jilly. 'I kept on bumping into
former clients who said they'd got over the divorce
and all they needed now was a new partner. Couldn't
I fix them up?'

Gillian's eyes were wide with interest.

'But where will you find the right sort of people?'

'They *are* the right sort of people. We've been going long enough that now we've got a huge pool of rich, successful, single-agains. I'm not going to match them one to one. That would be excruciating. What I'll do is organize parties, but really classy ones.'

'I'd love to be a fly on the wall.'

'I'll let you know when the first one is. If you can wangle it, you're welcome to come along.' Jilly smiled naughtily: 'But I don't know what Brian will make of husband swapping.'

Gillian smiled uncertainly.

'You're really lucky with Brian. He adores you,' added Jilly.

Gillian looked pleased, but embarrassed.

Like her, Brian had grown up in a council house in Aberdeen and had been the first in his family to go to university. He'd only a moderate interest in his studies and considered Glasgow a dark, chaotic place. But he'd scaled the local government career ladder to return to his home city exactly as he'd schemed it, as director of planning, residing in an imposing pink granite villa with award-winning roses along the North Deeside Road. It was the kind of home in which his father had once been gardener and handyman to fish merchants and timber importers, and later to helicopter pilots and oil company executives.

Jilly never ceased to congratulate Gillian on having found Brian. But on the rare occasions they all got together, Jilly never spent more than two minutes speaking to him.

'Pity he couldn't come down with you,' she suggested.

'Well, I don't like to ask Mum to take the kids too often,' said Gillian. 'Anyway, I really wanted a proper chat with you.'

'Yeah, it's great, isn't it? To have the chance for a proper natter.'

They each picked up their champagne glass and took a swallow then, at the same time, began: 'D'you remember—'

'You first.'

'No, you.'

'I was just going to say, d'you remember when we used to go to free concerts at the beach?'

'That was brilliant, wasn't it?' agreed Jilly. They smiled at each other. 'What was the name of that band?'

'The one where you got off with the lead singer?'

Jilly nodded.

'White Serpent. And he was called Neil. Neil McBain. He was from Wishaw.'

'How can you remember all that?'

'You went out with him for nearly a month.'

'I know. But *I* couldn't have told you his name.'

Jilly smiled and shook her head.

Gillian picked up her glass, uncrossed and recrossed her legs and completed the record: 'We walked into Ma Cameron's one night and caught him there with his girlfriend. She'd been in France. Grape picking. You had six Moscow Mules and were sick on the bus home.'

'Oh yes.' Jilly looked deflated. 'I remember it all

now.' She sighed: 'Six Moscow Mules? Really?'

Gillian smiled at her fondly. 'Really.'

Jilly reached for the champagne bottle to top up their glasses, but it was empty. She turned it upside down in the ice bucket.

'Don't you just hate it when that happens?'

The two women looked up to see a tall-enough, almost handsome man in casual-expensive clothes and sneakers designed to be collector's items.

'Hey Saul,' said Jilly. 'I thought you were in training.'

Saul held up the beer in his hand and smiled again.

'I am. I'm in training for John's stag night.'

'Gillian, this is Saul. Saul, this is Gillian, my best friend from school.'

'Really?' As his dark eyes assessed the two women, Gillian looked down at her hands.

'We've known each other since Primary One,' added Jilly.

'So you've known each other for twenty years. That's great,' said Saul, with a smile which embraced them both initially but settled on Jilly.

She acknowledged the compliment with a smile.

'What do you do?' asked Gillian.

Jilly grinned saucily: 'Saul's made more women sweat than Enrique Iglesias.'

Gillian gave Saul's perfectly honed body an appraising glance: 'You're a gym instructor?'

'He runs the biggest personal training firm in the country,' explained Jilly.

'I've got a friend in Aberdeen with a personal

trainer,' said Gillian. 'She's been seeing him for six months, £30 an hour, and I haven't seen any difference yet.'

'Sounds like we'll have to send Saul up there,' said Jilly. 'The Grey Granite City – where folk walk at an angle against the wind. Could you bear it?'

Saul grinned, but caught Gillian's frown.

'Anyway, this calls for a celebration.' He put down his glass and rubbed his hands together, then addressed Gillian first: 'What can I get you?'

'I'm fine thanks.'

Her glance was as welcoming as a shop assistant at closing time.

'Thanks, Saul. But it's a girly night tonight. It's such a treat for us to see each other,' soothed Jilly.

'Are you sure I can't . . .'

The look on Gillian's face was one Jilly had seen countless times before – from their first under-age outings to the student union to the last time they'd met up in a bar in Aberdeen and bumped into male colleagues of Gillian's who'd been so insistent about drawing Jilly into their company.

'Really,' Jilly told Saul. 'Any minute now we're going to start talking about lip gloss and kitten heels.'

'Not to mention the Sex in the City stuff,' added Gillian.

He held up his hands in surrender: 'I understand.'

He smiled politely. 'Good meeting you, Gillian. Enjoy your evening.'

Turning to Jilly, he paused, looked down, then smiled into her eyes: 'There's a barbecue at the gym next week. Saturday afternoon. I'll call to remind you.'

Gillian flicked a fleck of colour from her watch strap.

'Okay,' said Jilly.

'I don't know your number.'

Jilly shook her head and smiled, then delved into her handbag and handed him a card.

'See you, Saul.'

The two women watched him return to a group of mates.

'Bit smarmy,' declared Gillian.

'I s'pose so. Good fun, though,' said Jilly. She retrieved her purse from her handbag: 'Another bottle of champers?'

The look in Jilly's eyes was the same as when she'd dared Gillian to go shoplifting at Woolworth's, to slip away from the rest of the class on the school trip, to go into that sleazy nightclub in Cyprus.

'I've got to give a talk in the morning. I think I'll switch to mineral water.'

'Sure?'

'Sure.'

A couple of minutes later, as Jilly returned to the table, Gillian looked sharply at the drinks: 'You're having mineral water too?'

'Why not? I'm practising to be a wagonista.'

'A what?'

'A wagonista. It's what people in London are call-ing themselves to make giving up alcohol sound sexy.'

'I see.'

Happy Hour

Jilly clinked glasses: 'It's not really. It's vodka tonic.' She grinned conspiratorially. 'You know when I was up at the bar, I was just thinking, d'you remember that guy at uni who was always trying to get you to go back to his to see watercolours of his croft?'

'Alastair Macdonald.'

'That's right. The hunk from the Highlands.'

'I don't remember him being *that* hunky.'

'Well, I saw him the other week on *Who Wants to be a Millionaire?* and he was looking really fit.'

'As a contestant?'

'No, just in the audience. But I'm sure it was him. He hadn't changed much. Looked even better than at uni. Good hair cut. Nice tan. No beer belly.'

'He must've gone gay.'

'Doubt it. Not after the way he pursued you all year.'

'He only asked me back a couple of times.'

'Well, he seemed pretty smitten to me.'

Gillian smiled. 'D'you remember those guys who invited us back to theirs for a party and it turned out it was only the four of us?'

'A bottle of brandy, a box of Dairy Milk and Barry White on the cassette?'

'How could I forget?'

Gillian shook her head at the thought of it.

Jilly burst out laughing.

Gillian joined her.

Then she looked at her watch: 'Oh no! Is that the time already? Colin – you know, the senior partner I came down with – he's expecting me for dinner at eight o'clock. At Rogano's.'

'Rogano's. Lucky you. '

'Not really. It's just a bunch of clients. All men. If they talk about anything but golf all night I'll be seriously surprised.'

'Oh well. If it gets too boring, just bring on the Bolly.'

Gillian smiled.

'In fact,' Jilly drained her drink. 'Better safe than sorry. Just order champers straight off. That's what I do on a duff night.'

Gillian nodded thoughtfully: 'Right.'

She finished her mineral water, lined up the two empty glasses side by side, looked at her watch, but made no move to go.

'I'm sorry I've got to rush off.'

'That's all right. You told me you had to go on to dinner. I've arranged to meet some people in the restaurant upstairs.'

'Oh. Right. Is the food here any good?'

'It's brilliant. I come here all the time.'

'I think I read a really good review. Still, I'm sorry we're not having dinner together.' Like a cleric leading worshippers in prayer, Gillian awaited the appropriate refrain.

'Me too,' chimed Jilly. 'Next time we'll have to make a night of it.'

'That would be great.'

'And you'll have to come and stay at mine.'

'I'd love that. Actually—' Gillian reached for her shoulder bag, pulled out a Psion organizer and checked her diary: '– I'm going to be in Glasgow in October. Yes . . . from the twenty-second to the twenty-fifth.' Her fingers hovered above the keys: 'How does that sound?'

'Great . . . but I'm not sure whether I'll be here or in London.'

Gillian closed the lid of the Psion.

Jilly's smile was bright: 'Of course you can stay at mine anyway. If I'm not around I can always send you a set of spare keys.'

'Thanks. But if you weren't there I'd just stay at the Copthorne again.'

'You know you should've stayed with me tonight. Then we could've had breakfast together.'

'I know. I'm dying to see your new place. But it just seemed to make more sense to be at the Copthorne with Colin, since I'm having to go to this dinner.'

'Hmmm . . . So it'll be a slinky nightcap with Colin then?'

'If you could see Colin you wouldn't be saying that.'

'Oh well. He'll have his little mini bar and you'll have yours.'

'Exactly.' Gillian packed away her Psion and stood up: 'I'd better be going.'

Jilly stood up and hugged her friend.

'It was so great to see you. And to see you looking so fab – and so happy.'

'I'm sorry I've got to rush off,' repeated Gillian.

'I'll give you a call about October,' promised Jilly.

Gillian looked her friend straight in the eye and tilted her chin slightly upwards: 'And you know, you must come to ours sometime. If you can cope with two small children and total chaos.'

'There's *never* chaos at your place.'

Gillian acknowledged this with an uncertain smile.

'And it would be a real treat to see Cameron and Lauren.'

Gillian shrugged: 'Oh well. It's up to you. You're welcome any time.'

'And thanks for the champagne. It was so generous of you.'

Gillian made a dismissive gesture: 'It was happy hour.'

'Good. Well . . .'

Gillian turned the strap on her watch so the bald patch wouldn't show. Then she hoisted the too-heavy black leather bag – which clashed so badly with her pastel dress – onto one shoulder.

'Bye then.'

'Bye,' said Jilly.

At the very last moment her friend was still in reach, Jilly stretched out a hand to touch her arm, as though for luck.

For the first time that evening, their gazes met, and lingered. Jilly looked away first, then looked back, forcing her lips into a tight, awkward smile that was more like Gillian's than her own.

Gillian, pink-cheeked and shiny from the unaccustomed early evening alcohol, did nothing to stop a big, open smile sliding across her face and bursting into Moët-assisted radiance.

Then, like two people walking arm-in-arm who've

wordlessly stepped into the gutter rather than walk under a ladder, they shared, for a few heartbeats, a look of recognition.

'Bye. Till next time.'

'Till next time. Bye.'

THE CRUNCH

Carol Anne Davis

Born in Dundee, **CAROL ANNE DAVIS** left school at fifteen and was everything from an office junior to a dental nurse before going to university in her twenties to take a Master of Arts degree. She later moved to Edinburgh to study for a postgraduate diploma in Adult and Community Education. She currently lives in the south of England and writes full-time.

Carol is the author of three dark psychological novels, *Shrouded*, *Safe as Houses* and *Noise Abatement*, and two true crime books, *Children Who Kill: Profiles of Preteen and Teenage Killers* and *Women Who Kill*, which profiled fourteen female serial killers.

'Write about where you're going on holiday,' Miss Barrie says on the last day of term.

The half of the class whom she calls the Worker Bees get out their jotters and start writing but the Drones have mostly lost theirs and have to get pieces of paper. I'm in the row that's between the workers and the Drones 'cause Miss Barrie says I could go either way.

I get out my jotter and smooth back the anaglypta-papered cover. I write the same thing at the start of every summer: *This year we are going a day here and there.*

I was five and a half, half the age I am now, when Mum first said to tell the teacher we were going a day here and there. She said it was what people did when they didn't feel the need for a proper holiday. So I came off school for a whole seven weeks and Mum said every day that I could take my wee brother Mark downstairs to play on the washing green providing we didn't touch anyone's washing or let Mark fall off the wall.

One morning, just as we were getting ready to go downstairs and walk the wall, the doorbell rang.

The three of us jumped and Mum said that the place was a midden as usual and to throw everything behind the cushions. Mark started to put his cereal bowl behind the cushions but I stopped him because I knew what she meant.

I had just finished putting all her darning, the *People's Friend* and *Woman's Weekly* in the sideboard when she came back into the living room holding a square machine. 'Look what Mr Elder gave us.' We looked and looked until she added, 'It's his old record player as thanks for looking after his mum.' Mr Elder's mum had something wrong with her which made grown-ups whisper and my mum had popped downstairs to see her every morning for ages as the creaking door aye hings.

We asked Mum if we could have a record and she said wait-till-your-dad's-in-a-good-mood-then-ask-him so three months later we still didn't have a record. Mum sang 'It's A Man's World' and 'You Don't Have To Say You Love Me' and 'The Green Green Grass Of Home' all afternoon after they'd been on the transistor but she only knew a few of the words.

I already knew lots of words from my first year at school and was trying to learn more from the *People's Friend* when Mum wasn't reading it. She passed her copy on to Aunt Mina every Saturday, running down the stairs to meet her as she walked past our house on her way to work.

Only one Saturday Mum was ill and forgot so Aunt Mina rang our bell and as Dad was up a ladder painting the roof again I let her in. Dad said I was

The Crunch

a stupid wee bastard as it could have been Black Jock at the door and he thought he'd been given the wrong bairn at the hospital, and he came down the ladder in such a rush that I threw myself behind Aunt Mina's legs.

Aunt Mina said, 'She thought she was doing good, Bob,' and put me and Mark outside on the washing green while she went into the bedroom to see Mum. When she came back outside she said, 'How would you two like to come to my house for the day?' and when we got there she gave us big white tumblers of cream soda and wee bags of Smiths crisps which said that you could send off the crisp bags and get a record called *When It Comes To The Crunch*. I hadn't heard of the Crunch but I knew *The Top Ten Singles Of 1966* from the transistor and liked 'Bus Stop' where the Hollies shared their umbrella the best.

A while later Aunt Mina called round when Dad was at work and she brought the Crunch with her. It was so thin that I was sure it wouldn't work but Mum put it on Mr Elder's old record player and suddenly all this music and words came pouring out. 'When it comes to the crunch – crunch, it's Smiths, it is.' It was magic. Me and Mark danced up and down, then got Mum to put it on again and again. In the end we wore it out and Mum bought some Smiths crisps (don't tell your dad) and we sent for another Crunch. I had wished and wished for a record like the grown-ups on the TV had and before I was six I'd got the best one in the world for free.

Miss Barrie clicks her fingers in my face and I jump and my heart beats fast for so long that I think I'll die. When it slows down a bit, I look at what I've written so far: *This year we are going a day here and there.* Lorna is going to New York (which is in America) to visit her aunt. Clarissa's parents are taking her to Naples though I don't know where that is. 'Stuck-up bastards. Well, tell them you're going Nae Place,' Dad said from behind his wallpapering table when he heard. Even the Drones are going to Butlins or to Edinburgh Zoo or to Glasgow to see some of their many uncles. I am the only ten-and-three-quarter-year-old from Ancrum Road Primary School who will stay in Dundee for the whole seven weeks.

I pick up my HB again. *We may go to Camperdown Park again this year.* On my eighth birthday Mum said, 'I'll go mad if I stay in here and dry another dish. Bob, you can't take it with you. How about we take the kids to Camperdown Zoo?'

Dad said, 'Don't I spend enough on you lot as it is?'

Mum said, 'But Bob, she'll no be eight again.'

Dad said, 'No, but *he'll* be eight next year,' meaning Mark. 'Anyway, why don't *you* take them?' he asked.

I wanted to shout 'Yes!' but didn't risk it.

Mum said, 'The neighbours must already think we're no speaking and I'm no goin' a that way on the bus on me own.'

We were on the bus for over half an hour to get there 'cause Dad timed it. And when we got to

The Crunch

Camperdown Park it was so big that it had a road right through it and the bus drove us all the way in. We saw lots of grass and bushes before we walked to a metal whirly gate that gets you into the zoo.

The zoo had a brown bear who stood up on his back legs and white baby goats who ate penny dainties and sherbet dabs from a boy who laughed and laughed. But Dad had to pay through the nose for the ice-cream cones and did we think he was made of money and you could spit peas through that dress I was wearing and didn't I have the sense I was born with yet?

Mum took hold of my hand and Mark's and said, 'Lets hae a look at the Children's Section.' So we looked and after a few minutes a woman came along with her little girl and said we were allowed to touch. Her little girl sat on the low wall that went round the baby rabbits and she stroked their backs until they moved away into the tunnels that their mums must have built. Mark and me wanted to stroke them too but Dad was watching and we're the hashiest little bastards he's ever set eyes on so we didn't touch anything.

But when he went to the Gentlemen's Room, Mum said, 'Look at they tortoises. They could be really old.' So we looked at them too and I picked some grass and pushed it through the wire mesh towards the biggest tortoise. And when he came to the end his mouth sort of grazed my finger and it felt like bone.

I pulled my hand away just as I saw his shadow

darken the grass. 'Trust you – you can get diseases from they things,' he said in a loud voice and Mum said, 'Bob, people are looking,' and Dad said, 'She has to learn the hard way. I should knock her into the middle o' next week.'

I tensed my tummy in and backed away until I touched the sides of the Wishing Well. Mum had said earlier that it would grant three wishes but I just wished for the one thing three times.

More of the red paint has come off the HB pencil into my mouth. I swallow it down fast so that Miss Barrie doesn't notice. My last pencil had a rubber on the end and I was close to being moved to the Drones for eating it when I was miles away as usual in my head.

Aunt Mina bought me the pencil I'm using now with my full name on the end in gold swirly letters. She got me four of them in a see-through plastic case. Mark got four with his name on them too. Mum said that it was all right for Mina because her husband had died and she had a job where her boss was really good to her and she had no children of her own so it was easy for her to make ends meet.

Everyone else is writing really fast and one of the Worker Bees has borrowed the globe from the Our World desk next to Miss Barrie. I look at the Reading Cabinet and remember all the places that the Famous Five have been and start writing in my jotter again. *Or we may go on a Secret Trail, to Mystery Moor or Smuggler's Top.*

What we really do every day in the school holidays now that we're too old to play on the washing

The Crunch

green is go to the free children's show at Dudhope
Park. But Mum said not to tell Miss Barrie that or
she'd think we were all in the grubber. The children's show is on the outdoor stage unless it's rain-
ing and they hold it in the archway under the castle
instead. Aunt Mina comes with us every Wednesday
on her day off. She brings Mark and me dot-to-dot
books and wee knitted gollywogs and big panstick
lollies with polos for eyes and smiley candy mouths.

To get to Dudhope Park, we walk down the
Lochee Road past the butcher who has real dead
cows on the wall. The butcher also has a can with
a little crippled boy in a wheelchair on it but no
one ever seems to put in coins for him. Every time
Dad gets mad at us, Mum screams, 'Not their heads,
Bob,' and afterwards she says, 'You'll go too far one
day and put them in a wheelchair,' and I am very
scared that no one will give me and Mark any coins.

We go past the butcher and the fish shop and the
post office which has really cute wee cars and vans
in the window (but we're not made of money) and
then we look right, left, then right again, then cross
the road and go past the Dundee Rep where the
rich people go at night in their fur coats and no
knickers. Mum has a fur coat which Gran gave to
her but it is only for best and the best has yet to
come. I will be eleven in July, which is my second
year into double figures, but you don't get a fur coat
until you are really old. I am old before my time
according to Mrs Williams upstairs and I am a spas-
tic according to Gwendolyn who is only ten but
already wears a bra.

At Dudhope Park there are men and women on a stage and we call them Auntie and Uncle though they aren't really. They tell jokes and sing 'knock three times on the ceiling if you want me' while they knock in the air.

One Wednesday the Uncles dress up in big yellow macs and start singing 'Dedicated Follower of Fashion'. I put on my pretend smile when they sing that song and am glad I'm sitting at the back. Mum has bought me a big white blouse that I'll eventually grow into because Dad says money doesn't grow on trees and me and Mark don't know that we're born and we're spoilt useless. She has also taken up one of her old skirts for me and it sticks out funny at the sides.

'Sweetheart, you're looking hot. Why don't you roll your sleeves up?' Aunt Mina says as she taps her foot along to the song.

I do as she says, then see her looking at my arms. I look too and quickly pull my sleeves down again. I look over at Mark who is on her other side but he's not going to get us into trouble because he has on a sloppy joe which covers the marks on his back.

Aunt Mina looks at the ground for a moment and seems really sad. Then she says, 'Who wants popcorn?' in the same kind of bright high voice that Mum sometimes uses. We don't say anything 'cause that would mean we were being greedy little bastards but then Aunt Mina gets the popcorn out of her carrier bag and hands it to us, so that's all right.

After we've finished – and had Treetops juice from

the carrier bag too – Mark puts the popcorn bag over his head like a crown and Aunt Mina says, 'Don't put it over your face, love, or it could suffocate you.' I look at the bag more closely but realize that it'll rustle when pulled over a sleeping man's head. Then I wonder about causing Death By Tortoise but know I'll never find my way back to Camperdown.

I pick up my pencil again. *Aunt Mina may take me and Mark and Mum to Broughty Ferry beach.* Last year for our day here and there she took us to the beach and she and Mum sat on a wooden chair on the concrete whilst me and Mark tried to find Australia at the bottom of the sand. Aunt Mina bought me a red plastic bucket and spade and Mark a yellow one. She said that Mark was turning into a great wee man and that the dress Mum had made me was nice, though Dad said I looked like Teenie Frae The Neeps.

Mark and me dug and dug all afternoon until we'd made such a big hole that we could lie down in it. We could hear Aunt Mina and Mum and dogs' paws and ladies' heels on the concrete path above but no one could see us. We wanted to stay there for the rest of our lives.

Mum said, 'Did you see that shop sold single eggs? Toffs are careless,' and Aunt Mina said, 'They're great kids, May, but they're always bruised.'

'They fall a lot,' Mum said and I saw by the change in the shadows that she'd stood up like the bogles were after her.

'If you threw him out, the council would change the house to your name.'

'My bladder's turnin' into a nippy, sweetie. I'm off to the Ladies,' Mum said.

I went to the Ladies a few times too but apart from that we stayed at the beach all afternoon and had tea from Aunt Mina's blue and white flask and oyster cones from the wee stripy kiosk. And at night Aunt Mina bought everyone fish and chips wrapped in newspaper and a seagull ate the chips that Mark didn't eat and nobody seemed to mind.

At last it started to get dark and Aunt Mina said we'd better walk to the Broughty Ferry bus stop. I asked her if I could take some shells home to put on my dressing-table top.

'Course you can, love. Just watch out for the jelly fish. They can kill you if you stand on them with your bare feet.'

He was always going about the house in his bare feet. I wrapped the corner of my dress around the end of a white-grey blob and lifted it into my bucket, then put mussel shells and pink shells and big white shells on top of it so no one would see.

We got the bus all the way back to Lochee Road, then Aunt Mina stayed on as she lived another two fare stages away. We waved and waved till she was out of sight. It was the perfect day.

'He'll only have had a pie for his tea so don't tell him we had fish and chips,' Mum said as we walked up the stairs.

I don't know why she said that 'cause me and Mark never told him anything. We just kept our heads down and tried not to even look his way.

He was watching *The Benny Hill Show* when we came in. He looked over as we came in the living-room door and said, 'Oh aye.'

Mum said, 'It was great, Bob. The sun never stopped shining.'

Dad said, 'Well some of us have to graft to keep us out of Queer Street.'

Mum took a step towards him. 'It wasn't . . . Mina put her hand in her pocket for everything.'

'And I suppose she's going to buy *her* a new pair of Start-Rites?'

I was wearing my red sandals but knew he meant my school shoes where my toes were starting to poke through.

Mum said, 'I have to get them ready for bed.' Me and Mark had the same thought and were already out in the lobby.

'If you'd just get a job like other women,' Dad said.

Mum hurried us into our room. I knew that she couldn't get a job, as she'd had one before I was born and hadn't liked it. It was working in a grocer's shop (which is another word for food shop) and the lady had made her clean out the cat box in the back shop every day and Mum was sure that was how she got jaundice which meant she could never give blood.

'I did my bit before you two came along,' she said as she tucked us in. She was all pink in the face and her voice was funny.

'I love you heapers and heapers and heapers and

a wee bit more,' I said as that always made her smile when we were wee. But her mouth was still in a straight line so I added, 'I love you best in the world, Mum. Lorna Milne says she likes her dad better than her mum but she must be telling lies.'

'I never liked my father either. He wasn't good to Mina and me and he'd shout at us and sometimes he wouldn't feed us,' Mum said.

Dad always brings in the money to feed us but sometimes after he's gone for my head I bring the food back up and Mum says I haven't got the good of it. And other times he says, 'You'll bloody finish that soup before you leave this table,' but if Mum doesn't like it either he changes his mind.

'Night, night, sleep tight. Don't let the bogles bite,' Mum says before she leaves. But I'm not scared of Black Jock or the bogles. I'm only scared of what'll happen if the jellyfish doesn't work.

And it doesn't. I put on Mum's rubber gloves next day and get it out from under the shells and it's all sort of melted. So I flush it down the toilet but there must have been a shell sticking underneath and it stays.

He tells Mum he's away to re-tile the bit above the bath but he comes back into the living room while I'm reading the *People's Friend*.

'What the hell have you been putting down that toilet?'

I jump up. Mum always tells me to keep out of his way or run like the clappers but he's standing between me and the door.

My heart is beating even faster than when Miss

The Crunch

Barrie snaps her fingers at me when I'm away with the fairies as usual. 'Nothing,' I say.

'Don't give me nothing. There's sand and stuff in the bottom of the pan.'

There's no air behind my voice. 'It wasn't me.'

'So the sand got there by itself. Or are you blaming your mother?' He shouts for her and she appears, flushed, from the scullery.

'Did you put sand down the loo?'

She looks at me, then looks at him. 'Bob, she didn't mean any harm by it.'

His hands have gone into fists now. I look at the window but we're three flights up and I'd fall straight onto the concrete path. There's no escape.

He glares at Mum. 'Are you paying the plumbing bills now?'

'You wouldn't like it if I worked. You like your tea on the table when you get in.'

'Plenty women manage both.'

She looks back over her shoulder at the scullery. 'I've got to get on.'

He lunges at me. 'Have I not got enough on my plate without you screwing things up?'

He gets to me just as I back into the window.

'Not her head, Bob,' Mum shouts as she always shouts but it's too late.

I put my hands up to my head and turn away to protect my face but his fist catches one of my hands and sort of drives it into my eye. I slide down the wall as usual.

I hear Mum say to him, 'You don't know your own strength sometimes,' then she says to me, 'Why can't you just keep out of his way?'

'Just remember that you're playing with fire,' he says before grabbing his anorak and stamping downstairs to the washing green for an Embassy. I want to set him on fire and watch him burn away to nothing. But fire spreads and I could never let anything happen to Mum.

Mum goes all pink when she comes back from church the next morning and sees my eye. 'You can't go out like that.' So I have to stay in the living room and Mark doesn't want to go to Dudhope Park on his own so he plays on the washing green but shouts up every five minutes. Mum's so nice to me that it's like when I had the measles. She brings me a tumbler of Creamola Foam and a silver horseshoe that she kept from her wedding cake and a big peach from Fishie Willie's van.

On Wednesday morning, she runs down to the end of the close with Mark to meet Aunt Mina. I watch from behind the curtain as they talk, then Mum comes back up the stairs and says that her and me can watch the morning film on TV.

When the film comes to an end, Mum puts the white puddings under the grill and opens the marrowfat peas and puts slices of bread on the wee plate with the bonny thistles around it. I help by putting out four sets of forks and knives but then she says, 'No, your aunt's taking Mark to her house after the show to see the new baby budgies. There's just us three for dinner and for tea.'

I want to see a baby budgie and go to Aunt Mina's house where you can spill your juice without getting

The Crunch

into trouble and even put your feet on the settee.

'Why can't I go?'

Mum turns the blackening white puddings over and says, 'I don't know why I eat they things. They always come back on me.'

'We could take some seed for the budgies.'

She puts the gun that lights the cooker under the saucepan of peas. 'Just remember you're supposed to be sick.' Then she smiles and ruffles my hair. 'Look, we'll open the window wide this afternoon and pull the chairs over so we get the sun. And I got you a mint Yoyo from the co-op. Won't it be good, chumming with your old mum?'

He comes in and eats his white pudding. I know that she can't tell him about watching the film 'cause he doesn't like the TV going on until after teatime.

'I could get black puddings next week to ring the changes,' she says.

'Oh aye.' He looks down at the wee tea trolley that we sit around. 'I'll maybe knock through to the lobby press, give us a bigger recess, like. Then we'd have space for a gateleg table and chairs.'

Mum and I look at each other. He's always painting and polishing and fixing things and it never makes them better and it makes him swear all the time.

He goes back to work and she says, 'Where would I put my carpet sweeper if I didn't have a lobby press?' She also keeps the lucky black cat calendar in there which gives her the creeps but was given to us by Mrs Williams upstairs.

We chum until almost teatime, then she says, 'Oh

hell, look at the time,' and 'Go and fall afore him in the hall.'

No way am I going to fall afore him anywhere so she lets him in while I put tomatoes and cucumber and slices of ham-and-egg roll on three plates for our tea. Then we all sit around the tea trolley and I hold my elbows right back as usual so there's no way my arm touches his.

'The wee man not here?' says Dad.

He wasn't here at dinnertime either but he didn't notice. *Only if he's turned invisible,* I think.

'No, he's at Mina's. She said she'd have him back by seven.'

'Oh aye.'

I can hear them both chewing. I stare at the egg so hard that my eyes start to blur.

'They windows are needing cleaned again,' he says, his eyes narrowing. Me and Mum turn to stare at the glass but it looks fine.

'Mina's budgie has had bairns,' Mum adds, cutting a circle of cucumber in half.

'Oh aye,' Dad says.

I push the tomato seeds to the side of my plate cause they can drop off my fork and he bloody hates that. I hold my cutlery real tight and make sure that it doesn't scrape. My fingers and palms feel so tired that I'm scared to reach for my cup of tea.

Tea's at five-thirty and only an hour later there's a ring at the door.

'Oh hell, she's early,' says Mum. She looks over at Dad but he's just sat out on the window ledge so that he can wash the outside window-panes. Only his lower legs are in the living room, gripping hard to stop himself from falling back. I've wanted to push him so often. I'd only have to lift his knees and shove hard and he'd fall three storeys onto the concrete path below. But if he didn't fall out he'd get me and put me in a wheelchair and I'd never be able to run like the clappers away from him again.

'I'll keep her at the door,' Mum says to me. Mum usually keeps people at the door, at least when Dad is home.

I listen hard, as I always do, and hear Aunt Mina say, 'Can I pop in and see her for a minute?'

Mum says, 'No, she's in bed.'

Aunt Mina says, 'Poor wee lamb. Maybe you can let me know how she is tomorrow?'

Mum says, 'I'll get the *Weekly* finished early and bring it down to you.'

A minute later Mark walks into the living room. 'You should have seen these wee birds.'

I try to act like I don't care. 'Well, me and Mum watched a whole film and had a Yoyo biscuit.' I look back at the door. 'Where is she?'

'Gone to the loo.'

I wish I'd gone in first as she's always in there for ages on white pudding day. But whole armies used to march on their stomachs and they fill you up and they aren't as dear as dead cow from the butcher's shop.

Dad's chamois leather is making its usual horrible sound on the glass so me and Mark leave the room and go into our bedroom.

'We had all the budgies out of their cages for ages.' Mark takes off his shoes and lies down on his bed.

'Did you get to hold any of them?' I'm jealous as hell but I want to talk to someone.

His eyelids flutter and he turns on his side. I'm looking for an excuse to wake him up when the doorbell rings. 'I'd better get it,' I say after a minute when no one else does anything.

I open the door a wee bit and to my surprise it's Aunt Mina.

'I forgot to give Mark the lollies I got you both.' She takes a brown bag from her basket and I can just see the tops of the polo eyes.

Then she stares at me and I remember about *my* eye.

'Sweetheart,' she says in a different-sounding voice, 'do you want to take these into your room?'

I nod eagerly, say, 'thank you very much,' as I've been taught, then add, 'Mum's in the loo.'

'I'll wait,' she says and walks towards the living room. I go into the bedroom but Mark's still asleep. I set down his lolly on his bedside cabinet and put mine on my bedside cabinet just so we can look at them. Then I think I'll go and talk to Aunt Mina and see if the baby budgies would like another visitor soon.

I walk into the living room and at first all I see is her arms outstretched as she backs away from the window. Then I notice the bucket of water on the floor and remember that Dad was sitting on the window ledge washing the panes.

The Crunch

She turns around and sees me, stops and stares. Then she goes and sits at the tea trolley, picks up her basket and holds it close.

'Mum, Dad's fallen out!' I scream, racing back down the lobby to the loo.

She comes out and says, 'Oh he hasnae, has he?' and 'Kids, you don't want to see this.'

But we definitely do.

It's not on the cards though, so Aunt Mina gets Mum to stay with us whilst she goes downstairs. Then she goes partway upstairs again to use Mr Elder's phone and then she comes back up to us and shakes her head.

'I was always telling him no tae sit oot,' Mum mumbles as she tidies up her magazines. 'But would he listen?'

'Anything I can do at any time . . .' Aunt Mina says.

'You've always been so good to us, Mina,' Mum adds with feeling and I silently agree.

PRIVATE HABITS OF HIGHLY EFFECTIVE WOMEN

Abigail Bosanko

Edinburgh-based **ABIGAIL BOSANKO** is a professional whisky tasting tutor. Her first novel, *Lazy Ways to Make a Living*, published in 2002, was an instant bestseller.

It was Kirsty's thirtieth birthday. She was the only person she knew who had achieved everything she had set out to achieve by the time she was thirty. Been there, done that, thought Kirsty. She had ticked everything off her To Do List. There was no one whose life she envied and none of her friends earned more than she did. Sitting in her smart office, wearing her newest 'I-Deserve-It' suit, she felt supremely confident. The field in which Kirsty had chosen to express her ambition was Law. She knew how to merge, how to acquire, how to get and how to spend.

Such was her ambition and stamina that in the year she turned twenty-eight she not only had her first child, but started her own law practice, specializing in e-commerce business. Every sane, sedate and sensible Edinburgh lawyer thought that this was foolish, attention-seeking and doomed to failure. However, due to a combination of luck and professional brilliance, the practice thrived and the eponymous founder of Kirsty Cassini & Partners soon had a reputation for her audaciously successful approach to business. Kirsty had always been incongruous on the Scottish legal scene. Not least because she looked like a 1950s Italian movie star and the magnificence of her stilettos could make a strong man weep.

Kirsty came from a large, exuberant, Scottish Italian family, but her husband, Rory Mackenzie, was not Italo-Scossesi at all. He didn't have a drop of Italian blood in him. The most southerly blood he possessed came from Yorkshire, via a grandfather who had once been a slow-bowling county cricketer. Although Rory loved his wife, he sometimes found it hard keep up with her, to match her intensity or share her drive for success. Kirsty was now nine weeks pregnant with baby number two. Perfectly planned and conceived on schedule – just like everything else in Kirsty's life.

Kirsty didn't like surprises and for this reason, birthday presents had to be subject to prior approval. She always told Rory exactly what she wanted and he was quietly obliging about it. This year, according to instructions, her favourite perfume and a heavy gold bangle had been presented at breakfast, along with a glass of champagne. Last year Rory had uncharacteristically ignored her birthday wishes. Kirsty had asked for a diamond ring and he had given her earrings. Shiny silver hoops with a sapphire star suspended on each one. He explained that he had had them made especially for her. They were unique. But Kirsty had ostentatiously put them in the back of a drawer and never looked at them again.

Today, Kirsty was preparing for a meeting with

a client. She was feeling sick, but she didn't let that put her off her work. She had no qualms about her ability to manage a law practice and a family at the same time, having succeeded in the role of pregnant super-solicitor right up until the moment she had left for the maternity ward, briefcase in one hand, hospital bag in the other. In the long, horrible hours that followed, motherhood hadn't seemed like such a good idea, and for the first time in her life, Kirsty thought she might have made a bad decision. But she had been amazed at her ardent love for her daughter, despite the nastiness of giving birth. For a woman who had conceived her first child with due regard to next year's business calendar, who had fully intended to leap from her hospital bed to attend her new client's drinks party, all this came as a considerable shock. But being an all-or-nothing sort of person, Kirsty realigned her life's path like a planet responding to the pull of a mightier star. Now that she was a mother, there were new things to be determined about, but one of the most important was that motherhood should not prove to be life's sideways promotion.

Kirsty always worked fast – that was how she got so much done. She put the dictaphone in the tray for her secretary, together with a dozen annotated documents and three thick bundles tied with pink india tape, then reached into the bottom drawer for her Marmite sandwiches. Between the fifth and tenth week of pregnancy – the same as last time – they were the only things she was able to eat for lunch. They weren't even proper slices of bread, just soldiers, and even then she knew she'd be sick afterwards. Following her usual routine, she forced them down between sips of mineral water, wiped her fingers on a napkin and then walked briskly down the corridor to throw up in the ladies'.

Sometimes, when she was pregnant, Kirsty's schedule slipped. Like now, for instance. She needed some fresh air before she went to her meeting. She had scheduled appointments end-to-end all day and fresh air was not on her agenda, but then neither was fainting and some fresh air now might save her from that later humiliation. Stuffing a British Airways Club Class sick bag in her pocket, Kirsty set out on the short walk to her client's shop. The air was cool and welcome but she walked with one hand on the sick bag, just in case. She would be mortified if she were sick on her suit. Fortunately, being the kind of woman she was, she had learned to vomit with precision.

Kirsty's meeting was with 'Young Entrepreneur of the Year' Anna Grant, who had a business selling ambient music. Purple Heaven appeared to be a tiny shop in a narrow close just off Edinburgh's Royal Mile, but, as Anna liked to explain to local customers, the shop was merely the terrestrial base of a thriving cyber-enterprise and she herself was aiming for nothing else but dot com domination.

Anna greeted Kirsty in a warm but businesslike manner and invited her upstairs to the flat above the shop. This was a large, open-plan space, hung with the silk banners she had collected on her travels. There were purple candles on low wooden tables and batik-printed cushions on the floor. At one end of the room was Anna's four-poster bed – a bold, contemporary design constructed from metal scaffolding and made to Anna's precise specification. The bed was a multi-task piece of furniture and today it provided a display area for Anna's project management diagram. Draped over a scaffold pole was a white sheet with busy plans drawn all over it in washable felt-tip pen. Arrows and targets, dates and deadlines. Kirsty stood back to admire the overall effect. Over espresso and peppermint tea, these two highly effective women spent an efficient hour discussing the logistical details of organizational expansion. It was a productive meeting and Kirsty was able to overcome her nausea by a determined concentration on the task in hand.

One o'clock at Scottish Prosper Assurance and Kirsty's husband, Rory, was feeling pretty nauseous himself. The open-plan office was stifling behind sealed windows, the blinds drawn against the glare of the sun on computer screens. It was a very ordinary office: grey hard-wearing carpet, grey cubicles and reflected grey steel from the regulation lighting. The only colour came from plants struggling to be green, tended on an abandoned rota, doused by the odd cup of coffee, and wilting like the people around them. The twenty or so people in Rory's department felt equally pot-bound in their cubicles, and just as distant from their preferred natural habitat.

Rory Mackenzie, as the head of department, sat

in an especially coveted corner cubicle. His chair had arm-rests because he was considered by many to be a key player at Prosper Assurance. His jacket hung on a specially designated managerial coat hook and his corporate kudos was further enhanced by having the biggest banana tree in the building. He fiddled anxiously with his cuff-links – one was a little silver golf bag and the other, a disproportionately large ball. He took a swig of coffee from a chipped cup and diligently set about rearranging the figures on his computer screen. Things weren't going well for Rory. If he couldn't get the left-hand column to add up to the same number as the right-hand column, then he could forget about being seen as a dynamic young thruster. He leaned back in his chair and looked up, blinking as his tired eyes tried to refocus on the row of digital clocks on the wall. Each one showed a different time zone. He thought of the army of Prosper Assurance employees toiling around the world – enough coffee cups to stretch to the moon and back. Rory wanted to go home, to be allowed to live in his own private time zone, but it was only one o'clock, the figures didn't add up and there were still a few accounting ruses left to try.

An e-mail flashed up on the screen, marked URGENT. It was a line of bold, underlined block capitals, **ESSENTIAL I HAVE FIGURES NOW**. Rory swore under his breath. It was at times like these that he loathed his job, when he wondered how on earth he had ended up doing investigative actuarial accountancy. Perhaps it was his own fault or even his own particular fate: held to ransom by an effortless ability to get top grades in maths exams and an inability to think of anything else to do instead. And it was too late now to try to think of doing anything else. He and Kirsty earned a lot, but they spent even more. Their debt had blown up and risen out of their hands like a fat helium balloon. Rory had four personal loans that he serviced with credit card cheques. He had a child. He had a pregnant wife.

He was appalled to think that she was pregnant again. Rory felt duped. Kirsty had changed. It was as if the woman he loved and married had gone missing two years ago in Simpson's Maternity Pavilion at the Royal Infirmary and in her place was this other woman – someone who looked like her, wore her clothes and wrote busy lists in her handwriting, but who was, nevertheless, a postnatal impostor – a highly efficient, domestic fifth columnist, and all that was required of Rory was his acquiescence.

He recalled the pointless discussions he had had with her last week when he had tried to make her see that his job was getting him down. Rory couldn't understand why Kirsty worked the way she did. If he were Kirsty he would have gone home at the first sign of morning sickness. He imagined it would be worth the pain of childbirth not to have to go back to his cubicle at Prosper House.

Rory put his head down and tried working faster, fingers stabbing at the calculator. Despite his corner cubicle and the arms on his chair, Rory knew his future was as uncertain as the figures on the screen.

The phone rang, nagging as usual. He stared once more at the implacable numbers, then, with a last furious expletive, picked up his jacket and walked out.

It was liberating to be outside. He walked down Lothian Road and up Castle Terrace, putting some distance between himself and his wrong life. He would go for a solitary drink, before facing the grind of another late night at his desk. With each step away from the office he reclaimed the day. With each step he felt calmer and more himself. Down the High Street and left into Cockburn Street, and along the narrow close. He got to Purple Heaven and stopped. He always stopped here, just to see if she was inside, and this time he was in luck. There was Anna, his undomestic fantasy, sitting on the desk, flicking through a magazine, long brown legs dangling beaded sandals. Her dark curls spiralled wildly around her beautiful face and her eyes were roundly traced with sultry, inky-black.

When Rory entered the shop, Anna recognized him from many previous visits. 'Hello again,' she said. She looked at him from under her curls, making an effort to look bored. It was hard because he was smiling and she liked him. She didn't know he was married to her lawyer.

Anna left the desk and came towards him until she was only inches away. Rory could smell the slight waft of patchouli that always seemed to follow her about. 'What are you looking for?' she asked. 'Can I help you?'

Rory smiled, inanely. He felt a thrill at being this

close up. He could see the curving, Celtic tattoo on Anna's breast moving slightly with her breathing as she raised a silver-ringed hand to push back her hair and fixed him with an appraising look. Her eyes relayed a peculiarly intense message and all of a sudden Rory realized, with a start, what it was.

For a whole week, Rory did nothing. Then one night when Kirsty was out, he sat at the kitchen table, drank a few beers and finally screwed up his courage enough to ring the Purple Heaven phone number. There was only an answerphone. Over and over again, he listened to Anna's voice, right through to the end of her gently ambient, husky message and then hung up. When she eventually played the tape, she would only hear a series of empty bleeps where he had listened, but said nothing. He was restless and excited when he thought of Anna but couldn't see himself as being exciting to her. He was worried that, perhaps, she was just making fun of him. Perhaps it was all just a joke.

Rory felt his life stretching blandly ahead, an unrelieved monotony. As dull and predictable as the grey walls of his cubicle, blocking him into his desk. If he were lucky, he would probably avoid getting the sack and would last until his retirement in thirty years' time, whereupon he would probably be averagely unlucky and die of a heart attack. And then it would be all over, and what would he have to show for his time on the planet? What vestige of himself would Rory Mackenzie leave behind to show he had existed? He would pass on his genes, he supposed. His offspring might share his strengths and weaknesses. He had a two-year-old child who might turn out to be good at maths and a ten-week-old foetus who might turn out to be bad at football.

But what about me? thought Rory. On the wall there was a Family Organizer Calendar with a column just for him, with his name written across the top in Kirsty's neat, block capital letters. On a whim, Rory picked up a loaf of bread from the kitchen table and threw it petulantly at the calendar, which fell off the wall with a thump, the scheduled months crumpling onto the floor. He thought how annoyed Kirsty would be when she saw it, then he picked up the phone and rang Anna's number again. Four rings, the tape clicking in, her message in her sexy voice – only to be interrupted this time by the real, unrecorded, live Anna.

When Anna heard the hesitancy in his voice, she knew she had to keep things very simple and so she told him as plainly as possible what she expected of him. There was a sharp intake of breath from the man clinging to the other end of the line. 'But I'm married,' he blurted out.

She wondered, then, if she might have gone about it in the wrong way, if she ought to have led up to it more gradually, but she put the thought aside. Anna believed it was best to be frank. She explained that she didn't want to get bored waiting for him to come to a decision; she wanted to find out what he was like in bed, nothing more – and definitely nothing less.

'Do you want to or not?' she asked.

Private Habits of Highly Effective Women

In the long, long pause between her question and his answer, she listened to the quiet static humming of the telephone and thought of the coded electricity passing between them. His answer, when it came, was a half-whispered 'Yes'. A softly spoken crossing of boundaries. They arranged a time and a place. Anna made it clear she did not want to see him until then. And he mustn't change his mind; no second chance. He was married, so this was just going to be a one-off; it would not happen again; they were not having an affair; they were simply going to have a one-night stand for their mutual enjoyment. And if he thought it was going to be anything else, he should just forget about it right now.

After the phone call, Anna thought briefly, guiltily, of Rory's wife – whoever she was – but she crushed this little qualm of conscience with the thought that if Rory were really in love with his wife he wouldn't have just agreed to adultery, would he? No one could accuse her of breaking any marriage; this one was obviously already broken.

In the dark, Anna lit one of the candles she kept in a clutter by her bed and stared, absorbed, into its flame. She passed her hand across it and through it, quickly, without being burned, watching its flickering patterns on the wall and wondering at how the small flame changed the ordinary shape of things.

Kirsty sat up in bed with her Filofax, writing the next day's list. She turned to the section labelled

'House & Spouse' and checked the list she had written out for Rory. She hoped he wasn't going to be up all night working – wherever he was – in some hotel somewhere for a team-building session. If he were up all night he would complain that he couldn't do any childcare the next day, but he would just bloody well have to. After all, she did it all the time.

In the candlelit semi-darkness of Anna's flat, Rory was lying stretched out and naked on the bed. His eyes were half open and he was looking at Anna's breasts. He lazily raised an arm and traced his fingers round the curves. It was four o'clock in the morning and he had been there for ages. She was the first woman he had touched for seven years, apart from his wife, and she felt gorgeous. Her warm, slender body fitted next to his in a pleasingly different way to Kirsty's. The hand which she rested on his chest wore nail varnish in metallic blue.

Rory was exhausted and euphoric with sex. At first, he had been amazed to find himself there, just as he had been amazed at hearing his voice on the phone agreeing to the assignation in the first place. Now, he was glad; glad Anna had made him wake up to what he had been missing, but hadn't realized by how much. It was like not knowing how hungry you were, until you actually started to eat. Guilt lurked somewhere in the distant, logical, sensible part of his brain – the bit he had switched off in order to be there – but Anna had made him realize that he didn't want to spend all the hours of darkness desiring nothing more than an uninterrupted night's sleep. He now knew he didn't want to spend every night in a bed that smelled of stretchmark cream. Anna's bed smelled of patchouli, like Anna herself.

Rory and Anna's one-night stand of mutual enjoyment turned into several nights, several times a week. Fidelity in marriage is like a new virginity – secure in its completeness until the moment that it's gone. To Rory it seemed that his vow to forsake all others and keep himself only unto Kirsty was now about as distant and as quaint as an earlier promise to keep the boy scout law. The demands on his time were considerable; he found he had to work highly anti-social hours at the office, had more overnight stays than usual and quite a few lunchtime conferences in hotels, too.

Two months later, Kirsty attended a meeting where her opposite number capitulated to her arguments earlier than expected and so Kirsty found herself with unallocated time on her hands. Not wanting to waste it, she decided to pay Anna an unscheduled call. A 'hello-how-are-you?', good-client-relations kind of call. She would see if there was a chance of doing more business together.

Arriving at Purple Heaven, she saw that the shop window was taken up with an artfully posed photograph of a naked woman, sitting idly on a shop counter. It was Anna. The words *Ambient Aphrodisiac* were scrawled in pink at her feet. It was obvious that the photograph had been taken inside the shop and it gave the impression that if you walked in now she'd be there, waiting for you, looking just like that. A blatant publicity stunt, thought Kirsty, but she had to give her credit for her nerve.

She went in the shop and there, sitting on the counter, was Anna – not naked, but sparsely clothed in a purple string vest, drinking a can of Irn-Bru. There was swirly, smoothie music pulsing out. No doubt it was the advertised product.

When Anna saw Kirsty enter the shop, sharp-eyed and alert, stiletto heels clicking purposefully over the wooden floor, she felt a cold chill beneath her vest. 'Morning!' said Kirsty, with unnerving brightness. 'I just thought I'd drop by and see how you were getting on.'

Anna nodded and attempted to smile, but the attempt failed. She managed only a half-grimace. She had known for a few weeks that Kirsty was Rory's wife and shit, shit, shit, here she was! And pregnant. She hadn't looked pregnant last time she called. Rory hadn't mentioned she was pregnant.

'I see you're going down the aphrodisiac route,' said Kirsty. 'Useful to segment the market. What's the customer reaction been like?'

The ambience drained away into its own Technicolor vortex and Anna found she could not move to change the music.

Anna's discomfiture was interesting to observe, thought Kirsty. She wondered why her client didn't like to look at her, why she fiddled with the string on her vest instead. Why she kept running a hand nervously through her hair. Glinting among the curls there was a flash of silver and sapphire and Kirsty found herself staring very hard indeed. Silver hoops with a single, bright sapphire suspended from each one. Just like the earrings that Rory had given her for her birthday last year. The ones she had never worn.

At last, Anna managed to speak. 'I'd like to wrap up our business together,' she said, very fast. 'Could you work out the bill, please? There's bound to be a price to pay,' she gabbled.

Earrings just exactly like mine, thought Kirsty, tapping her perfectly manicured nails on the counter. The ones Rory gave me. A unique design, made especially for me. Immediately, from force of habit, her mind sought out the most unlikely scenario – the last resort. As she frequently told her clients, it was often the fastest route to an answer. A strange, icy feeling was creeping up the back of her neck and she realized, with a surprise, that it was fear. In the grip of her suspicions, the only course of action that presented itself to her was to roast the defendant and elicit a self-condemning reaction.

'I have earrings just the same as those,' said Kirsty, stabbing a finger at Anna's head. 'They were a present from my husband, but I've never worn them. Sapphires can only ever be a girl's second-best friend.' Anna was looking dazed. 'My earrings are exactly, precisely, totally identical to those.' And she pointed accusingly.

Anna realized later that she should have said

something like: 'Perhaps we share the same designer?' but under Kirsty's penetrating stare, she did something she hadn't done in years. She blushed. Not normally a very important thing, a blush, but for Kirsty, catching her breath, it counted as circumstantial evidence. The red face and a stammered 'M-maybe a limited edition . . . ?' were proof enough.

'I'll see to it that our account is drawn up,' said Kirsty, her cool, clear voice diamond-hard. Then she walked steadily out of the shop, across the road and straight into a pub. She was in shock but, being Kirsty, she was in control. 'My name is Kirsty Cassini,' she told the barman, 'and I'm about to faint. Please call me a taxi and I'd like a whisky and soda when I come round.' With that, she collapsed to the floor in a elegantly coutured heap.

Alone in the house, Rory sat in the kitchen, looking vacantly at the telephone receiver, where it lay stranded in the middle of the table. The operator's mechanical voice persisted: 'Please replace the handset. Please replace the handset.' He had taken the afternoon off work with the intention of spending it with Anna. He had come home to change, tired of always turning up in a suit, when, out of the blue, she had called him on the phone. 'I can't see you any more,' she had said. 'I shouldn't have started it in the first place.' When he had protested, she had been casual and dismissive. 'I've had enough of you now, thanks very much. It was very nice, but let's admit it, it wasn't the right thing to do for either of us. Let's end it here.' He had spluttered objections, but in the end he had accepted it. 'Bye, then!' she had said and then hung up. No lingering farewells. The click of the receiver had sounded so neat, so exactingly final, that he had been reminded of Kirsty. That, he thought, was just how Kirsty would end an affair – not that she would ever be able to fit one into her schedule. At last, responding to the operator's instructions, he picked up the phone, replaced it, and with a dull ping, it was over.

Perhaps it was all for the best. He had been feeling guilty about it for some time now. At first, the excitement of subterfuge had made his conscience easier to ignore. Then, as the weeks went by, his conscience made a stronger bid to be noticed. He had fought it off, but it was always going to get him in the end. Anna's phone call had just precipitated what was inevitable. Ah, well, it was all over now. He had had his respite from domesticity.

The front door closed with a loud bang. He looked up. Must be the cleaner, he thought. There was a thumping sound, like someone running up stairs. Rory swung back on his chair and reached into the fridge for a beer. (This was the only thing about Kirsty's ergonomic kitchen design that appealed to him.) Upstairs, he heard the noise of doors being flung open and slammed shut. Phew! he thought, that cleaner's in a bad mood today! He was feeling okay, himself, though. It was surprising, but only ten minutes after being chucked by his mistress, he was beginning to feel all right about it. Contented even! Was it, in an odd kind of way – a sense of relief? Perhaps it was time to get back to normal? Having had a holiday from the labours of family life, he was ready now to go back to work. He could face it again, revitalized, rejuvenated. He had lived a bit; he now knew what it was like to have spaced-out sex all night. Rory lolled back in his chair, smiling lazily . . . those urgent lunchtime meetings at that hotel, those nights spent at Anna's flat, in a hot and scented different world . . . and then there were all the things he had now done that he'd never tried before.

More crashing sounds from upstairs. Perhaps she was moving the furniture around? Upstairs there was a four-poster bed, but he had never been quite so attached to it as he had been to Anna's.

Kirsty stood on the landing, her face as livid as the crimson-tented ceiling of the dining room and her disbelief similarly suspended. Having established that Rory was not in any of the bedrooms – with God knows who, he might have any number of mistresses, nothing would surprise her any more – she had hauled his clothes out of the wardrobe, searching for solid proof to support her suspicions of his adultery.

She had already looked for her sapphire earrings and had found that they were gone. Kirsty believed in a place for everything and everything in its place. They were not in their place. And she bloody well knew where they were! The pockets of Rory's suits had yielded nothing but bits of lint.

It was unlike him to tidy up so efficiently. Back in their bedroom, she pulled the drawers out of the dresser and they fell on the floor with a bang. In a frenzy, she threw his cartoon boxer shorts around the bedroom – Tom & Jerry, Tweetiepie, Wallace & Gromit, the Simpsons and the stupid, stupid Valentine ones with the red love hearts, that she herself had bought him. She started to cry. How did this happen? How could he do this to her? Distraught, she wiped her tears on the pink cotton of the *Financial Times'* Black Wednesday share index, but her resolve returned when she picked up the green and white pair of boxers with the triumphant words on them: *I scored for Hibs*. Bastard! she thought. Bastard!

Abandoning Rory's underpants, she noticed his briefcase standing in the corner, where he had left it. She had told him time and time again not to leave it where it made the place look untidy. It had a combination lock. She had never opened it before, but she knew what the combination would be. Rory used his date of birth for every code, pin number and password he had ever had. So easy! The locks flipped open and she rummaged inside. Between pages six and seven of *Actuarial Accountancy Review* was a smaller version of the poster of Anna. Slowly and deliberately, Kirsty tore it up. And then it was easy to locate the briefcase's 'secret' compartment. The side snapped open and there, in the lining, was a zipped pocket. And inside the pocket, something else: a small, black, velvet drawstring bag. With shaking hand, Kirsty reached inside and found . . . 'Handcuffs!' she said in ringing tones like a fetishist Lady Bracknell. 'Handcuffs!'

Kirsty always worked fast. She believed in rapid reaction and the last resort first. She was deliberately quiet when she entered the kitchen and Rory didn't hear her. He was still swinging back and forth on his chair, a silly grin on his face. Then, in one shocking second, something was snapped around his wrist and the chair was kicked out from under him. An icy blast hit him in the neck. He twisted round to find himself attached to the cold metal of the deep freeze. In terror, he looked up to see his wife standing over him, steely smile on her face, steely scissors in her hand.

Very quickly, Kirsty's immaculate, ergonomically designed kitchen became a shocking mess of smashed crockery, sticky puddles, accusations, anger and apologies. There were multi-coloured splatter patterns on the wall behind Rory's head and at his feet lay the shredded remains of his suit. Kirsty stood at the other end of the kitchen with an armoury of hand-held tomato passata jars, pots of organic yogurt and free-range eggs. At school, Kirsty had been the only one to bowl over-arm at rounders.

'You're a lying bastard!' she shouted, tears in her eyes. 'I'll make you sorry!' She swore she would divorce him so fast he wouldn't hear the litigious bullet that hit him. She would take the house and everything in it – the cars, the shares, the cash, the designer cuff-links she made him collect – the whole damn lot, and she would sweep out of the drive in the Jaguar, leaving him with nothing but his underpants and his overdraft.

But Rory had begged forgiveness. He had begged for quite a while, handcuffed to the freezer, and it has to be said that Kirsty found that quite satisfying. However, forgiveness did not come easily. Although it was only a matter of hours before Rory was divested of the wretched handcuffs, for three months, forgiveness was withheld altogether. After a trial separation, much discussion, confession, and, oh dear, some punishment, Kirsty began to measure out very small amounts of forgiveness in inverse proportion to the adulterer's guilty pleading.

When she was seven months pregnant, Kirsty decided to take her husband back. Their first outing together was to attend a business awards dinner. She had read in *Vogue* that it was *de rigueur* for a pregnant woman to wear long, lycra tube dresses. This had made it difficult for her to climb the steps to the platform to accept a Women Mean Business Award (Legal Section), but for Kirsty that was merely a challenge, not a problem, and Rory had assisted. He waited at the foot of the podium while Kirsty basked in the warmth of the applause.

Kirsty realized now that she didn't want to divorce Rory. He had been so contrite and so eager to make amends; he was so essential to the smooth running of her domestic arrangements. Plus, it was good to have him on her arm at social functions such as this.

'Every successful woman needs a supportive man

at her side,' said Kirsty, with a fond glance down at Rory. 'Or at her foot,' she added. As everyone laughed, Kirsty noticed Anna sitting in the audience. For a second, their eyes met and they allowed themselves a brief smile of mutual understanding.

SCHOOL-GATE MUMS

Muriel Gray

MURIEL GRAY is a well-known media personality, the creator and presenter of numerous
radio and TV shows, including *The Tube*, *The
Media Show* and *The Snow Show*. She is also
the author of three chilling novels of the super-
natural, *The Ancient*, *Furnace* and *The Trickster*.

Muriel Gray lives in Glasgow with her
husband and three children.

'Ah, interesting,' said Lesley Henderson, her mouth contorting to articulate the words around the impediment of a half-masticated Bourbon biscuit. 'That must be Roger Rabbit's mum.'

The three women crunching biscuits and nursing plastic cups of tea craned their necks. A small, unremarkable, dark-haired woman waited in line at the trestle table for her own refreshment, her head turning occasionally to gaze at a wall barnacled with grotesque paintings of oversized heads entitled 'my mummy' that glared down on the hall's occupants like a surveillance device. Holding her hand was a small boy with curly hair and promi-nent front teeth.

Lesley leaned forward conspiratorially. 'Well, we're honoured indeed. Mrs Rabbit has clearly found time in her busy diary to come and see what young Roger does in her lengthy absence.'

The two other women smiled and moved their shoulders as though shrugging off invisible perching birds.

Dorothy Stevens gesticulated at Rosemary McKendrick beside her. 'Move Lesley's coat off that seat, Rose. Get her over here.'

A grey wool coat and an orange silk scarf adorned with a childlike pattern of bumble bees was hastily shifted from the one remaining vacant plastic seat to the floor beneath an occupied one. The dark-haired woman accepted a cup of tea from a plump parent helper behind the trestle, then bent down and kissed her son on the forehead. He ran off towards a group of boys at the back of the school assembly hall, his slapping feet joining the muted thunder that the boys' cavorting drummed on the scoured oak floorboards. She watched him go, then her shy gaze roamed the room in search of refuge before coming to rest on the three women staring at her. With a pause that betrayed it as a considered effort, she smiled with an accompanying upward nod of the head. Lesley raised a hand. The gesture was returned.

'Sorted,' said Dorothy under her breath.

Cautiously, the dark-haired woman threaded her way through the labyrinthine obstacle course of formally and sensibly arranged plastic stacking chairs that had been informally and ludicrously rearranged by the groups of women who now occupied them, gabbling together like startled geese and booby-trapping the way between them with handbags and jackets. In this sea of shrill femininity, only one or two ugly, gangly men, whose beards, wire-rimmed spectacles, cagoules and bicycle-clipped trousers advertised a very particular kind of personal failure, indicated that this was a parents' open day rather than a mothers' one. The dark-haired woman arrived at her destination and stood awkwardly, like a child called to a stern father's study, waiting to be asked to sit. All three seated women noted her discomfort with pleasure and said nothing.

'Hello,' said the standing woman quietly to Lesley. 'Are you Sandy's mum?'

Lesley grinned. 'Guilty!'

The dark-haired woman laughed politely, trying to look amused despite the weakness of the joke. Regardless of its disingenuous provenance, it was a nice laugh.

'I'm Thomas's mum, Irene. I think Thomas plays with Sandy quite a lot.'

The seated women exchanged furtive and amused glances.

'Why don't you sit down?' suggested Lesley, neither confirming nor denying Irene's statement.

'Thank you.'

'We don't see much of you at the school gates,' said Rosemary as Irene sat down on the prepared chair.

'No. I work. My mum drops off and collects Thomas most days. A childminder on the days she can't manage.'

'Ah,' said Lesley.

'Do you work?' asked Irene, pressing a finger to the top lip she'd just burned by sipping the unpleasant tea.

'At the hardest job they've come up with yet,' said Dorothy. Irene raised her eyebrows in polite enquiry, her head inclined to invite fuller explanation.

'It's called being a full-time mum.'

Irene nodded sagely, ignoring the heavy theatrical emphasis on the last three words.

'Yes, no one realizes how tough it is, all this, do they? Not until they do it themselves.'

Lesley snorted. Irene looked at her quizzically.

'So what it is that you do then?' demanded Lesley in a voice that was rather too rough for a pleasantry.

'I work in computers,' said Irene, her eyes drifting to the group of boys at the back of the hall, pushing and jostling by the tables where the projects they'd been working on were laid out for their parents to admire. The boys were growing rowdy, the high-pitched yelling giving way to a subtle but audible drop in key and tempo.

'Keep you busy?' enquired Rosemary with a barely concealed sneer.

Irene sipped her tea again, eyes still on the boys.

'Yes. I have to travel a lot. It's hard sometimes.'

Dorothy crossed her arms over the large breasts that were fighting to get out of a zippy-up fleece that advertised her husband's polytechnic by way of a badly designed embroidered logo.

'Well, of course there's hard and there's hard, isn't there?'

'Yes,' said Irene. 'There certainly is.'

A shout rang out from the back of the hall and then a scuffle. Irene was on her feet and over to the boys with a speed and agility that surprised the seated women.

Thomas was already on the floor, Sandy Henderson standing triumphantly amongst a small group of hooting admirers. Irene picked up her son and straightened out his crumpled uniform with quiet motherly efficiency. Neither mother nor son spoke, but instead looked intently at each other as the group of boys watched with shining eyes to see what Sandy would do next. But Sandy was looking at Thomas's mother's face. She moved her gaze slowly to meet his and his cheeks coloured.

'Buck-toothed freak,' he muttered to his nearest companion as he turned and walked away. Irene waited until she and Thomas were alone in the small space they had defined with crouched bodies, then put an arm around his shoulders and said something quietly into his ear. Thomas looked into her dark eyes, moved off, head bent, and began looking at the scrapbooks, poking at them to turn the pages with a limp disinterested finger.

The three women were quiet as Irene rejoined them and sat down, smoothing her grey suit skirt over short muscular legs. Lesley looked at her friends. All three exchanged mirthful glances, trying hard not to laugh.

'The projects are rather good, aren't they?' said Irene in a steady voice.

Alasdair Henderson didn't kiss his wife goodbye in the morning any more. Nor did he kiss or hug his two boys. For the last two years he had worked hard at making his exits from number fifteen Churchill Avenue as swift as he could manage, and now after a breakfast that had been punctuated with the usual sly, contemptuous insults from his sullen, brutish sons, fuelled by tiny encouragements from his wife, he was free and happy behind the wheel of his car. Sonya's flat had been broken into last night and he was going straight there to act as her saviour. His whispered comforts to her over the mobile in the garden last night at midnight had been well received, and his crotch ached at the prospect of the many ways he would relieve her anxiety when he got inside the small and trendy Hyndland apartment that he paid for.

He was not disappointed. She had calmed down, mostly because nothing had been taken, and it looked like kids had just kicked in the door. They took an hour to make each feel better about the whole thing and then the Alasdair that kissed her goodbye, and left for work for the second time that day, was a man who felt the world was on his side. As he accelerated through an amber traffic light and glanced in his mirror at some pathetic little white Japanese car behind him that hadn't his kind of horsepower to make it through, he felt like a real man, and one to be reckoned with.

Lesley walked a few steps out of her prime territory by the main gate and sidled up to the elderly woman. 'Am I right in thinking you're Thomas's granny?'

The older woman turned and regarded her over the top of her spectacles without warmth. 'Yes?'

'I'm the mum of one of his friends.'

'Which friend exactly?' said the woman curtly and with an accent of upper-class origin that took Lesley by surprise. This wouldn't do. Surely everyone realized that in school-gate hierarchy grandparents were only one step up the food chain from nannies, who were undisputed pond scum and not to be acknowledged under any circumstances. This granny was clearly getting above herself. Who did she think she was? After all, Lesley had made the effort to come and speak to her in full view of the troops. Gratitude would be appropriate. A snippy response was quite wrong, and the surprise of the woman's upper-class accent had thrown her. Lesley's pulse quickened.

'One of the few he has, I believe,' she said, working hard to elevate her middle-class status to a slightly higher plane with a mannered and clipped diction, her gaze deliberately leaving the woman's face as though already bored. 'Well, considering his rather noticeable orthodontic problems,' she added. 'You know how cruel children can be.'

'Indeed,' replied the older woman non-committally while consulting an elegant and expensive wristwatch, thereby trumping Lesley's semblance of boredom to a considerable degree. Lesley fumed. How dare the old cow treat her like this? She glanced over at the girls, still waiting, whispering to each other and smiling; anxious to see what titbit she would return with. Lesley composed herself.

'Is Irene working today?'

'What do you think?'

A rage boiled in Lesley's belly that threatened to affect her voice. That couldn't happen. The placid delivery of slights and covert insults was essential to their efficacy. She must remain calm. She breathed deeply. 'I imagine it must be rather hard, that's all. You know, for mothers who don't get to do much mothering.'

The elegant and expensively dressed old woman looked once more at Lesley over the top of her spectacles, her eyes and nose screwed up as though examining an offensive piece of graffiti on a wall. 'What are you, anyway? A dentist or something?'

Lesley could feel colour rising in her cheeks. 'No.'

'Then what is it you do exactly?'

'I'm a mother.'

'As are we all. But what do you *do*?'

'Isn't that enough?' There was a nervous laugh in Lesley's voice.

The old woman wrinkled her nose again and turned her gaze back to the playground with an air of finality. 'Self-evidently not.'

Thomas Barker's Monsters Incorporated lunch box travelled at least fifteen feet before coming to rest against the wall. It split open and spilled its contents onto the wet concrete. The small comforts of home – the ham sandwich and round, wax-coated cheeses, the chocolate bar and hard-boiled egg his mother had packed that morning as they'd laughed at something on breakfast telly – all lay like crash casualties in a muddy puddle as Thomas viewed them side-on from his own prone position in a similar body of water.

'Get up, you fucking rabbit-faced twat!'

Thomas pushed himself up on his palms and knees. His trousers were wet through and black with mud. His anorak had at least saved his torso from a soaking.

Sandy Henderson kicked at the puddle and splashed Thomas in the face. Thomas stood up, wiping his eyes.

'Say it. Go on.'

Thomas shook his head. Sandy's eyes narrowed. He gripped the smaller boy by the hair. 'Say, my mum has to work because she can't keep a man and she's a fucking moron.'

Thomas shook his head, eyes fixed on the ground. 'My dad's dead.'

Sandy snorted, just like his mother. 'Yeah? My mum says yours just works because she's a stupid lazy tart who can't be bothered doing the proper job of being a mother.'

Thomas didn't react. This was what Sandy hated the most.

As he contemplated another kick to Thomas's stomach just to get a response, Mr Strang appeared around the corner of the canteen block. The crowd of boys dispersed like mayflies on the wind. Thomas Barker watched them go, then wiped his mouth with the back of his arm and went to fetch his lunch box.

Lesley and Alasdair Henderson shook hands with the Reverend Paterson and exchanged a few pleasantries, mostly about the Scotland versus England rugby match the day before, while Sandy and his younger brother Andrew kicked at the gravel.

'Well, I tell you this, my old son, we'll give them what for next time,' said the reverend as he gripped the big man's elbow.

'Here now! Could you not have put in a word

with the boss upstairs?' grinned Alasdair.

Lesley hit her husband playfully. She was about to add her own little bon mot, but the reverend was already pumping the hand of the next exiting congregation member, making a joke about sailing. She composed herself and walked down the gravel drive of the church a few paces behind her children, concentrating on not ruining the heels on her new kitten-heeled shoes from Princes' Square. As they stepped out onto the street Sandy booted Andrew's ankle and he screamed.

'Stop that! Right now!' hissed Lesley through bared teeth, her eyes scanning the crowd of church-goers to check no one was witnessing this insub-ordination, only adding 'You little bastards!' when she was sure it was safe to do so. The children ran off down the street and started to swing on the low branches of a flowering cherry, pulling off the blos-som in handfuls and throwing it on the ground to wither and die. Following their progress made her miss Irene Barker's appearance from the door of a small white Nissan Micra, and so it took her by surprise when Irene stepped in front of her, her face calm, hard to read.

'Hello, Lesley.'

'Irene,' cooed Lesley. 'Were you in church? We didn't see you.'

'No.'

Alasdair slipped in beside his wife and took her arm, the grin of the village idiot painted across his face.

'This is my husband, Alasdair.'

Irene shook his hand.

'Irene's in computers, Alasdair. Thomas's mum.'

'Ah!' grinned Alasdair. 'Computers. Bloody brilliant. Keep telling Lesley that's the kind of thing she should be studying. Get her up off her bloody backside instead of drinking coffee in Fraser's all day with her pals while she spends my money.'

Lesley pulled her arm free of her husband's and ground her back teeth together. If he noted the movement, then Alasdair didn't register it, on his way as he was to slap the back of another church member standing on the kerb shaking some keys to a new BMW estate.

'Is Thomas with you?' said Lesley coolly.

'No,' said Irene. ' But I'd like to talk to you about him, if I may.'

This was good. Lesley liked this very much. She was coming to her to beg. That was the way it should be. It was the way it had to be. Lesley smiled, beatific, understanding.

'Do you want a coffee? We're just here.' She indicated one of the neat, identical, terraced Edwardian houses stretching away from the church that made up this dependably middle-class Glasgow district.

'Thank you,' said Irene. She locked the car with a key, as Lesley noted with pleasure the absence of central locking on the tiny vehicle, and together they walked quietly down the street.

'So what brought you to Jarrowhill then?' said Lesley as she placed the mug of coffee on the glass top of the low table.

'Well, I'm sure you know yourself the school has a very good academic reputation. And luckily my mother lives in the catchment area.'

Lesley sat down heavily and pushed a biscuit into her mouth. 'So you live with your mother then?'

'Just since John died. We're looking for something more permanent.'

'That must be hard,' said Lesley without feeling, as she washed down the biscuit with a gulp of coffee.

'Yes.'

'And where were you before?'

'We moved around. John's job, and now mine I suppose, takes us wherever the work is.'

'Ah,' mused Lesley. 'Difficult for Thomas.'

'Not really. He settles quickly.'

'Does he?' said Lesley sitting back, enjoying herself.

Irene looked at Lesley, unblinking, and Lesley looked back, trying hard to do the same. She really was a very plain woman, thought Lesley. The kind of face you would never remember in a crowd. Pretty enough, but so very ordinary. It made her feel good that she was considerably more attractive and certainly more notable in appearance. But then she worked at it. You had to.

'May I ask you a great favour?' said Irene quietly.

'Of course. Anything I can do to help.' Lesley hugged herself. Power was a wonderfully intoxicating thing. She knew what was coming, and she was going to savour it.

'I have to go away for ten days. To the States, on business.'

You show-off cow, thought Lesley.

'How exciting,' said Lesley.

'I wonder if, while I'm gone, Sandy could perhaps be a little kinder to Thomas.'

She had planned for this moment. It was a beautiful and delightful thing when an anticipated pleasure came to fruition so perfectly. Lesley savoured it before raising her eyebrows in surprise and leaning back as if in horror. 'I don't know what you mean, Irene.'

'I think there's a little tension between them.'

Lesley adopted a posture of placation, hand held shoulder high, patting the air. 'I'm sure you've got that wrong. It must just be schoolboy scrapping. Sandy thinks of Thomas as one of the gang.'

Irene nodded. 'Perhaps you're right. But if you could just ask him to be kind for this very short trip, it would mean a great deal to me.'

'Well, I mean, I'll have a word, but I really don't . . .'

Irene leaned forward. 'When I'm working away from Thomas,' she said in a voice so low that Lesley had to strain to hear it, I have to concentrate one hundred per cent on the job. One hundred per cent. It's important to me that I don't worry about what's going on at home. I don't like to make mistakes at work.'

Lesley was slightly discomforted by the peculiar and measured emphasis on her last sentence, but she sat back and half smiled. 'Then perhaps you shouldn't work away from home.'

'Perhaps not.'

'We all have choices, Irene,' said Lesley and drained her cup.

Irene Barker sat very still, waiting. It unnerved her.

'Yes. Well, of course I'll have a word with Sandy. But don't be surprised if he hasn't a clue what I'm talking about. He's a very friendly and popular boy, you know.'

Irene continued to stare for a moment, then got up. 'Thank you, Lesley.'

She left the room and Lesley followed.

As Irene's small figure walked back down the tree-lined road to her tiny cheap car, Lesley Henderson reflected on how good life was. It was good to be the strong one, the one in control. The one who'd done well for herself, with the wealthy popular husband, the two expensive cars, and two strapping boys. The one who people had to ask for help, who had the power to grant respite or the power to turn up the heat. It was good, in fact, just to be alive.

Sonya Fergusson fumbled through her drawers looking for the red lace bra and pants set that Alasdair had bought her, until she remembered with a smile what they had been through and knew they'd be in the wash. But curiously she didn't remember putting them in the washing machine. She thought for a moment with a mind befuddled with sleep and then dismissed it. They'd turn up. She opted instead for a black silk teddy, slipping it over her shoulders before looking at herself in the mirror to admire the way her small upturned breasts protruded through the smooth black material. Sonya yawned and went to start the coffee machine. Behind her in the quiet bedroom, the rummaged drawer remained open, and to an owner who might have been more interested, it revealed that not only was it short of a bra and pants set, but also missing were some six letters that Alasdair Henderson had clumsily composed, written and sent in the heat of his passion for the recipient. But more than that, beneath the chest of drawers on the floor, in the dark shadows against the skirting board, lay a crumpled orange scarf with bumble-bees.

Irene Barker looked in on her sleeping mother and then kissed her restlessly sleeping son goodbye before she left the house for Glasgow airport.

She carried only a small holdall as hand luggage as she caught the six-fifteen shuttle to Heathrow. On arrival at Heathrow she went directly to Costa Coffee and sat on a high stool at the only beech-wood table that was out of range of the video camera covering the catered area, on account of it being behind a pillar. The man sat beside her within five minutes. He read his paper from cover to cover, finished his coffee and left the envelope on the table. She picked it up and walked to the ladies' room. In the cubicle Irene Barker sat on the closed toilet seat, removed her new passport, the coded instructions and three credit cards in the name of Mrs Lindsey Scott.

On the flight to Denver she talked to a woman beside her who was going to visit her sister. She had the chicken, watched a movie about some rich people in a big country house and then slept for four hours. In Denver Irene hired a small car and drove to the address she had been given. The bag with her equipment and the mark's file was concealed in a log pile at the back of the house. In the car she read the file before destroying it. Cats, she thought.

Seven and a half hours later at a Holiday Inn in Colorado Springs, Irene phoned home.

'How are you, darling?' she said to Thomas.

'I'm fine. How are you?'

'Fine.' There was a silence.

'Is everything okay at school?'

'Yes,' said Thomas.

'We'll be moving on again soon, darling.'

'When?'

'Very soon. Mummy's big contract is nearly finished and then we'll live a little. I promise.'

'With Granny?'

'Yes. Granny's coming too this time.'

'He ripped up my spelling book today.'

Irene stared at herself in the smoked hotel mirror.

'That will stop.'

'I miss you.'

'I miss you too.'

The safe house was in a quiet street with neat square lawns but few trees for cover. It was clever and she admired it. He would see a car coming for miles.

318

Irene stopped at the hydrant outside his house to let the mongrel she'd just picked out from the town dog pound pee against it. She committed the layout of the house to memory, calculated the distance between the front door and the sidewalk, and paid especial attention to the garage door. Then she walked on with the happy animal, an unremarkable housewife walking a dog that couldn't believe its luck.

When he heard the cat screaming, he looked out of the side window of the study. The animal lay half on the sidewalk, half on the road, its back legs twitching. He felt his heart atrophy. The stupid fucking Americans and their fucking cars. Couldn't they see an animal when it crossed the road? He'd seen those bumper stickers, the ones that proudly declared 'I don't brake for critters' and they made him sick. They had no respect for life. For a second he hesitated. But he was a professional. He could smell danger. No one knew he was here, and this was simply a cat that needed help. He thought of Gammshead, his wife's white Persian at home, and how he would feel if someone failed to come to their beautiful pet's aid in such circumstances.

Carefully, he opened the front door, looked up and down the street, then walked forward quickly to the stricken cat. The neighbour across the road was watching him as usual from the window. He always watched. Of course he had routinely searched the man's house when he was out and found it safe. A nosy old interfering redneck, just irritated that the new neighbour who lived across the street had a better lawnmower and pick-up. Nothing to cause concern. He waved at the man and the figure stepped away from the window, embarrassed to be caught. The animal was in a bad way. By the time he bent down and gently picked it up, Irene was in the house, her latex gloves already on.

She let him close the front door and then stuck the needle into the back of his neck. His hand and arm flew up in the beginning of a killer defensive move but she was already three steps back and the drug was instantaneous. He fell, his legs folding beneath him like a shot deer. Irene quickly snapped the neck of the cat she'd maimed. It had done its job. No need to let it suffer. She took out two tiny castors from a deep pocket, placed them under his heels, then wheeled the man's body through the house to the garage and opened the car door. They could tell from the shoes these days when a body had been dragged. He was overweight and she was small, but she had been trained how to lift. She re-pocketed the wheels, propped him at the wheel, inserted the hosepipe to the exhaust and brought it round to the driver's side. Taking off her small ruck-sack, she opened it and found the bottle of vodka, the nasal gastric tube and a syringe. Inserting the greased tube up his nose and feeding it carefully down his throat, she syringed in half the bottle of vodka, taking her time, spilling nothing. She glanced at her watch. It was important he stayed alive enough long enough for the alcohol to enter his bloodstream. Removing the tube, she put the hose between his legs, wrapped his hands around them, turned on the ignition and shut the door.

Back in the house Irene checked her watch, quickly found the computer, inserted the disc and watched for a moment with mild curiosity to see what had been chosen to incriminate their target. As the files of hard-core paedophile porn downloaded onto the hard drive she raised an eyebrow, glancing over his desk and around the room at the tiny clues that told her instantly that this was unlikely to be the man's vice but would mean nothing to the lumpen FBI dolts who would be crawling over the house in the next twelve hours. It was the detail that mattered to Irene. The enigmatic decisions she acted upon without question, and the variety of the challenges kept her interest, but the detail was what kept her alive.

As the computer continued to consume pictures of inhuman depravity, she moved to the kitchen, fetched a glass he'd just used and filled it with a generous measure of vodka. She returned to his study, sat it by the computer as the disc finished its business, and then carefully knocked it over. She watched the vodka spill over the desk and dribble onto the floor as she removed the disc and pocketed it.

Irene folded the dead cat into her bag, checked that all the doors and windows were locked and secure from the inside, and returned to the garage. She looked out through the dusty strip of glass that revealed the street and the house opposite and checked it was clear. Reassured, she opened the car door, pressed the remote garage-door-opening device on the car keys and then closed the car door again. It took her seconds to slip out as it opened, and minutes while she hid, to watch it close again automatically, the engine of his modest Lincoln ticking over innocently on the other side. She walked away.

On the plane home Irene had the beef. She sat beside a man who had been on a fly-drive holiday and had very much enjoyed it. She watched a movie about wizards and elves, and before she went to sleep she took out her calculator. After this job, that would make her total savings in the bank accounts in Switzerland and the Caymans come to nearly nineteen and a half million pounds. It was enough. It was nearly time to stop.

'So, Thomas tells us you're moving on then?' said Lesley, adjusting her sitting position to the posture they taught at her Pilates class.

'Yes,' replied Irene, smiling. 'Next month.'

The stage in front of them started to fill with small boys and girls, clattering and shoving in their excitement about their impending performance. Thomas looked smart and proud, his curly head just visible in the back row of the choir. Rosemary and Dorothy came breathlessly along the row and sat down in the seats that Lesley had kept.

'Sorry,' said Rosemary.

'God,' said Dorothy. 'Nearly didn't make it. Who'd

be a bloody mum, eh?' She glanced sourly at Irene. 'I don't know how we manage, I really don't,' she said pointedly.

Irene smiled sympathetically. Lesley watched the choir assemble for a moment, studying Irene's face from the corner of her eye and registering the pride that shone there. Sandy hadn't made the choir. Sandy was handing out programmes. Sandy was only good at rugby, allowing him as it did to use his skills at knocking people over and hurting them. But even then he was only average. No one made Lesley proud. She relied on herself to do that. Lesley leaned into Irene's ear.

'I don't want this to sound the wrong way, Irene,' she whispered. 'But have you ever considered getting Thomas some cosmetic dentistry?'

'Yes,' said Irene, still watching her son. 'I have.'

'And?'

'There's plenty of time.'

Lesley raised her chin. 'Well, I don't know. You don't want him being made fun of again wherever it is you're going next, do you?'

'That won't happen,' said Irene.

Lesley sat back with a cruel smile playing on her lips. Maybe it would or wouldn't happen where they were going. She didn't care. But it was up to her if it was going to happen or not in the next month before snivelling Roger Rabbit and his smug working mum left for pastures new. But then the most intoxicating thing about power was the ability to withhold it. Would she withhold it? Would she call Sandy off or encourage him? It was up to her.

Power. She pulled in her pelvic floor muscles and relished the choice, although she already knew which it would be.

Alasdair Henderson turned off the television and took his whisky glass through to the dishwasher in the kitchen. He could hear Lesley thumping around upstairs getting ready for bed. He wondered if they should try have sex tonight in case she started to suspect him, then decided against it. The memory of Sonya's twenty-eight-year-old tongue licking the inside of his thigh quickly turned the idea of wrestling with Lesley's spongy bulk into a horror he couldn't face. He needn't have worried. Lesley had other things on her mind than the dull, predictable sex offered occasionally by her dull and predictable husband. She was thinking about strategy, about the placing and timing of small hurts and how good it felt to get them right. It was these thoughts that so absorbed her that she fell asleep without noticing that the kitchen knife she'd used to make a repulsive chicken casserole was not in the dishwasher where it belonged, but lying in the dark beneath her bed. Nor did she know that a dusty hat box on top of her wardrobe contained more than simply the garish green velvet affair she had bought for Amanda Findlay's ghastly cheap little wedding, but in fact a semen-soiled set of red lace underwear and some badly written love letters.

But then her husband's attention was no more acute than hers.

As Alasdair Henderson ripped open a dishwasher

tablet, leaving the packet on the worktop in a habit that he knew annoyed Lesley, stacked his glass, turned on the dishwasher and put out the lights, his thoughts were very far away. So far indeed, that as he went to lock and chain the front door, he failed to register the tiny breeze from the kitchen window that had been propped open with a pebble, the breeze that as he left the room nudged the discarded wrapper off the worktop and made it flutter gently to the floor.

THE SIX-STONE STACK

Sara Sheridan

SARA SHERIDAN was born in 1968 in Edinburgh, where she still lives. Touted as one of *GQ*'s BritLit talents in 1997, Sara is the author of three highly acclaimed novels, *Truth or Dare*, *Ma Polinski's Pockets* and *The Pleasure Express*. She was nominated for the 1999 Young Achievers of Scotland Award and in 2001 was commended by the Saltire Society for her novella, *The Blessed and the Damned*.

The stack was Mary's idea. She had read about it in a glossy magazine.

'It's a visualization technique,' she said. 'We need to have it in the kitchen.'

'It'll melt in this heat,' Bella pointed out.

It was mid-July and baking. The centre of Edinburgh had begun to resemble the South of France with sun awnings rigged up outside the shops and cafés spreading out over the pavements. It was the sun that really started the whole thing. Climbing up to sunbathe on the roof above Mary's aunt's flat Bella had got stuck. The window wasn't exactly small, it just wasn't large enough for Bella's frame, though, as she later pointed out, it had been large enough only the year before. The girls had lived in the flat rent-free since their university days. Now primary school teachers, they still had the luxury of long summer holidays that left them free to sunbathe at will. Not being able to get out onto the roof was a milestone. Below Bella, the daylight completely obscured, Mary had tried to push her best friend through the tiny hole and up onto the hot, wide slates. When that was unsuccessful, Mary decided that the best thing to do was retreat. She swung on Bella's legs until her friend fell down on top of her. The girls squealed with laughter as tears ran down their pink faces and Bella rubbed her ribs.

'Well, if you can't make it I'm not even going to try,' Mary gasped for breath.

When the laughter subsided though, the shock set in. They examined themselves carefully in the wide, full-length mirror in the hallway, playing with their dark curly hair and smoothing their eyebrows. Both stood sideways, pulling up to their full height and then turning straight on in the mirror.

Bella blew herself a dramatic kiss. 'Not *that* roly poly,' she grinned.

'I think we ought to measure ourselves,' Mary said, feeling slightly sick.

The tape in the sewing box was unrelenting. Bella's waist was almost forty inches with Mary coming in only an inch behind. Mary couldn't take her eyes away from the measuring tape. Her fingers twitched as she clasped it tightly at the thirty-nine-inch mark. Both girls' hearts were racing.

'Oh fuck,' said Bella, distractedly mixing a pair of bright green iced drinks with a pink straw apiece. Mary sipped as they slumped in the squashy old armchairs in the living room.

'Oh shit,' Mary said with the measuring tape lying like a dead snake at her feet. Her fingers felt weak now and the cocktail went straight to her head. Bella was chain-smoking an old packet of Rothman's that someone had left behind after a party. 'Speed up my metabolism,' she mumbled.

Over the several days that followed the girls tried to ignore what had happened. They baked trays of shortbread that they topped with whipped cream and raspberries. They drove over to Bruntsfield for ice cream at Luca's. They tanked back the beers outside the Pear Tree with their friends. If it hadn't been for the wedding they probably would have been able to brush off the whole incident with the skylight. But as it was, they had to buy outfits and it turned out that those outfits were going to have to be bigger than they had ever been before. In the ample changing rooms in Monsoon at the East End Bella crashed through the curtain obscuring Mary from the world.

'Oh God,' she said, clasping at the zip that gaped open down her left side. 'It's a sixteen. Look.'

Mary's eyes were filled with tears. 'I know,' she said, turning sideways and showing the zip of her dress, clearly impossible to pull up over the mound of smooth peach flesh. 'Me too.'

And that's how it came about that the girls realized they were officially fat. Size eighteens. The last two inches and the final straw. An unaccustomed gloom descended on the airy, top-floor flat. They slept in late, went to bed early and wore their darkest, loosest clothes. For days their worries remained unspoken between bouts of skipped meals followed by blow-outs of heroic proportions.

'I suppose we'd better weigh ourselves,' Bella said one day after breakfast.

And so at eleven o'clock on 18 July they took it in turns to step onto the bathroom scales. Mary weighed twelve stones. Bella was eleven stone twelve. Hands sweating, nervous, with lips quivering they consulted the chart that Mary had found in a drawer and discovered that they each had to lose in the region of three stones.

'But I was always eight stone ten,' Mary complained to the world in general. Bella didn't reply.

That evening they drove out to the twenty-four-hour Tesco near the airport and bought the lard. Six stones of it. A hundred and sixty eight blocks. Mary piled it up on the kitchen table. The stack reached up the wall as far as the old brass clock.

'We throw it away as we lose it,' she explained as Bella mentally divided the lard into two and imagined her side of it melting off her hips and stomach.

Within a couple of hours the stack had begun to sag at the edges in the muggy heat of the evening. The girls considered putting it into the fridge but then realized that with a fridge full of lard they would have nowhere to put the food they were intending to eat. Partially melted lard oozed out of the corners of the packs at the very bottom of the pile as Mary made low-calorie hot chocolate. They sipped it, sitting by the open window, the streetlights of the city stretched out before them.

'I love the smell of the summer air,' Bella said. 'It's so warm somehow.'

The Six-Stone Stack

Mary winced as she sipped the watery mixture in her mug.

'This dieting thing isn't going to be so bad,' she said. 'I mean, considering we never did it before.'

The girls raised their mugs in a toast. 'To bikinis next summer.'

Bella and Mary started with breakfast. Crispbread, tomato and black coffee. Mary made consommé for lunch. By the middle of the afternoon the girls were clutching their stomachs with hunger.

'Hunger is good,' Bella said, 'we're probably losing weight as we speak.'

Mary cut out pictures from *Vogue* and *Tatler*. They pasted Jennifer Aniston to the fridge and put Catherine Zeta Jones on the biscuit tin.

'I think Jennifer Aniston's too thin,' Bella said, as she passed the fridge.

Mary came over from the sink to have a look. She squinted critically at the cut out, judging Jennifer Aniston's proportions. The picture was taken from the side. Jennifer's waist couldn't have measured more than twenty-two inches in the flesh.

'It would be like going to bed with a skeleton,' Bella complained. 'Look at her arms.'

Mary didn't want to disagree – Bella could be dogged at times when she was defending her opinion – but Mary thought that Jennifer Aniston looked rather good.

At five o'clock the hunger got the better of them and by mutual agreement they caved in and had spaghetti with a cream sauce and then, consumed by guilt, did sit-ups on the floor of Bella's bedroom.

'Over a thousand calories,' Mary despaired and they decided to skip the low-calorie hot chocolate at bedtime.

The next morning, Mary woke up early. She wandered through to the bathroom, stepped onto the scales and then ran through to wake up Bella.

'I've lost two pounds,' she grinned, flush with her success, proud of herself despite the lapse with the pasta.

Bella nervously threw back the covers and walked through to try for herself. She stepped onto the scales and then stepped off again slowly.

'I'm just the same,' she mumbled.

'Oh,' Mary said. 'Don't worry. Sometimes it just takes a couple of days to kick in.'

But for the rest of the week, although they both stuck to semi-skimmed milk and slimline tonic with almost religious vigour, Mary lost a pound every day and Bella lost nothing at all.

On Sunday night Mary was occupied in pulling clothes out of her wardrobe. They were the kind of clothes that she hadn't worn for a couple of years and had been dispatched to the upper shelves because they had 'shrunk'. Now Mary was bringing them down again, trying on the T-shirts and jumpers and skirts as if they were long-lost friends. Bella was reading a book in the living room. Or at least, Bella was pretending to read a book in the living room. Really she hadn't been able to concentrate on anything for at least two days. Without any encouragement from her recalcitrant metabolism, she was beginning to find the diet tiresome. There didn't seem to be any point. While Mary had bounded around the aisles in the supermarket during their weekly shopping trip, reading the back of low-fat margarine packets with zeal, Bella had been quietly scanning high-fat produce and discreetly slipping it into a separate bag. She missed her mascarpone sandwiches and her dark chocolate ginger biscuits. She missed cooking chicken in melted butter and rosemary. She missed the delicious, dripping cheese on toast that she and Mary usually enjoyed on Sunday evening together. Mary bounced through from the bedroom.

'Look,' she grinned as she modelled a low-cut, sleeveless, green crochet top. 'I'd forgotten about this.'

Bella lit up a cigarette. 'Great,' she said languidly, raising her eyes only momentarily from the book in front of her.

As Mary skipped back out of the living room, for the first time ever, Bella thought to herself, 'What a complete bitch.' She got up out of her chair and crossed the hallway, making it to the kitchen with the steady pulse of a highly trained undercover operative. She opened one of the low cupboards and reached inside, stuffing her pocket with dark chocolate ginger biscuits that she had smuggled in earlier. Mary was singing in the bedroom. She had graduated onto swimming costumes and was examining herself in the mirror. She had the figure of a rather ample 1950s bathing beauty and she was posing around singing 'Let's do it, let's fall in love'. Bella glanced through the kitchen door and, realizing that she was safe, sank down onto the floor. She bit into one of the biscuits guiltily. God, it was fantastic. It was the best thing she had ever tasted. She reached up behind her without looking and switched on the kettle, continuing to savour the thick bitter chocolate and the exquisite spice of the buttery biscuit as it melted in her mouth.

'Make me a black tea, would you?' Mary called through, causing Bella to stuff the remaining quarter of biscuit into her pocket and jump instantly to her feet. Just in time as it happens because Mary sauntered through in a miniskirt and high heels.

'Don't think I'm quite ready to resurrect this,' she laughed, oblivious, and perched on the kitchen table.

'Do you know,' Mary said after a pause, 'I think that we should do some exercise. It'd be bound to, well, you know, speed it up.'

Bella poured hot water over a teabag and fished it out of the mug with a spoon.

'Sure,' she said, the gorgeous taste of the biscuit lingering in her mouth.

'It's so rotten, Bell,' Mary continued. 'I mean, you're still struggling. We should go swimming. If we really try, we have to be able to shift it.'

Bella cast her eyes over Catherine Zeta Jones as she poured herself a hot drink.

'Swimming,' she repeated.

Mary elaborated. 'Yes,' she said, 'we both want to enjoy this together. I mean, just because it's coming so easily to me I'm not giving up on you.'

'Thanks,' Bella managed, wishing that Mary would bog off so that she could have another one of those biscuits with her coffee.

Mary stood up and brushed down her mini-skirt. 'Won't be long,' she said with a wink. 'We can have our low-calorie cocoa soon.'

The light was only just fading out of the sky and the cocoa cups were only just drained and Mary was examining herself in the window, which, because of the balance of light in the room, had become like a mirror.

'It's amazing what a difference it makes,' Mary said. 'I was like a whale before. I feel completely different, you know.'

Bella sighed.

'Not that you're a whale. Not at all,' Mary continued. 'You're just a plump partridge.'

Bella looked at the bottom of her mug. She was still hungry and she wanted something more to eat.

'I could do with something for supper,' she said.

'Oh no,' Mary railed at her. 'No, Bell, you mustn't. I mean you're going to be thin,' she said with evangelist zeal shining in her eyes. 'You're going to be gorgeous. You have to hold on to that. No flabby tummy, no heavy legs, no chubby cheeks. No more wobbling flesh at all. Come on, Bell.'

And Bella didn't say anything because she

suspected that whatever she did say would be difficult to take back at a later date.

Late that night, when the flat was silent and dark, Bella sneaked back into the kitchen avoiding all the mirrors on the way as if she were some kind of vampire. She ignored the delights of the low cupboard, she sneered at Jennifer Aniston and picked up between thumb and first finger a size-fourteen-to-sixteen blouse that Mary had left on the table. Bella murmured to herself, 'That rotten cow,' as she dropped the blouse into the bin with a flourish, and then turned her attention to the fridge. 'Wobbly flesh,' she whispered to herself and quietly took out Mary's shopping. Decisively she scooped out the low-calorie margarine and mayonnaise and replaced the contents of each packet with high-fat produce she had bought herself. She decanted the semi-skimmed milk for full-fat pasteurized. She tipped spoonfuls of icing sugar into the no-sugar fruit squash that Mary had chosen and then shook it until the evidence dissolved. 'Flabby tummy,' she mouthed and then she sat up on the window ledge and surveyed what used to be the kitchen but had just become a battlefield.

The six-stone stack was sagging lamentably by the beginning of the second week. Ten packs of lard had been removed by Mary in the first seven days but the reduced weight at the summit of the stack did not seem to have helped. The bottom layer was squashed to half its size and the Formica of the tabletop was covered in a greasy smear of fat, which it seemed impossible to remove. On Monday morning Mary bounded through to the bathroom to weigh herself and then threw another pack of lard into the bin joyfully as she made herself some coffee and crispbread. Bella wasn't awake yet. Mary wandered through the flat packing a swimming bag as she went. They would walk down to Glenogle and do a few lengths, she thought. It was bound to be quiet first thing. She really should find out how many calories swimming used up. She had heard it was the best form of exercise. When Bella still hadn't stirred, Mary decided to do some housework. She would take out the bins. After all it was her turn. She was sure of it. She began to collect the waste-paper-baskets from around the flat, and then lifted off the lid of the kitchen swing bin, ready to tip in the refuse from each room, but as she did so she noticed the sleeve of her blouse. Her purple, stretchy blouse, emanating from under the pile of rubbish. Gingerly she reached into the bin and pulled out the garment, covered as it was in gunk. And then the nature of the gunk became clear. There were scoops of margarine and an empty full-fat Flora packet. There was a wrapper, just like the wrapper that came on those biscuits Bella liked. And down the side of the black bin liner there was what looked like mayonnaise. Mary put one and one together and got a lot of unnecessary calories. She opened the fridge. Inside she inspected the items she had bought the day before. The margarine wasn't smooth enough in the tub, the milk was too creamy, the mayonnaise jar was dirty around the top.

'That bitch,' said Mary out loud. 'How could she?'

Over the next few days Bella was somewhat perplexed by Mary's continued weight loss. The stack shrunk by a further seven packs and, usually content to let Bella work away in the kitchen, Mary seemed more interested in cooking for herself than she had ever been before. To make matters worse, Bella seemed to have developed a summer bug that had put her off her food and upset her stomach simultaneously. Though this meant that she couldn't accompany Mary to the Glenogle baths for her now-daily swim, it resulted in a further four packs of lard making their way into the kitchen bin.

'Oh that's good,' said Mary, 'it seems to be starting to work. Don't worry. I'll make the lunch.'

And strangely, it was always after lunch that Bella felt worst and had to rush suddenly to the bathroom.

This left Mary free to tidy up the laxatives that she had been grinding up and putting onto Bella's plate, hidden in the salad dressing or dissolved into the soup.

'I don't feel well at all,' Bella would complain when she finally emerged.

'Now you just go to bed,' said Mary. 'I'll bring you through something later. A little snack.'

But Bella couldn't face food much. The dark chocolate ginger biscuits languished in the low kitchen cupboard along with the full-fat Montgomery

The Six-Stone Stack

Cheddar she had bought. And by the end of the week Mary was a full stone down on her original weight and Bella was in hot pursuit.

'I know I'm losing more than you,' Mary said wickedly, 'but I think you're doing awfully well.'

Curled up in bed under an old pink quilt, Bella was thinking of taking a holiday. It was too bad she'd caught this summer flu. She was thinking of getting out of town and going to visit her parents in Perth. She would be able to recuperate there and if she stayed long enough, she thought, perhaps this whole ridiculous diet thing would be over.

And so she would have gone to Perth probably the very next week, if only she hadn't discovered the Ex Lax. Mary, needless to say, was out. She had decided to go and climb Arthur's Seat and then meet some friends for a drink and so Bella had been left to make her own supper. Cinnamon toast. But behind the cinnamon there was a small, pink packet that she had never noticed before and when she pulled it out and read the back she realized what had been going on. Hurriedly she poured herself a glass of cold water and gulped it down. This was something she never thought Mary would be capable of. It was shocking. She was being poisoned. Bella glowered at the decreasing stack in front of her as she leaned against the sink. Every fibre in her being was straining to go and deface both Jennifer Aniston and Catherine Zeta Jones. Instead she chewed distractedly on a piece of bread.

'Right,' she thought to herself, 'I'm not going anywhere except to eat out.'

And she went back to bed, clutching her stomach, optimistic that by the following day her summer flu would be cured.

Mary's degree had been in History, whereas Bella had a B.Sc. in Physics. This was not usually of any use to her in her everyday life. The five-year-olds she taught had no interest in high-blown Mathematics. However, when it came to fixing the scales, Bella was fully equipped for the job. She squatted on the bathroom floor as she had done so many times over the past few days but on this occasion she held a screwdriver in her hand as she carefully removed the outer casing. Then she examined the mechanism. It was simple. She only had to realign the balance very slightly and then test it to make sure. Four pounds. That was the most she felt she could get away with. Bella was going to see what this little trick would do to Mary's supercilious smirk. The next morning instead of a superior ten stone twelve (or whatever it was), that cow would be back above the eleven stone mark where she belonged. Bella screwed the casing back in place and caught sight of herself in the mirror. The weight loss, she had to admit, had made a small difference, but the laxatives had left her pale-looking and without her usual healthy glow. She pinched her cheeks and checked herself sideways in the glass touching her stomach.

Not bad, though, she thought to herself. And she

glided straight past the biscuit tin on her way back to bed.

The next morning, Bella woke to screams coming from the direction of the bathroom. She sat bolt upright and began to rush out of bed before she remembered and instead took the time to smooth down her hair and tie her dressing gown properly.

'What is it?' she asked as she emerged into the hallway.

Mary eyed her suspiciously. 'Nothing,' she said, her eyes darting from one side of the flat to the other. 'I didn't lose anything today.'

'That's all?' Bella asked. 'What did you scream for? It was bound to slow down, you know.'

She sauntered past Mary and dropped her dressing gown to the ground as she stepped onto the scales.

'Now I've lost a pound and a half,' she smiled, mentally making the necessary adjustments. 'That's three packets, isn't it? You could say that I've lost a pack for you, couldn't you? Don't worry. You'll lose tomorrow.'

Mary's eyes were still darting. She was very distressed. A bagpiper started up in the street below.

'Oh,' she said, 'it's the Festival, isn't it?' and she absentmindedly walked over to the living-room window and closed it.

'God,' thought Bella, 'she isn't even going to tell me that she's put on at least three pounds. Or thinks she has.'

Mary was pushing her gym clothes into a bag. 'I

think I'll do an extra forty-five minutes today,' she said nervously. 'Want to come?'

'Nah,' Bella smiled. 'I'm feeling much better, actually. I think I might go out for a walk and have something to eat. Haven't been out there in a few days, have I? Dreadful things, those summer bugs. Resilient.'

'Right,' said Mary, utterly self-absorbed as she disappeared out of the door. 'See you later.'

So for the next several days Bella mostly ate out and Mary worked out at the gym and had a swim after. And eventually the discrepancy in the bathroom scales ceased to matter because Mary came down to ten and a half stones, which was really even less, while Bella found herself not far behind, her appetite still quelled by the prolonged dosage of Ex Lax, and her need to stay out at mealtimes meaning that she found herself walking, often quite briskly, in the opposite direction to the flat. The Festival had started and the streets around the centre of town were populated by actors handing out leaflets for their shows. George Street was awash with cardboard posters stuck to the lamp posts and it was more difficult than usual to fight your way through the weekend crowds. Bella took her key to Queen Street Gardens wherever she went and was often drawn back there to lie on the grass, listening to the roar of the traffic on either side of the green.

'God,' she thought. 'This whole thing is crazy.'

The six-stone stack was down to nearly three

stones. Still oozing and unctuous, it made Mary's skin crawl whenever she noticed it. All that fat. It was disgusting. How she and Bella had let themselves go so much she would never know, but one thing was for sure – it was never going to happen again. And she'd fixed Bella. In fact, Bella ought to be grateful to her. Now she looked so much better and even though she could never tell, Mary was proud of her laxative soup. It seemed to have kick-started Bella's weight loss. Why, they were more or less halfway there and they both had to admit that they felt a lot better. As both girls glided down below the ten stone mark they picked the packs of lard from the bottom. Soft inside the greaseproof paper the melted lard dribbled down the side of the bin.

'Yuck,' said Bella as Mary got a soapy cloth and cleaned up. 'Look, it just coats your skin.'

'Better over the skin than under it, eh?' said Mary.

There were only about fifty packets left. Bella spread them out over the table in a single layer.

'Not far to go,' she grinned.

On Saturday night the girls were asked out to a drinks party in Great King Street. They spent a long time getting ready, lolling in the bath and choosing what to wear. Bella in particular, due to her extended stay in the bedroom, had hardly seen anyone since the diet had started. She wore a linen shirtdress with a pair of high-heeled mules and swept her hair back to show off her newly emerged cheek bones. Mary wore a pink mini skirt and a white blouse. As they left the flat, their low-calorie drinks in tow, it was like being twenty again and they felt close despite everything. They walked up Howe Street and along Northumberland Street arm in arm. The New Town was busy at eight o'clock on a Saturday evening, there were queues at Margiotta's wine counter and the crowds from the pubs spilled out onto the stone-slabbed pavement.

'Gorgeous evening,' Bella remarked, flicking her hair to one side.

The party was a hit. The girls drank gin with slim-line and danced near the open windows, enjoying the breeze. Mark Bevan pressed up against Mary in the kitchen and told her he liked the changes. Mark Bevan had been a particular crush of hers since college. Mary flushed. She almost dropped her drink. 'I'm going to lose more,' she said breathlessly. Bella was last seen with a guy who said he was in a play at the Assembly Rooms and was living in a boxroom somewhere down Leith Walk. She didn't arrive home until nine the next morning, stumbling into the hallway mumbling something about drinking after hours in a bar called the Red Lion that was entirely peopled by Irish comedians.

Before she crawled into bed she ditched her dress on the bathroom floor and stepped on the scales, jumping off to have a quick pee, and delighted, upon remounting, to find that she had lost almost a full pound.

She scooped two packs of lard off the kitchen table, chucked them into the bin and disappeared into her bedroom, not to be seen until the early evening.

During the festival dancing till dawn became a full-time occupation. The girls stayed up late at the Bongo Club, jeering the lousy acts, cheering the good ones and dancing until they were bodily removed from the floor. Their diet became increasingly liquid and they more or less gave up food altogether.

'I'm sure this isn't good for us,' Bella said, scientifically.

But as the lard kept disappearing neither of them complained. And finally on the kitchen table there were only a dozen blocks left.

Bella got up early and nipped over to Glass and Thompson where she procured take-out cappuccinos and buttery pastries. Back at the flat she laid out a tray, garnished it with a rose and took it through to Mary, who sat up, muggy with sleep.

'What's this?' she asked. 'A-zillion-calories-on-a-plate day?'

'Well,' said Bella, 'I thought we ought to celebrate.'

'We're not there yet, you know,' Mary scolded, but Bella just looked sheepish.

'Well, actually, Mary,' she said, 'we kind of are.'

When Bella explained about her tinkering with the scales Mary's colour heightened, but this was quickly overcome by the fact that It Was Over. They Had Made It. She jumped up and weighed herself and making the necessary changes pronounced herself perfect. In fact she was one pound under the ideal weight.

'Oh God,' she squealed, hugging Bella. 'Mind you, Bell, that was a rotten thing to do.'

And then Bella caught Mary's eye and they laughed until they were pink and Bella was clutching her considerably reduced sides.

'You learn a lot about your mates in a crisis, don't you?' she gasped.

'At least,' said Mary, 'I never took in the button on your jeans.'

'God, that would be wicked,' Bella replied. 'Sometimes you are scary.'

'Well,' said Mary, 'it's a lovely day. What are we going to do now?'

'I think,' Bella grinned, 'we ought to sunbathe. Up on the roof.'

A CHOC ICE DOWN THE SHORE

Morag Joss

MORAG JOSS completed a degree in English at St Andrews University before leaving Scotland to study at the Guildhall School of Music. She began writing in 1997 after her first short story won a prize in a national competition.

Morag is the author of three critically acclaimed Sara Selkirk mysteries, *Funeral Music*, *Fearful Symmetry* and *Fruitful Bodies*. Her first stand-alone novel, *Half Broken Things*, will be published in June 2003. Morag lives and works in the country, near Bath.

It's in the way she enters a room, for a start. She can't help entering the room as if she's absenting herself reluctantly from the other side, just stepping through the door for a moment to attend to what she might find in here. You know she's left her entourage of important things waiting outside. She's told them to be patient, she won't be long. She's left her real life like a little band of masked followers in carnival costumes with plumed hats and lutes and whistles and drums, and they're all waiting behind the door because, of course, the party can't go on without her. Already they're drooping with disappointment and starting to slump against the walls and wonder how long this is going to take. And so is she; she's checked her watch already, I saw her eyes slide over it as she took her coat off.

Oh yes, she takes off her coat, although when she's got it on she's doing more than just wearing it. It's a piece of costume too; a big statement, way beyond what a coat should be capable of. In the coat she is carrying her life, it shimmers with the story of the past she's shaken off, the chances she's seized, the success she's having. It's wide in the collar and made of some dark silvery material that makes a glassy, slipping noise. Removing it is a friendly act, a concession, I'll give her that. She's disarming herself as clearly as if she were unbuckling a sword. She is putting aside her glamour with the coat and laying it by, stepping from the life that she has now and that she naturally prefers (who wouldn't?) back into the old one that I am the only other survivor of. It's a concession unforced by me so her generosity in making it is another thing that this afternoon must expand to contain, I suppose, and already it's holding plenty. It's like a paper bag, this afternoon, being stuffed with more than it can take. It'll split.

'Mum?' she says. She says it like that, as a question. I hate that. What is it she's asking me? If I were anyone else, if she were anyone but my daughter, how could this room now be filling up so uncomfortably with what that means?

Come to think of it, was it so friendly after all, taking off her coat? She could hardly keep it on. The room's hot. They're always hot, these rooms.

'Hiya, there. Mum.'

'Hi yourself,' I say. I think I say. My voice is not as steady as hers but it is darker somehow. It comes, I think, from deeper down. No, perhaps I did not say it, for she is glancing back at the door. The door remains closed, but soon it will open. Somebody will be in with a cup of tea in a minute.

'Somebody'll be in with a cup of tea in a minute.' That was her voice. It doesn't require an answer.

A Choc Ice Down the Shore

She looks at the door again, expectantly. Was that a stray toot from a carnival whistle, a sigh, an impatient shake of a feathered headdress? She turns back and I can tell she is looking at my face.

I realize that my eyes are closed and I do not remember closing them. They must have been open when she came in, for how else could I have seen the coat? But now I am sure they are closed; and yet, thinking about it, I do not feel that anything escapes me. I know she's here. I know I am here. I know that outside a bleaching wind carries sand up from the shore and casts it like a veil over the pavements, that birds in a bleak sky are wheeling and swooping uselessly through the white of another afternoon. And I can still see this room, in my own way. I know I'm still surrounded by my 'own little bits and pieces'. That's what they call them. You are welcome, they tell you, to bring some of your own little bits and pieces, to help you settle in and make you feel more at home. Within reason, smaller items only. So I selected from a lifetime's accumulation of pointless objects a few 'little bits and pieces' to share this twelve-by-twelve-foot space with me, wondering at the same time how it all comes about. Who decides and how, the amount and the pace of this shrinking of one's allotted area now that one is old, what are the rules, I want to know? Is it a sliding scale? Forty and up to sixty: whole houses as big as you like, gardens generally available. Over sixty: smaller dwelling-units only, one bedroom, windowboxes. Seventy and over (pushing your luck by now) and it's a

single room with view of communal garden, shared
bath with use of hoist plus a few of your own little
bits and pieces. Is that it? Maybe it gets even worse.
Maybe eventually you're only allowed your bed.

There's a woman here has a soup tureen. It takes
up all the space at the side of her washbasin so she
has to keep her sponge bag on the floor even though
with her hip she can't bend down to it any more
for her flannel. She won't hear of keeping her flannel *in* it mind you, because, as she points out, when
all's said and done it's not for flannels it's for soup.
She has it, she says, because it reminds her of her
old Alloway days. Apparently the tureen is the only
thing she's kept from an eighty-piece dinner service. *I thought nothing of dinner parties for twelve*,
she'll say, sighing. She is convinced she was the
first person in Alloway to serve gazpacho. *In those
days*, she says, *a red pepper was a talking point. Four
courses for twelve single-handed and I'm talking
about when other folk had their tea at half-past five.
Even in the doctor's house. Of course the doctor's
wife, though a nice woman, could barely run to a
potato scone, on her own admission.*

I've a feeling she's losing her marbles, this
woman with the soup tureen. Myself, I brought
lightweight and meaningless things. They are all
still here.

'How are you feeling, Mum?' There's something
crawling over my hand. I move it away. She says,
'Okay.' There is a sigh, hers or mine, it doesn't
matter. 'Not feeling chatty. That's okay.'

The voice is fainter now and I decide I prefer it

A Choc Ice Down the Shore

from a distance. She has got up and gone to the window. I know what she can see. I believe I have always known what she sees. In this instance there is, in fact, no view of the communal garden because this room looks out over the back, across the roof of the extension to the drying green and the brick wall that the tall bins stand behind. There's a sign in red on the wall that says Arranview Home for the Elderly – Fire Assembly Point Only – NO PARK-ING. Outside, the light looks salt-scrubbed, it intrudes everywhere and washes out the shadows, it reaches into the corners of gardens in which not enough grows. Along the edges of the drying green there's nothing but a row of hebe, but she'll not know it's that. It's one of the few things that'll grow in a salt wind, and she'll not know that either.

Beyond, she sees the backs of other houses like this one, a row of them in another street that runs in a parallel line with this road down to the dunes and the shore. They're quite good-looking houses, large and handsome in a flattish kind of way. Well spaced out, they stand in lines in the teeth of the sea wind that comes off the firth, congratulating themselves that a builder on the make in 1969 thought a tasteful development of executive homes at Doonfoot (with breathtaking views of the Heads of Ayr) would go a bomb, and so put them here. Each varies a little from the rest in small details, so as to satisfy some aspiration to individuality, but not enough to threaten the others. There are plenty with patios and barbecues, and some have got those sun awnings that roll up flat against the wall above the French windows. And, this being the West Coast of Scotland in November, that's where they are; rolled up, redundant, with brownish-red streaks from their side fixings staining the whitewash like rust tears. A regrettable notion in the first place. There's a woman here was married to a surveyor, it's from him she knows what these houses are all about. Widowed now, of course.

The door opens and in comes somebody. It's the one called Irene, the one with broken veins like a tangle of red worms on her cheeks and a wristwatch the size of a ship's porthole. 'And how's Mrs Howie the day? How's my wee Janey?' she says. But I am not wee and I am not hers, and I say nothing. 'She's no' just been very bright last few days, right enough.'

'She's sleepy.' My daughter turns from the window and her voice is full of tears. 'She's too tired to talk, I think.'

'Aye, so she is. Here's a cup of tea for yous. She'll maybe take a cup of tea from you, even so.' She puts down a tray.

My daughter says in her weepy voice, 'Look. That seagull's been standing there a full five minutes. Down there on the green, standing on the tip of the clothes pole, it hasn't moved in over five minutes. It made me think if I looked away it would fly off. I thought, maybe it's me, maybe I'm keeping it there just by looking at it.'

'Oh aye, they're a pest. See last time there was a big washing oot? Wan o' thay gulls shat a' doon the sheets. We'd tae dae them again.'

A Choc Ice Down the Shore

So. So, I am the only person in the room who knows that what my daughter is really trying to say is that it is she who makes everything happen, or that it is she who prevents it. She wants this Irene to tell her that it's a responsibility all right, but not to worry. I may be managing to point this out. In any event I am suddenly the centre of attention.

'Mum? Hello, Mum – are you waking up, Mum? Mum, it's me, Catriona.'

'What's that, Janey, hen? D'you mind yon day with the sheets, is that it?'

There is silence. My own little bits and pieces sit listening to the silence: the tapestry picture of a girl in a garden, my Wedgwood posy vase, my National Trust back cushion, my Liberty spectacles case. My carriage clock is ticking almost inaudibly and the room swells with my daughter's dismay at finding me so deranged.

'Aye well, there you go, your mum's a bit confused. But she's comfortable, any road, she's still eating well. *Aren't you, eh? Eh, Janey?* She'll maybe wake up a bit for you. I'll see yous later.'

Some time after the door closes I open my eyes and see that Catriona's eyes are already fixed on mine. It's another thing I know, the slatey-blue film of guilt that shines over their surface, but I remember also her baby eyes and their earlier, trusting depths.

'You're awake.'

'Cup of tea,' I say, with a cough in the middle. I'm not finished yet. 'I like a cup of tea.'

This is quite true. I do like a cup of tea. When I

say I'm gasping for a cup I mean it; I like tea the way a fish likes water. Archie brought me a cup of tea in bed every single morning of our married life and every single morning I was grateful for it and I would say so, and he would smile and say it was just his appeasement tactics, anything to appease the missus. Jokingly, of course. Every single morning, that's three hundred and sixty-five times twenty-four plus extra for leap years, I can't do the sum but that's a lot of tea. I start to laugh, thinking about the lake of tea that Archie must have made, the torrents of it that have poured through me, and the laugh turns into another cough. Catriona fusses and yanks and in another minute I'm sitting up straighter with another cushion behind my back.

'Appeasement,' I find I have said.

'Appeasement?' Catriona looks round and back at me. 'Are you thinking about the war or what?'

'Tea,' I say. 'Your dad. Appeasement.'

'Are you meaning his war photo?' she asks. 'The one in his uniform?' She does seem to ask me so many things. Isn't she sure of anything? She gets up and goes to the windowsill and brings back a photograph in a frame and she holds it in front of me. It's a smooth-faced man with a thin moustache and slicked-back hair under a soldier's cap. He is gazing with rapt, visionary eyes out of the picture and away towards some high point in the distance. But apart from the implausibly hopeful eyes there is nothing of interest in it. His face is not even memorable let alone good-looking, and he is too young to be taken seriously.

A Choc Ice Down the Shore

'So am I getting my tea?' I ask.

No, it would seem I am not. She goes back to the windowsill and returns with another photograph. Full-length figures this time standing on some steps somewhere, same man but older and in a suit, and a girl much younger next to him wearing a long pale skirt and matching jacket. Hair rolled back and curly at the ends, big smiles. And she's holding a hefty bunch of flowers so I guess it's a wedding picture. I'm not so far gone I can't see that.

'Remember, Mum?' she says.

'I remember I want my tea,' I say carefully, and she smiles as if somebody's made a joke and then *she leans over and she ruffles my hair*. I let out a yelp and knock her hand away. Just who is she, anyway?

'I want my tea!' I say. It feels good to shout so I shout again. 'I want my tea. Where's Irene? Irene! *Ir-reeene!*'

Tea arrives and is placed in my hand.

I also remember this: I have one daughter called Catriona. She is in her thirties. She is divorced from a difficult man whom she ceased to please after a few years of marriage. She has no children. Now she is sitting on a small chair in this room with me and she also is having a cup of tea, or trying to. She has put down her cup and is busy pushing her glasses up on to her forehead and wiping her eyes.

'I hate to see you like this, Mum. I'm sorry I haven't been for so long.' She is now swiping at her face with a paper hanky that she has helped herself to from the box by my bed. *My* paper hankies. So it's theft now, is it, barefaced theft? Don't I put up with enough?

'Ir-eeeeeene!' I go again. On and on I go, several times, but I do not slop one drop of tea into my saucer. I fancy Catriona notices this.

'Stop it! Stop it!' she hisses at me. 'Just *stop* it, Mum! Just stop that noise, there's nothing wrong with you!' I drain my cup and hold it out for more. Our eyes meet. And then I suddenly see (in the way that you might set eyes on someone you hadn't seen for years and not recognize them at first, but then the old face you remember and the new unfamiliar one fuse together and you think, of *course* it's them), I suddenly see certain things about the younger Catriona, whose traces, even if they are no longer true, still sit in her eyes. That she was too good and dutiful a child, too inclined to agonize. She twisted herself into knots of conscience about everything. There was the Busy Lizzie she took home for the holidays when she was seven, that dropped all its flowers overnight and died; she went through a whole pad of Basildon Bond, spoiling page after page with dripped tears, writing a letter to her teacher about it. And when she was twelve she spent an entire afternoon alternately on the phone or in her room sobbing, all about which hair band to wear to a disco. She had two that had been given to her by rival friends and the giver of the unworn one would be offended, an unbearable prospect. She set out, poor innocent, with a desire only to make them both happy. She found after five hours and a dozen calls that she had promised each of them that her gift would be the favoured one.

And now I am looking again at the same sacrificial, puffy eyes. She nearly didn't go to the disco at all, but of course I made her, setting great store, as I did in those days, by seeing a thing through. Even as Archie was still thundering about the phone bill I remember watching her, laden with the obligation that being given things lays upon you, as she set off joylessly dressed up in her ra-ra skirt for the fun that I was instructing her to have and that she was far too depleted even to contemplate. She was carrying the hair band she wasn't wearing in her pocket with the idea that she could change it halfway through the evening. It was my suggestion, but I wish now that instead of providing a practical solution I had tried to rescue her from such seething oversensitivity. I chose to consider it twee and petty, thinking only of those silly hair bands; now I see there was something grander, even tragic, in her inability to tolerate the possibility of hurting anyone.

She refills my teacup, places it in my hands and I thank her, peacefully, and she smiles.

'I'm sorry I haven't been to see you before now.'

I nod. She's busy, though what it is she does I can't just this minute recall. It's in London, I think I've got that right.

'The business is doing well. Opening another branch. It's frantic.'

This reminds me of the silver coat, though just why I'm not sure. Maybe it's because Catriona in the silver coat is free from the ferocious grip of that compulsion to be kind that pinned her down and mauled her when she was twelve. Because of course all that sort of thing got knocked out of her when Archie died a few months after that. We both toughened up. We had to, in order to make do with less of everything. There seemed even to be less available air, as if Archie sucked quantities of it away with him when he went. Our lungs tightened; our breathing grew limited and we could not spare any for sentimental sighing over remembered little rituals with early morning tea, or Saturday afternoons crying over hair bands. Then the space for words shrank until there was room only for exchanges of information – the endless arranging of arrangements – which filled the gaps between our adversarial silences. Certainly we made sure that there was not enough space for words of proper farewell, never mind forgiveness, when she left home. I wonder if, when I see guilt in her eyes now, she sees the same in mine.

'Like what?' I demand. 'You hate to see me like what?' I don't really want an answer (I think I know what it is) but I am enjoying the sensation of being able to hold what she says in my mind for quite long stretches, perhaps up to a whole minute, if anyone's counting. It is a novelty to hold her words there, roll them around and come up with a lucid response, even if a little late. It seems to me that I have not managed this for a while.

'I want to go out,' I say. 'Out. Out down the shore.' Even from here I can see the cold lying thick in a patch of sky, and sense the wind. Yet I want to go out and see the sea. I must.

'Out? *Outside?* Mum, you can't go out, it's . . . well, it's not a nice day for one thing. It's really cold.'

I haven't been out of this room except to be wheeled along the passage and winched into the bath since I don't know when. Literally I don't know since when, because the walls between one hour (one day, month, year) and the next are so flimsy now. Time is measured only in the intervals between tea, and things to eat, and being dressed and sitting here and the folding back of bedclothes again, while all the time light enters and travels across this room before it slips away and is forgotten. A great deal strays from me in this way, floating between the two wide, spinning orbits of memory, and of the dementia into whose pull I have not yet irreversibly surrendered.

'Take me out. Down the shore. Please,' I say. 'Oh, please.'

I get my way, and a fine picture we make. A woman wearing shoes too light for walking and a long silver coat and glasses, puffing along behind a wheelchair holding a doolally old bat wrapped up in enough rugs for four people (you've never seen so much tartan mohair on one person). Although we could hardly look more different on the surface, I suspect that Catriona and I wear the same look of concentration on our faces; we are a unit. We are women with a mission. But there is nobody to notice or comment. We make our way down the deserted pavement of black tarmac into which, when it was being laid, white pebbles were thrown, one supposes for decoration. There's an assumption in it; that people will be walking with their heads down, inclined to notice a little aesthetic touch like a dotted pavement. It's a thing I have seen only in Scotland. It has always seemed foolish to me and in dubious taste but Archie used to say it raises an area. He knew about things like that. He was a surveyor, did I say? I've a notion Catriona's one as well. She was close to her dad.

Down past the end of the houses there's a path behind the dunes that's wide enough for the wheels. All I do is wave towards it and Catriona understands. Though the path rises and falls, she does not complain and on we go, it seems to me for a long time. We pass a man carrying a dog lead and he says 'afternoon', although not to me. Soon after that I nod off, I think. Then I can hear Catriona's breathing behind me, and when we stop I suddenly hear how far we have come and how alone we are. I hear the wash of the sea rasping sadly up the beach and sucking the shingle back; it seems that the pull of the tide itself is stretching into the air, yearning to become a sound, a sight, something describable. Catriona turns the wheelchair, and parks me facing the water. She comes round and stoops in front of me, takes another of my paper hankies, wipes a slick of drool away from my mouth and adjusts my hat. Behind her the sea and the sky are of no colour at all, as if the wind is blowing the colours right off their surfaces like dust.

A Choc Ice Down the Shore

'I'm sorry,' she says, and wipes my eyes, for tears are running from them. It's the wind does it, I suppose. I look at her in surprise.

'For keeping away.'

'Oh, you're busy, I remember that,' I croak. Who she is nearly swims away. I grab her back and concentrate. 'Is it Glasgow you stay?'

'London. I'm in London now. Anyway I don't mean that kind of keeping away, not just that. I mean I'm sorry, you and I . . . I mean, you never got over Dad, did you, Mum?'

Behind her a silver line has appeared between the sea and the sky. I can see that, even through tears. You get that here, sometimes.

'Do I know here? Have I been here before?'

'This is Greenan Shore, Mum, remember? You brought me here loads of times. You and Dad. Not remember the castle?' She points across the curve of the beach and there it sits, a pile of rubble and half a tower, an awful-looking thing. I don't.

'Do you remember, Mum,' she is asking in a quieter voice, 'd'you not remember we scattered the ashes in the sea? Dad's ashes.' She dabs at my cheeks with the hanky again. 'I know you thought the world of him. I know you never got over it, Mum.'

I never considered getting over it. My Archie. Fourteen years older than me and already thirty-eight when we got married, he'd been waiting for perfection, he said. I was his gorgeous girl, his wee bombshell. I was neat and good-looking. I'd been living in Glasgow, I knew how to dress. I learned how to turn a house to best advantage, how to garden and sew. I learned how to entertain. Oh, we were the golden couple all right. I wanted to keep it that way. I learned how not to fall pregnant (I truly thought of it as a fall) so that I could stay his gorgeous girl, his bombshell. In those days it was called keeping your figure, and it worked for twelve years. Archie just thought it wasn't meant to be, us having children.

'The thing is, Mum. The thing is, that night, the day he died, before Auntie Sheila came. I heard you. You cried and walked about your room the whole night. It sounded like you were in pain, I mean physically, in real agony. You cried all night, and I heard you, and I kept away. It was too much for me. I could've knocked on your door but I kept away.'

Archie was beside himself with joy when his daughter was born. So was I; I was shocked by my happiness. He was already fifty and I was thirty-six; that was old for a baby, then. Our daughter made us wonderful to each other, even amid the tumult and the hard work of it. When I saw that was how it was, I realized I had done something very wrong. I tried to atone. But even while I did my best to be a good mother and wrap us all up in the happy family stuff – trips to Greenan Shore and running up skirts for discos and all the rest of it – I knew I would not be allowed to get away with it.

Archie dropped dead of a heart attack. He dropped dead and his daughter was not yet thirteen. If I had not been so selfish, he would have known his child longer and she would have had a father to ease her on her way forwards, towards her own life. He would have relieved her of some of the sorrow that comes with leaving childhood. As it was, she was flung out of it in the course of a single day when she was twelve years old, and that was my fault. I must tell them what I did, that's what I must do. I must confess it to them so that I can hear them forgive me and say it doesn't matter.

Mind you, this girl is not twelve.

'How old are you now?'

'I'm thirty-six, Mum.'

'I'm sorry. I'm awful sorry.' If she's thirty-six that means Archie really is dead. I can't talk to him. He died before she was thirteen.

She says, 'I can live with it, Mum. I don't mind.'

'You know, your Dad, he never got over you. He thought the world of you. We both did.'

'I was just ordinary.'

'Oh no. You were not. Do you not remember, how you couldn't have anybody's feelings hurt? You always had to rush in and stop anybody getting upset, as if it was all up to you. You took it upon yourself.'

'I did, didn't I? I don't any more.'

'I'm sorry.'

'Oh well. It's one of those things you learn, isn't it? You can't make everything nice for everybody. I can live with it.'

She looks at me and I see that she can. There is a kind of gleam of strength and knowledge coming off her, and of course she is right. The night she lay awake listening to me she learned the sorrowful truth, that sometimes we are powerless and solitary. It grieves me that she learned it so early, and from me, but in the end who better to teach her, who else to show her that hearts do break?

'Mum, do you forgive me? For staying away the night he died?'

'But you weren't even thirteen. That's what it was all about, you should have had your dad longer. Oh, I was crying for me, but for that too. If anybody needs forgiving—'

My hands are like two blue-brown roots but she takes hold of them and rubs them.

'I love you, Mum.'

I am from Ayrshire where we are not given to that kind of talk. I say, 'Och away, your hands are freezing.'

But then I lift her hand and place it against my lips. 'I love you, too.' Her hand is a narrow thing without the swellings, like crocus bulbs just beneath the skin, that bulge out of my own. 'Catriona shiver-shins.'

I used to call her that, when we came here, Archie and Catriona and me. After she'd been in the water she'd just stand there shuddering and her eyes glassy with cold, and I would wrap her in a towel that was never quite big enough, strip the swimsuit off her and take her violent-pink-and-blue-patched hands with sand clinging to them and rub them and put them against my lips. I could taste the salt on them; I would blow a big raspberry on the backs of her hands and I would say, 'Catriona shiver-shins. Are you cold enough yet? Ready for a choc ice?'

A Choc Ice Down the Shore

And the thing was she always was. But I would have a thermos, and banana sandwiches in a paper bag, and I would make her drink something hot and eat a sandwich first (you shouldn't chill a child's stomach straight after bathing) while Archie went along the sand to the kiosk at the castle.

Today she laughs and says, 'You're *kidding*! A *choc ice*? On a day like this? I doubt if the kiosk's still there.'

It isn't. But when we get back from the dune path to the start of the roads of houses, the houses that were going up all during those years we came to the beach, Catriona heads away from the sea up a wide street where now there's a caravan park and a garage that sells choc ices. Then we trundle back, and Catriona finds a bench on the edge of the empty car park at the seafront. She sets me beside her and we sit with our choc ices, looking out while gulls twist down from the air and land near us. They poke around shamelessly, bigger than they should be. The silver line where the sea ends and the sky begins is still there.

Catriona points and says, 'That's Ailsa Craig, remember Ailsa Craig?' and I do. And I remember the Heads of Ayr, and Arran. She is clearly impressed.

Then, as sometimes happens here, the sky splits and shows not sun, but a simple rag of blue. Out of it spills light that falls over the water from horizon to shore in a widening, vibrating path of cracked and broken stars. It feels like the reason we came and sat waiting here in the wind.

'Would you look at that,' Catriona says.

At the sound of her voice I turn and wonder who she is. I feel as if I have made a mistake, no, several mistakes. I have wandered too far. For my own amusement I threw myself into the randomness of a dream in which anyone might be just anyone, and now I cannot get out, the wind is too loud in my ears and I cannot think in all this mayhem. Anything at all could happen, and here I am in the centre of the action without in the least understanding it. I am the star of its chaos. Then it's Catriona again and I sigh with relief.

'See the tureen? Take it with you when you go. I've no use for it.'

'The tureen? But you're fond of it. I wouldn't use it.'

'Och, you've got the rest of the set. You take it, I want you to have it now.'

I like a choc ice. But I am too tired to manage all of it, and Catriona has to take the sticky mess from me before it collapses out of the wrapper into my lap. She spits on her hanky and wipes my fingers. Then she removes the last frozen, melting glob of ice cream from the floor of my open mouth, wraps it in a tissue and looks for a litter bin.

'Time to go,' she says, and pulls up the wheel-chair brake.

'Time to go,' I agree.

Now I keep my head lowered as Catriona bowls us along, and when we reach the road going back up to Arranview Home for the Elderly I watch the white stones set in the black tarmac skim past beneath the lumps of my feet planted on the footrest. It's ridiculous. Why go to that trouble over a pavement?

'Run,' I say, and close my eyes.

'*What?*'

'Go faster. I want to go faster. Run!'

'Oh *Jesus*, Mum!'

And she groans, but I feel a surge through my back and my head lolls with the sudden push of speed. I open my eyes and look down, and then finally I see the point of the pebbles in the road. There is a point to them at last, a point no less ridiculous than the very fact of their presence but point enough, anyway, for me. Because they are, I decide, not pebbles but stars, stars whole and broken, constellations of white stars strung out across the pavement for us, strewn at random into boiling black stew and now fixed while we lumber along and leave them behind. I close my eyes and quickly open them again, and suddenly we are running through a blackness so thick and deep you could tar roads with it, we are propelling ourselves up the road and into the stars, away from frozen car parks and litter bins, away from rooms, houses, pavements; away even from the untidiness of things left too long unsaid and from our shame at our own shortcomings. We are splitting away from our pathetic inability, until the last possible moment, to talk of love. We are separating, thank God, from life and arrangements and pain and joy. I keep my eyes fixed on the ground. I hear Catriona's quick heavy footsteps and her breathing at my back. And the fun of it! Oh, the whole fun of it is they have disguised the stars as *stones*, just to have you believe that all that's happening is you're getting wheeled back up Ailsa Drive after a wee bit of afternoon air and a choc ice down the shore!

But Catriona is spinning me out of raw winter afternoons with the sting of sand and ashes cast by the wind, out of time itself, and I have no age, no weight, no grief, no ending; I am beyond all these. I am free, at last, of my own little bits and pieces. This is such a thrill I give a shout and remember that I still have hands. I pull them from my lap to see if I can clap them, pushing away their mohair wrapping which catches in the wind and sails away. Catriona snatches the scarf out of the air without breaking step and on we go. She tells me cheerfully I'm terrible and over my shoulder she starts up a song that I think is 'Step We Gaily'. We both laugh. I wet myself, I think.

Time to go.

I shall go at some point after Catriona leaves today. Maybe I will go in the next hour or two, or in a day, a month, a year from now. Maybe it will be in the night, or it may be at a time when sunlight slants through the window and falls across my shins while I lie under the bedclothes. Maybe I will go when Irene is in the room taking away a cup and saucer or lifting the sponge bag next to the basin while she wipes round. Maybe the very next time a seagull lands on the tip of the clothes pole on the drying green, the old woman in the upstairs back room will finally go. Whenever it is, I have the feeling that it will be unceremonious, even modest, but at a time of my choosing.

And after I am gone they will discuss me as they strip the linen off the bed and fold the blankets for the laundry, and they will say, 'Right enough, she was ready to go.'

'Seemingly she never got over the husband.'

'She was awful wandered, poor soul.'

'She was a character, though. Mind her and that bloody tureen?'

'It's a shame the daughter couldn't get here a bit more often.'

They will say the last thing behind her back, of course. But Catriona, sensing something of the sort in the air when she comes to collect my little bits and pieces, will tell them, 'The last time I saw her she knew me. That last time when I took her out down the shore and we had a choc ice and she made me run her back up the road? She enjoyed herself. She knew exactly who I was.'

YOUR TIME IS UP

Tania Kindersley

Born and brought up in the Lambourn Valley near Newbury, **TANIA KINDERSLEY** moved to the north-east of Scotland in 1997. She is the author of several bestselling novels including, most recently, *Nothing to Lose, Elvis Has Left the Building, Don't Ask Me Why* and *Goodbye Johnny Thunders*.

You called me yesterday. You said: 'I wanted to ask you what vicissitudes means.'

You know exactly what vicissitudes means. You are highly educated and you cross-examine people for a living; you wear a wig and gown for your work and I am the only one who finds that strange.

You said: 'You never call me any more.'

I said, heavy and blunt with irony, 'I wonder why that is.'

'Vicissitudes,' you said, and there was something sad in your voice. But not sad enough.

'Wilf,' I said. 'What did she do? Run off with a judge?'

It was six months on from that lost weekend, that stranded weekend when the snow came. The world outside my window is green now, and the white land is a falling memory. I remember too much. I remember everything that was said in those close, white days; I wish I didn't.

We had all been together for eighteen years, the six of us – how could it be that long? That was what we said; we had grown obsessed with time in our middle thirties, time was something strange and alien to us now; we were old but we felt young, or the other way round; we could never work out where those years had gone.

Eighteen years, and we thought we knew each other better than our own hands. Fernanda was there, that weekend, still wearing her outlandish name like an expensive coat; Fernanda, who used to be the wildest of us all, who once drove flat across America in an old yellow Chevvy and stopped off in Las Vegas to play the tables, and married Peter, her teenage sweetheart, in a cut-price chapel with a fat-period Elvis doing the honours, and the organist so drunk on tequila that he played 'Thanks for the Memories' instead of 'Here Comes the Bride'.

Peter was never wild, he only wanted to save the world; he marched and protested and got up petitions, and then one day he discovered money and all other drugs of choice went out of the window. Peter, the quiet revolutionary, made money, capital M Money, big cash, the kind you can't ever spend; my God, he made money; he piled it up until it had nowhere else to go, and then he made some more just for the hell of it, because he could, and Fernanda stopped writing and lost all that wildness that lived in her and became a trophy wife, which wasn't something any of the rest of us had ever seen up close.

Dino was there, still sexually confused, eternally promiscuous, wearing his one red shirt all weekend, because he had no money to buy another; Dino, who had been to bed with most of us at some time or another, and sometimes liked to make trouble about it. Ellie was at his side, his perpetual shadow, laughing at his jokes, the dark circles under her eyes cast into contrast by the thin pallor of her face and the black of her hair. Ellie was haunted by ghosts: a lost cousin, dead from drowning when they were fourteen, washed off a rock in northern France by a freak wave; later, as if fate hadn't done with her yet, the man she would have married drove his car into a stone wall in Ireland and was killed on impact. She was left with Dino, and they said that one day they might settle down together and have one of those alternative families that the tabloid newspapers hate so much.

Wilf was there, another one with an unlikely name; his father had been obsessed by the war poets, and sat all night drinking whisky and reading Wilfred Owen, hating himself because he had not been old enough for the second war. He joined up the day before the Armistice, so there was no action left for him, and for the rest of his life he felt he had failed. So Wilf got a dead name and an inheritance of debts and bitterness and pushed himself through law school and made words his weapons against an uncertain world. Or that was what he said. I sometimes thought he just liked dressing up in the preposterous clothes.

And I was there, because that was where I lived, high up in the north-east of Scotland, where the winters were long and low and spring never seemed to come. I was the writer, the one who was supposed to make sense of it all.

* * *

'I'm not going to answer that question,' you said.

'No,' I said. I suddenly hated you very much. 'Don't answer anything. Claim your constitutional rights. Just go on.'

'Six months,' you said, 'without a word.'

'Words are your business,' I said. 'You know how to bend and break the truth with plausible and professional language. I'm not playing that game any more. I'm tired of it, and I'm not playing.'

The first two days were just another weekend; old friends, who didn't see each other often enough because of time and distance and ambition and change, coming together and drinking and smoking and eating and staying up late. My high stone house with its scarlet carpets and white walls rang with laughter and remembering, and we were having a fine time. There were all the unspoken things, but that didn't seem to matter, we were used to that. We knew, with a certain delicacy, that there were things we needed to forget or ignore or bury, now we were of that age when nothing is very simple any more. Or perhaps it was just me who thought that.

The snow came in the night. It wasn't forecast, but it did that sometimes, blew in from the west without warning. I knew it before I opened my eyes on Sunday morning; I could feel the whiteness of it over my eyelids and smell the metal smell of it coming through the open window. We had drunk bourbon the night before, which was not something we did much any more, we were too old for the pain. My head was heavy and for a moment I thought Wilf was in the bed with me, and I reached out my arm for him, but the sheets were taut and empty. I felt a falling regret in my stomach before I could check it (*you know better than this, you should be better than this*, said the chattering voices in my head) and I opened my eyes onto the day to dispel it.

Wilf was the first one I ever loved, that tired old chestnut, the first love you never forget. He was angry in university, furious and full of invective, some of his father's disappointment twisted in him; too thin and with a fired intensity in his black eyes. He hated everything on principle, and that was the kind of thing that sent me swooning with desire, because I was young, and a fool. I wanted to gentle him, as if he were a fractious colt. I wasn't angry; I was that most unfashionable of all things, in those disaffected times, I was an optimist. He was scornful of that, but perhaps it touched him also, and perhaps it was that which drew him to me one black January night in a smoky basement bar. We had one of those rambling meaningless conversations that you can have when you are eighteen, one of those conversations that go on through the night and into the thin, cold, winter dawn. I remember him opening the shutters of his room at eight o'clock; I remember being startled because it was light. We stood very close together, looking out over the empty quad; there was a dog barking somewhere, and the air smelled of stone and woodsmoke; and then I stopped talking at last and he kissed me.

Five years later he stopped being angry. It had been leaking from him imperceptibly since he went into the real world and learned he had to impress people to get on; finally he turned it off like a dripping tap and that was the end of it. He married a woman in a ceremony in the Temple that I wouldn't go to, and she turned out to be angry enough for both of them. He became charming and liberal and saw each side of every argument; she grew more and more furious and finally left him for an expert in the bond market.

He came back to me and I let him, but he was battered and unsure from divorce – our first divorce. We were too young for it perhaps, still not thirty yet; it was something that happened to older people, our parents' generation, we weren't sure what to do now it had happened to one of us. Later, it turned out he was being comforted by several other women besides me. So that was my heart smashed all over again; I hated him then and wished him dead. But the thin line that pulled from his heart to mine could not be severed so easily, and I forgave and forgave, and pretended I was being adult (life is too short, people are starving in Africa and blowing themselves up in the Middle East, many other spurious and clichéd rationalizations).

So I let him back in, and he liked to call me up late at night after he had drunk a bottle of red wine and tell me I was the best friend he ever had, the only one who understood him, and I fell for it every time. So now we were friends again, and sometimes we slept with each other, and sometimes we didn't, and just lately he had taken to saying that he had a dream that we would end up together in some unspecified future, and I wasn't sure what I thought about that, and all the others said, laughing as if at an old joke, that I was still as big a fool as I had ever been, and I laughed too, and went along with it.

'Is it a game?' you said.

'I think that's what you are playing,' I said. 'I think you are playing something, but it's no game I ever heard of. I don't know the rules and I don't want to do it any more, and that's why there hasn't been a word, and I'm hanging up now.'

'Don't,' you said. 'Don't hang up.'

The snow changed everything. When I went downstairs, they were gathered round the ruins of the breakfast table, and they looked up at me like children, as if I could tell them what to do or how to be. Six characters in search of an author, I thought, because I am a writer after all, and we all have to have our little moments of fancy and pretension, that's what we're paid for, we don't like to let the public down.

I wish I could have made it turn out like a book. In fiction, I can get people to act how I want them to, and it all comes out right in the end. Even if the ending is unhappy, it makes sense, holds a shape and a purpose, some cohesion running through it like a steel hawser. You can do that in stories, but you can't do that in life, although perhaps I still held a hidden hope that I could. I had some fatal arrogance just then, about life; I thought I had cracked it. When they all called me a fool, with that indulgent fondness that old friends can freight insults with, as if admiring the flaws and failings that make us human and touchable, they weren't talking about that, even though that was the greatest folly of all. I laugh internally in shame and regret as I think of it.

It was the place, I think. Fifteen years in a grimy street in west London, a dim flat with a patch of garden which was always reclaimed by bindweed whatever I tried to do about it, and then, like a present or a revelation or a shooting star – the wide spaces of the north. Try to imagine it: like a bronco being kept in a narrow stable and suddenly released onto a wide plain. I think I was dazzled by the light.

The light itself did startle me; it was so different from southern light, English light. In the winter it was low and thick and yellow, like the kind of light they had in Verona or Naples, ancient Italian light. In the summer it had a green tint to it, from the colours of the hills and the trees; and in the autumn it was amber. I never saw light like it in my life. There were forests and rivers and a long snaking road I could follow over two ranges of mountains and see nothing but sheep and the rotting hulks of old crofts, abandoned when life grew too harsh there for soft modern people, unused to the wind and the weather.

In the shocking early weeks, I drove around the space and the grandeur of it and thought of the frantic streets I had left behind, and it was as if everything had fallen into place, like that game children play when they slot the square peg into the square hole. I thought this was the answer to everything. I had always wanted freedom more than any other single thing, and now I was free. I had time and distance and all this vast unending room, to move, to breathe, to think.

So perhaps I was a little cocky with it, imagining I had found the secret that everyone wanted; and a reason too, that's another thing we all search for, the *point* of it, the meaning of life. I thought the soaring acres of high, empty country were the point of it all, or if not entirely that, some solid clue to it, some intimation or suggestion; I believed in it like a god or an icon, all that outrageous beauty, and I had it on my doorstep.

And pride, and a fall, and going before, yes, yes; there is all that.

'Is it because of what I said?' you said.

'I don't remember what you said,' and now I was lying, even though I was the one who always insisted on holding such high regard for the truth. 'I don't remember at all.'

Maybe I did feel some kind of lethal confidence then, looking at them all, stranded and helpless – because Dino still couldn't decide if he liked boys or girls best, whether he wanted to go on picking up beautiful nameless men in Soho on a Saturday night, or settle down and have children and a dog, and Ellie was so scarred from the Irish wall and the smashed car that she had retreated from other

385

men and saw only Dino and devoted all her time to her work, and Fernanda spent her days trapped in one fad diet or another and kept secret the regret that ate into her like a canker, the regret of giving up her career to be a perfect wife and mother, and Peter had lost everything he ever believed in for the sake of a portfolio of commercial property and many mansions in the slums, and Wilf didn't know what he wanted and spent too many nights alone with a bottle and a pack of smokes; and I, *I* – had all this. I thought I had nothing else to wish for.

They were supposed to leave at lunchtime to catch the flight south, but there was no question of that. Peter had been on his mobile telephone, checking about.

'What are you going to do, Pete?' said Dino. 'Get them to come and chopper you out?'

Peter frowned, his forehead caught in the pattern familiar to it now, furrowed with deep care; he often walked into a room looking as if he had lost something and he wasn't sure what it was, or what he would do with it if he found it.

'The airport is closed,' he said. 'How can a whole fucking airport be closed?'

'You're a long way from the free market now,' said Dino. 'You're out in the sticks and they do things differently here.'

'Shut up, Dino,' said Ellie. 'Just because you don't have a job to go to.'

'I have a job to *get*,' said Dino. 'I have to go and talk to the nice lady at the labour exchange.'

'I don't think they have one of those any more,'

said Ellie. 'It's called career potential office or something nice and bland and politically correct.'

Ellie edited a magazine which dealt with sex and politics. It was only a year old and the circulation was soaring. 'I don't know why no one thought of it before,' she said. 'It's like horses and carriages and apples and pears.' She wrote scathingly ferocious editorials and her interviews were like watching someone forensically filleting a fish, until there was only the bare white skeleton left, the flesh picked clean away. 'I'm a cynic now,' she sometimes said. 'I was sceptical, and now I'm cynical, and it's rather a rest, to tell you the truth, I don't have to believe a single thing that anyone tells me any more.'

'What happened to that gig I got you?' Wilf said to Dino.

'The hours,' said Dino, reproachfully. 'Very bad for my complexion.'

Fernanda spoke, for the first time.

'What do we do now?' she said.

'You remember,' you said.

'No,' I said. 'No, I don't.'

It was my idea to play a game. It's strange, looking back now, because I was never one of those people. I hate games, and I hate jokes; I always thought both those things killed any gathering as dead as a stone. But the snow had rendered us static and awkward; the momentum had built over the week-end to this parting, this return to our normal lives, our other lives, and now the weather had stopped us, and the long snaking train of talk, which fed off eighteen years of jokes and indiscretions, had dried in our mouths, and it was as if we were strangers, trying to make polite conversation.

The morning dissipated; breakfast was cleared and Fernanda had spoken on the telephone to her children, who were happy with their grandparents, allowed forbidden pleasures of chocolate and all-night television. Peter and Wilf tried to go for a walk, but the blizzard was still blowing in and they turned back quickly. 'I'm not going to be Captain bloody Oates,' said Wilf, coming back into the house and shaking the snow off his shoulders. 'I'm beyond all that now.'

'Nobility and self-sacrifice?' said Peter. 'Did they used to be your strong suits?'

Dino and Ellie played backgammon and then it was past noon, and I made some lunch, and still we were stilted. The bags, which had been packed and left by the door in hope of departure, were taken back into bedrooms and opened again.

'You'll have to stay tonight,' I said. 'The gritters will come in the morning.'

By lunchtime the storm had blown itself out and the land was settled into anonymous white masses; the sky was low and pale and you could not tell where it ended and the hills began. Lunch gave us something to do, and I opened some wine to ease the stick; but by the time we had finished and were drinking coffee and smoking cigarettes, we were restless and stilted again.

'Come on,' I said. 'We'll play a game.'

Your Time is Up

We should have played Monopoly or Scrabble or something anodyne and harmless, but I remembered that the last time we played Scrabble Peter and Dino had fallen out over the word qi. Dino insisted it was a Vietnamese coin or some such thing, and Peter refused to accept it, and there was no dictionary in the house, and they fought so badly that Peter threw the board across the room at the wall, all the plastic letters making the sound of falling rain as they tumbled onto the stone floor. He and Dino didn't speak for four weeks after that, and Peter said cruel things behind Dino's back, that he was just a bitter old queen who was trying to fight destiny by occasionally going to bed with women and pretending that one day he and Ellie would set up house, when he should be brave enough to come out all the way and run away and live with the leather boys. They made it up in the end, but I never forgot those ugly things that Peter said and I wondered what it was about Dino that made him so furious and unforgiving.

'It's like the truth game,' I said. 'It's a variant.'

'Wilf won't like that,' said Ellie. 'He's a barrister.'

'Yeah, yeah,' said Wilf. 'But this is amateur hour for me, so I might be able to break the habit of a lifetime.'

'So we write six nouns on separate pieces of paper and then we pick them out of a hat, and you have to talk for two minutes without stopping or lying or prevaricating about your chosen subject,' I said.

I knew a farmer over the hill who read the *New York Review of Books* while driving his combine, and I had played this game at his house the week before and it had been funny and challenging and revealing, and I thought it would do well for us, in this trapped atmosphere. That was all I was thinking; that we could forget that we were here against our will, and we could start talking again and laugh and Fernanda would stop fretting about her two boys and Peter would forget about being late to the office and Ellie would lose the shadows under her eyes and Dino would forget about making trouble and Wilf would stop giving me the secret looks which confused me and made me remember too many things I would have rather forgotten. That was all I thought.

At first it was fine. We had snow, and drugs, and America, and fireman, and house. But then Dino, of course Dino, who had been stirring things since he was old enough to talk, decided it was too simple.

'A drinking game,' said Wilf, 'that's what we should make it,' and Dino saw the possibilities, and came in with the complications and riders.

'We should challenge,' he said. 'If we think someone is not telling the truth or hiding something. Yes,' he said. 'That's it. We can challenge, and if you lose the challenge, then you have to drink. And the challenger gets the subject for the rest of the two minutes, and whoever makes it to the end without interruption wins.'

'Like that game on the radio,' said Fernanda. There was a surprising delight in her voice, and I looked up, startled. She was very contained now, Fernanda, the wildness had burned out of her, been groomed out of her. She was beautiful now, polished and suitable; she did Peter credit, that was what she did. Her father had written plays; he liked to bring her out for show at theatrical parties in the seventies, when all the actors and directors and impresarios cooed over the olive Columbian looks that she got from her mother, who was dead. She had published a collection of poetry that won her prizes and sexual advances when she was in her early twenties, but then Peter turned himself into a tycoon and her father had three failures in a row and went to drink himself into oblivion in Tangier with an under-age mistress, and she gave it all up and started going to the hairdresser once a week and stopped eating. I missed the wild girl with poetry in her soul, but sometimes, just when I thought she was gone for ever, I got a fleeting glimpse of what once was, and I knew that she wasn't quite buried yet.

'Fuck it,' she said, and the light danced in her eyes. 'Let's do it.'

'It wasn't my fault,' you said.

'It's never your fault,' I said. Coldly furious, suddenly. 'It's always a freak of nature or an outside agency or some damn thing. But it's never, ever, you.'

The nouns went abstract.

Dino got innocence. 'Oh shit,' he said. 'Well, that's not my special subject.'

'Go, go,' said Ellie. 'No hesitations.'

'Innocence,' said Dino, 'is over-rated, some nostalgic tear in post-war eyes for a time when people had respect and the kids could play in the street and television wasn't invented.'

'Warning,' said Wilf. 'Muddling innocence with deference.'

'Innocence,' said Dino, shooting him a dangerous look, 'is a kind of deference, to the idea that there is a grand plan, some higher good or greater power that orders things the way they should be. And I am good and you are good and we all get what we deserve and life isn't a fucking Jane Austen novel.'

'Oh,' said Ellie. 'He's pretending he's read a book.'

'Penalties for heckling,' said Dino. 'Innocence is either a pose or a wish or a hypocrisy. Don't let's do it in the street and startle the horses.'

'You're rambling now,' said Fernanda. 'I think he's rambling.'

'I'm going to call a point of order,' said Wilf.

'I'm going to finish,' said Dino.

'You have to tell the truth,' said Peter, and his voice was low and quiet.

'Yes, yes,' said Ellie. 'Get personal.'

'I was never innocent,' said Dino. 'No one is ever innocent; children are like small Machiavellis and we imagine that they are wide-eyed and going to get a terrible shock when the realities of the world are revealed to them. And we all know that human beings are cruel and unusual and that to pretend otherwise is some Elysian liberal dream. We're all out for what we can get and we dress it up in nice clothes and spurious charm because we want to get laid; we pretend to be shocked at the things that other people do because we don't want anyone to find out that secretly we are capable of anything.'

'Oh stop,' said Ellie. 'Challenge, challenge. You are talking the most awful shit.'

'You're the cynic,' said Wilf, 'that's your job, don't go soft on us now.'

'You have to prove the challenge,' said Peter.

'All right,' said Ellie. 'Dino is not telling the truth, because really he has the greatest innocence of all, and he would rather die than admit it.'

'Blah,' said Dino. 'Wrong.'

'Oh yes,' said Ellie. 'Because you believe in happy ever after, against all the odds, and it kills you that you have no idea how to get it, and that's why you never stick with a job, or one sex, or anything that might be a real relationship, because you believe so hard in that happy ending and you are terrified that you won't know how to do it if you try for it. And there are no happy endings and I know that and you don't and that's why you are innocent.'

There was a pause. The light was fading so I got up for something to do and turned on the lamps and they cast the room in a low umber glow.

'I suppose we have to vote on it,' said Peter.

'You don't have to take it so seriously,' said Wilf, with the easy voice he used to avert disaster.

'Yes, we do,' said Peter. 'There's no point in playing otherwise.'

Ellie was staring hard at Dino and he looked away; so certain always, in his camp and his sharp lines and his care for nothing, he was uncertain now. I should have seen then, where we were headed, but I had opened three bottles at lunch, and the wine was in us, and the snow was banked up against the walls outside, and there seemed nowhere else to go.

'I think Ellie is right,' said Fernanda.

Peter turned his head sharply, and I remembered those accusations that he had scattered when he and Dino were not talking, and I thought something irreparable was going to come out and I didn't know how to stop it. Then he laughed, and a thin shadow of the boy we had known showed through the flint, and he said, 'Actually, I think she is too.'

Dino was astonished then, and he and Peter looked at each other, and I wondered if they were remembering the forbidden night they had spent, so many years ago, when Peter and Fernanda had broken up for three months, the night that none of us mentioned any more, not now. I wondered if it was the ineradicable memory of that night that lived in Peter and made him so touchy when it came to Dino and all Soho boys.

'All right,' said Dino, throwing up his hands. 'I admit it. I drink. I really do dream of happy endings, and some lovely butch professor of philosophy who will quote Spinoza at me and love me for ever, and all that happens is that I pick up twenty-year-old plumbers in Greek Street and we never seem to be able to make a go of it, don't ask me why. So fuck all of you, and if the prof doesn't turn up, then Ellie and I are going to have three children and separate bedrooms, so if that's innocence, then shoot me.'

'Drink,' said Ellie, laughing, 'to our future, if nothing else.'

Fernanda looked at her watch. 'You have thirty seconds, El,' she said. 'You have to finish the subject.'

'I don't need thirty seconds,' said Ellie. 'I was innocent, and then everybody died, so let's go on to the next one.'

'I remember what Ellie said,' you said. 'About everybody dying.'

'I did that one,' I said. 'You know that. That last time you wanted me to forgive you, and I said I would because you might die in a car smash like Stephen did and then I would have only regrets. I don't think that is going to work again, so there's no point in you trying. The possibility of random death just isn't going to cut it any more.'

'I'll try anything,' you said, and then I thought you were the one who was lying.

Ellie got sex. 'Bugger,' said Dino.

'You never said a truer word,' said Wilf.

'That was my special subject,' said Dino. 'Why didn't I get that?'

'You get that every night, you dolt,' said Ellie.

'Go on then,' said Fernanda.

I suddenly realized that for once I was the one not saying much, and I wondered why. I was the one who knew all about the truth; I had been chasing it all my life. I was the writer, I was the one with the words, and now I was not saying anything.

'Sex,' said Ellie, 'throws sand in your eyes and makes all your reason count for nothing and I should know better than that at my age.'

'We never know better,' said Dino.

Sex turned out to be our safest subject, which strikes me now as ironic. With all our history there in that room, who had gone to bed with whom, who wished to go to bed with whom, and on and on. But in that round there was just barracking and many disputed challenges as an excuse to drink some more and Dino threatened to give a demonstration of how it really went with him and the young plumbers.

'I can never get a plumber at the weekend,' said Peter, who seemed infected with some kind of recklessness, now he was stranded so far from the office. 'I don't know how you do it.'

'Charm,' said Dino. 'And technique, of course.'

Fernanda got childhood.

'Oh,' she said. 'Are we back to innocence? Who wrote these?'

'You did, you fool,' said Dino.

'Not that one,' said Fernanda. 'I wrote sex, if you must know.'

Peter looked as if he was about to say something, but stopped himself, and I wondered about that, afterwards.

'Oh,' said Fernanda, again, and her face was suddenly taut with something: distress or fear or memory. 'I have to tell the truth. Well, well, you see, I, ah . . . I thought it was something you could *give* someone; I thought that if I tried hard enough I could give it to my boys, all those things I never had. I thought that even though I had a fucked-up childhood, I could make it different for them. But now I don't know. I want to hide them from all the hard things in the world and I can't do that and it makes me feel as if I have failed.'

There was the silence of shock in the room, for twenty different reasons. Fernanda hadn't talked like this for fifteen years, but it was more than that. The incarnation she had invented for herself was so complete and sheened and gleaming that even though we all knew better, I think we had been half fooled by it. Women who looked like she did didn't have regrets or dark introspections or feelings of failure, they were too busy shopping for shoes or being seen in fashionable restaurants. Perhaps we had fallen for the surface, despite all that savvy and insight we prided ourselves on. Maybe we had been fooled into forgetting about the dead mother and the lush father and the husband, who had once loved her so extravagantly, who now stayed in his office for twelve hours at a stretch.

'You wanted the truth,' she said, and there was something in her that was defiant and daring now, some banked fury at us for having written her off so silently.

'And if you want the truth, it's more than that. I fret about my boys, but all mothers do that, that's a mundane truth, that's part of the deal. What I really think about childhood is it's the thing that none of us ever talks about, but now it's the only thing that keeps us together, that we have in common. I got the dead mother and the selfish father who is drinking himself to death; Wilf had a drinking father as well, bitter and obsessed with the failure to reach fighting glory; Peter left home at seventeen and has never talked to either of his parents since; Ellie had the drowned cousin and the mother who fell apart and took to pills; Dino was cut off for liking boys, which wasn't done in the suburbs; and Rita – well, Rita had the mother who ran away and the father who married five times after that, and each stepmother was drunker and stupider and more neglectful than the last, so she had feckless and careless when she was a child, which sometimes is worse than dead, and I think that is why she is hiding up here and pretending that she doesn't need anybody, even Wilf, who is the one she will always love, even though he won't love her back in the way she deserves.'

Black silence that time, the deep quiet of a stone falling into a bottomless pool.

'Is that my two minutes?' said Fernanda.

'How much have you had to drink?' said Peter.

'What?' said Fernanda. 'That was the point, wasn't it? The truth was the point.'

'You were only obeying orders,' said Wilf, trying to make a joke of it.

'Possibility of . . .' said Ellie.

'. . . too much information,' said Dino.

'You fuckers,' said Fernanda. 'You think I never say anything any more, and then when I do, you don't like it. Well, you asked for it, and there it is, unvarnished.'

'I don't think it was what I said,' you said.

'No, of course not,' I said. The fury was still packed tight in me, and the blunt irony was back, because I didn't know how else to face it.

'That's just what I think,' you said.

'There's nothing *just* about it,' I said.

Peter nearly saved the day with money. 'Well,' he said, 'that is my very own subject and I think this game was rigged.'

Fernanda and I were sitting on opposite sides of the room, on the two long sofas that faced each other. We couldn't quite look at each other. Wilf was lying against my legs, and I felt him there and wondered if what Fernanda had said was true.

'Yes, yes,' said Peter, and for once the crease that lived between his eyebrows lifted. 'You are all right. My name is Peter and I am a workaholic, and cash is my middle name, and it doesn't buy you love but it gets you lots of hot clothes.'

He made it through his time, fending off hecklers and challenges, refusing to give any quarter. He almost persuaded us that making money was the highest calling a man could dream of; he was on a roll, infused with some hectic evangelical fire. And just as he almost had us beat, he dropped his shoulders and said, looking across at the girl he had married in the gambling fever of the Nevada desert, I sometimes think that I started chasing all that

399

money because I wanted to impress Fernanda and show her I was worth something. I knew I could never write a play like her father could, or be adored by the beautiful people like he was, but I thought if I could make a ton of money she might think me a hell of a fellow.'

He put a spin on the last sentence so we laughed at it, but Fernanda saw right through it, and the gloss and the gleam left her, the perfect wife fell away, and the Vegas girl was there again for a minute, and she said, 'Oh you fool, I always loved you because you made me laugh and you were good at sex.'

'So now we're back to sex again,' said Dino.

Peter gave the small preen that men can't help when they have been told they are a great lay; there was surprise there too, a tight thrill of delight.

'We should do it more often,' he said.

'Ha,' said Ellie. 'So it is true that once you are married you never do it any more? I heard that.'

'Too much truth now,' said Fernanda.

'Do you think it strange,' said Ellie, who had a habit of going off on musing tangents once she had some drink in her, 'that of all of us you are the only ones that are married?'

'If we are telling the truth,' said Dino, 'and we are caught in that hellish rictus, then it's not odd at all. Wilf was married anyway, but that doesn't count, he only did it because everyone else was.'

'Point of order,' said Wilf again, who liked to think he was something of a radical, even though the blindest of blind men could see that he was nothing of the sort.

'You know that's true,' said Dino. 'And Ellie isn't because her fiancé died in a car smash and that's enough to put anyone off, and she has a Celtic streak of superstition in her that believes if she said yes to anyone else, they would be doomed to perish.'

'Perish is lovely,' said Fernanda, who seemed to have got her groove back.

'How did you know that?' said Ellie. 'We never talked about that.'

'I'm right though,' said Dino, 'aren't I?'

'Oh all right, yes,' said Ellie. 'Right on the money.'

'So,' said Dino. 'That leaves me, which is obvious, half in half out of the closet, dreaming of the possibility of a happy ending. And then Rita, who has a nice combination of fear of matrimony on account of the feckless parents, which she likes to think means nothing to her but means everything, and the unshakeable obsession with Wilf, who will always treat her badly.'

'Fuck off,' said Wilf. 'I was mostly perfectly charming.'

'Oh yes,' said Ellie. 'Until you swore you would love her till you died and married someone else; then, correct me if I'm wrong, went running back after the disaster of the marriage to the angriest woman in the world, begged our Rita to take you back, and then turned out to be fucking three other women at the same time.'

'Not at the exact same time,' said Wilf. I felt him shift uneasily at my feet; he moved away and leaned against the wall. The fire was burning low and cast a diffused light on his face, so I couldn't tell whether he was blushing or not. I wished they would all stop. It was the things we never said, and it was all true, and I hated it.

'It wasn't what *I* said,' you said.

'Are we back to that again?' I said. 'I don't really see any point to this conversation.'

'It was Ellie, I think,' you said.

'You just go on thinking, Butch, that's your job,' I said. I knew once I said it that it was a terrible mistake, because that was one of the lines we had together, one of the ones so old you can't even remember how they started; it was from an old cowboy film, but I can't remember how it became ours. Those are the treacherous waters in any old relationship: the words and lines and references that will always be yours alone, that no other person will ever understand. They fool you into thinking something is still there, something still *counts*, when all they are is old lost lines.

'That's my job,' you said, and I wished you hadn't.

So I got love.

'Peter is right,' I said. 'This game is definitely rigged. Rigged all the way to hell and back.'

'Come on, Rita,' said Ellie. 'You're the one of all of us who got something right.'

'You were always on Rita's side,' said Peter.

Ellie sat up straight and craned her neck in the way she did sometimes, when she wanted to intimidate a suspect. I felt rather admiring and detached watching her do it.

'Just what do you mean by that?' Ellie said, and she was back in her cynical voice.

'You know,' said Peter, 'perfectly well. The rest of us were lagging along being all screwed up and Rita was the true shining light.'

'Challenge,' said Ellie.

'It's not his round, you arse,' said Dino.

'You're a fine one to talk about arse,' said Ellie.

'Since it's the truth we're telling now, I resent it, that's all,' said Peter. 'Because she was the other one who chose to live alone and not get married and not have children, just like you, it means you would never hear one single word against her.'

'You are supposed to be her friend too,' said Ellie. 'You're not supposed to be spreading sedition, and if we're on to just because, *just because* she didn't choose to take the conventional route and worship Mammon and get her wife to be submissive and perfectly coiffed, maybe that's what's threatening you, so shut up before I punch you in the nose.'

'No, no,' said Wilf, with that voice again, the one he believed could settle all dispute. 'This is not the game.'

'Well, let's play the game,' said Fernanda. 'And I'm not so entirely submissive, if you don't bloody mind.'

'All I'm saying,' said Ellie, 'is that you all think of love as a sexual thing, but there are many kinds of love. There is friend love, love for music and books and mountains and I don't know what the hell else, all those other things that Rita loves, so lay off.'

I had always hated being told what I was; it made me feel unsure and unsettled, so I started talking, as if talk alone could help me impose myself on this strange day.

'Actually,' I said, hearing the word come out lamely into the room, which was dark now, and filled with the smell of peat and red wine, 'I don't know diddley about love.'

'Challenge,' said Wilf.

'*You* are not allowed to speak,' said Fernanda abruptly, and I looked at her and I thought that once she and I had known something about love, when we were very young and we still believed we would go everywhere together.

'I know something about those other kinds of love,' I said, 'the ones that Ellie talked of. I sometimes think I can believe in those; and love of place, of this place.'

Then it all fell from me and I wanted to stop and go back to the beginning, but it was too late, we had sat for too long together, drunk too much, talked too far, been trapped into something we didn't want or understand.

'The heart love, the sexual love,' I said, 'I never knew about that, I always felt I was making it up as I went along. I didn't trust it, I had no example. And I know you all think I am a fool, but I hoped one day I would grow out of that, and I thought I had, and I see now that I haven't, and perhaps there is a part of me that will always go on loving Wilf despite everything, because he was first.'

'Challenge,' said Dino.

'I'm afraid so,' said Fernanda.

It was odd, looking back, that they were the two who could see that I was lying; not quite lying perhaps, more not admitting the truth, whole and pure and clean and entire. I might have thought it would have been the other ones, but, in the end, it was those unexpected two.

I gave in then; the book opened wide and I could read it, without let. 'Oh, all right,' I said. 'I go on loving him because it is safe, because he will never quite love me back, so I have an excuse to stay alone.'

It felt as if a thorn had come out of my side and I wasn't sure what to do with the gap.

'Oh,' said Ellie. 'I never got that. So you and Dino are virtually the same person after all. Perhaps you two should be the ones who settle down in the alternative family.'

'I wanted to ask,' you said, 'whether you meant it, what you said that night.'

'Meant what?' I said, because I wasn't going to give in that easily, not after everything.

'You know exactly,' you said, because maybe you weren't quite going to give up either.

We almost stopped then. The night was black outside the windows; I had not closed the blinds and it seemed too late now. I had a sense that a low thaw had come and that by tomorrow the snow would be muddied and melting.

'It's a stupid game,' Wilf said.

'You're just saying that because it's your turn,' said Fernanda.

'It's late,' said Ellie, frowning in surprise. She went into the kitchen and brought back some bread and cheese and another bottle of wine. 'We've come this far,' she said. 'We're not innocent any more. Let's get really fucked up.'

'It's a stupid game,' said Wilf again.

And this time it was Peter who said, 'It's your turn. You can't duck out now, it's too late for that.'

I wonder now if Wilf would have gone on if it wasn't for Peter. For all that we mocked him, there was something about Peter's vast business drive that made us respect him; we pretended to have a disdain for money and the amount of soul you had to sell to get it, but all the same, we had no idea how to make it in those high numbers; we had neither the ruthlessness nor the diamond brilliance, so there was a hidden part of us which deferred to Peter, although we would have died rather than admit it.

I wondered too whether Peter said what he said because he wanted me to hear what Wilf might admit. In the first term at university, I had kissed Peter, one drowsy autumn afternoon, before Fernanda, before Wilf; one chaste, youthful kiss and nothing more, but because of it, even eighteen years later, there was some residual loyalty, more than just friendship and history, which could tip the odds, when it came to it.

So Wilf gave in and picked out his small square piece of paper. He got folly.

'This is a ringer,' he said.

'Go, go, go,' said Ellie and Dino.

'Well,' he said, and I could see, because I knew him so well, that he was debating whether to put on his wig and gown or just tell the truth and damn the consequences.

'You all know that my greatest folly was what I did with Rita,' he said.

'And what was that exactly?' said Ellie.

'All the . . . all, you know, everything you said,' said Wilf. 'All that stuff. All of it.'

'My point of order now,' said Dino.

'What happened to my two minutes?' said Wilf.

'Sod your two minutes,' said Peter.

'My point of order,' said Dino, 'which is: is it the case that while you are now officially friends . . .'

'Again,' said Ellie.

'Who sometimes sleep with each other,' said Fernanda.

'What is this?' said Wilf. 'The Star Chamber?'

'. . . officially friends,' said Dino, 'who sometimes sleep with each other, unofficially you are still telling her, when you have sunk a bottle of red, and you are alone in your chambers, and you pick up the telephone in the still watches of the night . . .'

'Poetic,' said Ellie.

'. . . you are still telling her that she is truly the only one for you,' said Dino, 'the one you will always love most, and can't forget, the only one who understands?'

'Stop,' I said, finding my voice. 'What about his two minutes?'

'Is that true?' said Dino, staring hard at Wilf.
'Remember the rules.'

'Yes,' said Wilf. 'That is true, and fuck you for
asking.'

'And is it also true,' said Peter, 'that you have, in
all that time, been chasing another woman, and
swearing undying devotion to her, and that you have
been sleeping with her for the past month and not
telling Rita a single thing about that in your late-
night telephone conversations?'

I didn't see that coming. I was the one who was
blind and I didn't see, that for all my talk of it, the
truth was the last thing I wanted.

'You should have been the lawyer, Peter,' said
Wilf.

'Is it true?' said Ellie.

'Yes,' said Wilf, and his voice was very quiet. 'Yes,
all right, it's true.'

I wondered how they all knew about that. I
wondered if they had been trying to tell me, not
knowing how, and now they had found a way to
bring it out into the light.

'You stupid bastard,' said Ellie.

'You always take her side,' Wilf said.

'*You* were supposed always to be on her side,'
said Ellie.

'I am in the room,' I said. 'You don't have to talk
about me in the third person.'

'It's always my fault,' said Wilf. 'All right, all right,
I'm the shit, I'm the fuckhead who doesn't know
what he wants and can't commit and says one thing
and does another.' It was as if the old angry boy in

him was resurrected for one last dance before the music stopped; it silenced us all for a moment. The logs spat in the grate and the walls groaned and settled with the night.

'I never wanted to be part of the construct,' Wilf said, and the words were spat out of him, from his gut, as if beyond his volition.

'I don't understand,' I said, and then he looked at me straight and told me.

'It was always on your terms,' he said. 'Do this, be that, believe the other. You were always so sure. And then you moved up here and you would never come back. You liked being alone, and you wanted me to fit into the corners of your life, a weekend here, a week there, and I can't do that. I don't know what it is you are afraid of, but I can't do that part-time thing, it's all or nothing at all.'

So that was the end of it. I knew then, instantly, after eighteen years, that was the end of it, because he was asking me to sacrifice the one thing I could never give up. I wished he had told me that before, right at the start of it, before it got so complicated.

'Oh well,' said Dino. 'It's after midnight and we are all wrong and twisted in the head and clearly need forty years on a nice couch in Hampstead before we can go out in public again, and this really is a stupid game.'

'It's a stupid game,' said Ellie.

'I quite liked it,' said Fernanda.

'Six months,' you said. 'And you remember it all, word for word.'

'I remember,' I said, giving in.

'Was it what I said?' you said.

'Yes,' I said. 'No.' I felt as if I didn't know anything any more, that I would never again be certain of any single thing. 'It was what I said. It was what we all said. It was the truth, which sometimes will set you free.'

If this was one of those stories with a neat ending there would be two possibilities: the expected and rewarding, the heart-warming and mildly sentimental; or the implausible *deus ex machina* where everything falls abruptly and surprisingly into place. I always remember that line in *Casablanca*: Humphrey Bogart in his weary worldly voice saying, 'Does it have a wild finish?'

I'd love to give a wild finish – the one where Fernanda and Peter yelled through a bitter divorce and she went to live on the Dalmatian coast with a red poet, where Dino contracted Aids and died in Morocco and the body wasn't found for three days until the smell disturbed the neighbours, where Wilf was the victim of a professional hit ordered by a jealous husband, and Ellie went to live in the fjords and sing a song of Norway with a forty-year-old woman.

Or the not-a-dry-eye-in-the-house Hollywood version, where it turned out that our friendships were forged in fire by that strange night, and Fernanda and Peter remembered how in love they had once been and had three more children and she managed to write sonnets in between the feeding and the nappy changing and still cook the perfect risotto (because she would have lost her fear of food, of course); and Dino realized he didn't really want a butch professor or a series of youthful plumbers but went down on one knee to Ellie, the one he always truly loved, and got his happy ever after, and Wilf and I made it up, and I lost my fear, and he lost his doubts and fury – and oh, there was orange blossom everywhere.

But there are no wild finishes in life, and everything went back pretty much to the way it had been before, and the same old arguments and doubts and secrets ran round the merry-go-rounds of our lives.

There was a difference; one difference, as if a light bulb had finally fused. I couldn't forgive Wilf, for what he had said, and I knew that was stupid and adolescent, because what they said about me was true too, or half true. Maybe I was alone because I was scared, perhaps it was true that I had chosen him because I knew he would never threaten that perfect solitude I had chosen. But I wasn't sure, and I could not forget the sudden venom in his voice when he said he never wanted to be part of the construct. I hated it that he thought of it like that; I wished he had told the truth, and not whitewashed me with all those sweet illicit words. I hated it that he had not told me about the other woman.

Perhaps it was more than that; maybe that strange, trapped day when it all came out made me realize that I could not go on blaming him for everything; I had a part in it too. But all the same, he had lied one too many times, and the tugging contract between us, that had endured so much, was finally broken. So that's why there was six months of radio silence; that's why I knew, the moment I heard his voice again, constrained and unsure, that all the old intimacy was dead. Perhaps that is the wild finish. It took eighteen years to die, and now I can say RIP and mean it, for the first time; for the last time.

'Was it the truth?' you said.

'What?' I said.

'What you said,' you said.

'You never knew much about the truth,' I said. 'I was supposed to be the one who knew all about that. But now I don't know anything much.'

I suddenly realized that it didn't matter any more, what was true, what was not. You were no longer the beating heart at the centre of my life; you were just a man I used to know. 'But,' I said, 'I think there was some truth in what was said, in all of it. It had the ring of authenticity to it. So that's why there is no point to this any more, and I am free now, and there's the difference.'

'I suppose,' you said, 'that is a difference.'

'Yes,' I said. 'I think it is.'

Your voice suddenly was tight and suspicious. 'Is it someone else?' you said.

I laughed then, genuine for the first time. 'No,' I said. 'You would think that, but no. It was too many things you never told me, and too many things I never admitted to myself, and everything else in between.'

'So this is the end,' you said.

'Yes,' I said.

That should have been the finish, but curiosity is the strongest human emotion, and I've never been much for the grand finale. So it was bathos, in the end, rather than tragedy.

'Go on,' I said. 'Did she run off with a judge?'

I could hear the telephone line sighing with other voices. 'Of course,' you said. 'What else would she do?'

'Oh yes,' I said. 'That's right. That's the last word.'

A DAY AT THE SEASIDE

Julia Hamilton

Born in Dumfries and brought up in Galloway, where her father was a hill farmer, **JULIA HAMILTON** now lives in London. She is the author of several bestselling novels including, most recently, *Forbidden Fruits* and *Other People's Rules*.

The manse at Garholm was a handsome cream-washed Georgian house with touches of Galloway vernacular about it in the green painted surrounds of the windows and the crow-stepped gables. It stood on a slight slope amidst an acre of lawn and shrubberies – policies, as these areas are known north of the border. To the left of the house as it faced the road, a lane led to farm buildings and outhouses where the minister, the Rev. Mr Wright, farmed the glebe, counting his bullocks of a morning as well as the souls in his church, a church in which the Elders sat under the pulpit facing the congregation, already one step ahead on the long road to God.

Inside, the manse was as large and four-square as it looked from the road and Lizzie, 'wee Lizzie Douglas', occasional best friend of the last child of the manse, Catriona Wright, loved to spend time there with Catriona, pretending (she was a child with a great deal of imagination) that she was also a child of the manse, the daughter of the Rev. John Wright and Mrs Wright.

Mrs Wright, a small, round cannonball of a

woman with a head of tight grey curls and spectacles that caught the light, taught infants at Garholm Primary School and was a figure of considerable authority, particularly when that authority was allied with her husband's: as a couple, they dominated the village, just as Catriona, their last child, dominated the playground at Garholm Primary. Catriona was as ruthless as any henchman of Lenin's: if you were 'in' you were in heaven, and if you were 'out', as Lizzie had often found herself, you were in hell. Today was heaven.

Mr Wright was a severe, pale-faced, rather humourless man whose unsmiling expression emanated a kind of sanctity, or so Lizzie thought. She was both frightened and fascinated by him. He represented the Protestant, all-knowing and unforgiving God who would eventually turn his scalding gaze on Lizzie's soul.

To Lizzie, whose father, Sir Eldred Douglas, was a large landowner and local grandee, the manse represented almost everything her own home didn't. For instance, the Wrights sat down to a large high tea at half past five every day and ate things that Lizzie never saw at home; slices of tongue with jelly round the edge and Spam (which Lizzie thought delicious); there was beetroot chopped into tiny cubes, coleslaw in little frosted glass dishes; there were 'tattie' scones and shortbread biscuits with icing and a great deal of bread and margarine and jam. Lizzie's mother disdained margarine. Lizzie knew her mother would disapprove of the way she smeared it on slabs of white bread, but that, of course, made it all the more delectable. Lizzie's own early supper, if she were at home, would consist of an omelette with chives or a piece of sole or possibly cold lamb and salad. She was allowed one piece of cake only and invited to choose fruit instead. At the manse, Mrs Wright pressed her to eat more of everything, particularly the sugary, delicious things that were banned by Lizzie's mother.

At breakfast on the day of the outing to the seaside with the Wrights, Lizzie had heard her mother murmur something to her father about Mr Wright that she couldn't quite understand, something about Mr Wright being seen 'yet again' at Nonie Macaskill's, the wife of one of her father's tenant farmers.

'One parish visit too many,' said Lizzie's mother in a tone of voice which Lizzie at eleven years of age was experienced enough to know (even if she couldn't name the term) was ironic.

'She's a good-looking woman,' said Eldred mildly, without looking up. 'I don't blame him.'

'Blame him for what?' Lizzie piped up.

'Nothing,' said her mother repressively.

'You never let me say that,' Lizzie replied. 'That's not fair.'

'Little pitchers have big ears,' said her father gently, so that Lizzie would know he was not reproving her. 'Now eat up or we'll be late.'

Lizzie's father, who cared nothing for cars, drove Lizzie to the manse in his old grey van which smelled of machine oil and wet dog; when they went round corners too fast, various nuts and bolts clattered and

slid across the tin floor in the back, with what dogs
there were – there was usually a collie or two, Jip
or Roy they all seemed to be called (the foot soldiers
of the stack yard) – huddled against the sides. They
discussed the fall of the Roman Empire, a subject
close to both their hearts. Lizzie's father would
sometimes read little bits of Gibbon to Lizzie of an
evening and was delighted by her interest.

The Wrights' car was a Rover, painted a sober
grey with red leather upholstery and a leather steering wheel. Lizzie loved this car, as opposed to her
father's smelly old wreck, and enjoyed travelling in
it, imagining that the people who saw them would
think she was Catriona's sister, a fantasy she enjoyed
indulging. Her only brother was at boarding school
and she was lonely a lot of the time. She'd always
wanted a sister.

Mrs Wright was wearing a tent dress in a bold
pattern of green and white flowers and was fuss-
ing over a picnic box in the hall of the manse when
Lizzie came in. Mr Wright was wearing *shorts* and
a short-sleeved shirt. Lizzie tried not to stare at his
rather hairy legs. For some reason, she had a strong
picture in her mind of Mrs Macaskill's glossy blonde
hair and red lips, the way her eyes crinkled when
she smiled.

'Come on now, Mary,' Mr Wright was saying,
glancing at his watch. 'The tide will be perfect if
we leave straight away.'

'I can't find the serviettes,' Mrs Wright replied.

'We don't need serviettes. We can wash our hands
in the water. Come on, woman.'

Catriona glanced at Lizzie and made a face. 'Let's get in the car,' she said conspiratorially, and Lizzie's heart leaped.

The beach was called Greenyard and was reached by driving down a long road that led through a farm, in fact the farm where the Macaskills had raised their three children, at least one of whom, Callum, had babysat Lizzie when she was smaller. Now these children were all grown-up and living away from home. Callum was learning to be a scientist in Edinburgh.

As the Wrights' Rover slid past the dyke surrounding the garden of the farm, Mrs Macaskill, as if by magic, appeared in the rarely used front doorway and waved. She was wearing a fitted blouse and slacks, plain clothes that showed off her trim figure to perfection.

'There's Nonie,' said Mrs Wright, waving back vigorously.

Lizzie, seated in the back, watched as Mr Wright failed to respond to this piece of information.

'Did you not see her, John?' asked Mrs Wright.

'Can you not see I'm driving?' replied her husband. He caught Lizzie's eye in the mirror and looked away swiftly.

One parish visit too many, Lizzie heard her mother's voice. She looked again at Mrs Wright in the front beside her husband, with her helmet of steel-grey curls and her fat, white, lardy arms and suddenly felt inexplicably sorry for her, although she wasn't quite sure why.

Mr Wright parked the Rover in the car park and

421

the two excited girls took their towels and swimming things and plunged ahead up the path to the beach, which lay over a dyke with a stile and through a glowing thicket of butter-smelling gorse. It was an exceptionally hot, blue day, as if some weather had escaped from the Mediterranean by mistake. The sea, normally the colour of sheet metal, was deep azure and shimmering; the water in the rock pools was the temperature of blood. Lizzie, pausing to admire some pale pink anemones, thought again of Mrs Wright's arms and the trim curve of Nonie Macaskill's hips in those tight slacks. She didn't know what to make of the proximity of the two images in her mind, but something powerful and dark stirred in her as if she had received a signal that she was too young to decode.

The tide was right up, and the sea had polished the sandy slope towards the ocean so that it was both firm and glistening. Running towards the water with her skinny legs going like pistons, Lizzie felt the shock of physicality that water induced in her. I'm *alive*, she thought, as she plunged into the salty water, *alive*, *alive*. Sometimes on horseback she had experienced the same piercingly visceral feeling, as if she and the horse were somehow one being.

Catriona and Lizzie swam and swam, diving in the cloudy depths and turning somersaults, salt water in their eyes and up their noses. Mr and Mrs Wright joined them at one point; Lizzie noticed Mrs Wright's flabby white thighs dappled with small veins, the roll of fat round her middle scarcely concealed by the swimsuit, the blind look her eyes had without her spectacles. Mr Wright's chest was as hairy as his legs and there was something puny about his upper arms that made Lizzie avert her eyes.

She realized that she disliked seeing these two people so nearly unclothed, but wasn't sure why. She dived again and forgot the problem.

When she surfaced, she saw that the Wrights were walking up the beach, Mr Wright steering his wife as if she couldn't see the way.

'I'm starving,' said Catriona, after another underwater swimming session. 'Shall we go and get our tea?'

Mrs Wright was sitting on the tartan rug next to the picnic box, but she wasn't her normal bustling, bossy self, the classroom disciplinarian. *Now, children, turn to page ten . . .* Instead, she gazed off out to sea and appeared to be talking to herself. She had on a towelling robe of a kind that was supposed to provide discreet cover to change underneath, but Lizzie could see from the damp patches that she still had her costume on, a disquieting note.

'I know he's been seeing her, I know, I know,' she was saying in a strange reedy voice to the air or to the view, but not to Mr Wright who was crouched next to his wife with his arm round her. To Lizzie, the gesture looked more as if he was trying to suppress his wife rather than to support her. He looked as if he would like to crush her to the ground or fill her mouth with sand to stop the hateful things she was saying.

'It's been going on for a while now,' she continued in the same unreal, alarming voice. 'They think I don't know but I do, they think I'm blind and deaf, that I don't have any feelings. And I bore him four children and all.'

'Here's Catriona now with Lizzie,' Mr Wright said desperately. 'Shall we lay out the food, Mary? The girls will need their tea.'

But Mrs Wright continued to address the view as if she hadn't heard. 'And there he is so holy of a Sunday with everyone looking up to him and going off to Balmoral to preach as if he were St Paul himself . . .'

'Your mother's not feeling well,' said Mr Wright, addressing Catriona, who stood looking down at her mother, shivering and dripping. 'Get a towel and dry yourself and get one for Lizzie.'

'What's wrong with her?' asked Catriona, her mouth dropping open. There were tears in her eyes. Glancing at her, Lizzie felt both compassion and a sense of triumph at seeing her friend (and her tormentor) brought so low. She also knew instinctively that it was dangerous to let the enemy know that you knew their weakness. She looked away for a moment as if to pretend she hadn't seen anything untoward.

'She's not well. I'm going to have to take her home and call Dr Macmillan. Now do as I say. Get a towel for yourself and one for Lizzie, then change into your clothes and we'll be on our way.'

'I'm hungry,' said Catriona, staring at her mother, as if willing her to get back into her normal role.

A Day at the Seaside

'Well, get something to eat out of the box, don't just stand there,' said Mr Wright, echoing his wife's customary briskness.

Mr Wright got to his feet and looked down at his wife. 'It's time to go, Mary,' he said. 'I think you need your bed.'

But Mrs Wright made no effort to move. 'We were girls together, Nonie and I,' she continued, addressing Catriona, who had squatted down to be closer to her mother. 'She was always the pretty one; all the boys were after her, including your father, the Reverend Mr Wright, but Tommy Macaskill got her instead and your father had to make do with me.'

'Don't talk nonsense, Mary,' said Mr Wright. 'It's upsetting for Catriona and for Lizzie,' he added. 'Lizzie is the daughter of Sir Eldred Douglas,' he continued, giving Lizzie's father his full name, in the hope, Lizzie felt, that he could distract Mrs Wright, as one might distract a dangerous dog with a tempting morsel.

'Sir Eldred?' asked Mrs Wright, turning his name over tenderly. 'Oh, but he was a handsome one. He loved her too, but she wasn't good enough for him. He had to marry that stuck-up bitch Cecilia.' She pronounced Lizzie's mother's name 'Cess-eeel-ia'. And we all know that she was after him for his title and his money, not because she loved him, oh no . . . and he was mad for her, he still is . . . what a fool—'

'Mary!' thundered her husband, causing picnicking groups in the vicinity to look round. 'That's enough. It's time to go home.' He turned to the two girls who were standing just behind him.

'Take something to eat and walk up the beach for five minutes and then come back, okay?'

The girls set off together in silence.

After a minute, Lizzie asked, 'What's wrong with her?'

'I don't know,' said Catriona miserably. Although she had a towel round her shoulders, she was still shaking with cold, in spite of the warm day. 'I think she's gone mad,' she added.

'Is it true, do you think?' asked Lizzie.

'Is what true?'

'Mrs Macas— Nonie and your father?'

'Of course it's not true,' said Catriona scornfully, 'she's mad, I tell you, just mad. Mad as a snake.'

'She said other things too,' said Lizzie, 'about my family, not just yours.'

Why should Catriona hog all the pain to herself? It was typical of her.

'I hate her,' said Catriona vehemently, 'I don't want to hear any of it.'

But somehow Lizzie knew there was some truth in it all somewhere. She felt as if she had been wounded by Mrs Wright's wild and dangerous words. They confirmed thoughts she had had herself about her parents but had not dared to examine.

In some ways, she agreed with Mrs Wright. Her mother *was* stuck-up. Lizzie was always hearing about the difficulties caused by her mother in the village. Lady Douglas was not popular and had no interest in playing Lady Bountiful. She did not attend church on Sundays, where Lizzie always went with her father and sat grandly in the family box pew, quite enjoying the stares and whispers. It was the one time in the week she felt invulnerable to Catriona.

And Lizzie had for some while suspected that her mother didn't love her father enough. There was often tension at meals with Lizzie talking to her father and her mother sitting in icy silence. The silences hurt Lizzie, but when she tried to explain that to her mother, she just looked away and waited for Lizzie to stop talking.

At the manse, on the other hand, Mrs Wright chattered throughout high tea. There were no silences there. And yet, thought Lizzie, gazing at the hyacinth-coloured horizon arranged in layers like swathes of gauze, maybe there should have been. Maybe Mrs Wright's chatter at tea was to cover the silence that lay beneath, the silence that stretched all the way to the pulpit or to the church at Balmoral where Mr Wright had famously preached on Matthew 13:24–43: *The kingdom of heaven may be compared to a man who sowed good seed in his field . . .*

When they got back to the rug where the Wrights had been sitting when they came out of the sea, there was no one there.

'Mebbe he's taken her to the car,' said Catriona, kneeling down to scrabble in the giant picnic box. 'Let's eat the cake quick before he gets back.'

They sat side by side in silence with crumbs falling into their laps, watching the sea.

'Are you worried about your mum?' asked Lizzie after a bit.

Catriona shook her head. 'She'll be okay,' she said. 'Elspeth says she's got the mennypose. She says it makes women crazy, but not to worry.'

Elspeth was Catriona's elder sister, now a student at Edinburgh University, and Catriona's invariable authority on all things reproductive. Lizzie envied Catriona Elspeth. She only had Oswald, her elder brother, who liked to shock with his tales of what went on between men and women. To Lizzie's mind it was all disgusting, but something always impelled her to listen. The Birds and the Bees, her mother called it, for some reason, handing her a leaflet containing strange line drawings of interior piping and tubing that Lizzie couldn't imagine were really accurate. She had a copy of Leonardo's drawings in her bookshelf and was particularly keen on the one where the mother's stomach opens like a nut to reveal the curled infant within. That she could grasp.

'What's that?'

'When your womb dries up, silly. You don't get periods any more. But you wouldn't know. Have you started yet?'

'No.' Lizzie shook her head. Catriona had had her first period when she was ten and Lizzie had been so jealous she could hardly bear to speak to her for a week.

'Oh well, you will soon,' piped Catriona, sounding to Lizzie's ears just like the nurse in Dr Macmillan's surgery whose first question was always 'Have you started yet?' to which Lizzie always had to say no, she hadn't, and blush with shame at the inability of her body to keep up with everyone else's.

Forgetting about their elders, the two girls swam again for what seemed like hours.

As they trailed up the beach shuddering with cold, they saw Mrs Macaskill coming towards them in her slacks and blouse. She was barefoot, her shoes dangled from her left hand, and Lizzie saw that her toenails were varnished bright scarlet. This seemed to Lizzie the height of sophistication, but she also knew that it was something her mother would turn her aristocratic nose up at.

'Your daddy's sent me,' she said to Catriona, 'as Mummy isn't well. She's had to go to the hospital in Kirkcudbright. She'll be fine, but she just needs to rest. He said to keep you until Eldred comes to fetch Lizzie and then you two can go home together.'

'Am I staying with Lizzie then?' Catriona cast Lizzie an indecipherable glance, which did not bode well, Lizzie felt. She could feel Catriona's favour retreating like the sun behind a cloud.

'I think that's the plan, dear. We'll sort out the things now and take them to our house, if that's all right. But you're not to worry, she'll be fine. She needs a night or two in hospital and then she'll be as right as rain.'

'Can we swim again?' asked Lizzie, reaching down for a sandwich.

'Do you really want to?' asked Mrs Macaskill, smiling down at her. 'You look a wee bit cold to me, dear. Why not come home and I'll run a lovely bath and then you two can watch the telly until Daddy comes.'

The thing about Mrs Macaskill was, Lizzie thought to herself, as she pulled off her sodden swimsuit and threw it on a rock, that she was nice, really, really nice. She was one of those women who exuded a kind of warm, toasty atmosphere, like the three-bar fire in Lizzie's father's study, which glowed a bright orange-red and which Lizzie liked to turn herself in front of during the coldest months, watching her white legs grow mottled in the intense heat.

The Macaskills' farmhouse was built in the same style as the manse at Garholm and was of the same period, only there were no crow-stepped gables and the window surrounds were painted black, a rule of the Douglas estate. The front garden behind the dyke was planted neatly with bright, orderly looking flowers, marigolds and tulips, and other things Lizzie didn't know the names of. Her mother was a keen gardener and Lizzie had already spent an inordinate amount of her childhood following her up and down other people's herbaceous borders whilst her mother admired various plants and asked for their names, English or Latin, which she wrote down in a little black book. Behind her, in an act of quiet rebellion, Lizzie would throw stones onto the grass. It was the only way of passing the time.

Mrs Macaskill led the girls into the kitchen on the other side of the house, a large, stone-floored room with a view over the ocean. There was an Aga on which their towels and wet swimming things were to be draped and, above the Aga, what Lizzie's mother called a hedge, a large, ridged, wooden drying rack attached to a pulley upon which Mr Macaskill's working trousers and shirts were hung to dry. It had been baking day and the kitchen smelled of pastry and iced sponge, making Lizzie's mouth water. An elderly labrador lay by the Aga and thumped its tail genially when it saw Lizzie and Catriona.

'Well, girls,' said Mrs Macaskill, 'shall I run you a bath?'

'We can do it ourselves,' said Lizzie politely, 'if you'll just show us where to go.'

'Thank you, Lizzie, that would be wonderful. I've got the tea to get, so that would be a great help.'

'Where's Mr Macaskill?' demanded Catriona suspiciously.

'He's still out, dear. You can probably see him from here.' Indeed, as she spoke, Tommy Macaskill came into view, a distant figure in the cab of his tractor, gulls screaming overhead.

'So, there's no one home then?' said Catriona, looking offended, an expression Lizzie dreaded. Once Catriona was in this mood, anything could happen. Such was her control of the playground that if Catriona deemed it, no one would speak to you for a week. Mrs Macaskill seemed, Lizzie thought, remarkably calm.

'Just me, dear, that's right,' replied Nonie Macaskill. 'It's lucky I was here, too, when he called in, considering what's happened to your mummy.'

'I suppose so,' Catriona replied cheekily. She was

looking very ugly, Lizzie thought. Her normally pale face looked peaky and her little eyes red-rimmed. Sometimes she realized how much she hated Catriona and the power she wielded in the playground. Having Mrs Wright as your mother and Mr Wright as your father amounted to supreme power amongst the under-twelves at Garholm Primary. Oswald, Lizzie's brother, thought Catriona squeaky, skinny and common. He had no time for her at all and Lizzie had wished she could share that view. But now it occurred to her suddenly that all that was changing. If Mrs Wright really was, as Catriona herself had said, as mad as a snake, then Catriona's influence would diminish; her power would wither and she would be as others, a mere mortal.

'You're upset,' said Mrs Macaskill, kindly, 'that's only to be expected. But I'm sure she'll be fine. Your daddy will ring soon and give us the latest.'

Catriona folded her arms and gave Mrs Macaskill a look, but she didn't appear to notice.

'I'll do the bath,' said Lizzie quickly, 'come on, Catriona.'

'I don't want a bath.'

'It'll do you good,' said Lizzie firmly, 'and, besides, you need to wash off all that salt.'

'I'm not having a bath,' said Catriona in her most frightening tone of voice.

'Suit yourself,' said Lizzie more chirpily than she felt, following Mrs Macaskill out of the room. Glancing over her shoulder, she saw Catriona looking surprised, almost as if she had been lightly winded.

When Lizzie came downstairs after her bath, she

found Catriona sitting on what she knew Mrs Macaskill called 'the settee' in the front room watching telly. Her mother banned 'settee' as a word from Lizzie's vocabulary. The object was a sofa, just as a 'serviette' was a table napkin. Sometimes Lizzie felt exhausted leading her double life, the burdens of which had been added to considerably by Mrs Wright's 'revelations' if that's what they were.

There was a whole set of other double standards among the adult world that matched the complexity of Lizzie's own playground hierarchy. She had thought things would become clearer as she grew up, as they plainly had to Oswald, who was not confused by life as Lizzie seemed to be, but in reality, Lizzie thought sadly, things became more obscured, like swimming in the sandy depths of the ocean.

Glancing at Catriona, she saw that she looked miserable and pinched. The streaks on her face suggested tears. But she wouldn't talk, so Lizzie went out again and sat in the kitchen with Mrs Macaskill and asked the sort of questions that her mother should ask but never did.

When her father arrived in his grey van, Lizzie's heart leaped. She watched closely as he greeted Mrs Macaskill, and there was no doubt in Lizzie's mind that her father found this woman attractive. He smiled more than he usually did and accepted a cup of tea, which she knew he didn't particularly like. He also refused to sit formally in the front room amongst the antimacassars and the glass-fronted cabinets containing the tea sets and moustache cups of previous generations, preferring the kitchen where he perched himself against the table, cup in hand.

'How is she?' he asked Mrs Macaskill. 'It's not the first time this has happened, I gather?'

'No,' said Mrs Macaskill, glancing meaningfully at Lizzie, but Eldred waved away her concern with a shake of his head. 'Lizzie might as well know,' he said. 'She can't remain a child for ever, can you, Lizzie?'

'No,' said Lizzie, leaning against her father, aware of the comfort she gained from his presence. It had been a day of shocks, she realized, surprised to find this realization somehow comforting, as if acknowledging pain somehow diminished it, instead of the other way round. And it was nice to be treated as grown-up for a change, instead of being chased out of the room or ignored as her mother did.

'I spoke to Wright and he said she was being monitored. Dr Mac has had her moved to the cottage hospital in Kirkcudbright. They may move her to the Infirmary, but they're waiting to see if she improves. They've put her on a drip.'

'Has she recovered her senses?'

'He didn't say.'

'She was talking a whole lot of nonsense on the beach, practically gibbering, John said.'

Eldred gave Nonie a considering look. 'Well, perhaps she's been under a bit of pressure lately,' he replied. 'She's not as young as she was and she still has a full-time job looking after this lot that

434

would wear any of us down,' he nodded his head at Lizzie.

'That's true,' said Nonie, smoothing her hips. 'Perhaps she needs a holiday.'

'They're going to Crieff Hydro,' said Lizzie, 'that's where they always go.'

'He should take her somewhere better than that,' said Nonie. 'She needs to go abroad, maybe to Majorca or the Costa del Sol. I wouldn't mind that myself.'

And Lizzie could see that she wouldn't: a picture came to mind of Nonie Macaskill in a fitted swim-suit and high heels, sipping from a glass containing complicated arrangements of fruit, topped by one of those adorable little paper parasols that Lizzie had seen in one of the stories in *Bunty* magazine.

'Crieff Hydro gives preferential rates to the clergy,' said Eldred. 'It's a bit of a bargain for Wright. But as it happens he could soon be in for something better,' he added, glancing into his cup as he spoke.

'Oh?'

'I hear he's climbing the greasy pole and may be in for a promotion.'

'He's never mentioned . . .' began Nonie and then stopped.

'And of course it would be better for his Mrs,' Eldred continued, as if he hadn't noticed Nonie's half-finished remark. 'She could give up work and relax a bit. He was a great success at Balmoral, you know, and it would be nice if he could build on that. He may even end up as minister of the church there, a nice little slot if ever I saw one.'

'Oh, I see.' Nonie put her cup down. 'Well, I wish him all the best,' she added, and Lizzie noticed with horror that her bottom lip was trembling as if she was about to cry.

On the way home, Lizzie's father stopped to have a look at some drainage works that were taking place in the lower fields of Bannerstoun Mains, the home farm.

'Do you want to come too?' he asked the girls, who were squashed together in the front seat. Catriona shook her head, she was still sulking, but Lizzie wanted to come. She liked walking about the land with her father, nodding her head as he mentioned various technical points, but this evening she also wanted to ask some questions out of earshot of anyone else.

'Mrs Wright said,' began Lizzie, as her father examined a trench where some pipes were to be laid, 'that you were in love with Mrs Macaskill when you were young. Is that true?'

'She said that, did she?'

'Yes.'

'She was a very pretty girl, Nonie Macaskill,' Eldred began, 'but I wasn't in love with her. She wasn't really my type. I like the intellectual ones, like your ma, for instance. I was always easily bored. Nonie would bore me after a bit. A cup of tea's enough.'

'She said other things too,' said Lizzie, 'about Mr Wright and Non— Mrs Macaskill.'

'Can you keep a secret, Lizzie?' asked her father,

putting his arm round her shoulders.

'I think so.'

'It means never telling anyone else. You understand that, don't you?'

'Yes,' said Lizzie gravely.

'Mr Wright and Mrs Macaskill are having a love affair. It's a foolish thing for both of them. She has a loving husband and three children and Mr Wright is an excellent clergyman who ought to know better.'

'Will he lose his job?'

'If anyone got to find out, yes.'

'But you know.'

'I know, but I'm not going to tell anyone, except you.'

'And Mum knows, doesn't she?'

'She suspects, but she doesn't know. And she wouldn't talk about it if she did.'

'Not even to you?'

'She might to me. Why, Lizzie? Was there something else?'

Lizzie hesitated and then, as the first act of her newly grown-up life, she said, 'No, there wasn't.' If Mrs Wright was correct in what she had said, then her mother hadn't loved her father but had married him for his position, something Lizzie realized she had long suspected. But she wasn't going to tell him that. He didn't need to know and knowing would only hurt him. And what if Mrs Wright really was mad? One had to make decisions, and Lizzie had decided. She would keep the rest to herself.

'I think we should go back,' she said, 'Catriona's on her own and she's pretty miserable.'

'Quite right,' said Eldred. 'It's been a hard day for her. I'm proud of you, Lizzie,' he added, 'you're growing up into a really thoughtful person.'

SILK AND STRAW

Helen Lamb

HELEN LAMB is an award-winning short-story writer whose work has been broadcast on Radio 4 and published in many literary journals and magazines. Her first poetry collection, *Strange Fish*, was published in 1997 and her first short-story collection, *Superior Bedsits and Other Stories*, in 2001.

Helen Lamb lives in Dunblane.

Gemma Bell, the girl next door, stood on tiptoes and peered over the fence. Her jet eyes rounded in fascination as Aileen tilted her head back and dangled the worm high in the air. The worm shrank upwards and seemed to shudder in the breeze, then slowly stretched as gravity pulled it, down and down, towards the black hole of Aileen's wide and waiting mouth. She stuck out her tongue and let it slither in, blinking at the first sharp tang of salt.

She swallowed it whole, eyes shut tight, all the better to savour the shimmy of jelly slip-sliding down her throat. When the wriggle finally reached her tummy, her lips closed on a satisfied smile. Her eyelids flew open and she stared straight back at Gemma Bell.

'What's it taste like?' Gemma asked.

Aileen cast around the garden until she found a really juicy one, short and fat with a bulging purple head. She held it out. 'Try one if you want to know.'

Gemma's hands clamped over her mouth. She had tiny spotless hands, shiny rounded fingernails. 'It's still alive,' she said.

Aileen nodded. 'They're best that way. Go down easier.' She shoved the worm through the palings.

Gemma took a swift step back. She shook her gleaming cap of sleek black hair and, through parted fingers, said, 'No, thanks. I'll just watch.'

So Aileen had to show her again. She fed the worm onto her outstretched tongue and, in one gulp, it was gone. Only, this time, Gemma hadn't seemed so impressed. 'D'you want to play?' was all she said.

Aileen said, 'Not today. I'm going in now.' There was *Jackanory* on TV and Gemma Bell was boring anyway.

When Aileen's dad got home, he had agreed. Gemma Bell was very boring and Aileen was his favourite girl. Maybe Gemma did have hair like silk and hers was more like straw but he had decided not to swap her for the girl next door.

He had thought about it, though. Aileen searched the creases in her father's smiling face. He had considered swapping her. That is what he meant.

'Don't you worry,' Aileen's mum said and handed her a chocolate biscuit. 'Your dad's just teasing.'

But Aileen knew that she had been compared and she had not come out the best. She bit into the biscuit and, deep down in her belly, she felt two little tickles. The worms were waiting to be fed.

Aileen's mum said to her dad, 'That Gemma's too good to be true. The way her mother's got her drilled – good morning and good afternoon, never just hello. It's not natural.'

She ruffled Aileen's hair of straw and handed her a second biscuit. Her mum only pretended to be friends with Gemma's mother and she was getting fed up hearing Gemma this and Gemma that. It was a competition she could never win. There was not a lot to brag about when it came to Aileen.

'Got her tying her shoelaces and the wee soul's just turned four,' Aileen's mum was snapping now. 'I will not turn my daughter into a performing seal.'

Aileen's dad picked up the paper. She was glad that he'd stopped listening. Aileen was five and three-quarters, already at the school, and she still had shoes with buckles and slip-ons for the gym.

She helped herself to a third biscuit, then a fourth. The worms were very hungry still. They needed her to feed them. One packet wouldn't be enough. She would have to eat and eat to keep the worms alive. They were her own two little secrets. Revolting things. Her mum would scream if she knew.

She had found Aileen one time, licking a wee baby worm. She had yelled over and over. *Dirty. Dirty. Dirty girl.* Aileen got such a fright, she bit right through the poor wee worm and one half of it died. She hadn't meant to hurt it. She was just saying hello. The worms had to be secrets after that. Revolting things. She swallowed them to keep them safe. She took good care of them.

The worms were her own private business and if they ever made her feel queasy or uneasy, if they wriggled and squirmed too alive inside her, a handful of biscuits would calm them down, a second helping of mashed potatoes.

She must have lost her taste for worms around the time she began to bite her fingernails. It was a nasty habit, her mum said. *Not nice.* Aileen's habits had never been nice. She got bitter aloes painted on her nails but she still could not stop chewing and she felt sick a lot.

'You've got no will power,' her mum said.

She gave Aileen a caramel wafer to take away the taste, had one herself while she was at it. 'Just this once,' she said.

Will power was what you needed when you went on a diet and she had been on a diet since the day Aileen was born. She had not got her figure back yet. She was still a wee bit fat. Aileen's dad would slap his wife's plump behind. He'd say, 'All the more for me.'

He promised he would never swap her for a slimmer model. But he must have considered it or he would not have said it. And Aileen got the feeling that her mother did not trust him any more than she did.

Every day, Aileen's mum squeezed herself into the extra-firm-hold corselet, that secret layer of armour that held her in and smoothed her out and kept those slimmer models at bay, while Aileen went on gnawing her nails, gnawed between meals and snacks, between all the extra consoling biscuits.

'Puppy fat,' her mother tried to reassure her as the pounds piled on. 'You'll take a stretch soon, don't you worry. Just look at the size of those feet.' Aileen didn't want to look. She was starving, starving all the time. And she did not believe that she would ever grow enough in the right direction to balance those gigantic, clumsy, size seven feet.

Silk and Straw

Her first cigarette brought a few hours' relief. The tar – hot on her tongue, a bitter layer of protection coating sensitive taste buds – dulling the eternal hunger. And Gemma had been there again, standing just a little outside the huddle of girls in the newsagent's darkened doorway.

Ten No 6 from the vending machine. They had all clubbed in, all except the aloof Gemma Bell. She looked on as they sparked match after match and the damp wind blew them back out.

Aileen was the first to get a draw. Worms of smoke burrowed and burned deep into her lungs. She held back the splutter as long as she could. She didn't like the way Gemma was watching her. Those black eyes. Diamond sharp. Curious. Critical. She was always watching but she never joined in. It was kind of weird, made you wonder what she was after.

The nicotine swirled and swam to her head and Gemma blurred. Aileen no longer cared what Gemma thought anyway. She took a couple more drags and offered her the cigarette. But Gemma didn't want to know. She shook her head and the sheen of the full November moon glinted in her coal-black hair. 'Maybe some other time,' she said.

'You're not going to tell, are you?' Aileen was worried now.

If Gemma's mum found out, it would not be long in getting back. She would just love to clype. Embarrass Aileen's mum. Land Aileen in it. Of course, she would say she'd thought twice about mentioning it. She didn't like to. But she was *concerned*. Gemma's mum was frequently concerned.

She cared about Aileen's welfare more than anyone.

'Why would I bother telling?' Gemma's tone was scathing. 'It's not as if it's all that interesting.' She didn't say she wouldn't, though. She had left it hanging. The cigarettes were Aileen's biggest secret yet. And Gemma could give her away any time she felt the urge – if Aileen was unfriendly, if she tried to shake her off.

Aileen had to let her tag along now, everywhere she went. Though why Gemma bothered was hard to figure out. She didn't smoke, did not see the point in starting either. She hardly spoke. But she still came, skipped school dinners and trudged down town in all weathers along with Aileen to the Café Rex. The smokers hung out there, the wildest boys, and casual girls who wore their shirts with all but a couple of buttons undone.

The Rex had a long, highly polished dark wood counter and dark panelled walls. Behind the counter, the clearest of clear mirrors shone with all the pride and elbow grease the owners lavished on it. A jukebox stood to one side, all gleaming chrome and flashing lights. In front – three neat rows of seven formica tables. The best seats were at either end of the middle row, backs to the wall. From here, you could see everyone who came in and everything that went on – without turning your head. That was the main advantage. You didn't want to look too interested. And you most certainly did not want to show the slightest interest in Gavin Urquart or any of that gang.

Gavin was not so easy to ignore though. He was

always glancing over, flashing his triumphant, cocky grin whenever he succeeded in catching Aileen's eye. Aileen would not let on she'd noticed. She would flick her cigarette, turn and try to chat to Gemma. Not that Gemma was much use as a distraction. She had nothing to say back.

One time, he'd stopped by their table on his way back from the jukebox. He took the cigarette from between Aileen's lips. 'You're not inhaling right,' he said.

He stood there, gazing down at her, with Jimi Hendrix, 'All Along the Watchtower,' smouldering in the air between them.

'Anyway, you shouldn't be smoking. It doesn't suit you.' He dragged deeply and stubbed the cigarette out in the ashtray.

Aileen's mum had agreed with him, after she'd been through the blazer pockets and found the cigarette and matches, the three half-eaten packets of Polo mints. She should not be smoking. In the end, it wasn't Gemma after all. It was the constant minty breath that had made her mum suspicious.

She wanted to know where Aileen got the money to indulge this latest filthy habit. She'd gone through every pocket, every drawer, Aileen's satchel. There was no privacy after that. She was always poking about, paying unexpected visits to Aileen's room in the hope of catching her out.

Aileen was constantly on guard and spending more and more time in the bathroom. Sometimes, she didn't even smoke in there. It was just a relief to lock the door and be somewhere no one could come barging in, intruding on her thoughts.

And lately there had been moments when she had needed to consider, needed to examine her reflection in the bathroom mirror. Ask herself important questions and watch the answer shaping on her lips, keep on asking until she got it right.

Like maybe she needed to know if she was nervous. And the first time she asked, the answer was no. She couldn't care less. Then the next time, she wasn't so sure. She had to ask again. And the answer was yes now. She *was* nervous.

Or maybe, one day, this boy just kissed her. And she needed to find out if it meant he liked her, and the answer kept changing. Maybe yes. Maybe no.

The face in the mirror hadn't looked like her face. She had to smile to make sure it belonged. And the smile that came back was so soft and so strange. It was hers. But not hers. She was a different person from the one that left the house earlier that afternoon.

She had wanted to brush her hair before she went out. But her mum said there was no time. The butcher's would be shutting soon and they needed mince for the dinner. Aileen would have to run.

'And come straight back,' she said.

Aileen hadn't hurried back, though. She had taken the slow, defiant way home, down by the river and over the bridge. She'd stopped in the middle and lit a cigarette. The water had been high today. High and loud. The roar had given the illusion of privacy. Behind the wall of sound, she had felt alone at last. She could relax, think her own thoughts better than she ever could in the quiet of her room at home. She was free to think anything she wanted and no one would even suspect.

The river kept coming and coming towards her. It came in countless streams. Fast and slow. Broad and narrow. Splitting. Joining up again. And always more to come.

The cigarette was almost done, just one more drag to go, when the dogs' barking interrupted the flow. A wolf whistle leaped through the air, a rude reminder that she was in a public place. Very rude. Embarrassing, actually. Aileen's cheeks had blazed.

When she looked round, Gavin Urquart was heading along the river bank, two great alsatians tearing ahead of him. He tried to call them back but they kept tearing on. They charged onto the bridge and he started running. His yells cut through the soft damp air.

Those dogs were almost on her before they finally obeyed. They didn't want to stop. They reared up before her, barely two feet away, their powerful necks jerking against the invisible leash of his command. They strained towards the poke of mince, scenting blood, ready to pounce if he relaxed his hold on them for even a moment.

Without taking her eyes off them, Aileen stuffed the poke inside her jacket and did the zipper up. She did not respond when Gavin said hello. She stood there transfixed, her gaze gripped by the dogs' throbbing jaws, bared teeth and steaming tongues. Gavin strolled between the dogs now, hands in pockets, calmly grinning.

'Now what did I tell you?' He took the cigarette end burning down between her fingers and tossed it in the river.

'You shouldn't be smoking. It doesn't suit you.'

Then he kissed her. The river raged beneath her feet. He was squashing into the mince and the dogs were all over her, sniffing and licking.

Gavin must have sensed her fear. He drew back. He snapped, *'Down.'* He said the dogs' names were Sacha and Sheba and they were just being friendly. She shouldn't be afraid. They wouldn't hurt her as long as he was there.

That meant they could – if he didn't stop them. If they were not restrained.

He kissed her again. Aileen didn't know what to do next. He had to tell her to open her lips. So she did. She didn't want him to get the idea that he was the first boy she'd kissed in her life. His tongue probed the secret depths of her mouth. Nothing would ever taste so dangerous or desirable again.

When she got home her mum was waiting for an explanation of why she had taken so long and how the mince poke got in such a state, burst on both sides, oozing blood. Aileen tried to tell her that it fell and rolled away back down the hill. It seemed a reasonable enough explanation. But her mum did not believe that mince would roll that far. She said that would defy the laws of physics. Mince was soft. It would change shape and flatten to the ground.

She said that it looked to her as if *somebody* stotted it all the way home. And she was still waiting for a proper explanation.

Silk and Straw

'It's the *secrecy*,' her mum complained when Aileen would not give her one. 'We worry, you know. We never know what you're thinking.'

The *secrecy*. The hissing suspicion in the way she said that word made Aileen's teeth clamp together defensively, caging her tongue. She was the guilty little girl again, the one who swallowed the worm, stomach churning, dreading the moment her secrets would be regurgitated from their deep dark hiding place into the light of her mother's disapproving glare. When she still wouldn't answer, she was sent upstairs to think.

'You make it hard on yourself,' her mother called after her. 'What on earth could be so bad that you can't talk to me?'

Aileen closed the bathroom door and drew the bolt against any more awkward questions. There were so many things she could not say even to herself yet, let alone her mum, so many feelings she did not have the words for. She examined the reflection in the mirror. It must be hers. But she had never looked this way before. She took up the hairbrush and drew it through her hair until every single stalk of straw was transformed to sheerest silk.

Maybe Gavin liked her. Maybe he thought she was pretty. Maybe she was.

Her lips looked distinctly kissed. All rosy, soft and swollen. Her eyes were dark and shimmering and full of secrets now. Gavin put them there. She could gaze into those eyes for ever and she would still not discover everything they meant.

BONNY IN SCOTLAND

Katie Agnew

Born in Edinburgh in 1972, brought up in Lasswade and educated at Aberdeen University, **KATIE AGNEW** has written for many magazines and newspapers including the *Evening Standard, Cosmopolitan, 19* and the *Daily Mail*. Most recently she worked as features editor on *Marie Claire* magazine, where she wrote a regular column, *What Katie Did Next*.

Katie now lives in Bath with her husband, John Latimer, their daughter, Olivia, and dog, Tilly. Her first novel, *Drop Dead Gorgeous*, has just been published.

1978

The little girl sat perched on a battered wooden bench on the promenade where her mother had left her with a firm, 'stay'. The seat was too high for her feet to reach the ground so she swung her tanned legs absent-mindedly, back and forth, back and forth, as seven-year-olds do. She stared past the group of kids her age, who were playing hopscotch with a squashed Irn Bru can, and out to sea with a worried expression more appropriate to someone five times her age. It was not the turquoise ocean she was used to and her tiny nose crinkled with distaste as she studied the filthy, litter-strewn excuse for a beach and the angry grey water beyond. It was summer, but the light was so poor and the cloud so thick that Fife was just a dark shadow on the horizon. She shivered in her yellow anorak and wondered why so many people were outside on such a miserable day. They all looked short and pale and sickly – especially the children.

Some miles to her right she could make out the monstrously scary form of Cockenzie power station. Later that night it would creep into her nightmares and she would wake up screaming in her camp bed in Granny's cramped front room. How could this be the place her mom had talked about with such longing? Was this dirty, grey city really 'home'?

Her mom was taking too long getting the ice-creams. The little girl looked desperately for the pretty, familiar face in the crowds but all she could see were strangers, talking with strange voices about strange things. She bit her lip hard and tried to halt the wobble but the tears came hot and fast, stinging her cold cheeks with salt and shame. 'Be a brave girl,' her mom had said but she couldn't be brave, not here. The little girl began to rock back and forth on the bench, quietly crying to herself, 'I wanna go home, I wanna go home, I wanna go home.'

'Are you greeting?' The blond boy observed her as he would an injured seagull on the beach, with a hefty dose of inquisitiveness and a small pinch of pity. He held a stick in his grubby hand and, when she failed to respond, poked her gently with it in the arm.

'You are greeting,' he persevered. 'Why are you greeting?'

'I beg your pardon?' The little girl wished to be left alone but was far too polite to say so.

'Oh, she's no from here,' said the boy excitedly to the two boys and three girls who stood behind him, watching intently.

'Gree-ting,' he repeated slowly.

The girl shook her head to show her lack of comprehension. The kids giggled.

Bonny in Scotland

'Crying,' said the boy in his most grown-up voice. He had been patronised often enough in his eight long years to relish this opportunity to talk down to someone. 'You're crying.'

'Oh, gee,' said the girl, wiping her face with her anorak sleeve. 'I wasn't crying. I just had something in my eye.'

'Are you a Yank?' asked the boy with wide, wide eyes which were the same steely-grey colour as the sky and the sea. 'You are, aren't you?' He recognized the accent from watching *Dallas* and *The Dukes of Hazard*.

The girl thought long and hard and then answered as she would have done if someone had asked her that question last week, back home in San Francisco.

'I'm Scottish,' she replied.

The assembled group of children dissolved into fits of hysteria.

'You're no Scottish,' laughed the ringleader once he'd pulled himself together enough to talk. 'Well, you're no fae Portobello anyhow.'

'I am,' said the girl firmly. 'I live just over there with my grandmother.'

She pointed to the grimy tenements which were now home.

'You dinnae sound like you're fae here. You dinnae look like you're fae here.' The boy's voice was more interested than cruel.

It was true that her clothes were different to the natives' attire. They wore nylon flares in various shades of brown, with black canvas plimsolls, and

457

green parkas with fur round the hoods. Their hair was in the classic bowl-cut shape. Their skin was as blue-white as the day they were born in Simpson's Memorial Hospital. The little girl was dressed in stripy, rainbow tights which her father had sent her for Christmas from Macy's in New York, with red leather clogs and a hand-embroidered smock dress from an Indian reserve in Nevada. Even her yellow anorak was all wrong, being covered in cloth patches from various rock festivals she had attended with her mother. Her black hair fell in one thick curtain right down to her bum and her skin was as smooth and brown as her Hispanic friends back home.

'Have you just moved here, like?' asked the boy. She nodded.

'Fae where?' he demanded.

'San Francisco,' replied the girl.

'Eh?' Six faces looked at her blankly.

'It's in the USA,' she explained. 'California.'

'America,' the boy explained knowledgeably to his friends. 'That's what I said. She's a Yank.'

'But I'm Scottish,' she reiterated. 'My mom's from Portobello.'

As if by magic her mom appeared, in a flutter of sky-blue kaftan and a tinkle of dangling jewellery. She grinned broadly with bright, white teeth and tossed her own mane of long, black hair over her slim shoulders.

'Wow,' said the boy. 'Is that your mum? She's awfie bonny.'

The girl smiled proudly.

'She is,' agreed the girl. 'And so am I because that's my name.'

'Eh?'

'Bonny. My name's Bonny. Bonny Lebowsky.'

Her new friend smirked to show that he thought that was a ridiculous name but there was no malice in his voice as he asked, 'Can you come out to play wi' us later?'

Bonny looked up at her mom with a hopeful gaze. 'Can I, mom?'

'Sure,' shrugged her mother. 'Don't see why not.'

'What's your name?' she inquired of the boy with the sea coloured eyes.

'Danny,' he said. 'Danny McVie.'

As Bonny and her mother wandered back towards their new home, licking their ice-creams and chatting about the trip they were planning to take around the Highlands, Bonny was aware that they were being followed at a distance by Danny and his small flock of adoring fans. Danny felt he had found an exotic butterfly on the beach and he didn't want to let it out of his sight.

'We need gas,' announced Bonny's mother as they approached Pitlochrie in their multi-coloured, hand-painted, hippie dippie VW Camper.

'Can we go to a gas station with a yellow sign, please?' asked the child politely.

'Why?' her mom glanced at her from behind her sunglasses.

'I'm collecting tokens for a World Cup tankard. It's a gift for Danny.'

'Oh,' said her mother with a knowing smile. 'All right.'

Bonny had learnt a lot since moving to Scotland. For a start, she now knew that football was not a game played by big men in hefty body armour in stadiums across the US; the *real* game – the beautiful game as Danny put it – was played in muddy fields by *real* men who were not afraid to take a tackle. American football was for softies. And no, she mustn't call it soccer. Only idiots like the English ever called the game that. Danny lived and breathed football. He was rarely seen wearing anything other than his Hearts strip and he seemed to spend most of his waking hours at the local Boys Club where he was star striker of the Under 11s team. Bonny was suitably impressed.

'This tankard has the signatures of all the Scotland team on it,' explained Bonny to her mother. 'Kenny Dalgleish, Joe Jordan, Danny McGrain . . . Danny will love it.'

'And how many tokens do you need?' asked her mom in amusement.

'Six,' said Bonny.

'Well, I'm sure we'll have enough tokens by the time we get back from our trip.'

'Do you want to hear my new song?' asked Bonny.

'Sure,' said her mom.

We're on the march wi' Ally's army
We're going to the Argentines
And we'll really shake 'em up
When we win the World Cup
Cos Scotland is the greatest fitba' team'.

The child smiled proudly at her mother, looking for praise.

'That's real great, Bonny, but you do know Scotland always lose, don't you?'

She was laughing and Bonny thought she was being unfair.

'Danny says we have a real chance of winning this time.'

'Oh, he would. He's a guy. Scottish guys always think we're going to win, but we never do.'

Bonny crossed her arms tightly over her anorak to show she was not impressed by her mother's lack of patriotism.

'And how would you know?' she demanded.

'Because I grew up here,' she smiled with fond recollection. 'I grew up watching my dad jumping up and down, swearing at the radio, and coming home from Tynecastle roaring drunk because Hearts had lost again. Scottish men take their football very seriously but they're not very good at it.'

'Danny is,' insisted the girl. 'He's going to be a professional when he grows up.'

'Well, Danny must be very gifted,' said her mother. She was still smiling to herself knowingly.

Bonny thought that she'd like to throttle her mother.

At Loch Lomond, Bonny started to understand why her mom loved this country so much. The Highlands looked kind of like Canada, only smaller. They arrived after dark and parked the camper van in a layby. It was so quiet that Bonny found it hard to sleep in the pull-down bed, next to her mother. She drifted off for a while and then woke up to find a shaft of light pouring in from behind the tie-dyed curtains. Silently, Bonny slipped from underneath the blanket and tiptoed gently out of the van. The sun had risen in a gloriously clear sky but it was too early to be warm. The surface of the loch was as still and black as polished ebony and it reflected the trees on its banks as clearly as any mirror. A heron perched like a statue on a branch which jutted out over the water. Suddenly the silence was shattered by the crunch of a breaking branch and as Bonny looked to her right she came eye-to-eye with a beautiful roe deer. They stared at each other for a moment and then the creature turned heel and ran. Bonny had to catch her breath.

'Woah, that was cool,' she said to no one in partic-ular and everyone in general.

'I love Scotland,' she shouted to the heron, who ignored her with studied majesty.

Bonny ran down the promenade towards the hooded figure leaning over the sea wall.

'Danny, Danny, I've got you a present,' she shouted.

It was a crystal-clear day, although the wind chilled the air, and the sea looked almost blue. Bonny noticed as Danny turned towards her that his eyes too looked more blue today. In the years to come she would learn that he had the eyes of a chameleon and that their colour would always change depending on his surroundings. In Jamaica they would be turquoise, in the south of France they'd be azure blue and in Goa they would be the same brilliant green as the ocean. It was one of the things that marked him out as special.

'I'm sorry Scotland lost,' said Bonny, gently, seeing Danny's dejected face. 'I thought this might cheer you up a bit.'

She handed him the glass tankard. It had a football on it with a thistle on top and was covered in the black scrawled autographs of the entire Scottish team.

'That's fab,' enthused Danny. 'I love it. Thanks, Bonny.'

Bonny shrugged.

'That's OK. I just thought you'd like it.'

She was already in love with the strange, enigmatic little boy with the rainbow eyes.

Bonny was thrilled to discover that she was in the same class as her new best friend when she started at primary school in August and wasn't at all surprised to discover that, despite her bohemian and worldly upbringing, he was the only child in the class who was brighter than she was. By the end of the academic year, she'd lost her American accent and Mom became Mum, much to her father's amusement when she visited him in New York the following summer. Her father, David Lebowsky, was a bigwig attorney who lived in a vast apartment in Midtown Manhattan and worked on Wall Street. He'd been a hippie, briefly, after studying at Yale and it had been during this phase that he'd met her mother, Alison. The result of their summer dalliance in a Californian commune had been Bonny. There was never any talk of marriage, but both David and Alison were proud of their 'mistake'.

'You're an American,' David teased his eight-year-old daughter when she said 'Aye' and 'Och'.

'You're Jewish!' cried her paternal grandmother, wringing her hands in dismay.

'I'm Scottish,' thought Bonny with certainty. She couldn't wait to get home.

Alison had started her own business – a vegetarian wholefood café just off Princes Street. She and David had always remained friends and she took his business advice to heart.

'It's the way forward, Ali,' he'd promised her. 'Health food stores are big news in New York. It's the way forward.'

The café's popularity took everyone by surprise, not least Alison, who had to question her long-held hippie beliefs as the money rolled in. By 1982, she owned three cafés and a restaurant. In 1984 she opened Edinburgh's first organic bakery. She bought a vast house in Morningside and Bonny was enrolled at St Margaret's School instead of Portobello High.

'You look like snot,' said Danny, huffily, as he watched Bonny parade up and down in front of the full-length mirror in her new green uniform.

'I ken,' agreed Bonny with a frown. 'I wish I was just going to normal high school wi' you.'

She flopped onto her double bed beside him and

looked round her huge, interior-designed bedroom.

'I didn'ae want all this,' she insisted.

Danny shrugged.

'You're no like me any more,' he said sadly.

'I am,' Bonny said. 'We'll still be best friends.'

There was a pleading, desperate quality to her voice.

'Maybe,' shrugged Danny. 'Maybe no.'

He jumped off the bed and announced, 'I'm going home.'

Bonny lay for a long time staring at the high celling of her room. Tomorrow she'd be the new girl again, the nomad, the one with no home. She missed Portobello.

1996

The woman sat at her computer on the thirty-third floor, subconsciously stroking her perfect black bob with manicured red nails. It was four forty-five p.m. and she'd just made three billion pounds for a greedy multi-national pharmaceutical corporation from the comfort of her desk, high up in a glass and steel tower, deep in the bowels of the City of London. It was enough for today, she decided. She would kill time for fifteen minutes and then she'd head for King's Cross. It was Friday, after all, and she was excited about seeing Danny.

Twenty minutes later, Bonny sat impatiently at the wheel of her black Porsche in a traffic jam on Farringdon Road, chain-smoking Marlboro Lights but being careful not to drop ash on the buttery cream leather of the upholstery. She hated being late and she tapped her long nails angrily on the steering wheel as the car crawled at snail's pace towards King's Cross, its powerful engine complaining at having to be driven at five m.p.h. It was hot and she had the roof down. The petrol fumes were giving her a headache. When she did eventually screech into the tiny car park beside the train station, there were no spaces, just dozens of battered mini cabs milling around. Bonny bumped up onto the pavement, ignoring the double yellow lines, and put on her flashers, before skidding into the station on black stiletto heels.

Danny was waiting in the middle of the concourse, eating a burger and watching the frantic goings on of a Friday evening in London with amusement. His train from Edinburgh had arrived half an hour ago but he was a patient man and he was happy to sit on his holdall waiting while the world hurried by. He spotted Bonny before she saw him and smiled to himself at the thought that the glamorous young woman in black was looking for him. He noticed the way that every man's head turned in her direction and how women of all ages would stop mid-sentence as she passed to look her up and down. She was half-running from platform to platform, sliding on her high heels. He saw her check in the pub – an obvious place, fair enough. Then she squinted up at the information board, looking for some sign of where he might be. Danny knew he was being mean, hiding there at knee height in the crowd, so he stood up and at last she saw him. Her beautiful face broke into a huge grin and he could see the tension drop from her shoulders. She was wearing a well-cut suit with a very short skirt. Danny thought she looked like a model in a mobile phone advert – the perfect embodiment of the modern career girl.

'Bonny,' he thought. 'You do make me laugh.'

When Bonny's eyes found Danny's, she felt her heart skip as it always did. He was dressed in baggy jeans, Adidas shell-toed trainers and a second hand tracksuit top. His blond hair was long and flopped sexily into his chameleon eyes. When he bent over to pick up his bag, his white Calvin Klein boxer shorts poked out from above his belt. Danny had a way of being cool without trying. He should have been the lead singer of a band, or an international footballer at the very least. Bonny always noticed that boys from indie bands dressed like him, not the other way round. He did it first and then they seemed to follow. She wasn't quite sure how he did it but he always knew what was going to be trendy next, long before *The Face* cottoned on. She always dressed a bit more 'safely', preferring to look smart and sexy rather than risk trying to be cool. She had a sneaking suspicion she might fail.

'Hiya gorgeous,' said Danny with outstretched arms.

'Hello,' said Bonny falling into them greedily.

He kissed her platonically on the cheek and as always Bonny tried to hide her disappointment.

'You're having a laugh, right?' asked Danny as

she unlocked the Porsche with a flick of the button on her keyring.

'What?' she was confused.

'You've gone and got yourself a Porsche?'

'So?' Bonny blushed.

'You flash bastard! We don't get many of these at the garage.'

Danny shook his floppy blond hair in disbelief. He was a mechanic who owned his own little garage in Leith just round the corner from his flat. One of the perks of the job was getting a good deal on second-hand motors but Bonny's new wheels made the five-year-old Jeep he'd just bought look like a Tonka toy.

'So, what is it,' he continued. 'Two point eight?'

Bonny looked at him blankly and shrugged.

'I don't know, Dan. I just get in it and drive.'

There was a parking ticket on the windscreen of the Porsche which Danny waved at her solemnly as if it was a big deal.

'Just bung it in the glove compartment with the rest,' she told him nonchalantly as she prised her long legs back behind the wheel.

'Bonny, you really are something else.'

When he walked into her swanky Thames-side apartment and took in the exposed brickwork, polished walnut floors and imported Italian furniture, Danny whistled his approval.

'Jesus, how much did this place set you back?' he asked in astonishment.

'My entire Christmas bonus,' admitted Bonny, failing to add that that was over a quarter of a million pounds. 'But it's not very big. It only has one bedroom so you'll have to sleep on the couch.

Danny looked at the white leather sofa with trepidation.

'I'll have to make sure I don't dribble in my sleep,' he said, only half joking.

He wandered around the open plan apartment, fingering the marble sculptures of naked men and gazing with a bemused expression at the modern art which decorated the brick walls. Bonny watched him nervously, hoping he would be impressed. Then he spotted a photograph which looked totally out of place in this stark, minimalist setting – it was too personal, too twee, too endearingly human. It was a picture of Danny and Bonny with their tanned limbs around each other, toothy grins looking ultra-white against their brown skin, his naked torso gleaming with suntan oil, her full, young breasts fighting to escape from a black crocheted bikini.

'Goa!' announced Danny in delight. 'Those were the days, eh?'

'Those were the best days,' replied Bonny with an indulgent sigh.

When Bonny left St Margaret's, she had decided to defer her place at the London School of Economics and take a year out to travel. Danny had just finished his mechanics apprenticeship and, having never ventured further afield than the Costa Brava, he was keen to join her. The only problem was money. How was an apprentice going to afford the trip of a lifetime?

The two had remained the most unlikely friends throughout their teens. Bonny's accent had become clipped and Anglicized. She wore expensive loafers, shirts with the collar turned up and cashmere cardigans slung over her shoulders. By the time she was sixteen her crowd were already drinking Chardonnay at chic little wine bars in the West End. She got five As in her Highers, played the cello at concerts in the Assembly Rooms and holidayed in the Hamptons with her father and his new wife. She had a string of boyfriends with floppy hair who played rugby at Daniel Stewart's, Merciston or Fettes. Danny was a football casual who knew the local constabulary well. He was bright but he constantly bunked off school and left with only six O Grades to his name. ('Folk like me don't go to university, Bonny,' he explained when she asked why not.) Danny smoked dope with his mates on Leith Links and snogged nameless girls in the Kangaroo Club at the weekend while off his face on speed. And yet when the two of them met on a Wednesday evening in the City Café (it was neutral territory in that it was frequented by both their ilk), they blethered and belly-laughed and drank themselves stupid while their fellow drinkers looked on, wondering what that Sloaney girl was doing with the casual – or vice versa.

Then one Wednesday Danny arrived at the pub with a broad grin on his cheeky face.

'What are you looking so pleased about?' asked Bonny.

'My Nan's dead,' he announced.

'Dan,' she scolded. 'That's terrible. You should be upset.'

'I ken, I ken, I am,' he insisted, still smiling. 'But the old dear left me two grand, so now I can come wi' you on your trip. It's what she would've wanted, like.'

'Why?' asked Bonny innocently. 'Was she keen on travelling?'

'No really,' deadpanned Danny. 'She never went any further than my Auntie Bella's hoose in Dalkeith.'

And so the odd couple set off round the world. They worked in a surf shop on Bondi Beach, crewed a yacht round the Caribbean, got stoned for three months in Jamaica, stopped off in New York where they got under her father's feet and up her step-mother's cosmetically-enhanced nose, and then finally they 'did' India, rounding off their year with six weeks in Goa, where they blew the last of their money (and several thousand brain cells apiece) on Es and beach parties.

'Best days of my life,' said Bonny wistfully.

'Listen to you,' laughed Danny. 'You're twenty-five. It isn'ae over yet.'

Bonny certainly hoped not.

'OK, so let me get this right,' said Danny solemnly, as he gulped down the freshly squeezed mango juice Bonny had prepared for him in her chrome juicer. 'We're going to watch Scotland play England in the European Cup at some poncy bar in Clapham with a bunch of Chelsea fans?'

'Uh-huh,' nodded Bonny. 'Another croissant, Dan?'

'Bonny, are you totally, fucking mental?' Danny looked at her in utter astonishment.

'Pardon?'

'I cannae watch a Scotland England match, especially one of this, this, this –' he searched for the right word, 'magnitude! I cannae watch a match of this magnitude with a bunch of Chelsea supporters. I'll end up decking one of them. Can't we just stay here and watch it on telly? Please, Bon.'

Bonny chuckled into the apricot conserve. 'Don't be silly, Danny,' she said. 'It's just my new boyfriend Damian and a few of the boys from work. You'll like them. I promise.'

Danny's face turned purple as he choked on a particularly flaky croissant.

'Bonny. Dah-ling. Mwa, mwa, mwa. You look utterly ravishing. As always.'

Damian Aldridge always gave three kisses, like the French. He was very sophisticated, or so he liked to believe. He was sitting at a table surrounded by his colleagues Jeremy, Nigel and Piers. Each of them wore brand new, bright white England shirts with the collars turned up which had obviously been purchased especially for the occasion of Euro 96. Danny doubted any of them had ever enjoyed a Saturday afternoon in the park up to the arsehole in mud. On the table was a huge silver wine cooler containing a magnum of Champagne.

'And you must be Daniel.' He shook Danny's hand limply. 'Bolly, old chap?'

'Nah, I'll stick to lager thanks,' said Danny, thinking, *What a wanker*.

'They only do bottled beers,' piped up Jeremy, a chinless wonder of a stockbroker with an unhealthy fondness for cocaine.

The building reverberated with the chant of 'Three Lions on My Shirt'. Danny stood awkwardly by the table (there were no chairs left in the overcrowded bar) in his well-worn Scotland top and wondered what Bonny was doing sitting on the knee of such an idiot. And then the whistle blew and the match started on the wide-screen TV in front of him and Danny forgot all about the stuck-up City boys he'd found himself with and felt that familiar nauseous knot of nerves form in the pit of his stomach as his team faced the old enemy.

When Shearer scored the first goal, the bar exploded into rapturous yells of English glee. Danny pulled his fingers through his long, blond hair and breathed deeply. There was time yet. They could pull it back. He noticed how Bonny was thrown off Damian's knee as the Englishman jumped up to celebrate. She stumbled and fell, disappearing beneath the feet of a dozen England fans. She reappeared a moment later looking slightly dazed and fought her way to Danny's side, suddenly desperate to be with her friend and ally.

'English bastards,' she whispered, squeezing his hand in mutual commiseration.

When Scotland were awarded a penalty, the entire room groaned except for Danny and Bonny who jumped up and down in anticipation of a

Scotland comeback. And then McAllistair missed.

'Bollocks,' shouted Danny. 'McAllistair you fucking donkey.'

'Yeah!' shouted the rest of the bar.

Bonny put her arms around Danny's neck and kissed his cheek fondly.

'It'll be OK,' she promised. 'There's still time.'

Damian bristled as he watched.

It was Gazza who put the nail in the Scottish coffin, scoring a second goal for England moments after the missed penalty chance. Bonny clung on to Danny's arm for dear life as the English fans erupted around her.

'ENGERLAND! ENGERLAND!' they chanted.

Bonny had supported Scotland passionately since World Cup 78 but even she was surprised by the surge of pain she felt as her team went further behind. As the minutes ticked by, tears of indignation pricked her eyes and the Champagne high that had given her such a buzz just half an hour earlier turned flat. Danny watched a fat, round tear trickle down Bonny's cheek and drip onto the floor. Her bottom lip pouted and quivered. He hugged her to him and kissed the back of her shiny, black hair – a tiny Scottish island of misery amidst a sea of English glee. The last few seconds of injury time were counted down by the entire bar.

'Ten, nine, eight, seven, six, five, four, three, two, one, yeah . . . !!!!'

Scotland were out of Euro 96. England went through to the next round. Damian, Jeremy et al clinked Champagne glasses with an air of such self-importance that you'd have thought they'd been on the pitch themselves.

'Let's get out of here,' shouted Danny to Bonny. 'Before I murder someone.'

Bonny looked nervously towards Damian and his friends.

'We're supposed to be going on to a party with them,' she mumbled.

'Oh, bugger them. They're a waste of space,' said Danny impatiently. 'Look, you do what you want, but I'm off, all right?'

Bonny shouted, 'No!' a bit too desperately and then said no again, but calmer this time.

'I'll just tell Damian I'm leaving, OK? Wait for me.'

Danny watched Bonny lean over the table and whisper something into Damian's ear. He was nodding. Then he kissed her roughly on the lips and slapped her bum twice. All the while he kept his eyes on Danny as if to say, 'See this piece of ass? It's mine.' Danny saw Bonny handing a key to her boyfriend and then she was by his side.

Outside it was a hot, bright summer's day. Clapham High Street was teaming with drunk England supporters singing 'Three Lions' and congratulating each other.

'Where now?' asked Danny.

'Back to mine?' suggested Bonny. 'It's a small Scottish enclave. No Englishmen allowed.'

'Sounds good to me,' he said.

'This way,' indicated Bonny, grabbing her friend's hand and dragging him against the tide of bodies toward Clapham North tube station.

They fought their way through the seething mass of English bodies, all singing and celebrating and chanting 'ENGERLAND'. A few of them spotted Danny's Scotland shirt through a haze of alcohol and shouted abuse.

'You fucking Sweaty loser,' said a bald guy with a beer gut which made him look pregnant.

Danny let go of Bonny's hand to push the fat bloke out of his face.

'What's a Sweaty?' asked Danny blankly once his tormenter had staggered on up the road.

'Sweaty Sock – Jock,' explained Bonny with a shrug. 'I've heard it all before.'

'Nice place to live, Bon,' said Danny.

The friends continued with grim faces down the street towards the tube station, shoving England fans out of their way as they went.

'I hate this,' shouted Danny over the din. 'Why the fuck did I let you talk me into coming down here this weekend?'

'Sorry,' mouthed Bonny, glumly.

She could feel a ball of anger well up in her belly. Why did Scotland have to lose – again? There was nothing worse than being stuck in London on days like these. She should have gone to Edinburgh for the weekend instead. At least there she and Danny could commiserate in style. Suddenly she felt a pair of unfamiliar arms grab her from behind and spin her round. A smug, pock-marked face that she'd never seen before was approaching at speed.

'Give us a kiss, darling,' said the ugly Englishman. 'To celebrate.'

The ball of anger exploded. Bonny pushed the
man away with all her strength and screamed, 'I'm
Scottish!' so loudly that several people stopped in
their tracks and stared. Afterwards her throat hurt.

The guy backed off in surprise.

'All right, love. Keep your hair on,' he muttered
before disappearing into the throng.

Bonny looked at Danny. He was laughing so hard
he was doubled over.

'That was classic,' he spluttered. 'The laddie's
face was a picture. I'm Scottish!' Danny did an
impersonation.

'We're Scottish!' shouted Bonny again, randomly
this time, at all the approaching English.

'We're Scottish!' repeated Danny.

They continued their chant all the way to the tube
station, down the escalator and onto the platform.
Only once they'd collapsed onto their seats on the
train did they stop.

'That confused them,' laughed Danny.

'It certainly did,' grinned Bonny.

Back at her flat, Danny and Bonny collapsed in
a heap onto the leather sofa. Bonny fell comfortably back into the crook of Danny's arm and he
kissed her hair gently.

'That wasn't such a bad day after all,' he said.

They must have fallen asleep like that, curled up
together on the couch, because when Damian let
himself in several hours later, that's where he found
them.

'Not interrupting anything, am I?' he sneered, as Bonny rubbed her sleepy eyes.

'Don't be silly, Damian,' she replied. 'Who wants a drink?'

The unlikely threesome spent an awkward couple of hours, making stilted conversation over a take-away curry and bottle of red wine.

'I don't get you and him?' whined Damian later, once he'd got Bonny alone in the bedroom.

'What do you mean?' she asked, knowing exactly what he meant.

'Well, he's such a Prole.'

'And you're such a snob,' said Bonny in disgust. 'He's my oldest friend. I love him to bits. It's as simple as that, so get over it.'

'You've never . . . you know . . . ?' muttered Damian. He was watching Bonny hungrily as she undressed.

'What?' snapped Bonny impatiently.

'You've never slept with Danny, have you?' Damian asked this question accusingly.

'No,' she replied. 'I haven't.'

This wasn't strictly true. There had been one night in Goa, perhaps it was the same day that photograph was taken, Bonny couldn't quite remember. The whole thing had been a bit like a dream. They'd been wrecked and it had felt like the most natural thing to do, there on the beach, Bonny and Danny, friends since childhood, a love story waiting to happen. Bonny had felt it was the most amazing experience of her life but the next day Danny had acted as if nothing had happened. Neither of them had mentioned the incident since and sometimes Bonny wondered if she'd made the whole thing up out of wishful thinking. So the official line was no, she'd never slept with Danny. Only in her head, a million or more times. Damian's attempts to seduce her that night were the pathetic fumblings of a drunken man and she found it easy enough to fight him off. His pumped-up bulk of body took up more than its fair share of the king-sized bed and Bonny fumed silently in the dark as she clung to the edge of the bed, listening to him snore.

In the morning she found Danny in his Calvin Kleins, drinking coffee and watching football on TV. It struck her as always how beautiful his physique was – lean, muscular, strong. It was as if any more flesh would have been surplus to requirements. He'd been made in the image of the ideal man. Everything looked as if it would work perfectly, like an expertly-tuned engine. Damian bumbled into the living room also wearing boxer shorts. Bonny thought how badly his gym-sculpted mass compared to Danny's lean frame. Quite frankly, there was just too much of him, she thought. It was as if he were trying to take up as much room on the planet as possible. Danny had been right, Damian was, quite literally, a waste of space. Bonny decided she would dump him later, once Danny was on his train.

Back at King's Cross, Danny gave Bonny a brotherly hug.

'I've had a good weekend,' he said. 'But I don't think much of this place.'

'Och, it's all right,' shrugged Bonny. 'You get used to it.'

'But it's not home.'

'It's not your home, Dan. But you're forgetting, I'm a nomad. I don't really have a proper home. So, London's as good as anywhere for me.'

'But you're Scottish,' teased Danny, impersonating Bonny's chant from the day before.

'I'm Scottish!' she shouted, hoping it would make him laugh, always eager to please.

'You're a doll,' smiled Danny, ruffling her perfectly-groomed hair.

Bonny stood on the platform and watched the train roll out of the station on its long trip back to Edinburgh. Suddenly she felt very alone.

2002

The chic New York businesswoman leaned elegantly back in her chair, drawing slowly on a cigarette. Her imposing, expensively-dressed (if grossly overweight) father sat opposite, nursing a glass of Cognac. They were sitting at the best table of the most exclusive restaurant in downtown Manhattan, having just finished a $400 lunch.

'You seem down, Princess,' said David Lebowsky in his deep, throaty drawl. 'What's up?'

Bonny shrugged, 'I dunno, Dad. Things just aren't the same any more.'

David nodded his understanding. They'd both lost friends on September 11th and some of the buzz of working on Wall Street had certainly been lost since that catastrophic day. Only six months had passed and New York was still licking its gaping wounds. Things certainly weren't the same as they had been before.

Bonny had been living in New York for four years, having been poached from the City of London by a top Wall Street firm. At first it had seemed to David that his daughter had thrived in his home city and he'd been proud to watch her blossom, both socially and professionally, under his watchful and loving gaze. He'd introduced her to the sons and daughters of his powerful friends and she'd slotted perfectly into their glossy world. She'd even had a two-year relationship with a brilliant young attorney from his firm. Bonny had never really explained to him why she'd finished that relationship, out of the blue, last Christmas. All she would say was that she didn't feel 'at home' with him. David worried about Bonny. She would be thirty-one in a few weeks and he desperately wanted her to find a good man, get married and give him grandchildren. It needn't ruin her dazzling career, he figured. Half the attorneys in his office were women who 'had it all' – husband, kids, a place in the Hamptons. Hell, that's what nannies were for. Most of all, David didn't want his beloved daughter to end up like him – over fifty and all alone in his penthouse apartment. Despite three marriages, the one thing he'd missed out on in life was true love and, with the help of his therapist, he'd recently come to the depressing conclusion that that might have been the one thing that would have brought him real fulfilment in his life.

'I think I might go home,' announced Bonny suddenly.

'Sure, Princess, let me just get the check,' said David.

'No, Dad, not home to my apartment. Home to Scotland.'

David's hefty shoulders dropped and he let out an involuntary sigh. 'Gee, Bonny, that's a bit of a bombshell. What's brought this on?'

Bonny shrugged. 'Just stuff. I don't want to talk about it.'

David's big heart was gripped with fear. He had been so much happier since Bonny came to live nearby and the thought of losing her terrified him. He would be left with nothing but a gaping hole.

'I don't know what I'd do without you here,' he said, sadly.

'You managed just fine for twenty-six years,' Bonny reminded him sharply.

She saw the hurt in his big brown eyes and immediately felt guilty. This had nothing to do with her father. He had been a rock for her during the last few years and she loved him desperately but he couldn't give her the one thing she wanted, the one thing she now knew she could never have.

'I'm sorry, Dad,' she said gently. 'This has nothing to do with you.'

It had everything to do with an E-mail she'd received the day before. An E-mail from Danny.

Bonny in Scotland

'Hi Bonny,' it had started innocuously enough.

Long time no see. How's life in the Big Apple? Still busy making millions of dollars? And how's the Big Lebowsky doing? I'd love to see your old man again some time. Say hi to him from me. I bumped into your mum in Jenners the other day, by the way. She seemed well. Everything here is cool. The garage is doing well and I've just bought a house in Gullane. Think I must be getting old because I've had enough of living in the city centre. The new place has got a view of the sea and I plan to spend my weekends walking the dog on the beach. How sad is that? But the big news is, I'm getting married! To a great lassie called Grace. She's a hairdresser from Haddington. You'd like her. Anyway, I know it's short notice but the big day is in two weeks time (just a registry office job, Grace didn't want a fuss) and I'd really love it if you could come. I'll totally understand if you're too busy with work but don't say you can't afford the air fare – I know that would be a lie. Let me know how you're fixed. It would be great to catch up.

Love from Danny x

Bonny had read the E-mail five times and as the words sank in she felt the bottom drop out of her world. Danny was the one. He'd always been the one. Bonny had grabbed life with both hands and had never been afraid to reach for her dreams. She'd been brave and confident and she'd succeeded in everything. Everything apart from

Danny, that is. In twenty years, she'd never found the words to tell him how she'd felt and now she would never know if they might have stood a chance.

Back in his apartment, after the meal, David Lebowsky poured himself a Scotch and picked up the phone.

'Ali?' he said. 'It's me, David. I'm worried about Bonny. We need to talk.'

David was still very fond of his daughter's mother. He wondered sometimes what would have happened if they'd got married when she was pregnant with Bonny. It was what her parents had wanted. He couldn't imagine that their relationship could have been any less successful than the three marriages he'd had subsequently and it would have been good for Bonny to have both parents around, a steady home life, real roots. He admired the woman Alison had become – independent, successful, strong. Who would have thought that two hippies would have changed so much over the years and yet stayed so much the same. They both had full bank accounts and empty beds.

As usual, Ali knew exactly what was wrong with Bonny. She told David about her chance meeting with Danny the week before. He'd told her he was getting married and that he was planning to invite Bonny to the wedding. Ali had smiled and said congratulations but she'd been panicking inside. She knew this would destroy Bonny. It had been obvious to Ali for two decades that her daughter was smitten with the boy.

Bonny in Scotland

'What should I do?' asked David. 'And what should I tell Bonny to do, more to the point?'

'I don't know, David,' replied Ali, sadly. 'I've never been very good with that whole love thing. I mean, you were the only man I ever really loved and I haven't seen you in thirty years.'

David couldn't help smiling to himself as he put down the phone. He was the only man Alison had ever loved. It made him feel all warm and gooey inside.

Bonny was due some holiday. Hell, after years of working late, she was due about six months' worth of days off in lieu. So she told her boss she would be away for a fortnight and booked a plane ticket to Scotland. She still didn't know what she was going to do when she got there, maybe she would do nothing, as usual. All she knew was that she had to be there to see Danny before he walked up the aisle and out of her life for good. She'd sent him an E-mail, telling him that she'd be on Portobello seafront at three p.m. on Friday. She hoped he would be there too.

Bonny sat on the bench where it all started and stared out to sea. It was a nothing kind of a day in March. The sky was dirty white and the sea was murky grey. Fife swelled up like a black splodge on the horizon. Portobello looked grubby and unloved. Bonny smoothed her cream cashmere coat self-consciously and realized how alien she must look – a New York career girl, perched on a battered old bench on Portobello promenade. It was five to three.

She could hear her heart beat loudly above the gentle lapping of the waves and the tortured screams of the seagulls. She had butterflies in her stomach. And then she saw him. He was striding purposely towards her, beaming a smile that lit up the pale grey sky. The years had been kind to Danny and she thought, as she watched him, how he'd retained the air of someone very important in the world.

As he got closer, she noticed the faint beginnings of lines on his handsome face – laughter lines around his eyes which today were dove-grey.

'Bonny,' he said, arms outstretched. 'I can't believe you're here.'

He hugged her hard and she stayed there for a long time, suspended in the moment, breathing in his smell. When he released her from his arms, she took a deep breath and then she began to tell him what she'd been holding back for so long.

'I need to say something to you that I should have told you years ago. And I'll understand if you just want to listen and then walk away and get on with your life. My timing's appalling and I'm probably being utterly selfish and . . .'

'Bonny, you're scaring me,' laughed Danny.

She put her finger to his lips and said, 'Shoosh, Dan. Just listen.'

He nodded and they both sat down on the bench.

'I'm in love with you,' she continued. 'It's as simple as that. I've always been in love with you but I never had the nerve to tell you before. The truth is, I don't want you to marry Grace. I want you to marry me and, and, and . . . and that's it, really.'

Once he had scraped his jaw off the bench, Danny spoke. 'You're right, Bonny. Your timing's terrible. I'm supposed to be getting married on Saturday. Jesus Christ, talk about a bombshell.'

Bonny stood up.

'I'm sorry, Danny,' she said. 'I shouldn't have come here. I just thought I'd explode if I never told you how I felt. I can see you don't feel the same.'

Danny pulled her back down beside him.

'You're wrong, Bonny,' he said with a strange look on his face, somewhere between pleasure and pain 'I feel exactly the same, always have done. I just thought that someone like me would never stand a chance with a girl like you.'

'But that time in Goa,' whispered Bonny. 'The next day, you acted as if nothing had happened. I thought you regretted it.'

'Regretted it? Christ, no. That was the best night of my life. I just assumed that it was a drunken mistake on your part. One night of passion with your bit of rough.'

'So?' asked Bonny.

'So?' repeated Danny.

'What now?'

'Now I do what I should've done years ago,' said Danny, pulling her towards him.

As Bonny felt his warm lips on hers, she let herself fall into him forever. The butterflies in her stomach were replaced by a warm, comfortable glow that would stay there always and finally, finally, she knew she'd found her home.

'What about Grace?' said Bonny quietly, aware that her dream was someone else's nightmare.

Danny shook his head solemnly. 'I'll go and see her tonight. I'll tell her everything. She's a great lassie. She deserves to know the truth.'

Bonny nodded and then she lost herself in his lips again.

Grace stood some way off, watching her fiancé kissing the glamorous woman on the wooden bench, and felt the warm tears trickling down her cold cheeks. She had always trusted Danny and following him was not something she would normally do. Not if it had been anyone else but Bonny. She'd heard all about his super successful, beautiful best friend. She'd seen the photos, heard the stories and reigned in her jealousy as best she could. Grace wasn't stupid. She'd always known that Danny loved Bonny most and that, if it came down to it, he would choose her over Grace every time. Not that he'd ever admitted it of course. It's just the sort of thing a woman knows, deep down. But Bonny had been in America and Grace had no reason to suspect that she might be in love with Danny too. Bonny was going to be a ghost that Grace accepted in their marriage, she wasn't supposed to turn up here, the week of their wedding, in the flesh. And oh, what glorious flesh. Grace could see quite clearly from where she was standing that Bonny's looks far outshone her own. She watched the embracing couple for a few moments longer and then turned and walked away. It was over now. She had lost him. There was no point in fighting. Not now. Not with Bonny in Scotland.